Praise for the novels of Sherryl Woods

"Sherryl Woods writes emotionally satisfying novels about family, friendship and home. Truly feel-great reads!"
—#1 *New York Times* bestselling author Debbie Macomber

"During the course of this gripping, emotionally wrenching but satisfying tale, Woods deftly and realistically handles such issues as survival guilt, drug abuse as adolescent rebellion, and family dynamics when a vital member is suddenly gone."
—*Booklist* on *Flamingo Diner*

"Woods is a master heartstring puller."
—*Publishers Weekly* on *Seaview Inn*

"Once again, Woods, with such authenticity, weaves a tale of true love and the challenges that can knock up against that love."
—*RT Book Reviews* on *Beach Lane*

"Woods…is noted for appealing character-driven stories that are often infused with the flavor and fragrance of the South."
—*Library Journal*

"A reunion story punctuated by family drama, Woods's first novel in her new Ocean Breeze series is touching, tense and tantalizing."
—*RT Book Reviews* on *Sand Castle Bay*

"A whimsical, sweet scenario…the digressions have their own charm, and Woods never fails to come back to the romantic point."
—*Publishers Weekly* on *Sweet Tea at Sunrise*

SHERRYL WOODS

Sweet Magnolias

WELCOME TO SERENITY

mira

ISBN-13: 978-0-7783-8630-8

Welcome to Serenity

First published in 2008. This edition published in 2022.

Recycling programs
for this product may
not exist in your area.

Mira
22 Adelaide St. West, 41st Floor
Toronto, Ontario M5H 4E3, Canada
www.Harlequin.com

Printed in Lithuania

MIX
Paper from
responsible sources
FSC® C021394

Dear friends,

Originally the Sweet Magnolias series was conceived as only three books, but reader response was so terrific and I loved writing about these women so much that I just had to continue the series! *Welcome to Serenity*, Jeanette's story, kept calling to me. And because it was originally written for release during the holiday season, it also made sense to make that a part of the book.

But unlike my own absolute love of the holidays, Jeanette clearly has long-standing issues with the season. Exploring her past and matching her with a man who has his own bad memories of the holidays seemed exactly right for stirring up conflict in Serenity, South Carolina, a community that loves its holidays, Christmas most of all.

No matter when you read this story, I hope it will rekindle a few of your own special memories from seasons past.

So, welcome back to Serenity and to the Sweet Magnolias. I hope your own friendships are as rich and rewarding as those found in these pages and in the hit Netflix original series based on the books.

All best,

Sherryl Woods

WELCOME TO SERENITY

CHAPTER ONE

The relaxing scent of lavender in the hand cream that Jeanette Brioche was massaging into her cramped fingers did absolutely nothing to calm her jittery nerves. A few hours ago Maddie Maddox, her boss at The Corner Spa, had scheduled a meeting for six o'clock, immediately after Jeanette was due to finish with her last client. Maddie hadn't said what it was about, but her grim expression suggested it wasn't a celebration, something she and her friends Dana Sue and Helen organized at the drop of a hat.

Since Jeanette tended to be a worrier who saw disaster around every corner, she decided to get this over with even though it wasn't quite six. Her stomach knotted with dread, she walked down the hall to Maddie's office.

After tapping on the partially open door, Jeanette stepped inside to chaos. A disheveled Maddie was holding a wriggling six-month-old Cole in her arms and trying to feed him, while two-year-old Jessica Lynn ran wildly around the room, knocking everything in sight onto the floor. Maddie's usually well-organized folders were in a chaotic heap, and samples from their suppliers were scattered everywhere. A topless bottle of hand lotion had been upended.

"Help!" Maddie said to Jeanette, who promptly scooped up Jessica Lynn and tickled her until the child dissolved into giggles.

"Having a bad day?" Jeanette inquired, feeling her stomach unknot as the toddler patted her cheek with sticky fingers that smelled of rose-scented hand lotion. The more time she spent around Jessica Lynn and Cole, as well as Helen's little girl, however, the louder the ticking of Jeanette's biological clock seemed to get. The alarm hadn't gone off yet, but she sensed it was about to when the scent of baby powder started to smell better to her than the herbal aromas in the spa.

"A bad day, a bad week and more than likely a bad month," Maddie replied.

The weary response pretty much confirmed the reason for her earlier grim expression. Maddie had already had three children when she'd married Cal Maddox a few years ago and now had two more. Her oldest son, Ty, was a sophomore at Duke and star of the school's baseball team. Kyle was in high school and finally regaining his equilibrium after Maddie's divorce from his dad, and Katie had just turned nine and was only marginally impressed with being a big sister, rather than the baby of the family.

There was no question that Maddie had her hands full, even without taking into account that she ran The Corner Spa, which was a thriving fitness club and day spa for residents of Serenity, South Carolina, and beyond. Jeanette couldn't imagine how she juggled all those balls in the air. Most days she did it with aplomb. Today she looked completely frazzled.

"Want me to take our girl here and give her a beauty

treatment?" she asked Maddie, even as Jessica Lynn struggled to break free.

"Actually, Cal should be here any second to pick them up," Maddie replied. "Then you and I can talk."

Just as she spoke, the man in question strode into the room, sized up the situation with a grin and took the squirming Jessica Lynn from Jeanette.

"How's my favorite girl?" he asked, tossing the toddler into the air, then planting a loud kiss on her cheek that had Jessica Lynn squealing with delight.

"I thought *I* was your favorite girl," Maddie grumbled with feigned annoyance.

Seemingly oblivious to his wife's mussed hair, lack of makeup and formula-splotched blouse, Cal set the two-year-old down and then leaned down to give Maddie a long, lingering kiss. "You are my favorite *woman*," he told Maddie. "And that is much, much better."

Jeanette watched enviously as Maddie touched his cheek in response and their eyes locked. It was as if the two of them were alone in the room. Dana Sue and Ronnie Sullivan, and Helen Decatur and Erik Whitney were equally smitten. Never in her thirty-two years had Jeanette experienced anything like the love these couples shared. It was little wonder that Jeanette almost sighed aloud with longing whenever she was around any of them.

In fact, their happiness was almost enough to convince her to give relationships another try. She'd been out of action for three years now, ever since she'd dumped the guy who'd resented her commitment to The Corner Spa. With Cal, Ronnie and Erik all devoted to their wives and supportive of their careers, Jeanette knew it was possible to find a man like that. She simply hadn't been that lucky yet.

Finally, her cheeks pink, Maddie tore her gaze away

from her husband. "Nice save, Coach Maddox," she said, referring to Cal's role as the high school's baseball coach and her son's onetime mentor. "Now, would you get these two little munchkins out of here so I can have an intelligent conversation with Jeanette?"

"Sure thing," Cal said, putting baby Cole in his stroller and then hefting Jessica Lynn back into his arms. "Want me to pick up something from Sullivan's for dinner?"

Maddie nodded. "I've already called. Dana Sue will have a take-out order waiting for you. Just park in the alley and poke your head in the kitchen. She or Erik will bring it out."

"Got it," Cal said, grinning as he gave her a mock salute. "See you later. Have a good evening, Jeanette. Don't let her talk you into anything."

"Hush," Maddie ordered, giving him a stern look, then shooing him out of the office.

Jeanette regarded Maddie suspiciously when she shut the door behind her husband. "What are you planning to talk me into?"

"Oh, don't listen to him," Maddie said, though her expression remained vaguely guilty. "It's no big deal."

Which meant it was, Jeanette concluded. She knew Maddie pretty well after working with her to get the business opened. Now it ran like a well-oiled machine thanks in no small measure to Maddie's ability to minimize the difficulty of the assignments she was handing out to the staff. She could sweet-talk with the best of the southern belles. Jeanette had learned to be wary of that dismissive tone.

"Talk," Jeanette ordered.

"Now that I think about it, it's too nice to stay inside. Why don't we get a couple of glasses of sweet tea and talk on the patio," Maddie suggested, already striding out of the office and straight for the little café that was part of the spa.

Jeanette trailed along behind, the knot of dread back in her stomach.

After they were seated in the shade of a giant pin oak, which blocked most of the rays of the setting sun, Maddie took a long sip of her tea, sighed with contentment, then gave Jeanette a bright smile that seemed a little forced. "How's business?"

Jeanette almost laughed aloud. "You probably know the answer to that better than I do. Come on, Maddie. Just spill it. What's on your mind?"

Maddie set her tea carefully on the table and leaned forward, her expression earnest. "You know I pretty much have my hands full lately, right?"

"Of course I do," Jeanette said. No sooner were the words out of her mouth than real alarm set in. "You're not quitting, are you?"

"Heavens, no," Maddie said. "The Corner Spa is as important to me as it is to Helen and Dana Sue. I'm proud of what we've accomplished here, and I'm including you in that. You've done an amazing job with the spa services. I have no intention of abandoning ship."

"Thank goodness." Jeanette sat back with a sigh of relief. She'd run the spa both times that Maddie had been on maternity leave. She knew she could handle the day-to-day operations, but she didn't want to. Being in charge of spa services was enough responsibility to suit her. Massages, facials, pedicures and manicures, those were all things she'd been trained to do, treatments she understood. As far as she was concerned, the gym was little better than a torture chamber best left to the excellent personal trainers on staff. And the paperwork and marketing involved with keeping this place on the cutting edge in the region were beyond her expertise. Besides, she liked the daily interaction with the clients. Maddie rarely ever got to leave her office.

"Okay, let's back up," Maddie said. "All I was trying to say is that Jessica Lynn and Cole require huge amounts of attention right now, to say nothing of keeping Kyle and Katie on track. And I'm still more or less a newlywed." She grinned. "Or at least Cal always makes me feel like one."

"I can see that," Jeanette said wryly.

"Bottom line, my time's just not my own."

"Okay," Jeanette said cautiously.

"The Corner Spa's now one of the most successful businesses in town, which gives us a certain responsibility," Maddie continued. "We need to be community leaders, so to speak."

Jeanette nodded.

"Which means one of us needs to be involved in town activities and events." She regarded Jeanette earnestly. "We can't get away with just writing a check or participating. We need to take a leadership position, serve on committees, that kind of thing."

Jeanette's eyes widened as understanding finally dawned. "Oh, no," she said, the knot tightening. "You're not about to suggest what I *think* you are, are you?"

Maddie regarded her innocently. "I have no idea. What are you thinking?"

"Christmas," Jeanette said, barely able to utter the word without a shudder.

Like all holidays, Christmas in Serenity was a very big deal—decorations to rival anything ever seen in a staging of *The Nutcracker,* the arrival of Santa, musical performances by local choirs, candy canes and small token gifts for every child in town. The whole town sparkled with lights, and lawn displays ranged from tasteful to garish.

The residents of Serenity loved it all. They embraced the season with the wide-eyed enthusiasm of a five-year-old.

Not so Jeanette. Christmas in her life was something to be endured, a holiday season to survive, not a time for rejoicing or celebrating or mingling with neighbors. It had been that way for years now. In fact, most years she tried timing her vacation to the holiday season and spending it holed up with DVDs of all the movies she'd missed the previous year.

"No way," she told Maddie now. "Not a chance. I am not getting involved with the Christmas festival."

"Come on, Jeanette, please," Maddie begged. "It's a few meetings, making sure that lights are strung up, trees are lit, the church choirs invited to sing. You've been here long enough to know the drill. And you're one of the most organized people I know."

"And the least likely human being on the planet to want to do this," Jeanette said just as earnestly. "Really, Maddie, you do not want me anywhere near the town's holiday plans. I give new meaning to bah-humbug. If it were up to me, we'd cancel Christmas."

Maddie looked genuinely shaken. "Why? How can you not love Christmas?"

"I just don't, okay?" Jeanette said tightly. "I can't do this for you, Maddie. I can't. Anything else, but not this. I'll watch your kids, take on extra duties around here, whatever you need, but I won't be involved with the festival."

"But—"

"I won't do it, Maddie, and that's final."

And for the first time in her three years at The Corner Spa, Jeanette stood up and walked out on her boss, leaving Maddie openmouthed with shock.

* * *

Tom McDonald had been town manager of Serenity for one hour and fifteen minutes when Mayor Howard Lewis walked into his office, plopped his pudgy body into a chair and announced, "Let's talk about Christmas."

Tom leveled a withering gaze at him that was intended to nip that idea right in the bud. "Don't you think we should be focusing on the budget, Howard? That comes up for a vote at the next council meeting and I need to be up to speed on what the priorities are around Serenity."

"I'll tell you what the top priority is," Howard replied with single-minded determination. "Christmas. We do it up big here in Serenity. Needs to be done right, so you need to call a meeting now. Get those chamber of commerce people and a few business leaders involved. I'll give you some names."

While Tom tried to figure out the best way to say no, Howard's expression turned thoughtful.

"Look," Howard said, "we could use some new decorations for the square, now that there are a few new businesses downtown. Maybe some of those big lighted snowflakes. I'm thinking downtown is where this year's celebration ought to be, just like the old days. The park's great, but there's something about a town square that just goes with an old-fashioned Christmas, don't you think?"

Tom ignored the question. "Are new decorations in the current budget?" he asked, trying to be practical and to avoid the quagmire of admitting his own distaste for the holidays.

"I doubt it," Howard replied with a shrug. "But there're always a few dollars here and there that can be used for emergencies. Discretionary funds, isn't that what you call them?"

"Snowflakes hardly qualify as an emergency purchase," Tom told him, wondering if he was going to have many discussions like this during his tenure in Serenity. If so, it was going to be a frustrating experience.

Howard waved off his objections. "You'll find a way, I'm sure. The point is to get started on this now."

"It's September, Howard," Tom reminded him, his dread growing in direct proportion to Howard's unwavering determination.

Howard waved off the reminder. "And it takes time to get things organized, especially when you have to rely on volunteers. Surely you know that. Your résumé cited all that organizational experience you have. Use it."

"It seems to me that since you have so much enthusiasm for this project, you should be the one in charge," Tom said, unable to keep the desperate note out of his voice. Another minute of even *thinking* about pulling together a Christmas celebration and he'd be sweating openly.

He'd grown up in a household that began holiday preparations not much later than this, complete with decorators who made every downstairs room in his family's Charleston household a designer's Christmas showcase before the round of social occasions began right after Thanksgiving. Heaven forbid that he or his sisters actually try to unwrap one of the packages on display under any of the lavishly decorated trees. Most were nothing more than empty boxes. Like a lot of things that went on in the McDonald home, it was all about show, not substance.

He was aware that Howard was studying him with a narrowed gaze. "You got something against Christmas?" the mayor inquired.

"In the religious context, absolutely nothing," Tom said quickly. "I'm just saying that organizing a bunch of decorations and such is not an effective use of my time. Then there's the whole issue of religious displays on public property, separation of church and state and all that. We need to be careful. The courts are ruling against a lot of these displays."

"Nonsense," Howard said. "This is Serenity. Nobody here objects to Christmas." He stood up. "I'll want to see a report on your progress with this before next Thursday's council meeting. Understood?"

Tom barely resisted a desire to close his eyes and pray for patience. "Understood," he said, tight-lipped.

Putting him in charge of the celebration, he thought sourly, was a little bit like turning it over to Scrooge.

If Jeanette had been a drinker, her conversation with Maddie would have sent her straight to a bar. Instead, it sent her fleeing to Sullivan's for a double serving of Dana Sue's famous apple bread pudding topped with cinnamon ice cream. The order—or a report on her sour mood from the waitress—immediately drew Dana Sue out of the kitchen.

The owner of Serenity's highly successful, upscale restaurant and part owner of The Corner Spa set down the oversize bowl of dessert and took a seat opposite Jeanette.

"What's wrong?" she asked, her expression filled with concern.

Jeanette winced. She should have known that coming here was a mistake. All of the Sweet Magnolias—the name that Maddie, Dana Sue and Helen called themselves—were too darn intuitive, to say nothing of nosy and meddlesome. "What makes you think anything's wrong?" she replied, digging into the bread pudding.

"For starters, you almost never order dessert, much less a double serving of it. Then there's the grim expression on your face." Dana Sue studied her. "And the fact that Maddie called here and told me you were upset about a conversation the two of you had. She had a hunch you'd head this way."

"Is there one single thing the three of you don't share?" Jeanette inquired testily, shoveling in another mouthful of the homemade cinnamon ice cream that was melting over the warm dessert. If it weren't for her state of mind, the combination of tender apples and rich ice cream would have sent her into raptures.

"We've had our secrets," Dana Sue assured her. "But we also rush right in whenever one of us needs backup. You're one of us now, you know that, don't you?"

"No, I'm not," Jeanette protested, though her eyes grew misty. "I didn't grow up here. You three have known each other all your lives. You've been doing things together practically forever. I'm an outsider. I can't be a Sweet Magnolia."

"For goodness' sake, it's not as if we have a bylaw against it. You are if we say you are," Dana Sue countered. "Which means we get to worry about you and meddle in your life. So tell me what happened with Maddie."

"She didn't fill you in?"

"All she said was that it had something to do with Christmas. Frankly, she wasn't making a lot of sense. Nobody goes into a tailspin over Christmas." Her expression turned thoughtful. "Unless they've put off shopping until Christmas Eve. But that can't be it. It's only September."

"It's definitely not about shopping," Jeanette concurred. If she could have, she would have dropped the subject right there, but judging from Dana Sue's quizzical expression, that wasn't going to happen. Jeanette uttered a sigh of resignation. "She wants me to be on the town's Christmas committee."

"Okay," Dana Sue replied slowly. "I don't see the problem. Don't you have the time?"

"I could make the time if I wanted to do it," Jeanette admitted grudgingly. "But I don't want to."

"Why?"

"Because I don't. Isn't that reason enough?" She stuffed another spoonful of bread pudding into her mouth. She'd already eaten more than she should have. All that sugar was beginning to make her feel a little queasy.

"If you're that opposed to serving on the committee, I know Maddie won't force it," Dana Sue reassured her. "But maybe you should tell her why."

Jeanette shook her head. If she explained, she would have to dredge up way too many painful memories. "It's not something I want to talk about. Can't we leave it at that?"

Dana Sue studied her sympathetically. "You know Maddie is a mother hen. She'll worry if she doesn't know the whole story, and she'll nag you until she knows what's going on. My advice is, just spill it and get it over with."

"No," Jeanette said flatly. "You guys hired me to run a day spa. Christmas was never part of the deal. If it's going to turn into this huge issue, maybe I don't belong here."

"That's ridiculous!" Dana Sue said, her expression alarmed. "Of course you belong here. We love you like a sister. You are not going to leave just because you don't want to serve on the town's Christmas festival committee. Maddie will figure something out. Maybe Elliot can do it. Or one of the other employees."

Jeanette's eyes brightened at the mention of the spa's top-notch personal trainer. "Elliot would be good. Now that he and Karen are together, he gets all mushy about every holiday on the calendar." She warmed to the idea. "Plus, he'd be great at climbing ladders and doing all the physical stuff that'll need to be done. Not to mention what excellent eye candy he is. All the women in town will be volunteering to serve on the committee."

"Good points," Dana Sue said with a grin. "Be sure to mention them to Maddie. Now, why don't I get you a real dinner. The catfish is especially good tonight."

Jeanette shook her head, shoving away the half-empty bowl of bread pudding. "I'm stuffed."

"And feeling better?" Dana Sue asked.

"A hundred percent better," Jeanette confirmed. "Thanks, Dana Sue."

"Anytime," she said as she slid out of the booth. "But before you make a final decision about this whole committee thing, there's one thing you should probably consider."

Jeanette froze. She'd thought the matter settled. She'd go to Maddie, recommend Elliot for the job and that would be that. She eyed Dana Sue warily. "Oh?"

"The new town manager will be running the committee."

"So?"

"He was in here with the mayor the other night," Dana Sue told her. "He's a real hottie." She grinned. "And I hear he's single."

Jeanette's gaze instantly narrowed. "Is that what this is about? Are you and Maddie matchmaking?"

"Wouldn't dream of it," Dana Sue replied innocently. "Just reporting what I know so you can make a fully informed decision."

"I've made my decision," Jeanette said emphatically. "And I'm not looking for a man. You've just given me one more reason for saying no to this."

Dana Sue smiled knowingly. "I seem to recall Maddie saying those exact words not long before she walked down the aisle with Cal. Helen's protests were even more forceful right before she married Erik. And I was pretty fierce about declaring I had zero interest in remarrying Ronnie. Just look at us now."

Jeanette blanched. "But I'm serious."

Dana Sue chuckled. "So were we, sweetie. So were we."

After the mistakes she'd made in choosing men, Jeanette's life had been refreshingly calm lately. Peaceful. She liked it that way. She really did. Oh, she might envy Maddie, Dana Sue and Helen their solid relationships, but guys like theirs were few and far between. And she knew for a fact they weren't the kind she attracted.

She gave Dana Sue a stern look. "Stay out of my love life."

"I wasn't aware you *had* a love life," Dana Sue responded.

"Exactly my point. And that's the way it's going to stay."

"Famous last words," Dana Sue said as she walked away.

"I mean it," Jeanette called after her. "I do."

Dana Sue merely waved. Even though Jeanette couldn't see her face, she knew the other woman was smirking. She resolved then and there to take up drinking margaritas like the rest of the Sweet Magnolias. Then the next time she had a crisis, she could head for a bar instead of straight into a hornet's nest of sage advice and friendly meddling.

CHAPTER TWO

◆────◆────◆

Tom was still seething over his meeting with the mayor when he left the office and headed for the Serenity Inn. The prospect of a long, empty evening in his hotel room held little appeal. He needed some exercise, something so strenuous that it would drive all thoughts of that ridiculous conversation from his head.

On his way to his room, he stopped at the front desk and asked Maybelle Hawkins if there was a health club in town. She frowned at the question.

"Well, now, there's Dexter's Gym, but I'll tell you the truth, the place is a dump. I hear Dexter has real good equipment over there and once in a while he slaps a fresh coat of paint on the walls, but that's the extent of any renovations he's done in the past thirty years. Men don't seem to notice, but the women complained for years, for all the good it did."

"So Dexter's Gym is my only choice?" Tom wasn't averse to the smell of sweat or even a shabby decor, but he questioned whether a place like that would keep its equipment in good repair, despite what Maybelle said. "I thought

I'd read something in a regional magazine about a place called The Corner Spa."

Maybelle's eyes lit up. "Now that's another story," she said. "Just walking through the door is a soothing experience. The owners took an old Victorian house at Main Street and Palmetto Lane and turned it into something special. I haven't used any of the fancy machines, but I've had a facial and a mud bath. Mud! Can you imagine such a thing? To tell you the truth, though, I never felt better."

Tom nodded. "Sounds like the perfect place," he said. He seemed to recall that the article had been equally glowing.

"It is, but you can forget about it," Maybelle said, an oddly triumphant glint in her eyes.

"Why is that?"

"It's only open to women. After all those years of pleading with Dexter to fix his place up, they finally have a place of their own."

"You're telling me that The Corner Spa discriminates?" he said, his ire stirring. "And nobody's sued?"

Maybelle gave him a blank look. "Why would they? It's a spa for women. You men have had your private clubs and private golf courses for years. Now a few women get together and open something just for women and you want to sue? Give me a break."

Tom winced. His father had belonged to several of those private, men-only clubs, in fact. That wasn't the point, though. This was a business, supposedly open to the public.

"Come on," he said. "You know it's morally wrong, probably illegal." He'd have to research that, look into those law books his father had bought in the hope that Tom would one day open his own law office in Charleston, actually use the law degree he'd earned.

Maybelle didn't seem the least bit impressed with his argument. "You'd have to take that up with one of the owners, but I'll warn you about that. Helen Decatur's the smartest attorney in town. Nobody with any sense goes against her."

Tom nodded slowly. Given his current annoyance over the way his first day on the job had gone, the prospect of challenging a business that blatantly discriminated based on gender held a lot of appeal. He could channel his sour mood into *that* fight, instead of waging a fruitless battle with Howard over the Christmas festival.

Then again, if one of his first acts as a resident of Serenity was to sue a popular attorney and business owner, it might mark the beginning of the end of his career as town manager. He'd have to give that some thought.

He gave Maybelle a distracted smile. "Thanks. I appreciate the information."

After a quick trip to his room to change into jeans, an old University of South Carolina T-shirt and sneakers, he headed downtown at a brisk pace. He'd probably wind up at Dexter's, but first he wanted to get a good look at this fancy spa.

He made a few wrong turns, but eventually he found it. There was something classy and welcoming about the old Victorian.

He climbed the steps to the porch and peered in a window. The equipment inside looked top-notch. A dozen or so women were using the treadmills and the elliptical cross-trainers, and he spotted a couple of men in there, as well. Hoping Maybelle had gotten the membership restrictions wrong, he was about to open the door and step inside to find out, when he heard brisk footsteps behind him.

"May I help you?" a woman queried, halting him in his tracks. Despite the slow Southern drawl of her voice, somehow she made the question sound more like a challenge than an offer of assistance.

He turned and faced a pixie of a woman with very short dark hair and huge, dark eyes. If he hadn't heard that drawl in her voice, he would have guessed her to be European. Her clothes had a French flair about them. Even though the outfit—really only jeans and a T-shirt—could easily have come from the local discount store, the low-heeled, ballet-style shoes and the artful twist of the scarf at her neck reminded him of the innate fashion sense he'd seen on the Left Bank in Paris during the summer he'd spent there after college. He had very fond memories of those days—and of the women he'd met.

He gave her his most winning smile. "That depends. Do you happen to have any pull at this place?"

"I'm not one of the owners, if that's what you're asking. Maddie meets with all prospective suppliers. I can give you her card."

"I'm not a supplier. I want to join."

"Sorry. We're only open to women."

"But I see a couple of men inside," he protested.

"Personal trainers. They're the only men allowed inside during business hours. I'd be happy to give you directions to Dexter's, if you don't know your way around town."

"I can find it," he said tersely. "You know, the women-only rule is probably illegal."

The suggestion didn't fluster her in the least.

"I seriously doubt it," she said, looking amused. "I'm sure that Helen Decatur—she's also an owner—covered that when she incorporated the spa. I can give you her card, too, if you'd like."

Letting the legal issues pass for the moment, Tom studied her speculatively, allowing his gaze to linger in a way meant to disconcert her. "When do you offer me *your* card?"

"I don't, unless you happen to be peddling skin creams, aromatherapy products or spa attire. Unfortunately, we've already established that you're not."

There was a gloating note in her voice that irked him. Instead of letting his irritation show, he turned on his charm. "That is a shame, isn't it? Maybe we can find something else we have in common."

The amusement in her remarkable eyes vanished. "I doubt that," she said coolly. "Have a good evening."

She opened the door, stepped inside, then shut it very firmly in his face. He had a hunch if the spa hadn't been open for another hour, she'd have turned the lock, as well.

Tom stared after her. His annoyance over the spa's discrimination against men had suddenly taken a backseat to his fascination with the feisty woman who'd just brushed him off. As the presumed heir to the McDonald fortune, he hadn't had a lot of experience with rejection, especially in the upper echelons of Charleston society. He discovered he didn't like it. Coming on top of his losing battle with the mayor, it really soured his mood.

His father would say that the day he'd just had in Serenity was no worse than he deserved for not following the more illustrious career path that had been chosen for him at birth. It was the image of the gloating expression he'd likely find on his father's face that stiffened his spine and made him resolve to make tomorrow better. He had a lot to prove, not just to his father, but to himself.

He'd come to Serenity because he cared about towns like this. He thought he had something to offer. His years as a planning administrator and as a chief financial officer in another community had prepared him to run Serenity and deal with whatever issues might face the community. If he had to do battle with a demanding mayor and suffer a little rejection at the hands of an intriguing woman, he could handle it.

He cast one last, longing look through the window of The Corner Spa, decided to skip a workout at Dexter's and jogged back to the Serenity Inn for an unappetizing meal of beer and takeout.

After her disconcerting encounter with the man on the porch, Jeanette retreated to her office to try to make a dent in the mountain of paperwork on her desk. It was as good a time as any to deal with this unpleasant aspect of her job.

Unfortunately, she couldn't seem to focus on it. Images of the man she'd just met kept intruding. The thought of him taking on Helen in a fight made her smile. He'd sounded so sure of himself. It would be fun to watch Helen teach him a thing or two about the law.

And even though she'd sworn off men, basking in the undisguised admiration of a sexy man for just a couple of minutes had given her a faintly quivery feeling in the pit of her stomach. It had been a long time since a man had looked at her like that. Or maybe it had just been a long time since she'd been aware of it and felt anything in return.

Not that she intended to do anything about it, she reminded herself sternly, turning back to the paperwork on her desk with renewed determination.

She'd completed her monthly report for August when El-liot tapped on her door and stepped inside. With his gleaming black hair, glowing olive complexion and well-muscled body, he was a walking advertisement for fitness. He was also one of the nicest guys around. He came from a large, exuberant family and was about to marry a single mom, who'd had a very tough couple of years. He and Karen had weathered their own stormy issues thanks to his rigorously Catholic family's initial disapproval of him marrying a divorced woman. Karen had finally won them over.

"You're here awfully late," he said.

"Catching up on paperwork," Jeanette replied with a grimace. "Is it time to close up? I've lost track of time."

"I sent the last of the clients on their way and locked the doors five minutes ago. If you're ready to go, I'll give you a lift home."

Jeanette gave him an odd look. "That's okay. I can walk. It's not that far."

Elliot immediately shook his head. "Not tonight. There was some guy peering in the windows here earlier. I've never seen him around before. It made a couple of the women nervous. They were about ready to call the sheriff, but when I checked outside, he was gone."

Jeanette smiled and shook her head. "I talked to him on my way in. He's harmless. He wanted to join the health club, but I told him he couldn't. I guess he's new in town. He left after we spoke."

Elliot's frown didn't fade. "I still don't like it. Did he give you a name?"

"No, but I didn't ask. Stop worrying. I'm a halfway decent judge of people." Okay, not men, but this was different. "This guy was clean-cut and well-spoken. He's not a threat to anyone."

Even as she uttered the assurance, she wondered if it was entirely true. The man probably wasn't dangerous in the way Elliot was thinking, but he might very well pose a threat to her. Before her cool dismissal of him, she'd responded to his fleeting attempt at flirting. She hadn't wanted to, but she had.

He was attractive. Okay, very attractive. Sexy. He didn't have the kind of muscular body Elliot had, but he was fit in a lean and lanky way. His eyes were more gray than blue and they'd sparkled with mischief. His neatly trimmed brown hair had the kind of golden highlights that came from spending time outdoors. And he had a dimple when he smiled. That dimple had knocked her socks off, which had been a shock. She'd thought herself immune.

His clothes had been casual, but she could easily envision him in a shirt and tie. A tailor-made suit. He was a professional man, if she was any judge.

Elliot didn't appear convinced. He moved a stack of papers from the extra chair, then sat down, propped his feet on her desk and pulled out a cell phone.

"What are you doing?" Jeanette demanded.

"Calling Karen to let her know I'll be late."

"Why?"

He grinned. "Because I'm not leaving here without you. It would tarnish my sterling reputation as a nice guy. Last time I let one of the Sweet Magnolias out of my sight when my gut told me not to, she nearly got herself killed."

Jeanette winced. She recalled the incident. "You weren't responsible for what happened to Helen. Her client's husband was determined to get even with her. No one was going to stop him."

"Not entirely, no," he agreed cheerfully. "But I'm not taking any chances."

Jeanette saw the stubborn set of his jaw and gave in. "Oh, for pity's sake. I'm not going to be responsible for you turning up late at Karen's." She stood up. "Let's go."

He gave her a smug look. "Good choice. Want to come have dinner with us? I'm cooking Mama's famous seafood paella."

"You're cooking?" Jeanette said incredulously as they stepped outside. "Your wife works in a restaurant."

"Which is why she shouldn't have to cook at home on her day off."

Jeanette regarded him with wonder. "Why don't you have brothers, instead of all those sisters?"

Elliot chuckled. "I have cousins. Want to meet one of them? I'm the best of the lot, but there are one or two who come close."

"Are their egos as big as yours?"

"Twice the size," he declared.

"Then, no. I think I'll continue to fly solo."

Elliot shook his head. "That's a pity. You're a beautiful woman with a good heart. You should share your life with someone special."

Jeanette sighed. "Once upon a time, I thought the same thing."

"Don't say that," Elliot chided as he tucked her into his car. "The right person could be right around the corner."

Jeanette couldn't help thinking about the way she'd felt earlier with the stranger's eyes on her. Maybe Elliot was right. Maybe it *was* a little too soon to give up on love.

Mary Vaughn Lewis had her jam-packed day planner spread open on her desk and was trying to transfer all of the information into her new BlackBerry, something her daughter, now a sophomore at Clemson, insisted she needed. Since she was about as computer literate as her Persian cat, Mary Vaughn wasn't so sure. Still, in this day and age, she couldn't afford to be left behind. People had certain expectations of the most successful Realtor in Serenity. Add to that her role as president of the Serenity Chamber of Commerce, and she desperately needed something to keep her schedule straight. Rory Sue swore this gadget was the answer.

When it rang, she was so taken aback she almost dropped it on the floor. It took her a minute to find the right button and answer.

"Yes, hello, Mary Vaughn Lewis," she murmured distractedly, still reading the directions as she spoke.

"Mom, it's me. Am I your first call on your new Black-Berry?"

"You absolutely are," Mary Vaughn told her daughter, brightening at the sound of Rory Sue's voice.

"No wonder you sound so weirded out. You're going to love it once you get the hang of it. I promise."

"Yes, well, we'll see about that. What's up, sweet pea?" Mary Vaughn suspected this midweek call had nothing to do with checking on her technical prowess and everything to do with a plea for money for shopping. Rory Sue would continue to shop even if the store was burning down around her. And somehow she'd talk the clerk into giving her a fire-sale discount while she was at it. It was a skill she'd learned at her mama's knee, though Mary Vaughn would have preferred if she'd learned a few Southern graces instead.

"I wanted to talk to you about Christmas," Rory Sue said.

"You want to talk about Christmas? In September?"

"Yes, well, I thought I'd better ask about this now and not hit you with it at the last possible second."

Mary Vaughn's antenna shot up. "Hit me with what?"

"I was thinking that since we don't really have a traditional celebration, you know, the way we used to when I was little…"

In other words, before Sonny had divorced Mary Vaughn

and ruined their daughter's life, she thought sourly as she waited for the other shoe to drop.

"Anyway, I was thinking that maybe you'd let me go away over the holidays," Rory Sue concluded in a rush. "To Aspen. Jill's family goes there to ski every year and she's invited me to come along. I have to let her know right away, though, because if I can't go, she wants to ask someone else."

"No," Mary Vaughn said without giving it a second's thought. "People spend Christmas with their families. It's not a time to go gallivanting off with strangers."

"Jill's not a stranger. She's been my roommate for two years now."

Mary Vaughn could have corrected her with a reminder that the second year was just starting, but she didn't waste her breath. Instead, she said, "You hardly know her family and I don't know them at all."

"You're just worried about how it will look if I don't come home for Christmas," Rory Sue accused. "You're afraid that people will think you're a failure as a mother. That's it, isn't it? All you care about is your image in that stupid town."

To Mary Vaughn's regret, that was part of it. She hated that her own child, whom she loved more than anything, didn't even want to spend Christmas with her. How pitiful was that? She simply didn't want people in this town to feel sorry for her the way they once had. She'd spent her entire adult life trying to change the way people looked at her.

But the other part, the most important part, was how lonely she'd feel. What would she do if Rory Sue didn't come home? Sit in that big ole house of theirs and stare at the walls? Light up that little ceramic tree she'd inherited from her mother and drink eggnog until she forgot she was all alone? No, the bleak picture she envisioned simply could not happen.

A couple of years from now Rory Sue might well be living on her own in some city far away. She might be unable to get back home for the holidays, or she might even have a family of her own and Mary Vaughn would have to go to some strange city to celebrate, but not this year. This year, Mary Vaughn wanted her daughter right here in Serenity. She wanted a traditional Christmas and she intended to have it, even if Rory Sue hated her for insisting on it.

"No," she said again, flatly.

"You won't even consider it?" Rory Sue pleaded.

"No, absolutely not. And don't call your father and try to get him on your side, either. I won't have you trying to play us off against each other. That might have worked when you were ten, but it won't work now. We're older and smarter."

To her relief, Rory Sue actually giggled. "You really think so?"

"I *know* so," Mary Vaughn said emphatically. "I love you, and I promise we will have the very best Christmas ever right here in Serenity."

"That is *so* not possible," Rory Sue retorted. "Bye, Mom."

"Bye, sweetie."

As she disconnected the call, Mary Vaughn resolved to find some way to make good on her promise, even if she had to start speaking to Rory Sue's beloved daddy—and her very estranged ex-husband—to accomplish it.

Jeanette had been avoiding Maddie all morning. She knew the subject of her involvement on the town's Christmas festival planning committee was far from over. There was also bound to be a discussion about why Jeanette was so opposed to participating in anything related to Christmas. In fact, she fully expected Maddie to call in the big guns—Dana Sue and Helen—before all was said and done.

When it came to something like this, the Sweet Magnolias were a team. Jeanette might be a member, but they could pull rank on her. When one of them fell out of step for any reason, the others rallied. She'd seen it happen more than once. She was dreading it. Last night's encounter with Dana Sue had been a mild precursor to what today was likely to hold. And the more she'd thought about trying to convince Maddie to turn the project over to Elliot, the less she'd believed the suggestion would be taken seriously—especially if Maddie was matchmaking.

"You don't seem to be your usual perky self," Mary Vaughn Lewis said as Jeanette smoothed moisturizer onto her throat and face.

"Sorry," she said, forcing a smile. "My mind's been on other things all day." Then she deliberately changed the subject. "How's your daughter doing? Is she happy being back at school? She's at Clemson, right?"

Usually asking about Rory Sue was enough to send Mary Vaughn off and running, and today was no exception, though Jeanette could sense an underlying tension in her client as she spoke about how well her daughter was doing at college.

"You're saying all the right words," Jeanette said after a minute. "But something's bothering you. Do you think she's unhappy?"

"Unhappy with me," Mary Vaughn admitted. "I won't let her go skiing in Aspen over Christmas."

"Why not?"

"Because the holidays are meant to be spent with family," Mary Vaughn said as if it were the law.

"Not necessarily," Jeanette said carefully. "I mean, sometimes it's great, if everyone gets along really well, but half the families I know are totally dysfunctional. They'd all be much happier if they didn't spend ten minutes together over the holidays."

"Is your family one of those?"

"You have no idea," Jeanette said, then clamped her mouth shut. She'd already revealed too much. She needed to get the focus back on Mary Vaughn and her daughter. "Maybe you could go to Aspen, too. Then you'd both get what you want. You and Rory Sue would be together and she'd be able to ski with her friends. What's really keeping you in Serenity?"

"Tradition," Mary Vaughn insisted. "And it would break her daddy's heart not to have her home for the holidays. When it comes to Christmas, Sonny is all about family. So is that daddy of his."

"You mean Mayor Lewis," Jeanette said.

Mary Vaughn nodded. "I swear that man spends the entire year thinking about playing Santa for all the kids. Serenity's Christmas festival is his very favorite thing on earth. Now that I'm president of the chamber of commerce, I'm going to have to serve on the festival committee, and I'm here to tell you it is not something I'm looking forward to. Howard and I are like oil and water on a good day, and believe me, good days are few and far between."

Jeanette regarded her with genuine sympathy. "Ever thought of delegating?"

"Send some underling and imply that the festival committee isn't the absolutely most important thing in my life? Are you kidding me? I'd never hear the end of it from Howard."

"Maddie wants me to represent The Corner Spa on the committee," Jeanette admitted. "I said no."

Mary Vaughn's eyes lit up. "You didn't!" she protested. "You *have* to do it. You'll save my sanity. Please, Jeanette, promise me you'll change your mind. If we're on the committee together, it'll be fun."

Jeanette couldn't imagine how Mary Vaughn could say that, especially knowing she'd have to deal with her former father-in-law, who was one of the most pompous residents of Serenity.

"Maddie might let you off the hook," Mary Vaughn continued, "but I won't let you say no to me. I want you to commit to doing this right this second. Please. We'll have a ball. You and me trying to keep all those stuffy old men on their toes. I know you love a challenge as much as I do. Say yes." She regarded Jeanette hopefully, then waited.

Jeanette sighed. "Maybe," she said at last. It was as much of a commitment as she was prepared to make. A flat-out no, sadly, was getting harder and harder to say.

CHAPTER THREE

Tom had one more meeting on his calendar for Friday and then he intended to head to Charleston for a command appearance at one of his mother's charity events. He'd promised to spend the night, but he intended to be back in Serenity first thing on Saturday so he could start looking for an apartment or a house.

His phone buzzed. "Cal Maddox is here to see you," Teresa chirped with her unflagging cheeriness.

"Am I supposed to know who he is?"

She sighed. "I'll be right in."

"I didn't ask you to come in," he muttered, but he was talking to a dead line. His office door was already opening…and closing.

With her short, steel-gray hair, rounded figure and penchant for flowered blouses and pastel slacks, Teresa looked as if she ought to be home baking cookies, but she ran this office with the efficiency of a drill sergeant. Right now she was regarding him with motherly dismay.

"If you and I are going to get along, you have to pay attention when I talk to you," she scolded. "Or at the very least, read what I write on that calendar I give you every morning."

Tom winced. "Sorry," he murmured, shuffling papers until he found the neatly prepared schedule for his day that he'd barely glanced at. He'd jotted his own notes on an At-A-Glance calendar. This meeting wasn't on that.

"Okay, here it is," he confirmed, finding it on Teresa's schedule. "Cal Maddox, high school baseball coach." He stared up blankly. "Why does he want to see me? I don't have anything to do with the school system."

Teresa gave him an impatient look and gestured toward the paper.

"Regarding starting a Little League program in the town," he read aloud.

She nodded. "I do my job. You need to get used to my system."

Tom barely contained a grin. In most places he'd worked, it was the boss who got to devise the system. "I'll try," he promised dutifully.

She regarded him with blatant skepticism. "We'll see," she said with a little huff. "Shall I send Cal in now?"

"Please do."

A minute later, the coach walked in, a grin on his face. "What'd you do to tick off Teresa?"

Tom hesitated, then shrugged. "Almost everything I do ticks off Teresa. Most recently I failed to read her notes."

Cal held out a callused hand, shook Tom's, then said, "Just so you understand, Teresa's been essentially running Serenity for the past fifteen years. You're an interloper."

"She was town manager?" Tom asked, startled by the information. "No one mentioned that."

"No way," Cal said, laughing. "But your predecessors

pretty much let her run the show. If you actually expect to do this job your own way, you'll have to ease her into it."

"I'll keep that in mind," Tom told him, grateful for the insight. It put a new spin on the uneasy relationship he'd had with his secretary since his arrival. He gestured toward a chair. "Have a seat. What can I do for you? Teresa's note said something about starting a Little League program."

Cal handed him a folder. "It's all in there. I've described the benefits to the town, the costs, the businesses who've committed to sponsoring the teams, the other communities that have similar summer programs."

"What do you need from me?"

"Start-up funding," Cal said. "That figure's in there, too. And I need another coach. I figure we'd have enough kids for at least two teams, one for the younger boys, another for the older boys."

Tom gave him a questioning look. "You're suggesting I coach?"

Cal nodded. "You did play ball at Clemson, didn't you? First base, as I recall."

Tom gaped. "How on earth do you know about that? I only played college ball for a year before I was injured and had to give it up." Then his eyes widened. "Cal Maddox?" he said, the name finally sinking in. "You played for the Atlanta Braves?"

Cal nodded. "Briefly. I was sidelined by an injury, too, but I was there when the scouting reports on you came in. You were a hot prospect, which I figure qualifies you to coach Little League in Serenity. Will you think about it?"

"First you need to have a Little League program in place," Tom said. He gestured toward the folder. "I'll go over your proposal this weekend and see if it fits in with the budget the town's about to finalize, then we'll talk again."

"Fair enough," Cal told him, standing up to leave.

"Hey, before you go, you're an athlete. Where do you go to get a good workout in this town?"

The confident man before him looked oddly disconcerted by the question. "If you swear never to repeat it, I'll tell you," he said at last.

"Confidentiality is my middle name," Tom assured him.

Cal leaned closer as if he feared Teresa or someone else might overhear. "I sneak into The Corner Spa after hours."

Tom stared at him incredulously. "You're kidding me! I've been told in no uncertain terms that the place is off limits to men."

"It is," Cal confirmed. "I'm married to one of the owners. She pretends not to notice that I borrow her key from time to time. Of course, if anyone ever catches me in there, I suspect my wife would throw me to the wolves and deny knowing me, much less admit she gave me tacit permission to sneak in."

Tom laughed. "Sounds like an interesting relationship."

"You have no idea," Cal said. "Maddie's a fascinating woman and the best thing that ever happened to me. I'm sure you two will cross paths before too long, especially if we get this Little League thing pulled together."

"I'll look forward to it," Tom said. "And I'll be in touch within the next week or so about your proposal."

"Thanks. Enjoy your weekend."

Tom thought about the formal event ahead of him tonight and the inevitable lecture from his father likely to be on tomorrow's agenda. Enjoyment didn't enter into any of it.

Jeanette had gotten through yet another day without crossing paths with Maddie. She was hoping to keep it that way. She'd picked up her tote bag and purse and was headed out the side door when Maddie appeared.

"Sneaking off?" she inquired lightly.

Jeanette grinned. "I was trying to."

"Can you stay for a minute?"

"Is that a request or a command?"

"A request, of course," Maddie insisted. She held up two glasses of tea and a clear box that held two cranberry-orange scones, Jeanette's favorite. "I brought bribes."

Jeanette released a sigh and turned toward the outdoor patio, Maddie following on her heels.

After they were seated, Jeanette took a bite of the light, flaky scone, then frowned. It was still warm. "Where'd this come from? I know we didn't have scones in the café today. I checked."

"I asked Dana Sue to whip up a batch and send them over," Maddie admitted. "They just arrived a few minutes ago, straight from the oven."

"You really are desperate for me to serve on this Christmas festival committee, aren't you?" Jeanette said as she savored another bite. Between the comfort food and Maddie's bribes she was going to be as big as a blimp.

"At the moment, I'm more interested in why you're so opposed to the idea. I've been giving you some space and thinking about our conversation, and I don't believe your reaction had anything to do with taking on a little extra work for a couple of months. Am I right?"

When Jeanette remained silent, she prodded, "So what was it about?"

Because she absolutely didn't want to get into that, Jeanette looked Maddie in the eye. "I'll do it."

Maddie appeared taken aback. "Do what?"

"Be on the stupid committee," Jeanette grumbled. "Isn't that what we're talking about?"

Maddie did not appear nearly as pleased by her capitulation as Jeanette had expected.

"Forget the committee for the moment. Tell me why Christmas upsets you," Maddie said. "I've just realized that you always take your vacation at Christmas, but you don't go home to visit your family, you don't go away, you just hole up in your apartment. I checked with Helen and Dana Sue, too, and none of us can recall you accepting a single invitation to a holiday celebration with any of us. There has to be a reason."

"I'm antisocial," Jeanette said.

"No, you are not," Maddie said, dismissing the reply. "You've come to lots of things—Fourth of July barbecues, margarita nights, Thanksgiving dinner. No, this is all about Christmas. You have an aversion to that specific holiday and I want to know why."

"It's my business," Jeanette replied stubbornly. "I know you want to help, but there's not a problem. I just don't like Christmas holidays." She scowled at Maddie. "And don't you dare tell me that *everybody* loves the holidays."

"Well, they do. At least around here."

"Then I'm an exception to the rule. Look, I said I'd serve on the committee. That should be enough."

"What changed your mind?" Maddie asked.

"Boy, you really don't know when to quit, do you?"

Maddie merely lifted a brow.

"No, of course you don't," Jeanette muttered. "Part of it was to get you off my case and part of it has to do with Mary Vaughn. She begged me to do it because she has to do it."

Maddie stared at her incredulously. "You're doing this

for Mary Vaughn? After the way she tried to steal Ronnie from Dana Sue?"

"He and Dana Sue were separated at the time," Jeanette reminded Maddie, feeling the need to defend her client. "Besides, she never had a chance with Ronnie, and everyone except Mary Vaughn knew it. The point is, she's a good customer and she asked me to do this."

"I'm your boss and *I* asked, and you didn't have any problem saying no to me," Maddie groused, then shook her head. "You're doing this for Mary Vaughn. Wait'll I tell Dana Sue and Helen."

"I'm mainly doing this to get you off my case," Jeanette corrected her. "And that hasn't worked nearly as well as I'd expected, so I'm going home before I change my mind."

Maddie opened her mouth, but Jeanette held up her hand. "Leave well enough alone, okay?"

"I was just going to say, if you ever want to talk about anything, all of us are here for you, understood?"

To her regret, Jeanette's eyes misted. "Understood," she whispered, and then bolted before she could make a complete fool of herself by bursting into tears.

Tom couldn't wait to get on the road back to Serenity on Saturday morning. The charity function had been everything he despised about Charleston's social scene. He could only imagine what the budget had been for the formal dinner and dance that his mother had organized for years. If that money alone had been donated directly to the cause, it probably would have equaled the amount raised. Whenever he mentioned that, she looked at him as if he'd uttered a blasphemy.

"This is what's expected," she'd told him more than once.

"When you hold a position in society, it is your duty to do good works."

"I'm just saying it would be more cost-effective to write a check," he'd argued.

"An event brings attention to the cause. And it supports local businesses. Where would the caterers, the florists, the printers and so on be if we stopped holding these fund-raisers?"

"So this is all about supporting the Charleston economy?"

She'd frowned at him. "Oh, for heaven's sake, you know it's about more than that. I know you think what I do is frivolous and unnecessary, but one of these days I'll reduce it all to dollars and cents for you and prove my point in a way you can understand."

He'd grinned at her. "I'd appreciate that."

"You're incorrigible," she'd declared.

"But you love me."

"Most of the time," she'd agreed. "Now, if you would just marry and provide us with an heir to the McDonald legacy, I could forgive all these silly arguments."

"Mother, you have six lovely granddaughters to dote on. The next generation is off to a fine start."

"None of them will carry on the McDonald name," she'd reminded him. "Even if one of your sisters has a son, he won't be a McDonald."

"So I'm to marry and have a son, is that the plan?"

She'd given him a stern look, though there was a decided twinkle in her eye. "I'd appreciate it," she'd said.

If his mother was gently persuasive with her marching orders, his father was downright dictatorial, Tom thought as he finished the eggs, ham, grits and redeye gravy the cook had prepared for him. It seemed he'd never had a conversation with Thomas Barlow McDonald that didn't end with one of them walking out in a huff. He'd give anything to avoid that this morning, but trying to slip away without paying his respects to his father would just lead to a tearful phone call from his mother later in the day. If arguing with his father was tedious, then listening to his mother's guilt-inducing lectures was worse.

It was too late to escape, anyway. His father strolled in, already dressed for his regular Saturday-morning golf outing at the private country club where McDonalds had been members ever since the eighteen-hole course had been carved out of the countryside.

"I thought you were taking off first thing this morning," his father said as he filled his plate from the serving dishes on the antique sideboard.

Tom swallowed the desire to answer honestly and admit that he'd considered doing just that. "We didn't have much chance to talk last night," he said instead. "I thought we could catch up this morning. How's your golf game?"

"Still better than yours, I imagine," his father replied. "You playing at all, or do they even have a course in that place you're living?"

Tom clung to his patience by a thread. "The town is Serenity, Dad, and yes, there is an excellent golf course nearby and another one being built just a few miles away. If you and Mother would take a drive over one day, you'd discover there's a whole big world that isn't Charleston."

"So, you *are* playing," his father said, sticking to his favorite topic with characteristic tenacity.

"Actually, I haven't had the time," Tom told him. Or the desire, for that matter. Golf wasn't active enough to suit him, or maybe he just played it badly. At any rate, the prospect of coaching Little League was much more appealing.

"Are you determined to turn your back on everything I do?" his father inquired, finally hitting his stride on his favorite complaint about Tom.

Tom was way past the stage of wanting to rebel against everything his parents stood for. "I'm just making choices that work for me, Dad. I wish you could understand that."

"What I understand is that you're wasting opportunities. You could have put that law degree of yours to good use right here in Charleston. You'd be making the right connections at the club. In another year or two, you'd be in a perfect position to run for governor or even Congress. That's your destiny, Tom, not counting the pennies in the treasury of some nothing little town."

"Seems to me the folks in Washington could do with a few lessons in counting pennies," Tom commented dryly, drawing a scowl from his father.

"You know what I mean," Thomas McDonald scolded. "You're way overqualified for this job. You have an undergraduate degree in business, a law degree and all the right connections to make something of yourself. You won't do that in Serenity."

Tom pushed aside his plate and sat back with a sigh. "I'm sorry that I'm not ambitious enough to suit you. I like knowing the people in my community. I like seeing the results of decisions I've made when I step outside my office. I like solving problems for individuals and for the town."

"What the hell do you think politics is about?" his father bellowed. "It's all that, but on a much grander scale."

"Maybe so," Tom conceded. "When it's not about raising enough money to win an election or taking the most popular stance to win the next election or doing the expedient thing to get the backing of some organization. I'm not saying there aren't decent, hardworking politicians who can do a lot of good, but I don't have the patience to deal with all the rest of it. I'm sorry. Obviously you and I will never agree about this. I hope we're not going to have this same discussion every time we see each other."

"I can't promise you that," his father said sourly. "I'll never give up trying to talk some sense into you."

Tom sighed heavily, wishing he could understand why this mattered so much to his father. Since figuring out what made his father tick seemed unlikely, he settled for trying to make peace.

"I don't suppose you'd like to drive over to Serenity one Saturday and play golf with me there, take a look around? We have a first-class restaurant, too. I think you and Mom would like it."

His father looked as if he was about to dismiss the suggestion out of hand, but his mother came into the room in time to hear the invitation.

"We'd love to do that, wouldn't we, Thomas?" she said, giving her husband a fierce look.

"Whatever you want," he mumbled. "I need to go. I have an early tee time."

"Shall I expect you for lunch?" Tom's mother inquired.

"No, I'll eat at the club." He was halfway out the door, when he turned and said, "Good to see you, son."

"You, too, Dad."

After he'd gone, Tom turned to his mother. "Well, there was no bloodshed. I'd say that's an improvement."

She shook her head and sat down facing him. "I don't understand why the two of you can't see eye to eye on anything."

"Because I won't bend to his will. I know he wants what he thinks is best for me, but one of these days he needs to listen to what *I* want."

Clarisse McDonald gave him an amused look. "Oh, I think you've made yourself abundantly clear. He just disagrees. He had such hopes for you."

"I know, and I understand that it's normal for a father to want certain things for his son, but Dad seems obsessed with getting his way, no matter how many times I explain that I'm happy with the path I've chosen."

"You know why that is, don't you?"

"Because he's a stubborn old coot?" Tom suggested.

His mother frowned. "He doesn't deserve your disrespect. Someday you need to come down off your high horse, Tom, and really talk to him. Life wasn't as easy for him as it has been for you."

Tom was taken aback. "The McDonalds have had wealth and a place in Charleston society for generations."

"No thanks to your grandfather," his mother said with obvious distaste.

Tom regarded her with surprise. "What does that mean?" He barely remembered his grandfather McDonald beyond the fact that he'd always tucked a quarter into Tom's hand, then chortled when he'd said, "Don't spend it all in one place."

"Ask your father about him," his mother said. "Perhaps then you'll understand him a little better."

"Couldn't *you* just tell me?"

"I could, but the two of you need to learn to communicate," she informed him. "Now, tell me about this little town you're running. Are you happy there?"

"I'm still getting a feel for the place," he admitted. "But I think I'm going to like it." He thought of the woman he'd met on his visit to The Corner Spa. "It definitely has some intriguing residents."

His mother's expression brightened. "A woman? One in particular?"

"Possibly."

"Tell me," she commanded, leaning forward with interest.

"There's not much to tell. I don't even know her name. I ran into her outside a women's spa. We exchanged a few words and then she shut the door in my face."

His mother sat back, her expression indignant. "Well, that doesn't sound very pleasant. She must not have very good breeding."

Tom grinned. "I didn't inquire about her pedigree, Mother. She was already annoyed enough."

"I'm just saying that a lady does not go around shutting doors in people's faces."

"I'll explain that to her when we cross paths again." And they *would* cross paths. He intended to see to that. He figured Cal Maddox might have some ideas along that line since the woman in question must work with his wife.

Thinking of Cal reminded him of the Little League proposal. Wanting to change the subject, he decided to mention that. His mother had always been a big supporter of his interest in baseball, even though she'd embarrassed the daylights out of him by coming to his games outfitted as if she were going to tea with the queen.

"Wait till you hear about this," he said, and described his meeting with Cal Maddox.

"There's a former professional ballplayer living in Serenity?" she said, clearly stunned. "I had no idea."

Tom laughed at her expression. "You'd probably be surprised by a few more of the people you'd meet there. Ever heard of Paula Vreeland?"

"The artist? Of course. Her works are displayed at some of the finer galleries here in Charleston."

"She lives in Serenity."

His mother shook her head. "You must be mistaken. I'm quite sure she lives here."

"Nope. The mayor pointed out her home and studio when he drove me around town. And this spa I mentioned has apparently received a lot of acclaim around the entire region, as has Sullivan's for its gourmet spin on old Southern favorites."

"Obviously I need to see this place for myself. Sit right here while I get my calendar. We'll pick a date and I'll come for a visit."

"With Dad?"

She cast him a wry look. "Perhaps I should come alone the first time. Scout it out, so to speak."

"That suits me," Tom said. If his open-minded mother left with a favorable impression, perhaps she could get through to his father. Their years of marriage had been achieved through an interesting balance of power. His mother, remarkably, wielded most of it.

She bustled from the room and came back with a bulging day planner that he knew was stuffed with business cards from her favorite florists, printers, dressmakers and caterers, along with those from newly opened businesses hoping to capture her attention. She flipped through the pages, muttering under her breath as she did.

"Two weeks from today," she said at last. "It's the best I can do. I'll have to cancel my luncheon and bridge plans, but there's time enough for them to find a fourth."

"Two weeks from today will be perfect." He stood up and bent down to kiss her cheek. "Thank you, Mother. I'll look forward to it."

His words were totally sincere. He wanted her to see Serenity as he did, as a lovely town to live in and a place with a promising future. And though he hardly dared to say it to himself, as a stepping stone to an even better job down the road. Contrary to what his father thought, he was not without ambition. He merely planned to take a different path than the one Thomas McDonald had charted for him.

CHAPTER FOUR

❖

Because so many of her best clients were working women who could only come in for treatments on Saturday, Jeanette rarely had an entire weekend to herself. She liked it that way. Sundays seemed endless, especially the ones when she didn't go to church. The day stretched ahead of her with too many empty hours.

How long could she possibly spend doing laundry or stocking her refrigerator for the few meals she ate at home? Serenity didn't have a movie theater and she wasn't interested in golf, kayaking or any of the other activities available in town. It was the one drawback she'd found to living in a small community after spending several years in Charleston. Despite all its other charms and the wonderful people, the peace and quiet of Serenity got on her nerves from time to time, especially with no one special to share her life.

This Sunday seemed worse than most. She had way too much time to think about Christmas and her family and all the reasons the holiday had lost its meaning for her.

By three o'clock she was going a little stir-crazy. She glanced at the phone next to her and thought about how long it had been since she'd spoken to her parents. They lived less than two hours away, but she hadn't seen or spoken to them in months. After leaving home, she'd soon learned that if she didn't initiate a call, it wouldn't happen. It was almost as if they forgot her very existence unless she reminded them.

Impulsively, she picked up the phone and dialed before she could talk herself out of it. It rang several times before her mother picked up.

"Hi, Mom."

"Jeanette, is that you?"

She wasn't surprised that her mother wasn't sure. "Yes, Mom, it's me. How are you?"

"Doing well enough," she said, not volunteering anything additional.

Despite the terse response, Jeanette pressed on. "And Dad? How is he?" Her father was nearing seventy, but seemed older. Working outdoors had weathered his skin and what her parents always referred to as "the tragedy" had aged him before his time.

"Working too hard, as always," her mother replied. "The farm's too much for him, but it's the only life he knows."

"Did he hire any help this year?" Jeanette asked, determined to keep the conversation flowing and hoping to spark even a smidgen of real communication.

"He had several day workers when vegetables were coming in, but he's let most of them go now that the only crop left is pumpkins. He loads those up himself and takes them to the market on Saturdays."

"Is he there? I'd like to say hello," Jeanette said. At one time her father had doted on her the way Cal doted on Jessica Lynn. All that had changed in the blink of an eye, and while she understood the reason on an intellectual level, the chasm between them didn't hurt any less.

"He's outside working on the tractor," her mother replied, not offering to get him. After a slight hesitation, good manners kicked in and she added, "But I'll tell him you called."

Jeanette barely contained a sigh. She couldn't even recall the last time her father had spoken to her. Her mother always had some excuse for why he couldn't come to the phone. Some rang true, like this one. Others didn't. Sometimes she thought he'd simply stopped talking to anyone after her brother had died.

Forcing a cheerful note into her voice, she asked, "Tell me what you've been doing, Mom. Are you still baking for the church receptions every week?"

"Took a coconut cake in today," her mother said. "I'll do chocolate next week. That's everybody's favorite."

"Mine, too," Jeanette said. "Maybe I'll drive down for a visit soon and you can bake one for me."

There was another unmistakable hesitation before her mother said, "You just let us know when you're coming, Jeanette."

This time Jeanette didn't even try to stop her sigh. Just once she'd hoped for some warmth, some sign that her parents missed her and wanted to see her. Instead, her mother sounded more as if she needed to be *warned* if her daughter was about to appear on the doorstep. Or maybe Jeanette had simply grown too sensitive to the nuances in her mother's voice. She'd come to expect rejection and found it in every word.

"I'll let you know, Mom," she said, resigned to ending another disappointing call. "Good to talk to you."

"You, too," her mother said.

It was only after she'd hung up that she realized her mother hadn't asked a single question about how she was doing or what was going on in her life. The lack of interest stung, even after all these years. She still recalled a time when she'd run in the back door after school, filled with news of her day, and her mother had put cookies and milk on the table and listened to every word. She'd seemed to treasure those afternoon talks as much as Jeanette had. Now they could barely manage a five-minute conversation and most of that one-sided.

"If I sit here one more minute, I'll start wallowing in self-pity," she muttered aloud, grabbing her purse and heading for the door.

Two hours later she was sitting in a Charleston multiplex with a giant box of buttered popcorn, a diet soda and a box of Junior Mints. The movie, a heavily promoted action flick, barely held her interest. Even so, it was an improvement on sitting at home all alone on a Sunday afternoon thinking about her dysfunctional relationship with her parents, a relationship she had no idea how to mend.

As she was exiting the theater, she heard a familiar voice and turned to see Maddie's son Kyle and several of his friends, accompanied by Cal.

"Wasn't the movie awesome?" Kyle asked her enthusiastically.

Cal interceded before she was forced to reply. "Something tells me Jeanette might have preferred a romantic comedy."

Kyle looked puzzled. "Then why did she go to see this movie?"

Cal met her gaze. "I don't know. Why did you go to see this movie?"

She shrugged. "I figured it would be fast-paced and exciting."

He gave her a knowing look. "Which appealed because it would keep your mind off other things?"

She frowned at him. "You realize, don't you, your intuitive questions are sometimes almost as annoying as your wife's."

Cal laughed. "What can I say? Maddie's rubbing off on me. By the way, we're going for pizza at Rosalina's on the way home. Maddie's meeting us. Want to come along? It'll kill a little more time, if that was your goal."

The idea held some appeal, but the drawbacks outweighed the benfits. "And subject myself to further interrogation? I don't think so."

"Hey, are you kidding? With this gang, plus Jessica Lynn and Cole, the adults will be lucky to be heard. Come on, Jeanette. No questions allowed. I'll make sure of it."

She grinned. "When Maddie's on a mission, there's no stopping her. And lately she seems to be determined to pry into my life."

"Obviously you're not aware of the toddler effect. Maddie is too busy chasing after Jessica Lynn to have time for much else. Mealtimes are no longer the serene part of the day you may recall, especially with Kyle's friends along." Jeanette noted that Cal seemed perfectly happy with that, content even. He'd taken to being a stepfather and then father to his own two little ones without missing a beat.

Based on his promise and a memory of the amount of chaos Jessica Lynn had created on her last visit to the spa, Jeanette relented, partly because the popcorn had hardly been a substantial meal and partly because the prospect of good company was a vast improvement over staring at the

TV and rehashing the unrewarding conversation she'd had with her mother.

"In that case, I'll meet you there. Pizza sounds good."

Cal gave her a considering look. "It's a long drive, lots of time for second thoughts. Do I need to have Kyle and a buddy ride along with you to make sure you show up? Once I've told Maddie you're joining us, I don't want to have you renege."

She frowned. "I won't change my mind. You don't need to send an escort."

He nodded, satisfied. "See you there, then."

Jeanette watched as he strode off with the teenage boys, then went to her car. Outside the parking garage, she lowered the convertible top, popped in a CD and let the music blast. By the time she hit the outskirts of Serenity, she was windblown, but her mood had improved by leaps and bounds.

Good thing, too, because the first person she spotted when she entered Rosalina's was the sexy stranger who'd been on the porch at The Corner Spa...and he was seated with Maddie.

Tom was holding the doll Jessica Lynn Maddox had shoved into his arms when he looked up and saw his mystery woman standing just inside the door. She was staring across the room directly at him, and for just an instant he had the distinct impression she was about to bolt.

Instead, Maddie Maddox was out of her seat across from his and charging across the room, Jessica Lynn on her heels, screaming, "Jeanette, Jeanette," as if they were long-lost friends. He was left to warily eye the baby sleeping in his carrier next to him. He had plenty of experience with his sister's kids, but mostly after they were past the diaper stage. He'd never bought the idea that infants weren't as fragile as they looked.

By the time Maddie returned to the table, her hand clamped rather firmly around the other woman's wrist, Tom was on his feet.

"Jeanette, I'd like you to meet Tom McDonald, the new Serenity town manager," Maddie said, almost shoving Jeanette's hand toward his. He clasped it instinctively. "Tom, this is Jeanette Brioche, who runs the spa operations at The Corner Spa."

"Hello again," he said, holding her soft hand just a little too long. Her smooth skin was a walking advertisement for the spa's treatments.

Though her dark eyes were wary, she smiled and said, "Nice to know my first impression wasn't too far off the mark."

He blinked. "Oh?"

"I told Elliot, our personal trainer, that you looked trustworthy," she explained. "Even though you'd been peering in the windows of the spa alarming the women."

Maddie regarded him with shock. "You did what?"

Tom winced. "It wasn't the way it appeared. I was looking for a place to have a good workout. I was told the spa was only for women, but I wanted to see for myself if I could join. Jeanette intercepted me outside and made it very clear that I couldn't."

"Sorry," Jeanette said, though her voice lacked sincerity. "Just enforcing the rules."

"Maybe you and Cal can team up and get something similar going for the men in town," Maddie suggested. "That way I won't have to pretend I don't know he sneaks in there late at night."

"I don't suppose you'd let me sneak in with him, would you?" Tom asked wistfully.

"Not a chance," Jeanette said sharply, drawing a look from Maddie. "I just mean, Cal's one thing. He's married to an owner. But if we let you sneak in, then someone else will ask, and the next thing you know we won't have a special place for women."

He grinned at her rapid-fire explanation. "For a minute there, I thought maybe you had something against me personally."

"How could I?" she said. "I don't even know you."

"We could change that," he suggested, and had the satisfaction of seeing her blush.

"I don't think so," she said tightly, though yet another sharp glance from Maddie had her adding, "Thanks, anyway."

He just stared at her for a moment before pulling out the chair next to his. Before Jeanette could sit down as he'd hoped, Jessica Lynn scrambled onto it and tugged on his arm. "I'm hungry," she announced. "Where's my doll?"

"Right here," he said, picking it up off the seat of his own chair and handing it to her. Conceding the fact that Jeanette would be sitting elsewhere—probably as far from him as possible—he leaned down and confided to Jessica Lynn, "I'm starving, too."

"Count me among the starving," Jeanette chimed in, surprising him.

"Then let's order," Maddie said. "Cal should be here any minute with the boys."

"Where's Katie?" Jeanette asked.

"At a friend's house, in theory doing homework. I have my doubts—the Grahams have a pool."

Tom regarded Maddie with curiosity. He'd already digested that there was an unmistakable age difference between Maddie and her husband—probably a good ten years—but it also sounded as if they had a large family. And Cal was only around his age—early to midthirties. "How many children do you have?"

"I have five," Maddie told him. She gestured at Jessica Lynn and Cole. "These two are mine with Cal, but I have three from my first marriage. Ty's a sophomore at Duke. Katie, as I mentioned, is with a friend tonight, and Kyle will be here any minute with Cal."

"And you manage the spa full-time?" Tom asked, impressed.

"And does an amazing job of it," Jeanette added. "Women are great multitaskers."

Tom frowned at the note of censure in her voice. "I'm aware of that. I'm just trying to learn who does what in Serenity."

After shooting a bewildered look in Jeanette's direction, which suggested there would be questions for her later, Maddie said, "Well, you'll be happy to know that Jeanette is an organizational wizard herself. She'll be our representative on the Christmas festival committee. Will you be chairing that?"

"Yes," Tom said. Suddenly the prospect of planning the town's holiday celebration didn't seem as dismal as he'd anticipated. He still thought there were better uses of his time, but if it threw him together with Jeanette, it couldn't be all bad. Right now, though, she was regarding him with undisguised suspicion.

"Since you and Maddie clearly don't really know each other, what are you doing here?" Jeanette asked as if he'd crashed the party.

Maddie's expression went from bewildered to dismayed

at Jeanette's rudeness. "I invited him," she said. "And before you ask, it was Cal's suggestion. He called on his way
home and said he'd run into you at the movies and invited
you to join us. He thought it would be nice for Tom to get
to know a few people in town."

Jeanette didn't look entirely satisfied with the answer,
but she sat back and hid behind her menu. The continued
high color in her cheeks was the only thing that gave away
her embarrassment.

Once Cal arrived with the boys, the tension at the table
dissolved, primarily because there was no way Tom and
Jeanette could be expected to communicate with each other.
It wasn't until they were on their way out to the parking lot
that he had a chance to speak to her privately. As the others
drove off, he deliberately lingered beside her.

"I'm sorry if my being here tonight was a problem," he
said, studying her intently. "Have I offended you in some
way? When Maddie called, I had no idea who else would
be here. I was just tired of staring at the four walls of my
room at the Serenity Inn, so I seized on the chance to get
out for a meal and some conversation."

She sighed heavily. "I'm sorry. I know I've behaved like
an idiot, but you don't know Maddie that well yet, or her
partners. They...meddle."

Ah, the picture was getting clearer. "Inveterate match-
makers, huh?"

"You have no idea. It was amusing when they were focused on each other, but now they seem to be turning their
attention to me. It's humiliating, to say nothing of unwelcome. And it's really embarrassing to see you put on the
spot the way you were tonight."

"I wasn't embarrassed. It made my day when I looked

up and saw you crossing the restaurant. I'd been hoping to run into you again."

His response only seemed to aggravate her. "I don't date," she said emphatically.

Tom wasn't half as put off as she'd clearly intended for him to be. She'd inadvertently created a fascinating challenge for him. He'd always excelled when told that something was beyond his reach.

"I imagine there's a story behind that," he said, holding her gaze until she looked away.

"Several of them, unfortunately."

She started to walk away, but he stayed in step with her. "We'll have to get together sometime so you can tell me about it."

Her lips twitched. "Wouldn't that constitute a date?"

"Not if we don't want it to," he said seriously. "Two friends commiserating over a good dinner and a bottle of wine could be perfectly innocent."

"Not if one of those 'friends' is you," she said. "I may be wrong, but somehow I don't think there's anything innocent about you."

Tom didn't even try to deny it. "It's the dimple, isn't it?" he said with exaggerated dismay.

"You, Mr. McDonald, are entirely too full of yourself. Something tells me you're a player."

"I was always told that self-confidence is a good trait. Did I get that wrong?" he asked worriedly.

"You say self-confidence," she teased. "I say arrogance."

"I'll work on that," he promised.

"We'll see."

"Hey, I'm all for self-improvement, especially if it means you'll eventually say yes to having dinner with me."

"Self-improvement should be its own reward," she said. "Good night."

"Do you need a lift?" he asked hopefully.

"No, thanks. I have my car."

"Then, can you give me a lift?"

"What about the car in which you just offered to drive me home?"

He shrugged. "I'll get it tomorrow."

For the first time all evening, she laughed. "You're incorrigible."

He shrugged, unrepentant. "You're not the first person to tell me that this weekend."

"Apparently the women in your life are all on to you."

"The other one was my mother," he admitted.

"Well, I rest my case. She would definitely know."

She climbed into her sporty little convertible, gave him a jaunty wave and drove off, leaving him in her dust. Being rejected by Jeanette Brioche was getting to be a little hard on his ego, which of course only made him more determined to win her over. He had a hunch he knew the rules of this game far better than she did and, in the end, he never lost. Not when something mattered to him.

Despite knowing that the Christmas committee would throw him into contact with the elusive Jeanette, Tom had hoped Howard would back off for a while. Unfortunately, when he arrived at work on Monday morning, it rapidly became evident that this was one area in which the mayor was highly efficient. Tom's secretary beamed at him.

"The committee's waiting for you in the conference room," Teresa announced. "I've had coffee and doughnuts brought in."

Tom frowned at her. "What committee? I don't have a meeting on my calendar for this morning."

Her smile never wavered. "Oh, dear, I must have forgotten to make a note of it on that calendar you insist on keeping yourself. It's on the one I keep."

"What committee, Teresa?" he repeated impatiently.

"Christmas festival, of course. I know Howard discussed it with you. He asked me to set it up."

Sneaky SOB, Tom thought uncharitably. And as for Teresa and her annoying tendency to take orders from people like Howard Lewis, she did know more than anyone else about how this place operated. He needed her. Otherwise his career in public service in Serenity was going to be very short-lived. That might make his folks happy, but he didn't want his career to falter even slightly because he'd offended a knowledgeable secretary within his first two weeks on the job.

"Okay, give me a quick rundown on the committee members," he said, grimly determined to see this through. Once it was over, perhaps he could reconsider whether he was at all suited to a life of public service, after all. It had sounded darn noble once upon a time, but that was before he'd been confronted with making decisions about hanging snowflakes on the town green or whether Santa's chair needed to be repainted with gold and adorned with glitter or whatever other little crises this committee dreamed up to waste his time. He was pretty sure nothing like this had ever been mentioned in any of his public-administration courses. And he definitely hadn't run into this sort of thing during his tenure in the planning and finance departments of the other towns in which he'd worked.

He listened as Teresa described the makeup on the committee. In addition to Howard and Jeanette, the other two members were Ronnie Sullivan, who owned the hardware store on Main Street, and Mary Vaughn Lewis, the president of the chamber of commerce.

"You'll want to watch out for Mary Vaughn," Teresa added. "She's bound to make a play for you. It's what she does."

Tom appreciated the warning, though he couldn't help wondering if another woman's interest might be just what he needed to spark a little life into the relationship he hoped to have with Jeanette. Then again, plans like that tended to backfire, he thought as he prepared to go to the meeting.

Jeanette sat at the conference table tapping her pen impatiently on the mahogany surface. She was thoroughly annoyed that she'd had to switch her entire schedule around at the spa to be here, but to make things worse, Tom was nowhere to be found.

Not that she was anxious to see him again. Dinner the night before had been awkward enough. She'd been rude, and she wasn't likely to hear the end of it from Maddie anytime soon, either. Nor was she looking forward to more of Tom's advances. She had a hunch he was persistent.

She turned to Mary Vaughn. "This is a waste of time," she groused. "You could have sold another house this morning and I could have done two or three treatments. If the town manager isn't here in five minutes I am out of here."

Across the table Ronnie Sullivan, Dana Sue's husband, winked at her. "Settle down, sugar. Things move at a slower pace in Serenity."

"Tell that to Maddie," she retorted.

He grinned. "The way I understand it, Madelyn is the one who sent you over here. I'm sure she knew what to expect."

Discovering that Ronnie was on the committee had been a surprise. Dana Sue had never mentioned that. She wondered if Dana Sue had any idea that Mary Vaughn was on the committee, as well. No way, she concluded. If Dana Sue had known, she'd have been here herself, protecting her turf: Ronnie.

Jeanette stole another glance at Mary Vaughn, who was wearing one of her expensive designer suits, chunky gold jewelry and a diamond-encrusted watch that cost more than Jeanette made in a month. Suddenly she was struck by the thought that Mary Vaughn and Tom McDonald were an ideal match. Both professionals. Both go-getters. And both, apparently, on the prowl. Yes, indeed, that was the solution to her problem. Once those two met, Tom would give up on Jeanette and move happily on to more available prey.

Astonishingly, the idea didn't hold nearly as much appeal as it ought to.

Finally Tom came into the room, looking no happier than she was to be here. She had to admit that dressed up for work in neatly pressed navy slacks, a blue-gray shirt the exact color of his eyes, gold cuff links and a tie that he'd already loosened, he managed to give a little jolt to her system even though he was definitely not her type. She preferred sexy, blue-collar guys who had absolutely no pretenses. Of course, based on past results, her taste was pretty questionable.

"Morning, folks," Tom said in a slow drawl that gave Jeanette another jolt to her system. Darn the man. He smiled, introduced himself and shook hands with everyone at the table. His attitude was friendly enough with most of them, but turned a little frosty when he reached the mayor. "Howard," he said curtly.

"Good morning," Howard said, oblivious to the undercurrent. He and Ronnie seemed to be the only people one hundred percent happy to be here.

Next to her, as anticipated, Mary Vaughn was studying Tom with a look suggesting he might well become her next romantic diversion. Jeanette noted the way Mary Vaughn honed in on Tom's left hand, obviously noting the lack of wedding band. She suddenly perked up, readjusting her suit jacket to expose a bit of cleavage. Jeanette sighed. Could she be any more obvious?

"Howard, since you called this meeting, why don't you get it started," Tom suggested. "I'm sure you have an agenda. Since I'm unfamiliar with the traditions here in town, I'll just take notes today and chime in if a suggestion comes to mind."

His tone hinted that any suggestions he might want to make right now wouldn't be offered in the spirit of the holidays. Jeanette totally sympathized.

Howard, however, took the ball and ran with it. Within an hour, he'd assigned Mary Vaughn to speak to all the choirs in town. Ronnie had been designated to investigate new decorations. That had left dealing with prospective vendors for Jeanette.

"Tom, you'll work with her on that, right?" the mayor said, to Mary Vaughn's obvious disappointment.

"Of course," the town manager said, giving Jeanette an impudent wink.

"Then I'd say we're well on our way to having the best Christmas festival Serenity has ever seen," Howard chirped cheerfully. "Good job, everyone. Same time next week."

"We're meeting weekly?" Jeanette asked, horrified.

"Well, of course we are. We have to stay on top of this, don't we?" Howard replied. "I might be Santa around here, but I can't do this without my little elves."

Tom looked as if he wanted to jab his ballpoint pen straight into the mayor's heart. Jeanette understood the emotion.

"He's not worth the time in jail," she murmured as she passed by.

To her surprise, his lips twitched. "You sure about that?"

"Now that you mention it, no. Check with me again next week. I might supply the pens."

CHAPTER FIVE

When Jeanette finally made it back to The Corner Spa, she was edgy and more annoyed than ever with Maddie for getting her involved in the Christmas festival. Two hours wasted every week from September all the way until the event itself in early December! Ridiculous. On top of that, Maddie had gently chided her just now for her attitude toward Tom on Sunday night. She'd expected it, but that hadn't made the experience any less annoying. She was still muttering about it when she ran into Helen in the café.

"Ah, there you are," Helen said cheerfully. "How did the committee meeting go? I hear the new town manager is very hot."

Jeanette scowled at her. "Not you, too," she grumbled, turned on her heel and marched into her office. "I've heard all the rave reviews I can bear from Dana Sue and Maddie." Along with that humiliating lecture on her rudeness Sunday evening and how inappropriate it was for someone in business in Serenity to be unwelcoming to the new town manager.

Before she could shut the door, Helen stepped in behind

her. "Okay, I obviously said the wrong thing. Mind filling me in on why?"

"Here it is in a nutshell," Jeanette said, working herself back up to a full head of steam. "I do not want to be fixed up. I do not want Maddie, Dana Sue and you getting any crazy ideas about me and Tom McDonald. If and when I decide I want to date, I'll find my own man."

Helen's shrewd eyes twinkled with amusement. "Got it," she said.

Jeanette's scowl deepened. "You are not taking me seriously. Why don't any of you take me seriously?"

Helen's expression sobered at once. "Oh, sweetie, we do. Believe me, when it comes to anything you have to say about running a spa, we take you very seriously."

"But not about this," Jeanette accused. "Not about my love life."

"It's just that you sound so much like we did right before we landed in marital bliss," Helen said.

Jeanette sighed heavily. "Yeah, that's what Dana Sue said, too."

"We've all been there."

"Where?"

"In denial."

"How can I be in denial? I've crossed paths with Tom McDonald three times. He's not my type. He's a little too uptight and stuffy." The comment was far from the truth, but there was no way she was going to say he had a cute dimple and a charming way about him: it would only add fuel to the fire.

"That's not how Maddie described him. Or Dana Sue, either."

"How did they describe him?" she asked, her curiosity piqued.

"Tall, handsome, smart and sexy. He has a dimple. I think it was Maddie who noticed that."

"Oh, I never noticed," Jeanette lied. "But anyway, I don't think that's enough on which to base a lifelong commitment."

"Probably not," Helen concurred. "Did I mention rich? Word is, his family's loaded. I think I've crossed paths with his parents at some charity events in Charleston."

"That is not a recommendation," Jeanette said. "If I cared about money, I'd have stayed at Chez Bella in Charleston. Besides, if he's really rich, why is he here in Serenity working for peanuts? Did they disinherit him? Or is this his good deed for the century? And what would a rich man want with a woman who gives facials?"

"And massages," Helen added, clearly fighting a grin. "Don't forget you also give excellent massages, and I can certainly see the appeal of that. Erik has suggested more than once I take lessons from you."

"Oh, for heaven's sake, you know what I mean. A rich man, especially one from old money, would want some debutante, a woman with social connections, which I clearly do not have."

"Good," Helen said. "I have no idea why Tom McDonald does anything. We've never met. Why don't you ask him?"

"Because that would imply a level of interest I don't have," Jeanette said stubbornly. "Now, if you don't mind, I need coffee with caffeine, not the herbal tea we serve here. I need to brew it behind closed doors. And I have clients waiting."

Helen grinned. "On my way. Never let it be said that I stood in the way of this place making more money." She was about to leave, when she turned back. "Hey, why don't you come over for Sunday dinner next week. Everyone's coming."

Jeanette narrowed her gaze. "Everyone?"

"Maddie, Cal and the kids. Dana Sue and Ronnie. Maddie says Ty might be home, and Dana Sue's trying to see if Annie can get home from college for the weekend. And in case you had any doubts about it, Erik will be cooking, not me. We won't die of ptomaine poisoning."

"Good to know." Jeanette debated the merits of attending a party where her love life could be examined yet again. Of course, the advantage would be that she could defend her position and keep them from pulling anything sneaky. "Okay, sure," she said at last. "Can I bring anything? Wine? Soda? Lemonade? A pie?"

"Forget the pie. Erik's a pastry chef. Any pies or desserts on the premises are his. I tried bringing home a frozen cobbler one night and didn't hear the end of it for a month. How about some tequila? I'm making margaritas."

"Oh, boy," Jeanette said. "The lethal ones?"

Helen grinned. "Are there any other kind? Especially since none of us is pregnant or nursing at the moment. See you around four, okay?"

"Works for me," she said, though she didn't entirely trust Helen's recitation of the guest list. Something told her that Helen wouldn't be above inviting Tom just to see if the rumors about his good looks were true—and maybe to initiate a little meddling of her own.

Mary Vaughn sashayed past an outraged Teresa and into Tom McDonald's office just before lunchtime without an appointment.

Her plan was to ask him something about the Christ-

mas festival, then work her way around to asking if he had
lunch plans.

As she stepped across the threshold, though, she came to
an abrupt stop. He wasn't in his office. She whirled around
and glared at Teresa.

"He's not there."

"I could have told you that if you'd slowed down for half
a second," Teresa said, a glint of satisfaction in her eyes.

"Where is he?"

"He had a meeting out of the building."

"When will he be back?"

"It's hard to say. Shall I tell him you stopped by?"

Mary Vaughn debated what to do. If she didn't explain
what had brought her, it would be all too obvious to anyone with half a grain of sense that she was here on a personal mission. She knew perfectly well that everyone in
town thought she was man-crazy. The truth was there'd
only been one man in her entire life who had made her a
little crazy and that was Ronnie Sullivan. Now that she'd
lost him twice to Dana Sue, it was pretty much past time
to give up on that particular dream. It had caused her nothing but heartache.

Her marriage to Sonny Lewis had been totally on the re-
bound, a fact she regretted every single day of her life. She
hadn't been a bit surprised that their marriage had barely
lasted ten years. What *had* surprised her was that sweet,
easygoing Sonny was the one who'd ended it. She'd had
a daughter she adored and a successful career that gave
her financial independence. Being married to Sonny had
given her the respectability she'd craved since childhood.
She probably would have drifted along contentedly for a
lot longer if Sonny hadn't forced the issue.

"You made up your mind yet?" Teresa asked, snapping her back to the present.

"About what?" Mary Vaughn asked blankly.

"Do you want me to tell Tom that you stopped by or not?"

"No," she said. "Thanks, Teresa. I'll catch up with him sooner or later."

Teresa murmured something that sounded a whole lot like, "I'll be sure to warn him," but her expression was perfectly innocent when Mary Vaughn turned to give her a penetrating look.

"You have a good day," Teresa said.

"You do the same," Mary Vaughn said with even less sincerity.

Outside Town Hall, she was about to cross Main Street when she saw Tom getting out of his car. She brightened immediately.

"Hello there," she called out. "I was just looking for you."

For an instant he looked confused, but then recognition apparently dawned. "Mary Vaughn, isn't it?"

"You have a wonderful memory," she said. "I'm sure it must be so confusing when you first move into a new town. Not that I'd know, of course. I've lived here all my life. There's not a nook or cranny of Serenity that I don't know like the back of my hand. The same with the people who live here. I know all their dirty little secrets."

"Oh?"

She flushed under his vaguely disapproving gaze. "Not that there are that many dirty little secrets, of course. I just meant that I know everyone real well. I could give you a crash course, if you like. In fact, if you have the time, I'd love to buy you lunch over at Wharton's or Sullivan's. Sullivan's is the best we have to offer. Have you eaten there yet?"

"I have," he said. "It's terrific and I appreciate the invitation, but I've had a jam-packed morning and the afternoon doesn't look much better. I'm just going to have a sandwich at my desk. I think Teresa has already ordered it."

Mary Vaughn backed down at once. "Another time, then. How's your house hunting going, by the way? Howard told me you've been looking. I'd be happy to show you some properties. I could fax over the material on the ones you might like."

"Do that," he said. "But I'm not sure when I'll get to them. I'll call you, okay?"

She bit back a sigh. She was striking out on all fronts today, but she'd live to try again. After all, that's what she did. She put on a cheerful smile and survived. She'd been doing it her whole life and there wasn't a soul in town who'd ever guessed how good she was at covering up her problems.

"Call anytime," she told him with her sunniest smile.

Then she walked away with her back straight and her pride mostly intact.

"Did Mary Vaughn get her claws into you?" Teresa asked the minute Tom walked into his office.

"What?" he asked distractedly. "Mary Vaughn? I just ran into her on the street. I'm not even sure what she wanted."

"You," Teresa said, following him into his office. "She wants you. Didn't I warn you about that the other day? Trust me. I've seen that glint in her eyes before. Last time, she was after Ronnie Sullivan, but Dana Sue put a quick end to that."

He looked up. "Teresa, I'm not interested in gossip."

But he had been aware of Mary Vaughn's interest. She'd asked him to lunch. Her offer to show him real estate had seemed like an afterthought.

He had no interest, however, in sharing this with Teresa. "The only thing she's interested in," he said, "is selling me a house."

Teresa rolled her eyes. "Men!" she muttered with a huff. "Your sandwich is on your desk. Ham and cheese on rye. I had 'em add some lettuce and tomato, so you can pretend it's healthy."

"Thank you. Give me fifteen minutes before you put any calls through, okay?"

"It's my lunch hour, too. I'm sending the calls to the answering service," she informed him.

Better yet, Tom thought. He took a bite of his sandwich and the lukewarm soda Teresa had left with it, then picked up the phone, dialed the number for The Corner Spa and asked for Jeanette. He had legitimate business to discuss and a new strategy for rattling her. He was looking forward to giving it a try.

When she picked up, she sounded frazzled.

"You busy?" he asked. "This is Tom."

"I'm in the middle of a treatment. Can I call you back?"

"Will you?"

"Of course," she said, sounding miffed. "Unless, of course, you're calling to ask me out, in which case, I'll say no now and save us both the time."

He laughed. "While I would love to ask you on a date, I'm not sure my ego could withstand another rejection. I wanted to get together to discuss this vendor business for the festival."

"Really?" She sounded skeptical.

"Cross my heart," he said. "Howard's going to be on my case about this any day now and I want to be prepared."

"You want to meet about business," she repeated. "In your office?"

She sounded suspicious, but also perhaps a little disappointed. That was exactly what he'd hoped for.

"Or wherever suits you," he said blithely. "I can come there or we can meet for coffee. I don't think that could be construed as a date. Your choice."

She was silent for so long he thought maybe he'd lost the connection. "Jeanette?"

"I'm thinking," she said. "Come here at six o'clock. We can have some iced tea on the patio. The place is pretty quiet at that hour."

"You're going to let me come into The Corner Spa?" he asked with feigned amazement.

"Actually, I'm not. You're going to come around the outside and meet me on the patio. There will be no males sneaking into this place on my watch."

"Darn. So close," he said with not-entirely-feigned disappointment. "I'll see you at six."

"Right," she said, already sounding distracted again.

"Jeanette," he said, "I'm looking forward to it."

He was already hanging up the phone, when he heard her shouting, "This is business!"

"Whatever you say, darlin'," he murmured as he hung up. "Whatever you say."

"Business!" Jeanette muttered to herself at least fifty times as the afternoon sped by. If Tom was coming over here on business, she'd eat a jar of their most expensive moisturizer. He'd used the festival to get past her no-date rule, the sneak! Well, she was on to him. If he didn't start talking business five seconds after his arrival, she was kicking him out. She might have to call on Elliot to provide the muscle, but he'd be so out of here.

"You look ticked off," Maddie said, popping her head into Jeanette's office just before six. "Anything I need to know?"

She was not about to explain that Tom was coming to the spa for business. Maddie would laugh her head off.

"Nope. Everything's under control."

"Okay, then, I'm heading home on time for once. See you tomorrow."

"Have a good evening."

"You, too. Any special plans?"

"Just a business meeting," Jeanette replied, and then could have kicked herself. While she had a certain amount of autonomy in running the spa services, she usually kept Maddie apprised of any decisions or meetings on the horizon. She should have avoided mentioning the stupid meeting at all.

To her dismay, Maddie halted in her tracks. "What kind of business meeting?"

"Not spa business," Jeanette told her. She sighed. Might as well spit it out. "Christmas festival business."

Maddie's eyes immediately got a wicked gleam, which was exactly why Jeanette hadn't wanted to tell her. She didn't need the amusement or the speculation.

"You're meeting with Tom, aren't you?" Maddie said gleefully. "Good. Maybe you can make amends for the other night."

"Don't you dare make anything out of me seeing him tonight," Jeanette ordered.

"Wouldn't dream of it," Maggie said, grinning. "You can tell me all about it tomorrow."

Jeanette glared at her retreating form.

On her way to the patio, she stopped to pick up a couple of teas and the last two scones in the case. If Tom wasn't on time, she intended to eat both of them.

Fortunately for her dress size, he slipped around the side of the building right on the dot of six. He cast a dramatically wary glance around. "Is it safe? Any wild and naked women out here?"

"You are so not funny," Jeanette said.

"Well, you have to admit that closing a place to men just invites all sorts of speculation about what goes on here," he said as he pulled out a chair across from her and sat down. "Is one of those scones for me? Preferably the one that has more than three crumbs left?"

She shoved it ungraciously in his direction. "Traditional scone with real currants, not raisins."

"Excellent."

He gave her a slow, lingering appraisal that made her blood heat.

"How was your day?"

"Busy," she said tersely. Then mindful of Maddie's admonishments, she asked politely, "And yours?"

"Busy," he echoed. "Mary Vaughn came to call."

Despite herself, Jeanette bristled. "Oh? What did she want?"

"Teresa says she's after my body. What do you think?"

"I wasn't there. I couldn't comment," she said more irritably than she intended. It shouldn't matter to her one darn bit what Mary Vaughn and Tom did. And hadn't she thought they'd be a perfect match?

"I thought she was there to try to sell me a house," he admitted.

"Men!" Jeanette murmured.

He chuckled. "That's pretty much what Teresa said."

"Why are you telling me this?"

"You asked about my day."

"So, no nefarious reason, like trying to make me jealous?"

"If you're absolutely certain you don't want to go out with me, how could I possibly make you jealous?" He actually managed to utter the question with a totally innocent expression.

"You can't," she assured him. "That doesn't mean you won't keep trying to change my mind."

"My ego's far too fragile to keep risking rejection," he said.

"Ha!"

"Well, it is," he insisted.

"You swore you were coming here to talk business," she reminded him. "Talk."

"I'm not sure I can talk on an empty stomach. Isn't it time for dinner?"

"I just gave you a scone. That should tide you over for the fifteen minutes you're going to be here."

"We're on a timetable?"

"I am."

"You are one tough cookie, you know that?"

"I pride myself on it," she said.

"In that case, let's get to it." He snapped open an expensive leather briefcase and shoved a list across the table.

She noticed that his hand was large and just a little callused, not the hand of a man who spent all of his time behind a desk. She could imagine this hand touching her. The thought made her blood heat again.

Oblivious to her reaction, Tom went on, "I found this in

a file. It has the names of vendors going back for the past ten years. Any reason not to ask them all back?"

"None I can think of," she admitted, a little taken aback that he'd actually listened to her and gotten down to business. She forced herself to focus, as well. "Should we put an ad in the area newspapers or send out a press release soliciting some new vendors? Otherwise it may start to seem as if no one else can participate. Plus, it's always good to have new blood. It helps to shake things up. The more vendors the better, I always say. It gives people a reason to come back year after year to spend their money."

Not that she was one of them. She hadn't attended the Christmas festival once during the three years she'd lived in Serenity. Even so, as hard as she tried, it had been impossible to tune out all the chatter about it.

"Good idea about getting some fresh faces in here," he said approvingly. "We'll probably have to go the press release route, since I don't think there's money for that kind of advertising. We need to spend that budget on promoting the event itself."

In exactly fourteen minutes, he snapped his briefcase closed and stood up. "Well, my time's about up. Thanks for meeting with me."

Jeanette was completely thrown by his abrupt end of the discussion, though she couldn't imagine why. She was the one who'd put a time limit on the meeting.

"Did we cover everything you wanted to cover?" she asked.

"Pretty much. I'll keep you posted on the responses. I suppose at some point we'll have to start thinking about mapping out locations for the vendors to set up, but there's no hurry on that. Howard would probably prefer it be done tomorrow, but realistically November's soon enough. We should have all the vendor responses in by Thanksgiving."

"Okay, then. Have a nice evening."

"You do the same." His gaze sought hers and held it. "Oh, hell," he muttered, then bent down and kissed her, not on the cheek as she'd anticipated, but on the mouth… with feeling.

Before she could react, maybe slap him silly, he was gone. She released a deep sigh. It was probably just as well. One more second and she'd have kissed him back like there was no tomorrow. So much for her theory that she was totally immune to men in general and this man in particular. Apparently her hormones had not enjoyed the drought.

CHAPTER SIX

❦

His impulsive decision to kiss Jeanette had been a very bad one, Tom concluded as he left The Corner Spa. He was restless and edgy with no way to work off the sexual tension. Since he wasn't dressed for running, he decided he could at least walk back to the Serenity Inn, though he doubted that would help. If anything, it would give him too much time to think about how soft her lips had been beneath his, the way she smelled of flowers and sunshine, the little sound she'd made in the back of her throat that proved she wasn't immune to him, after all.

"Damn," he muttered, getting stirred up all over again. This was bad. He had plans for the rest of his life and they didn't include staying in Serenity forever. He'd been very careful in the past to keep his relationships casual and un-complicated. Jeanette had *complication* written all over her.

Thankfully, before he could get too worked up over the unexpected twist of fate, his cell phone rang, promising a distraction.

"Yes, hello," he said, hoping he didn't sound as desper-ate as he felt.

"Tom, it's Cal."

He nearly sighed with relief at the distraction. "Cal, I meant to call you earlier about your Little League proposal. I wanted to let you know that I haven't had time to get to it, but I haven't forgotten."

"Not a problem," Cal assured him. "Actually, I thought maybe you'd like to hang out with Ronnie Sullivan—you know him from the festival committee, I think—Erik Whitney from Sullivan's and me tonight. We're going to toss around a football in the park, maybe have a few beers after. Interested?"

"How soon?" he asked eagerly.

"Twenty minutes," Cal said. "We'll be by the gazebo. Can you meet us there?"

"Absolutely," Tom said. "I just need to drop off my briefcase at the inn and change."

Thank heavens, he thought as he stuck his cell phone back in his pocket. He hoped these guys took their games seriously. He figured it would take a solid hour of hard sweat and a whole lot of inconsequential guy talk to work the memory of that smoldering kiss out of his head.

Two hours later, Tom was drained of thoughts and energy. These guys played even a casual game of football with an intensity that had challenged him. He was also on his second beer, which had loosened his tongue.

"So, what's the story on Jeanette?" he asked before he could think through the consequences of bringing up her name with these particular guys. "You all know her, right?"

Cal, Ronnie and Erik exchanged amused looks.

"Told you," Cal said, holding out his hand to the others. "Pay up."

Tom frowned. "Told them what?"

"That you had a thing for Jeanette and that it wouldn't

take more than two beers for you to start asking questions about her," Cal said.

"You bet on this?" he asked incredulously.

"We bet on everything," Ronnie said, handing over five dollars to Cal. "Keeps us on our toes. We're a very competitive bunch."

"I'm paying you under protest," Erik said as he gave Cal his money. "The deck was stacked in your favor. You've seen the two of them together. We haven't."

"Stop whining," Cal told him, seizing the five-dollar bill. "I know perfectly well that Helen and/or Dana Sue has clued you in about this. Probably both of them. And Ronnie's on the Christmas festival committee, so he's at least seen them together once."

Erik grinned. "Well, maybe I had heard something, but I'm busy when I'm at Sullivan's. I don't always pay attention to whatever Dana Sue's going on about in the kitchen."

"And your wife?" Cal taunted. "Do you tune her out, too?"

"Helen?" Erik said. "Impossible! She makes sure I hear every word she says. It's the lawyer in her."

Tom held up a hand. "Can we back up the train a minute? All of you, your wives included, have been speculating about me and Jeanette?"

"True," Ronnie said, giving him a commiserating slap on the back. "Welcome to the world of the Sweet Magnolias."

"Damn," Tom muttered. "She told me they meddled, but I had no idea to what extent."

"Take it from the three of us, these women work as a team," Cal reported. "You show a little interest in Jeanette, they're going to be all over it."

"I'm not sure if that's good or bad," Tom said. "It seems

to be scaring off Jeanette. She claims she has zero interest in me specifically and in men in general."

"Trust me, they were all skittish when we came into their lives," Cal reported. "With Maddie and me, it was the age thing, plus my job was threatened by the whole supposed scandal of her dating a younger man, who also happened to be her son's baseball coach. With Ronnie and Dana Sue, let's just say there was some history he had to overcome the second time around."

"That's putting it mildly," Erik added, giving Ronnie a playful punch in the arm.

Cal continued, "As for Erik here, well, he was just about as reluctant to get involved as Helen was. Ronnie and I had a great time watching the mightiest of the mighty fall."

"So what's made Jeanette so skittish?" Tom asked, probably too eagerly.

"Beats me," Cal said. "She was flying solo when she got to town and that hasn't changed in the time we've known her."

"Hold on," Ronnie said. "Wasn't there some guy she was living with before she moved here? I think Dana Sue said they broke up over her working so much and wanting to leave Charleston."

"Jeanette used to live in Charleston?" Tom asked. "I didn't know that. Is that where she's from?"

"No, she's from someplace south of here," Erik said. "Another little town."

Ronnie shoved another beer in front of him. "Okay, let's get to the point, man. Are you serious about her or are you just looking for a distraction?"

Tom stared at him. He'd been here less than a month, known Jeanette for a couple of weeks and they wanted to know if he was serious? "Come on," he protested. "Serious? As in looking for a wife?"

"That's the one," Cal confirmed.

"I barely know her." Tom shrugged. "And if she has her way, it'll stay like that."

"We could help you out," Cal offered casually. "*If* we thought you were serious."

"Help me out how?" Tom asked, suspicious of anything these three might be plotting. Obviously they were doing it with the blessing of their wives, which pretty much gave him hives.

"For starters, everyone is coming to our place for dinner on Sunday, including Jeanette," Erik said meaningfully. "I could invite you."

"But only if my intentions are honorable," Tom concluded.

All three men nodded somberly.

"Otherwise, you hurt her and we'd have to beat you up," Ronnie said, his expression still totally serious.

Tom laughed, but not one of them seemed to share his amusement. He sobered. "Okay, then, message received. Jeanette has three men looking after her."

"And three tough women," Cal added.

"Dana Sue lifts weights," Ronnie warned. "She's very fit these days."

Tom shook his head. "Maybe I should consider going out with Mary Vaughn, after all."

Again, the men exchanged a look, though this time there was real worry in their eyes.

"I think we may have come on too strong," Erik said.

"Possibly," Cal agreed.

Tom stared at them. "So this was basically a test," he said.

"Pretty much," Ronnie told him, looking vaguely chagrined.

"We were under orders," Cal explained.

"Did I pass?" Tom asked, more curious than offended.

"Beats me," Cal said. "You seem like an okay guy, but I don't think my opinion counts."

"Well, I think you'd better come on Sunday," Erik said. "The women will let you know if you pass muster."

Tom wasn't at all sure he wanted his love life subject to the scrutiny of these so-called Sweet Magnolias. He already knew Jeanette wasn't one bit happy about it. Still, if he won the rest of them over, there was a very good chance they'd give Jeanette a little shove in his direction. It couldn't hurt.

"Count me in," he said at last.

"Brave man," Cal said approvingly.

"Gets points in my book," Ronnie said.

Erik just grinned sympathetically, like a man who'd once been in the same spot he was in.

Tom shook his head and gulped down the rest of his beer. What the hell had he gotten himself into? One mind-blowing kiss and it appeared he was neck deep in quicksand.

The Sweet Magnolias were having one of their increasingly sporadic margarita nights. These occasions gave them a chance to catch up on spa business and on each other's lives. Normally Jeanette loved the casual gabfests, but something told her when she first walked through the door at Helen's that tonight was going to be an exception. The buzz of chatter died on her arrival.

"What?" she demanded.

All three women regarded her innocently. Helen immediately filled a margarita glass to the brim and held it out. Jeanette accepted it warily, then took a seat on the floor.

"Somebody needs to tell me why you all shut up the second I walked in," she said.

"She's right," Maddie said. "She should know."

"Of course she should," Dana Sue said, turning to Helen. "You masterminded this. You tell her."

"I did no such thing," Helen protested.

"Tell her," Maddie and Dana Sue said in unison.

"Tom's coming for Sunday dinner," Helen admitted. "The guys asked him last night."

Jeanette studied each of her friends in turn, then settled in on Helen. "And this was your idea?"

"Not exactly," she said, regarding the others with a touch of defiance. "We all wanted to get a look at the two of you together. Okay, not Maddie. She's already witnessed the fireworks firsthand, but Dana Sue and me."

"And how did the guys just happen to see him and invite him?" she queried.

"Oh, you know guys," Dana Sue said. "They were getting together to play a little football. Cal called Tom. Then they had a couple of beers together. Guy stuff."

"They were checking him out, weren't they?" Jeanette accused. "This wasn't some innocent little get-together. I know how you operate."

"We were just protecting your interests," Maddie said. "We know how you feel about getting involved with anyone and we figured if you're finally ready, it needs to be with someone trustworthy."

"I am not getting involved with Tom," Jeanette said for the umpteenth time. "Why won't you listen to me?"

"Because you don't sound convincing," Helen said. "I'm a lawyer. I know when people are lying to me…and to themselves."

"Okay, fine," Jeanette said in disgust. "You all conduct

your independent review of the new town manager. I don't have to be there."

"You can't back out now," Maddie protested. "Come on. We want you there."

"And I invited you first," Helen reminded her. "And you said yes."

"Did I really? I seem to recall you assuming that I would come."

"You're bringing tequila," Helen said. "I made a note of it."

"Of course you did," Maddie said, patting her hand. "You make notes on everything."

"Especially since I had the baby," Helen said with a sigh. "I can't remember anything if I don't write it down."

"Try having five kids," Maddie said. "I make lists of my lists."

"The bottom line," Helen said, gazing directly at Jeanette, "is that you're coming. If you absolutely insist, we'll simply tell Tom to stay away."

She frowned at them. "You know I can't do that. It would be totally rude to have you take back your invitation to him. He's new in town. He probably doesn't know a lot of people. In fact, why don't you invite some others? Mary Vaughn, for instance. I have it on good authority that she's interested in him."

"Then I'd have to stay home," Dana Sue said flatly. "And keep Ronnie there, too."

"Ronnie doesn't give two figs about Mary Vaughn," Maddie said impatiently. "He never did."

"Not the point," Dana Sue said. "I don't trust her near my husband." She frowned at Jeanette. "And you shouldn't want her anywhere near Tom."

"How many ways do I have to say that I don't care about Tom McDonald?"

Maddie's expression turned thoughtful, though her eyes sparkled with amusement. "As many as it takes to convince us. You're not even close yet."

Jeanette clamped her mouth shut. There was no point in belaboring this. It was a debate she couldn't possibly win.

Helen beamed. "Good, then we're agreed. It's going to be a great evening."

Jeanette didn't want to burst her bubble, but from her perspective, it promised to be hell. The memory of that kiss she and Tom had shared made her blood sizzle every time she thought about it. She was going to have to resist any repeat of the experience, and the sad truth was, she wasn't sure she had the willpower.

Tom was in the middle of an incredibly steamy dream about the elusive Jeanette when his phone rang on Sunday morning.

"Oh, honey, I didn't wake you, did I?" his mother inquired.

He sighed as the last image of Jeanette faded from his mind. "It's okay, Mother. I need to be up soon, anyway, if I'm going to get to church on time. What's up?"

"Your father and I were just talking. I know you weren't expecting me until next week, but the plans we had for today have been postponed, so we thought we'd drive over to Serenity to have lunch with you and take a look around your little town. Will that work for you?"

Tom bit back a groan. She made it sound like an excursion to a not-very-respectable amusement park. He'd planned on looking at a few houses this morning, doing some work on revising the budget, and then getting ready

to go to Erik and Helen's at four. Of course, his mother had
mentioned lunch. That would put them here around noon
and he could probably send them on their way by two. That
should work. And at least it would put this hoped-for, but
much-dreaded, visit behind him.

"Sure, Mother. That would be great. We can have lunch
at Sullivan's. We need to be there early, though. It's usually packed right after church and they're only open until
two on Sundays."

"That will work for us. We're going to the early service
at church and we'll leave from there. We should be there by
eleven. That should give us enough time to tour the town
and be at the restaurant before noon."

"Perfect," Tom said. "Why don't we meet at the town
hall. It's centrally located."

"Oh, but we want to see where you're living," she protested.

"It's a small inn, Mother. I have a room. There's nothing to see. I still haven't found a house."

"I know it's an inn, but I'd like to see it," she said stubbornly. "That way I can picture you there, even if it is only
temporary."

It was one of her idiosyncracies that she liked knowing
the details of her children's living arrangements. She'd visited every dorm room, every sorority house and fraternity,
every tiny apartment each of her children had resided in.
Tom should have expected she'd want to see the inn.

Still, he argued against it. "Mother, you're not going to
be here that long. Let's not waste the visit on a tour of my
nine-by-twelve room."

"I suppose you're right," she agreed reluctantly, then said
with enthusiasm, "Perhaps we should help you look for a
house while we're there."

"Absolutely not," he said more sharply than he'd intended. "I've seen almost everything that's on the market. I'm just trying to narrow it down."

"Then we could help," she persisted. "It's no trouble, darling. I've always been able to see the potential in places. In fact, once you've chosen something, I can come over with my decorator and help you whip it into shape. You'll need something large enough for entertaining, and it should be in the best neighborhood. After all, you *are* a public official."

"Mom!" He needed to get her attention. "Enough. I don't need anything fancy. I can slap a little paint on the walls if it needs it. The last thing I need is a decorator."

"Well, surely you'll want some of the family heirlooms," she continued, undaunted. "That awful place you had in the last town was nowhere for priceless antiques, but I'm sure you can improve on that."

Tom would rather live in a tent than be surrounded by the ornate McDonald treasures. "We'll discuss it when I see you," he said. If he put his foot down in person, she might actually hear him. Then again, that had never worked for his father. She'd been running roughshod over him for their entire forty years of marriage.

Jeanette exited the church, stopped for a moment to speak with Pastor Drake, then turned and bumped straight into Tom.

"You!" she said, taking a step back.

Had he been in church? That would explain his perfectly tailored navy blue suit, crisp white shirt and polished Italian loafers. She couldn't help recalling what Helen had said about him coming from money. He looked every inch the scion of some old Charleston family. Of course, the dimple in his cheek and the twinkle in his eye also made him seem sexy and accessible. It was a potent combination.

"Well, this is an unexpected surprise. You're just the person I needed to see," he said, seizing her hand and drawing her away from the crowd.

Jeanette tried to yank her hand away, but he had a surprisingly strong grip. Warm and solid. The kind of grip that would feel reassuring if circumstances were different.

"Will you let go of me?" she demanded.

"Will you at least hear me out?" he asked.

"Why wouldn't I hear you out?"

He shrugged. "Good question, but our brief history suggests you're not always open to spending time with me."

"You're not asking me on a date again, are you?"

"Not exactly."

"What does that mean?"

"It means my parents are arriving here in approximately fifteen minutes and I need backup."

She stared at him blankly. "Backup? Why?"

"My father hates everything about my being town manager here and my mother wants to choose my new home and decorate it," he said, sounding a little frantic.

Jeanette's lips twitched. This vulnerable side of him was oddly appealing. "You're scared of Mommy and Daddy?"

"You won't say it like that once you've met them. My father is a tyrant and my mother is a force of nature."

"And you want me to meet them after you've made them sound so charming?"

"Okay, bad planning on my part. The point is that they are always on their best behavior around strangers. I can feed them at Sullivan's and have them on their way by two if you'll help me out by tagging along. I swear it's not a date. I just need you as a buffer."

Jeanette found herself enjoying his discomfort. She actually wanted to meet the two people who could throw this self-confident man into such a dither. And it might be nice to see another dysfunctional family in action. It might be reassuring, somehow, to have proof that she wasn't the only one on the planet who had parental issues. And it wasn't as if they were dating and meeting his parents was a major moment. As he'd said, she'd be merely a buffer. No big deal.

"There's just one thing," she said. "How would you explain me?"

"As a friend," he said at once. "That's the truth, isn't it? We're friends, or at least getting there."

"Casual acquaintance is more apt, but I get why you'd need to call me a friend if you're including me in this lunch." She hesitated, then nodded. "Okay, then, as long as there are no hints…" She gave him a stern look. "None, whatsoever, that we are anything more than friends, understood? I don't want to hear even the tiniest suggestion that we might be friends with benefits."

"Of course not," he said solemnly. "Then you'll do it?"

"I'll do it."

He snagged her hand again. "Good, we're meeting them at the town hall—" he glanced at his watch "—in less than ten minutes. The one thing you don't ever want to do is keep them waiting. It's important to make a good first impression."

Something in his voice alerted her that he hadn't been entirely honest with her. "Why do you care what kind of impression I make? I'm a buffer, that's it. It might be even better if they hate my guts on sight."

"Possibly," he conceded. "But there's no point in either of us enduring a ten-minute lecture on the lack of respect implied by tardiness."

"Agreed," she said, amused.

Her oddly upbeat mood lasted until she spotted Mr. and Mrs. McDonald—surely it had to be them—emerging from a shiny black car almost the length of a city block. They'd parked across the square from the town hall, which put them some distance away, but she knew in her gut she wasn't mistaken about who they were. Her horrified gaze barely skimmed over the man, but the woman...she would recognize her anywhere. An image of that artfully colored blond hair, pale complexion and the arrogant lift to her surgically perfected chin was burned into her memory.

"Those are your parents?" she asked. "Over there, getting out of that limo?"

Tom shot a quizzical look at her. "Yes. Why do you look like that? You're pale as a ghost."

"I can't meet your parents," she whispered, frantically trying to get him to release her hand so she could bolt. Why hadn't she made the connection before now? It wasn't as if she'd never heard his last name or didn't know he was from Charleston. She just didn't believe in coincidences, that was all. Or she hadn't wanted to believe in this one. It had been too awful to contemplate.

Tom was still staring at her as if she'd lost her mind. "Why can't you meet my parents? Jeanette, what's wrong? Is it the car? They have money. So what?"

"It's not the car," she said in an oddly choked voice. "Believe me, that car is the least of it."

"Then, what? Tell me quick, because they've seen us, so it's too late for you to run."

"It's your mother, Tom," she said, still struggling to break free. "I know her. And you do not want us face-to-face. You need to trust me about that."

He stared at her blankly. "You know my mother? How?"

"Do you really want to waste time chitchatting about the details? I need to go before they get over here. I can explain later."

"Tell me now," he said tightly.

"I know her from Chez Bella's in Charleston. I gave her a facial once."

He still looked blank. "Are you embarrassed about that for some reason? You shouldn't be."

"It's not about being embarrassed," she said indignantly. "She sued Bella. Claimed I almost destroyed her skin. That suit could have cost me my job, my reputation. The only reason it didn't was because Bella had heard that she'd done the same thing at another spa in town. She's allergic to some ingredient. Her dermatologist has explained it to her, but for some reason she refuses to accept that she can't have the same treatments that all her friends have, so she just moves from spa to spa, raising a ruckus along the way. She freaks because her skin breaks out in hives. Now, will you let me go before she and I have this out right here?"

Tom was staring at her incredulously. "My mother sued you?"

"Not me, the spa. She probably doesn't even remember me, but I remember her. Now, let me go."

This time when she jerked away, he released her. Jeanette didn't wait around to see whether his mother recognized her or not. All she cared about was getting away before she yanked the woman's perfectly coifed, bleached blond hair out by its roots.

CHAPTER SEVEN

———— ✦ ————

"Who was that young woman and why did she run off?" Tom's mother asked the instant they reached him. "She looked vaguely familiar."

Tom wasn't about to bring up the Chez Bella incident, not until he'd heard the whole story from Jeanette. It would be just like his mother to make a federal case out of something like a skin rash, even if she'd been responsible for causing it by not disclosing her allergies. She'd had a habit of denying anything that didn't suit her. It didn't surprise him that she might ill-advisedly ignore her dermatologist's warnings just to have the facial her friends were raving about.

But if it had been such a big deal, why hadn't Jeanette mentioned it before now? Surely she must have wondered if his mother and the woman who'd filed the suit were related, if not one and the same person. He had a whole lot of questions and no answers, so for the time being he just forced a smile.

"She didn't run off. She's on my Christmas festival committee, so we were discussing a few details. She didn't want to intrude on our family get-together. She knows we don't have a lot of time."

His mother looked as if she wasn't buying a word, but his father was clearly disinterested in the whole discussion.

"So," he said, a scathing note in his voice, "this is it? What we're seeing right now is Serenity? Not much to it, is there?"

"This is the downtown," Tom said, trying not to sound defensive. "Those big-box stores over your way all but destroyed small, family-run businesses, but it's coming back. The drugstore weathered the tough times, the hardware store has reopened under new management, and two other spaces have been leased since I got here. A clothing boutique is opening in one and a florist in the other. One of my main priorities is trying to attract a few more businesses into this area. And the local garden club has organized a beautification program. They're installing all the pots of flowers at the doorways of businesses and will maintain them. Give us another couple of years and we'll have this area rejuvenated."

"Waste of time," his father scoffed. "These little shoe-string operations can't compete."

"They can under the right conditions," Tom countered. Before his father could argue, he held up his hand. "Let's take a tour. Would you like to walk through town hall? It was built in the early 1800s. It's on the National Register of Historic Places. Someone in town had the good sense to fight to preserve it. All the renovations through the years have been done with great attention to the original detail."

His mother's expression brightened. "I'd love to see it."

"Don't know why you care about a pile of old bricks," his father grumbled, but he kept pace with his wife and son as Tom described the Colonial-style architecture that had been the inspiration for the small, brick building with its white columns out front. It was set at one end of Town Square, right in the heart of what had once been the thriving hub of Serenity. Its sweeping lawn was well manicured, and several towering old oaks shaded both the structure itself and the carefully placed benches. The garden club tended the beds of flowers around the perimeter. Just recently they'd replaced the summer blooms with bright yellow chrysanthemums.

Inside on the left was an open area where residents could pay their tax bills. On the right was a large meeting room for the monthly council sessions. A wide staircase toward the back led to the handful of offices housing town officials, including Tom's large corner office overlooking the square. The office wasn't huge or lavishly furnished by Charleston standards, but it was impressive just the same. And the furnishings had been chosen with care, most of them at least a century earlier. The desk immediately sent his mother into raptures.

"Oh, just look at this wood," she murmured, rubbing her hand over the smooth, dark surface. "It's quite remarkable to be in this condition after so many years. It must make you think about all those who've worked here before you, Tom."

"Don't know how you can get so worked up over a piece of furniture," his father groused. "When are we going to eat? I'm starving."

Tom tried not to let his father's attitude get under his skin. "If you don't mind a little exercise, we can walk to Sullivan's from here," he told his parents. "There's no point in moving the car."

"Whatever you say," his mother said, then cast one last approving look around the room. "You know, dear, it would be so much lighter in here with new drapes. What do you think? I'd love to do that for you. Something bright, but tasteful, of course."

"I'm not sure I could accept that," Tom said.

"You can't accept a gift from your own mother? That's ridiculous. It's not as if I'm expecting special treatment in return. I don't even live here."

He smiled at that. "Okay, perhaps I'm being too much of a stickler for the rules. First let me see if anyone would object to new drapes for the town manager's office. I'll let you know."

Back outside, they set off for Sullivan's, his father striding ahead, even though he didn't have the slightest idea where they were headed. He finally paused at the corner and glanced back. "Right, left or straight?"

"Straight ahead. It's two blocks up on the left," Tom told him.

His father gave a curt nod of acknowledgment and walked on.

"I don't know what gets into him," his mother commented with a rueful shake of her head. "He was looking forward to this, but he's not going to admit that to you."

"I wouldn't expect him to," Tom said dryly. Anything less than a suite in the congressional office building in Washington wouldn't meet with his father's approval.

His mother fell silent, her expression perplexed. "I still can't get over the feeling that I've seen that young woman before. How odd, since I've never been to Serenity." She brightened. "Oh, well, I'm sure I'll figure it out eventually."

Tom hoped not. The last thing he wanted was for his mother to have some preconceived impression of Jeanette that she couldn't get past. Then again, it was already plain as day that Jeanette held her own impression of his mother, and it most definitely wasn't a good one.

* * *

"That woman all but accused me of deliberately scarring her for life!" Jeanette said to Maddie, still steaming from her near miss with Tom's mother. "And to think that Tom is that awful woman's son!"

"You're not going to blame him for what his mother did, are you?" Dana Sue asked as she put the finishing touches on a huge bowl of fresh fruit.

"No, of course not, but can you imagine what would have happened if she'd seen the two of us together? She'd probably have skewered me with whatever sharp object she could find in her purse."

"I don't think rich society matrons from Charleston carry a lot of sharp objects," Helen said wryly.

"You never met Mrs. McDonald," Jeanette grumbled.

"Actually I have," Helen reminded her. "Years ago at a charity event."

Jeanette waved off the comment. "I'll just bet she carries some kind of weapon around in that Gucci bag of hers." She leveled a look at each of her friends in turn. "I hope this puts an end to any matchmaking ideas you all have. Clearly there is no way I can date the spawn of a woman like that."

Helen laughed, but then swallowed it guiltily. "Sorry. I couldn't help it. *Spawn?* Who says that about a man, especially one as gorgeous as Tom?"

"You know what I mean," Jeanette retorted. "I cannot possibly date him, not when I want to stab his mother in the heart."

"You seem a little obsessed with the whole sharp-objects thing," Maddie said. "Here, have a margarita. You'll feel better."

"And you'll be more mellow when Tom gets here," Dana Sue added. "It's probably not wise to let him see you like this, especially when the person you're so worked up over is his mother."

Jeanette took a gulp of the very strong drink, but it did nothing to settle her nerves. Struck by a thought, she turned to Dana Sue. "They were having lunch at Sullivan's. You worked today. Did you see them?"

Dana Sue nodded reluctantly. "Tom introduced us."

"And?"

She shrugged. "They raved about the food."

"Well, of course they raved about the food," Jeanette said. "It's fabulous. Watch your back, though. If her stomach gets the least bit queasy in the next twenty-four hours, she'll probably sue you, too."

Maddie patted her shoulder. "You're not getting mellow. Have some more of your margarita."

Jeanette took another swallow of the icy, tart drink and waited for the alcohol to kick in. "I should have confronted her, that's what I should have done. Instead, I ran off like a scared rabbit."

"You were trying to avoid a scene that would embarrass Tom," Dana Sue said. "There's nothing cowardly about that."

"Besides, the lawsuit incident is behind you. Bella backed you up, so no harm was done," Helen said. "Of course, if you want me to file a suit against her for defamation of character, I can probably do that."

Jeanette stared at her. "I can sue her?"

"Well, you could have at the time," Helen said. "I'd have to check the statute of limitations."

Maddie scowled at Helen. "Would you stop stirring the pot? Nobody's suing anybody. The whole thing is over and done with."

Jeanette was beginning to feel the effects of the alcohol at last. She sighed. "You're probably right."

"Of course I am," Maddie said. "Besides, a lawsuit would be bad publicity for The Corner Spa."

Helen winced. "I should have thought of that. What's wrong with me? I'm spending way too much time at home playing mommy and not nearly enough in a courtroom ripping apart the bad guys. My head for business is turning to mush."

"We love the new, more serene you," Maddie soothed. "You finally have some balance in your life."

As if on cue, Sarah Beth's cries could be heard from the baby monitor on the kitchen counter.

"I'll get her," Jeanette offered, wobbling just a little as she stood. "Boy, I really do need to move around."

She grew steadier as she walked down the hall to the baby's nursery, which was as lavishly decorated as anything ever seen in a decorating magazine or designer showcase. Helen might have waited until her forties to have her first child, but she'd gone all out once she'd had Sarah Beth. Every piece of pristine white furniture was top-of-the-line. Every pink accessory had been chosen from the fanciest boutiques in Charleston. A dresser was filled with designer clothes that the six-month-old girl would outgrow in no time. And, like her mother, she already had an assortment of shoes for every occasion, from mary janes to tiny sneakers in every color of the rainbow.

The baby had pulled herself to a sitting position, her blue eyes filled with tears. Her soft curls were in a tangle, her diaper sodden. Jeanette's heart melted at the pitiful sight.

"Hey, angel, looks to me as if you could use a diaper change and some fancy duds for the party," she said.

Sarah Beth held out her arms to be picked up, a tearful smile breaking across her face.

Jeanette made quick work of changing her, then put her into the ruffled pink gingham dress that Helen had laid out. She added lace-trimmed socks and shiny pink shoes, then ran a soft brush through her curls.

The interlude calmed her nerves and pushed the near miss with Mrs. McDonald to the back of her mind.

"Okay, baby girl, let's go to a party," she said, picking Sarah Beth up and holding her close just to breathe in the powdery scent of her. The powerful emotions that swept through her whenever she held Sarah Beth, Jessica Lynn or baby Cole scared the daylights out of her. She wanted this. She really did.

Just not enough to risk her heart.

It was after dinner before Tom was able to corner Jeanette alone in the kitchen. She'd been very adept at avoiding him and now he called her on it.

"I have not been avoiding you," she claimed defensively. "I've been helping Helen and Erik."

"The table's been wiped clean, the dishes are in the dishwasher and everyone has an after-dinner drink," he said. "I think they can spare you for a few minutes."

"Okay, fine. What do you want to talk about?"

He gave her a wry look. "Gee, what do you think? The weather?"

"I am not discussing your mother with you."

"Do you want me to get the story from her?"

"I'm surprised you haven't heard her version already."

"She didn't recognize you," he said.

"Of course not," Jeanette scoffed. "I was just some little

nobody who ruined her life, at least for the day or two it took for the hives to go away."

Tom's lips twitched.

"It wasn't funny," Jeanette said.

"No, I'm sure she didn't think so," he agreed.

"I wasn't exactly roaring with laughter myself. She could have ruined my career, Tom. Baseless accusations or not, Bella could have fired me and word would have spread about what happened and not one single reputable spa would have risked hiring me. Women talk. They spread the word about stuff like that, and pretty soon, there wouldn't have been a spa in the state that would have wanted me anywhere near their clients."

"But none of that happened," he reminded her.

"Not the point," she said, her tone unyielding.

He studied her hard expression. "Bottom line—is this going to be a problem for us?"

She frowned at that. "There is no *us*. There never will be."

"Really?" he said, trying not to smile.

"Absolutely not."

"I could prove you wrong." he said, and watched indignation stir in her eyes.

"Really?" she mimicked.

He backed her up until she was trapped between him and Erik's professional-grade Sub-Zero refrigerator. "Really," he said, his gaze locked with hers. "Want me to tell you how, or should I just show you?"

She swallowed hard and alarm flared in her dark eyes. "Don't do this," she whispered.

"What? This?" he asked, lowering his mouth to hover over hers. He waited as she sucked in a nervous breath, then covered her mouth, plunging his tongue inside, tasting her, taunting her. With one hand braced on either side of her and nothing touching except their lips, he kissed her until she melted against him, her fingers digging into his shoulders, her hips swaying into his.

Then, when he least expected it, she shoved him away. "No," she said, all but quivering with outrage. "No more. This can't happen."

He held up his hands and backed off. "Jeanette, you were as into that kiss as I was."

"A gentleman wouldn't remind me of that."

"Darlin', I never claimed to be a gentleman."

She studied him with a perplexed expression. "Why are you doing this? You hardly know me."

"I've been trying to change that," he reminded her.

"Why?" she asked, looking mystified.

He thought about it. "You intrigue me," he said eventually. "You're strong and stubborn, smart and beautiful. I have to be on my toes around you."

"In other words, I'm a challenge—especially since I keep rejecting you."

"It's not just that," he insisted. "I want to know everything about you. I can't explain it any better than that."

"Well, you're going about it all wrong. Getting me into your bed is about sex. People getting to know each other start by dating."

Tom struggled to hide his amusement. "You vetoed that idea, remember? So I had no alternative but to go at this from another direction."

"By trying to seduce me?"

"It was a kiss, not a seduction."

"Well, it felt like more than a kiss," she retorted.

"If you want, I could go for a full-fledged seduction so you can do a comparison," he offered.

"Absolutely not!"

He grinned. "Oh, well, it was worth a shot. I'm trying to be cooperative."

"Cooperative?" She chuckled despite herself. "I suppose that's one word for it." She shook her head. "What am I going to do with you?"

"I have a list," he told her. "And a head full of some pretty provocative ideas."

"I'm sure you do, but I doubt I'd approve of most of the things you're thinking."

He saw an opening he doubted she'd been aware of. "Most? Does that mean there might be one or two things I could get away with trying?"

"Tom!" Again, she regarded him with bewilderment. "Why are you pushing this? And no flip answers this time. I really want to know."

His expression sobered at once. He wasn't entirely sure he could explain it himself, but he could see that he needed to try.

"Because from the very first time I saw you, I was drawn to you," he began. "And every encounter since then has raised more questions than have been answered." He touched a finger to her cheek, brushed back a curl of dark brown hair. "I'll be honest with you. Finding a woman was not in my plans when I came to Serenity. I wanted to spend a few years here being the best town manager possible, and then I wanted to move on."

She froze at that. "I see," she said stiffly. "So I'm supposed to provide a convenient diversion for however long you choose to stick around and then wave goodbye when you take off? I don't think so."

"That is not what I meant," he protested.

She brushed past him. "Oh, I think you made yourself perfectly clear."

"I'm not finished."

"Oh, believe me, you're finished," she said.

He stood where he was, staring after her retreating back and trying to figure out how it had all gone so terribly wrong. By the time he went outside to join the others, Jeanette was nowhere in sight. Worse, six pairs of accusing eyes were homing in on him as if he'd suddenly morphed into pond scum.

"What happened in there?" Helen demanded. "You upset her."

"Not intentionally," Tom said, feeling compelled to defend himself. "I was in the middle of explaining how attracted I am to her, how I wasn't expecting to meet anyone like her when I came here, when suddenly she took off."

"And that's all you said?" Helen demanded. "I don't believe you. Jeanette doesn't overreact."

"Well, she did this time." Tom sighed. He wasn't going to win over this crowd, not tonight, anyway. "I should go."

At least he would see Jeanette in the morning at the Christmas festival meeting. Maybe between now and then he could figure out exactly what he'd done to upset her and how to make things right.

Jeanette was counting jars of skin moisturizer when Maddie walked into her office on Monday morning.

"Isn't there a festival meeting this morning?" Maddie inquired.

"Not going," Jeanette said succinctly, avoiding Maddie's gaze.

"You can't hide from him," Maddie told her. "I have no idea what went on between the two of you last night, but

Serenity is a small town. You will run into each other. You might as well make peace with that."

"I'll go next week or the week after," Jeanette assured her. "Just not today."

"Was what he said or did so awful that you don't even want to be in the same room with him?"

"I'm not discussing this," Jeanette said. "You're my boss."

Maddie looked as if she'd been slapped. "I'm also your friend."

Jeanette sighed and reached for her hand. "I'm sorry. I know you are, but you can't help. I don't even know myself why I'm so upset, at least not entirely. The man infuriated me. I'll get over it eventually."

"I could help you figure it out, if you'd talk to me," Maddie offered, giving her hand a commiserating squeeze.

"Thanks, but there's nothing to figure out. Not really. I just hope this will finally put an end to any matchmaking plans you and the others have. Tom and I are doomed. Period."

"Okay," Maddie said, surprising her.

"Okay? Just like that?"

"You've made yourself clear. Do you want some help unpacking that shipment?"

"No. I need something totally mindless to occupy me this morning."

"So you won't think about whatever happened last night?" Maddie asked. "Or so you won't imagine Tom's reaction when you don't show up this morning?"

Jeanette gave her a chagrined look. "Both, more than likely."

"Okay, then, I'll leave you to it. My door's open if you change your mind about talking this through."

"Thanks," she said, then added, "And, Maddie, you are a really good friend."

"I must not be that great if you're so miserable and there's nothing I can do to fix it."

"Fixing it isn't up to you, but I appreciate you wanting to try."

After Maddie had gone, she put down the jar of moisturizer and sank into the chair behind her desk. This mood of hers was ridiculous. Tom wasn't the first man she'd been attracted to. He wasn't the first man that she'd known at first glance was a dead-end road. But last night when he'd flatly declared his intention to leave Serenity—and therefore her—behind, it had shaken her more than she wanted to admit.

It had stirred memories of too many other instances when she'd unwittingly been the short-term interlude. This time, at least, she knew in advance. If she allowed it to happen, if she gave her heart to a man who already had one foot out the door, then the heartache was all on her.

And no way in hell was she allowing that to happen again.

CHAPTER EIGHT

❖◆❖

Mary Vaughn had been looking forward to the festival committee meeting all weekend. Dealing with her ex-father-in-law was a small price to pay for a chance to spend time with the new town manager, who was without doubt the most promising male to hit Serenity since Ronnie Sullivan had returned.

She'd spent an extra half hour this morning choosing just the right suit—a lightweight turquoise wool that would be fine as long as the early-October temperatures didn't sky-rocket. She'd added the perfect accessories—silver-and-turquoise earrings and a matching bracelet from a trip to New Mexico—and a pair of strappy high heels that showed off her shapely legs. Her hair was artfully tousled to suggest the way it might look if she'd just left a man's bed. The total effect was sexy, yet professional, a look that was darn hard to pull off, but one she'd mastered years ago. Few men were immune to it.

When she sashayed into the meeting room at Town Hall, Ronnie Sullivan gave a low whistle and winked at her.

"Got your sights set on a new man, darlin'?" he asked impudently.

"Go to hell, Ronnie." She deliberately went to the opposite end of the table, even though it meant she was farther away from Tom's seat than she would have preferred.

No sooner was she seated than her BlackBerry rang. She'd finally figured out how to use it, so she snatched it from her purse with more confidence than she might have a few weeks ago.

"Hello, this is Mary Vaughn Lewis," she said in the practiced low purr she'd perfected just in case there was a male on the other end of the line.

"Mom, that tone is wasted on me," Rory Sue teased.

"Oh, sorry, sweetie. I didn't look at the caller ID. What's up? I'm in a meeting that's about to start," she said, keeping her gaze fixed on the door that led to Tom's office. She deliberately adjusted her jacket, opening another button to reveal a bit more of the lacy black camisole underneath, then caught the glint of laughter in Ronnie's eyes and buttoned it right back up.

She realized then that she'd missed half of what her daughter was saying. "Sorry, hon, tell me again."

"You didn't hear anything I said?"

"Afraid not."

"Why? Is there a man in the room?"

Mary Vaughn blushed at the question. "I only have a minute," she reminded Rory Sue, deliberately ignoring her daughter's impertinence.

"I wanted to talk to you again about my going skiing," she said. "Now that you've had some time to think it over."

"I didn't need to think it over," Mary Vaughn said. "I've already told you no and I'm not going to change my mind."

"Do you really want me to be miserable during the holidays? I'll be bored out of my mind in Serenity."

"Your friends will be home. You'll find plenty of things

to do right here. And you know how much your daddy and granddaddy love having your around for the holidays. They always make a huge fuss."

"I talked to Dad. He said it would be okay with him if it was okay with you."

Damn Sonny! Mary Vaughn thought. Couldn't he agree with her about anything? He'd probably been finalizing some car deal while Rory Sue was talking and hadn't even heard her request. It wasn't like him to give up time with their daughter, unless he'd done it just to rile her—although she was pretty sure he wouldn't waste the energy bothering with that now that he'd moved on.

"Well, it's not okay with me, which you knew before you called him," she told Rory Sue. "We're celebrating the holidays right here and that's final. Look, why don't you plan a big party so you can catch up with all your friends as soon as you get here. You can have it at our house or the club, whichever you like. Then you all can make lots of holiday plans together. Your schedule will be so full you won't have a minute to even think about skiing."

"Bor-ing!" Rory Sue intoned. "The club is way too stuffy and if we have it at the house, you'll freak over every detail."

"I'll stay completely out of it," Mary Vaughn bargained. "You can plan the entire party yourself. You can make sure it's not boring."

"How? Will you let me bring in beer?"

"Absolutely not. You and most of your friends are underage. No drinking."

"Then what fun will that be?"

"You don't need alcohol to have fun," Mary Vaughn scolded. "Come on, Rory Sue, meet me halfway here. I promise you'll have a great time. Have I ever broken a promise to you?"

"The most important promise of all," Rory Sue retorted without missing a beat. "You told me I'd always have a family I could count on. That hasn't been true in years."

The barb stung. Flushed, Mary Vaughn turned away from Ronnie's penetrating gaze and her former father-in-law's frown. "You can always count on me and your daddy and your granddaddy," she said in a hushed but emphatic voice. "Just because your daddy and I aren't married does not mean we don't love you as much as ever."

"If you loved me, you'd let me go skiing."

"I have to go now, Rory Sue. And don't you dare call your daddy and beg him to change my mind. I intend to have a talk with him today and make sure he knows exactly how I feel about this." The truth was, she should have had that talk with Sonny after Rory Sue's first call, but she hadn't quite figured out what to say to him. Now she knew exactly where to start. "I mean it, Rory Sue. This is settled once and for all."

"Fine," Rory Sue said in a huff and cut off the call.

Seconds later, her ex-father-in-law's phone rang. Howard answered and his face lit up. "Darlin' girl, how are you?"

Mary Vaughn made a dash around the table and yanked the phone right out of his hand. "Don't you involve your grandfather in this!" she snapped to Rory Sue, then handed the phone back to Howard.

"Problems?" Ronnie inquired as she went back to her seat.

"Nothing I can't handle," she replied.

"I'm familiar with the divide-and-conquer technique. During her recovery from anorexia, my daughter Annie tried it all the time with Dana Sue and me until she figured out it was counterproductive to her real goal of getting us back together."

"How'd you handle it?" she asked, even though she didn't really want advice from the man who'd spurned her twice.

"Dana Sue and I compared notes. We presented a united front."

Mary Vaughn considered that. She and Sonny hadn't had a conversation in months. They hadn't been united over anything. They acted, in fact, as if they barely knew each other, much less had ten years of marriage behind them and a daughter in common. If Ronnie was right and they went on like that, Rory Sue would do her best to take advantage of the situation every chance she got.

Much as she hated the idea, she really did need to talk to her ex-husband and come up with a plan. Maybe at the same time they could devise a way to make this Christmas Rory Sue's best, so she'd be glad she'd come home to Serenity.

"Thanks for the tip," she told Ronnie grudgingly.

Just then Howard clicked off his cell phone and scowled at her. "What are you and Rory Sue fussing about that you don't want me to know?"

"She didn't tell you?"

"After you'd busted in and told her not to, no. She just filled me in on what's happening at school. Now you can tell me the rest."

"She doesn't want to spend the holidays here," Mary Vaughn told him. "She wants to go skiing with her roommate's family."

Howard looked crestfallen. "Not home for Christmas? Of course, we can't have that. This is where she belongs."

"For once, we're on the same page."

"What does Sonny say?"

"He told her it was okay with him if it was okay with me."

Howard shook his head. "I'll talk to him."

"No," Mary Vaughn protested. "I'll handle this. Sonny and I need to present a united front, for a change."

"You tell him it just won't be Christmas without our little gal here. And if you need backup, you let me know."

Though on most issues, Howard would rather eat dirt than support her on anything, Mary Vaughn wasn't totally shocked by his backing on this. He adored Rory Sue. "I appreciate it," she told him sincerely. "It would break my heart to have her so far away."

"Mine, too," he said, giving her hand a pat. "This is all going to work out, Mary Vaughn. Don't you worry about that."

His confidence bolstered her spirits, but not quite as much as Tom's arrival. Even though he looked as if he'd rather be miles away from this meeting, he was the handsomest thing in a suit she'd seen in a long, long time.

She suspected he'd look even better out of it.

Tom didn't even try to hide his disappointment over Jeanette's absence from the committee meeting. He'd been peeking into the room for the past ten minutes, hoping to delay his entrance and the start of the meeting until she arrived. By nine-fifteen, he was forced to accept that she wasn't coming and that the others were getting restless.

"Good morning, everyone," he said, taking his seat. "Sorry I'm late."

"Punctuality is a sign of respect," Howard said, sounding very much the way Tom's parents would have sounded under similar circumstances. "None of us have time to waste sitting around here."

"Of course not," Tom said. "It won't happen again. Let's

get right to those reports. Mary Vaughn, how are you coming with contacting the church choirs?"

"We have commitments from the First Baptist Church and the Methodists," she reported. "I know we've never asked the choir at Main Street Baptist to participate before, but I think it's time that changed. This is a new era and the whole community should be represented."

Tom nodded approvingly. "I totally agree. Howard, do you foresee any problems with that?"

Howard looked taken aback at first, then shook his head. "To tell you the truth, I thought they'd been invited in the past and turned us down."

"You know that's not so," Mary Vaughn contradicted. "You and everybody always tiptoed around it, but the truth is, nobody wanted to take the chance of stirring up trouble. We ought to be long past such discrimination in Serenity, if you ask me."

"For whatever it's worth, I agree," Ronnie said. "They have an excellent choir and they ought to be included. Race shouldn't even be an issue in this."

"That's settled then," Tom said. "Mary Vaughn, you'll speak to their choir director and report back next week."

She smiled at him. "I'll call you or stop by and let you know as soon as I've spoken to her," she told him.

"Okay, then. Ronnie, what have you found out about decorations?"

For the next hour they looked at pictures of a variety of options, from lighted snowflakes to banners for light poles. From Tom's perspective, it was much ado about nothing, but Howard and Mary Vaughn carried on as if the entire success of the festival hinged on the selection.

"Budget, people," Tom said at last. "I've only been able

to find a very small discretionary fund we can use for this. We can't afford to go overboard."

"If we decide on the snowflakes, I can negotiate a discount," Ronnie offered. "I stock a lot of merchandise from this supplier. I think he'll cut me a deal."

"Then it's decided," Howard said, looking pleased. "We'll have snowflakes lit up all over downtown, along with twinkle lights in the oaks and palmettos, plus the town Christmas tree we'll light on the first night of the festival. Ronnie, you'll supervise a town crew getting everything in place, right?"

"I can do that," Ronnie agreed.

Tom covered his vendor report in under a minute, then adjourned the meeting. As the others were leaving, he beckoned Ronnie to follow him into his office.

"Where's Jeanette?" he asked.

Ronnie gave him a sympathetic look. "No idea. You must really have ticked her off last night for her to blow off a commitment she made to Maddie to serve on this committee. What'd you do?"

"I have no idea. How am I supposed to fix a problem if I don't know what it is?" He was frustrated by the situation and by the fact that Jeanette's behavior mattered at all. He'd been so careful all these years to avoid romantic entanglements for precisely this reason. They were an unnecessary distraction. And yet he couldn't seem to let go of his fascination with Jeanette. Lust was certainly part of it, no question about it, but there was more. She touched him on some level no other woman ever had.

"You could ask her why she's upset," Ronnie suggested. "Or you could just start groveling and see how it goes."

"I've never groveled in my life," Tom protested, then winced at the implied arrogance in the comment.

"You ever have a woman as mad at you as Jeanette seems to be?"

"More than likely," Tom admitted ruefully. "It's just never been this important before." He had zero experience with a woman capable of twisting his insides into a knot the way this one did.

"Well, if you want my opinion, a man's never too old to learn all the ways to apologize to a woman. Believe me, I had plenty of practice with Dana Sue." He slapped Tom on the back. "And look at us now. We couldn't be happier."

Tom nodded. "Flowers or candy?"

"Jeanette strikes me as a hard sell. You'll need to be more inventive than that."

"I'll work on it," Tom said.

For the rest of the morning, Tom wrestled with the town's budget and with possible ways he could make amends with Jeanette. He was so distracted by the latter that Teresa finally called him on it.

"You aren't paying a bit of attention to anything I say," she accused, taking a seat across from him. "Not that that's anything new, but would you mind telling me what's more important than your job?"

"It's a personal matter," Tom said.

"Must have something to do with that argument you and Jeanette had over at Helen and Erik's last night."

He stared at her incredulously. "How on earth do you know about that? None of her friends would be out spreading rumors first thing this morning."

Teresa regarded him benevolently. "You have a lot to learn about Serenity. Grace Wharton's cousin lives next door. She saw Jeanette storming out of there and you not far behind. She put two and two together and told Grace, who's probably told everyone who stopped by to have breakfast at Wharton's this morning."

"And you heard it from one of these people?"

"No, I heard it from Grace herself. I have a bowl of oatmeal at Wharton's every morning so I know the latest on what's going on around town. Nothing much gets past Grace or me."

"Does this town even need the weekly newspaper?"

"Not really, though I will say the reporters over there tend to stick with the facts and don't put a lot of interpretation on 'em. At least, not since they tried to spin what was going on between Maddie and Cal at the spa before that place opened. Once they'd stirred up that hornets' nest, things changed. Now it's pretty dull reading."

"Well, thank heaven for that," he muttered.

"So, is that what's on your mind?" Teresa asked. "Because it seems to me you'd get a lot more done if you just took the time to go over to the spa and settle things with Jeanette before you waste the entire day, instead of just the morning."

He stood up. "You know what, Teresa? For once, you and I are in total agreement about something. I'll be back in an hour."

"A smart man might consider stopping by Sullivan's to pick up some of that apple bread pudding she loves or maybe a selection of scones," she advised as he was going out the door. "I'll call Dana Sue and tell her you're coming. They're not open yet so just poke your head in the kitchen when you get there, if she's not around out front."

He considered balking at Teresa's interference, but concluded she'd come up with an excellent plan. "Thank you."

"Take your time coming back," she said. "I'll keep things running around here."

"I don't doubt it," he said.

He'd made it as far as Sullivan's when he was accosted by Mary Vaughn.

"My goodness, twice in one day!" she said, tucking her arm through his. "How lucky am I? I see you're heading to Sullivan's. Will you join me for lunch? They won't be open for a few minutes, but I'm sure they won't mind if we get there early."

Oh boy, he thought. This time she didn't even attempt to disguise the invitation by mentioning real estate. He needed to handle the situation diplomatically. Maybe he just needed to turn her down enough times that she'd get the message without getting any hurt feelings.

"I'm afraid I can't," he said, edging away from her. "I'm grabbing some takeout that Teresa called ahead to order. I have a meeting to get to."

"You're certainly busier than any town manager we've had before," she grumbled, not even trying to hide her disappointment. "I suppose I'm just going to have to call and make an appointment if I want to spend any time with you."

"I'm pretty tied up these days," he said carefully, hoping that would dissuade her from any further attempts to hook up with him. "There's always a lot to learn on a new job." He glanced deliberately at his watch. "Sorry, Mary Vaughn. I really do have to run."

As Teresa had directed, he went inside and dashed directly into the kitchen, picked up the bag Dana Sue had waiting for him and paid her for it, then glanced toward the back door. "Any chance I can get out of here that way?"

"You hiding from someone?" she inquired.

"Mary Vaughn," he said in a low voice.

"Enough said," she said, gesturing toward the door. "The

alley runs parallel to Main Street. In fact, if you take it to the end, it will take you all the way to Palmetto."

He gave her a sharp look. "Oh?"

"That order is for Jeanette, isn't it? Ronnie told me you were trying to come up with some way to make amends. When Teresa called, I put two and two together."

"Is everybody in this town good at that kind of math?" he asked testily.

She beamed at him. "Pretty much. Good luck, by the way. Jeanette's a wonderful woman, but she doesn't say much about herself. We've known her three years and none of us have ever met her family or even heard much about them. From the amount of time she spends at the spa, I get the feeling she's a bit of a loner."

"You think there's a reason for that?"

"Isn't there usually?" Dana Sue said. "I just think she's erected some pretty thick barricades around her heart. Don't try tearing them down if it's just a game to you."

He heard the warning and understood it. "I can't say this with a hundred percent certainty, but I don't think it is."

"Maybe you ought to be sure," she said.

"How can I be without getting close enough to find out just how well suited we are?"

"Fair enough," Dana Sue said, though she didn't look entirely happy about it.

Tom left Sullivan's, cut down the alley all the way to Palmetto, then happened upon a flower vendor. He grabbed a huge bouquet of summer flowers to add to his offering for Jeanette, then made his way over to the intersection with Main where The Corner Spa was situated. The parking lot out back was full, he noted as he walked around the building to the front.

Now that he was at the spa, he realized that the one thing

he hadn't considered was the no-men-allowed rule. Would one of those personal trainers try to toss him out on his backside before he ever made his way to Jeanette? He'd just have to risk it. Right now he was determined enough to fix things with her that he'd happily deck anyone who tried to prevent it.

Keeping his eyes straight ahead, he walked inside and headed for what looked to be a suite of offices. He'd made it about ten paces into forbidden territory when Maddie stepped into his path. Even though she was obviously trying to look stern, a smile tugged at her lips.

"You know you're not supposed to be in here," she scolded.

He shoved the flowers into her arms. "Couldn't you bend the rules for about ten minutes?" he pleaded.

"You think you can win Jeanette over in ten minutes?"

"I plan to give it my best shot. Is she with a client?"

Maddie shook her head. "She's taking a break on the patio. I don't think anyone will get too riled up if you go out there." She grinned. "Other than Jeanette, of course. I can't speak for her. She seems fairly annoyed with you."

"Believe me, I get that." He leaned down and pressed a kiss to her cheek. "Thank you."

"You're welcome," she said, and handed the flowers back to him. "Something tells me you're going to need all of this and more. Good luck."

"Who needs luck?" he asked jauntily. "I have flowers, scones and bread pudding."

Outside he found Jeanette reading a dog-eared copy of a romance novel. He found that encouraging. Apparently she wasn't totally immune to love, even if she preferred the fictional variety.

"Does the guy get the girl?" he inquired, sitting down next to her.

She looked up from the book, then blinked. "What are you doing here?"

"I came to see you."

"I meant in the spa, during regular hours. Maddie will have a fit."

"Actually I'm here with her blessing," he said. He tried to hand her the flowers, but she ignored them. He gave up and set them on the table. "I brought bread pudding and scones, too."

Her gaze narrowed. "From Sullivan's?"

"Of course."

"Whose idea was that?"

"A number of people reached a consensus," he said.

"Meaning?"

"Ronnie suggested I grovel. Teresa mentioned the bread pudding and scones. Dana Sue added her two cents when I picked up the order. I spotted the flowers on my way over. I tried giving them to Maddie as a bribe, but she said I'd probably need them for you." He studied her hopefully. "Is any of this working?"

She managed to keep her expression unyielding for another minute, but then she eyed the bag he'd set on the table. "Did you remember the ice cream on the pudding?"

"It might be soup by now, but I believe it's on there."

"Okay, then," she said, reaching eagerly for the bag. She took a deep breath as she opened it, then sighed. "Is there anything better than the scent of cinnamon or freshly baked scones?"

"I think whatever that scent is you're wearing is better," he said candidly.

She looked startled by the compliment. "Lavender?"

"Is that what it is? I just know I've developed an affinity for it recently."

"Tom, you have to stop saying things like that," she said.

"Why? It's the truth."

"You're very big on truth and honesty, aren't you?"

"I try to be."

"Which is why you warned me last night that your stay in Serenity is just temporary."

He blinked at the accusatory note in her voice. "Is that what sent you flying out of there?" he asked incredulously.

She nodded. "For once in my life I have no intention of starting something that can only end badly."

"It might not end at all," he said. "We won't know unless we spend some time together."

"We *do* know!" she countered. "You've already said you're leaving. Maybe not tomorrow or next week, but someday."

"And if that time comes, what's to prevent you from coming with me?" he asked, perplexed by her attitude.

"It won't work that way," she said. "You know it won't."

He held up his hand. "Slow down, sweetheart. We're getting way ahead of ourselves here. How about we go on an actual date before we start discussing breaking up?"

"Because I can already see down the road and it's not one I want to take," she said stubbornly. "You want to be friends, I can handle that. Anything more, forget it."

"I think those kisses we've shared prove there's something more than friendship between us."

"Come on, Tom. We're both adults. We both understand how chemistry works. Maybe we can light up the night sky for a few weeks, but eventually it'll die down. And one of us will get burned, more than likely me."

"You are, without doubt, the most pessimistic woman I've ever tried to date."

"With good reason."

"So I take the blame for whoever's mistreated you in the past?"

"Not at all. Just think of me as a woman who's finally learned her lesson."

He sat back. "You're not going to bend on this, are you?"

"Nope," she said, sounding proud of herself. "For once, I'm not."

He wondered if she had any idea how seductive it was to hear her make such a claim. "That sounds an awful lot like a challenge," he told her, then winked. "I've warned you about this before, but I'll do it again. I have never turned down a challenge. I'll be in touch, darlin'."

He saw the quick flare of alarm in her eyes right before he stood up and walked away. Good, he thought. She was on notice. Changing her mind had just become his personal mission. He had a hunch it was going to be more fun than anything he'd done in years.

CHAPTER NINE

⁂

Jeanette listened as Mary Vaughn recited the list of attempts she'd made to get the town manager to notice her, all to no avail. Jeanette couldn't help but be gratified that he wasn't succumbing to the woman's considerable charms.

Maybe his interest in her was serious, after all. She'd have to give that some more thought, she decided as she laid warm towels on Mary Vaughn's face at the conclusion of a treatment.

"Do you suppose he's gay?" Mary Vaughn said, her voice muffled a bit by the towels. "That would explain a lot, wouldn't it?"

Even though Mary Vaughn couldn't see her face, Jeanette had to turn away to stifle a laugh. Tom might not be right for her, but he was all male. There wasn't a doubt in her mind about that. Those remarkable kisses they'd shared confirmed it. Maybe she should describe them in detail to put Mary Vaughn's mind at rest.

Bad idea, she told herself at once. That news could feed the rumor mill in Serenity for a week.

Apparently, though, her silence had gone on too long,

because Mary Vaughn took it for agreement. "You think so, too, don't you?"

"No, not at all," Jeanette replied. "In fact, I'm trying to figure out how you could come up with such a crazy idea. You can't go around saying things like that about the man, Mary Vaughn. Who knows what kind of trouble you might stir up for him. This is a pretty traditional town."

"Oh, hogwash!" Mary Vaughn retorted. "It's not as if there's anything wrong with being gay."

"Some people might not feel that way, including Tom. My point is, you've jumped to this conclusion based on very little. You hardly know him."

"I have good instincts when it comes to men," Mary Vaughn insisted. "Besides, like I just told you, I've asked him out for lunch or for coffee or a drink a couple of times now and he keeps turning me down. Always has an excuse." She pulled aside the towel and met Jeanette's gaze in the mirror. "Oh, don't look at me like that. I know women are supposed to wait for men to make the first move, but if we did that, we'd spend way too many nights at home alone. I didn't ask the man to marry me, for heaven's sake."

"Do you even know if he's available?"

"Well, of course I do. I had a friend in the clerk's office look at the paperwork he submitted his first day on the job. He's definitely not married now, and as far as I can tell from asking around, he's never been married."

"He might have a fiancée or a girlfriend in Charleston or in the last place he worked," Jeanette improvised, not wanting to suggest he might be interested in someone else right here in Serenity. "For all you know he takes off every Friday afternoon to spend the weekend with a woman he's planning to marry."

"I suppose that's possible," Mary Vaughn conceded,

her expression thoughtful. Then she waved the suggestion aside. "Come on, Jeanette, he's in his midthirties and he's never been married. Don't you think that's strange?"

"I've never been married," Jeanette responded. "Is *that* strange?"

Mary Vaughn dismissed that idea, too. "Heavens no, sugar. I can tell you're just choosy. You're not going to settle for any ol' man who comes along, and why should you? With your looks, you can have any man you want."

"If only that were true," Jeanette commented dryly.

Not a single one of her supposedly serious relationships had led to marriage. She'd played second best to other women, to sports, to a career, and in one disastrous instance, to the man's mama. She'd finally resolved to break that pattern and never be anyone's second best again. If a man couldn't put her first, she didn't want him. And based on Tom's declaration about his own plans to move on, to say nothing of his unfortunate tie to a woman who'd tried to ruin her, a relationship with him didn't seem like a good route to go.

Determined to change the subject, she replaced the warm towel over Mary Vaughn's face. "Leave that there," she instructed. "I'll be right back. Try to relax and let those moisturizers do their thing."

Mary Vaughn murmured something Jeanette couldn't understand, which was probably just as well. She liked Mary Vaughn well enough most of the time, but one of these days the woman was going to make some nasty comment about someone Jeanette liked and she was going to lose control and stuff that towel right down her throat!

Tom looked up from the pile of requisitions on his desk to find his mother standing in the doorway, her expression uncertain, her arms laden with fabric samples.

"Mother, what on earth are you doing here?" he asked as he rushed to relieve her of her burden.

"I told you I was going to buy new drapes for your office," she said with a touch of impatience. "I brought a few samples so you can choose what you like."

Tom had forgotten all about the offer and his promise to make sure that no one in town would object. "I'm afraid you've wasted a trip," he told her, dumping the fabric onto a chair. "I haven't even spoken to the mayor about whether it would be appropriate for you to do this."

"Well, where is he? Let's ask him right now. Surely no one can object to your own mother paying for drapes."

Truthfully, they probably wouldn't, but Tom didn't give two hoots about what kind of material hung by the windows in his office. Ironically, he wasn't entirely convinced his mother did, either, despite her apparent enthusiasm for the project.

"Sit down," he said. "Talk to me. What's this really about? Normally you're so busy I don't even hear from you for weeks on end. Suddenly all you can focus on are my drapes. I don't get it. Are you bored, Mother?"

"Heavens, no. I have so many obligations, sometimes I can't fit them all in." Despite her convincing words, she avoided his gaze as she spoke.

"Then why are you wasting time choosing drapes for my office?"

She squirmed uncomfortably. "Because you're never around and I miss you," she admitted finally. "I know you want to avoid your father and his constant criticism, but that means you don't spend any time with me, either. You're my youngest, and my only son."

He grinned at her. "And your favorite," he teased.

"Don't start that with me, young man. Mothers don't have favorites."

"Then why isn't it enough for you that my sisters and their families are all right there underfoot?"

"Because they're older and they're settled. They've made good marriages and are filling their homes with children. You're all alone. I worry about you. I won't be around forever. You need someone in your life, a woman of substance who will challenge you and see to your needs."

Tom barely contained a sigh. "Not this again, Mother. I'll marry when I find the right woman." Then he thought about her offhand comment about not being around forever. "You're not ill, are you?"

"Of course not," she said at once. "It's just that you said something in Charleston to suggest that you might have met her," she reminded him. "But when your father and I came over here hoping for at least a glimpse of her, the only woman we saw was the one who scooted off before we could even be introduced."

"I told you—"

"I know, she's on some committee with you," his mother interrupted, clearly exasperated with him. "But is she the one?"

"Mother, you're getting way ahead of yourself. I swear to you that if I get serious about anyone, you'll be the first to know." He walked over and pressed a kiss to her forehead. "And no more talk about you not being around forever. You're not even sixty, for goodness' sakes. You'll be pestering us all for years to come."

She gave him a wan smile. "I hope so."

He bent and picked up the samples. "Why don't I haul all this fabric back to your car and then take you to lunch at Sullivan's."

Her eyes lit up. "Do you have the time? The meal we had there was surprisingly good. I've mentioned it to several of my friends."

"I'm sure Dana Sue will appreciate that," he said wryly, knowing that the restaurant was already booked to capacity most evenings.

They took his mother's silver Cadillac over to Sullivan's, where the parking lot was already jammed with cars. Dana Sue greeted them at the door, looking frazzled.

"Obviously, you're not part of this invasion by the Red Hat Society," she said to Tom. "Hello again, Mrs. McDonald. It's nice to have you back. We're a bit crowded, but if you'll give me two minutes I'll get a table set up for you in the bar area. Will that be okay?"

"It'll be fine," Tom assured her. "Thanks, Dana Sue."

His mother was gazing around the packed room. "I've heard about these Red Hat women," she said. "They look as if they're having fun, don't they? And I love all those red hats and purple accessories. They're a bit garish, but very lively."

"They sound lively, too," Tom said, listening to the roars of laughter.

"I've spotted several groups like this around Charleston at various restaurants," his mother commented. "Most of the women seem to be my age or older. I wonder what they do."

"Maybe Dana Sue can tell you that," he suggested just as she returned to lead them to a table as far from the commotion as possible. "Dana Sue, do you know anything about what these Red Hatters do?"

"I don't know that they *do* anything in particular," Dana Sue said. "I just know they come in once a month for lunch and seem to have a wonderful time. I've always thought everyone should take that kind of break from their hectic lives, get together with friends just to catch up and laugh. Helen, Maddie, Jeanette and I do that from time to time, but not nearly enough these days."

A young waitress rushed up. "Dana Sue, crisis in the kitchen!"

"I'm on my way," Dana Sue assured her. "You'll have to excuse me. Someone will be over to take your order in a minute."

"Go, we're in no hurry," Tom said.

He glanced up then and saw Jeanette rushing through the front door. She smiled when she saw him, but the instant she spotted his mother, dismay flashed in her eyes and she bolted.

"Mother, I'll be right back," he said, hurrying after Jeanette as she sped toward the kitchen.

He entered the kitchen right on her heels to find chaos as Dana Sue, Erik and their sous chef tried to keep up with the rush of orders. Dana Sue spotted Jeanette first, then Tom.

"If you two need a quiet corner to talk, this isn't it," she said as she dished up chicken salad with walnuts and grapes on a row of plates. "Go in my office."

"I'm just here to pick up Maddie's order for the café," Jeanette said, ignoring him. "She's tied up with a vendor."

"Five minutes," Dana Sue said. "And out of my kitchen, both of you."

Tom exited at once, then held the door for Jeanette. "Since you have to wait, now's the perfect time for you to say hello to my mother. Perhaps you can both put that unfortunate incident behind you once and for all."

Jeanette frowned. "Unfortunate incident?" she said, her voice low. "Please. I won't let you try to minimize what happened, Tom. Your mother tried to ruin me. If I'd worked for a boss other than Bella, she might have succeeded."

He was about to tell her not to be so dramatic when his mother stepped up beside him.

"Is everything all right?" she said, her words directed at him, but her gaze locked on Jeanette.

Tom saw the precise instant recognition dawned. His mother looked as if she'd just tasted a sour lemon.

"You!" she said, practically quivering with indignation. "I'm not entirely surprised to find you in this nothing little town. I imagine Bella ran you out of Charleston."

Bright patches of color darkened Jeanette's cheeks. She shot an apologetic look at Tom, then drew herself up to face down his mother. This wasn't going to go well. He could tell even before she opened her mouth. Since he couldn't decide which of them to drag away, he was forced to let it play out.

"Actually, Bella supported me one hundred percent," Jeanette told his mother. "I'm in Serenity because I had the opportunity to manage spa services at an exceptional new spa. I've been here for three years. We've gotten rave reviews from the media and our customers." She fixed her gaze on his mother. "And you know the most amazing part, not one single customer has ever complained about her skin care here. Do you know what that tells me? It tells me I'm darn good at what I do and that if someone had a problem with a treatment, just maybe it was because she never told me she was allergic to certain ingredients."

Undaunted by Jeanette's suggestion, Tom's mother gave Jeanette her haughtiest glare. "You are a very rude young woman," she declared. "And incompetent, as well. I have half a mind to call your current boss and report exactly what you did to me."

"Mother," Tom protested, "you've known about your allergies for years."

"That's not the point!" his mother huffed.

"It's exactly the point," Jeanette said. "You knew you were in the wrong, but you tried to get me fired anyway. What gives you the right to toy with someone's life that way? Is it just because you're rich and you think you can get away with it? People like you make me sick."

Tom winced. Jeanette was obviously out of patience and way beyond thinking about the consequences of her words. He was tempted to clamp a hand over her mouth, but in her present mood, she was likely to bite it.

"Forget about trying to make trouble for me again," Jeanette continued. "My current boss has heard all about you and, believe me, none of it was flattering. For another thing, you spreading these lies amounts to defamation of character and my attorney has already advised me I should sue."

His mother regarded her with shock. "You wouldn't dare!"

Jeanette's eyes blazed with righteous indignation. "Try me," she said, not backing down an inch.

His mother blinked rapidly, then turned on her heel. "Tom, suddenly I'm not at all hungry. We should go."

"I'll be right there, Mother." He met Jeanette's gaze. She was looking just a little shaken. "Did you really have to do that?" he asked mildly.

She winced. "What? Stand up for myself? Yes, I believe I did. It was something I should have done four years ago when the *unfortunate incident* happened."

He shook his head, then gave her a quick kiss. "Just so you know, you were formidable. I'll call you later."

And then he left to try to make amends with his mother, not on Jeanette's behalf, but on his own. He probably should have jumped to her defense, but he'd been so taken aback and, yes, impressed by Jeanette's tirade, he hadn't been able to interrupt. The woman was amazing…and just a little scary!

Outside, he found his mother in the passenger seat of her car, all but quivering with outrage. "How well do you know that little trollop?" she inquired.

"Careful, Mother," he warned as he slid behind the wheel. "Jeanette is a friend."

His mother looked horrified. "Well, I forbid it!" she declared.

Tom laughed. "I'm a little old for you to be deciding who my playmates should be."

"I'm telling you that woman is a menace. I don't care what she says, I'm calling her boss to report her."

Tom's expression sobered at once. "No, Mother, you're not doing that."

"I most certainly am. I believe I'll call the licensing board or whatever it is that regulates that business, as well."

"You do that, and you and I are done," he told her quietly.

She looked startled for an instant, then her gaze narrowed. "Why do you mind? You should be grateful that I'm taking care of the matter before she stirs up bad publicity for one of your businesses here in town. Unless this woman means more to you than you've admitted."

"Let's leave my friendship with Jeanette out of this," he said. "Don't you think that you trying to get her fired will stir up bad publicity? Come on, Mother, that's exactly what you want. You're hoping to publicly humiliate her, even though you were the one at fault."

She touched a hand to her cheek. "If you'd only seen what she did to me," she said, her expression miserable.

"My face was covered with these huge red blotches. And I had to attend a major event that night wearing so much makeup I'm surprised my face didn't crack."

"You could have stayed home," Tom suggested. "You've had hives before when you've tried a new skin lotion that contained whatever ingredient it is you're allergic to. Jeanette was absolutely right about that. You should have told her about your allergy."

His mother regarded him with dismay. "Why are you taking her side against your own mother?" she asked, then gasped. "She's the one, isn't she? She's the woman you're interested in."

Tom debated giving an evasive answer, but what would be the point? They might as well have this out here and now. "Yes, she is. And I would consider it a personal favor if you would drop this whole ridiculous matter. You were more at fault than she was, and you know it."

"Thomas Winston McDonald, don't you even consider getting involved with that woman!" she commanded. "Aside from my issues with her, she is beneath you. She does facials, for heaven's sake. You need to find a woman who's your social equal, not some little trollop who's probably a high-school dropout."

Tom regarded her with pity. "I warned you, Mother," he said quietly, opening the door and exiting the car. "We're done here."

"Thomas, get back in this car," she demanded.

He closed the door and walked away. He knew this wouldn't be the end of it. By nightfall, his father would know all about his ill-advised choice of female companionship and then things would really get out of control. On days like this, he wished they'd just write him off and stay the hell out of his life.

* * *

When Jeanette returned to the kitchen to pick up Maddie's order, she felt sick to her stomach. She had never in her life talked to anyone the way she had to Mrs. McDonald. On one hand, she was exhilarated to have finally spoken up to a woman who was little better than a bully. On the other, that woman was the mother of a man she was attracted to.

She wove through the chaos in the kitchen, found a stool and sat down out of the way. Sighing, she grabbed one of the huge iced red-hat sugar cookies Erik had made for the group's dessert and bit into it.

"Don't let Erik catch you with that," Dana Sue murmured, pausing next to her, several boxes of baked goods for the spa in her arms. She set them down. "Are you okay? You look a little flushed."

"I told off Tom's mother," she admitted.

"Oh boy," Dana Sue said, regarding her with sympathy. "How'd that go?"

"Let's just say I don't think she and I will ever be bosom buddies," Jeanette said wryly.

"How about Tom? Whose side did he take?"

"I think he was too stunned to say much, but he didn't seem mad at me." She grinned, despite her mood. "To tell you the truth, I think he was on my side. He said he'd call me later."

"Good for him," Dana Sue said. "Some men have trouble choosing a woman they like over their own mother."

"Been there, done that," Jeanette told her. "Tom gets real points with me for not jumping immediately to her defense and for keeping an open mind."

"Enough points to get you to go out with him?"

Jeanette sighed. "I don't know. Maybe."

Dana Sue pulled up another stool. "Okay, I have about

two minutes. Let's talk about this. You're attracted to him, right?"

Jeanette nodded.

"Then what's holding you back?"

"I already know how it's going to end."

Dana Sue's eyebrows shot up. "Really? Do you tell other people's fortunes, too?"

Jeanette chuckled at her feigned amazement. "Okay, stop. You know what I mean. Just look at the kind of family he's from, to say nothing of the fact that he's flat out told me that this job is a stepping stone, not a final destination."

"You have a problem with him being rich and ambitious?"

It sounded ridiculous when put that way. "Of course not, but come on, Dana Sue, we're talking about his family and his future. I don't really fit in with either one. I'd say this little blowup I had with his mother makes that plain."

"You fit in if he says you do," Dana Sue countered. "Where did you get this crazy idea that you don't measure up or aren't worthy of having a good man in your life?"

Jeanette thought of the history that had proved exactly that, but she was changing, or trying to. She was starting to value who she was and what she had to offer, which was exactly why she didn't want someone in her life who wouldn't put her first.

"Tom might have chosen me over his mother today, but I can't count on him always doing that."

"Always, no," Dana Sue conceded. "Look, no one can promise you this won't end badly, but the only way to find out is to give it a chance. Good men don't come along every day. All of the evidence isn't in yet, but Tom may be one of them. Don't leave him for someone like Mary Vaughn to get her claws into."

"Mary Vaughn thinks he's gay," Jeanette confided.

Dana Sue stared at her with openmouthed shock, then they both dissolved into giggles at the absurdity.

"Because he won't go out with her, I'll bet," Dana Sue said when she could speak again.

"Bingo," Jeanette confirmed.

"Well then, I think you have a moral obligation to show the world otherwise," Dana Sue told her with mock seriousness. "Start making out with him on every street corner in town. You owe him that in return for him standing up to his mother for you."

"Oh, yeah, that'll be good for his reputation," Jeanette said.

"It can't hurt," Dana Sue insisted with a wink. "And it might be a whole lot of fun."

Jeanette considered her past experience with Tom's kisses and concluded that her friend was right. It would be a whole lot of fun.

It would also be the start of a whole lot of trouble.

CHAPTER TEN

❦

Even though he'd told Jeanette he'd call her, Tom had found a hundred excuses not to. His reluctance had nothing to do with his mother's edict. He was still a bit shaken by how strongly he'd reacted to his mother's attack on a woman he hardly knew. He'd been furious. He'd felt this overwhelming desire to protect Jeanette, to leap to her defense, something he'd never before felt with another woman.

Not that Jeanette needed his protection. She might look like a vulnerable waif, but she'd more than held her own with a woman who many rich and powerful people considered formidable. He wasn't entirely sure, though, that Jeanette understood the potential for fallout. His mother had a wide circle of friends and an unfortunate vindictive streak. She might have been in the wrong in the incident at Chez Bella, but her vanity had been offended and she would blame Jeanette for that no matter how ridiculous the claim.

He thought he'd tied his mother's hands a bit with his own edict, but he couldn't count on that preventing her from stirring up trouble forever, especially if she got his father involved. Between them, they knew how to make someone's life miserable—he could attest to that firsthand.

The real reason he'd been reluctant to make that call was fear. When Jeanette looked at him with those big brown eyes, something inside him shifted. He lost focus, which had never once in all of his thirty-five years happened to him before. It scared the daylights out of him.

All those years of steering clear of marriage-minded debutantes had kept him footloose. He'd always dated aggressive, sure-of-themselves women like Mary Vaughn, who was a little old for him, frankly, but obviously willing to have some sort of fling. He'd just about run out of excuses for turning down her invitations and found it oddly disturbing that he felt he *needed* to. He knew it was because of his feelings for Jeanette. He'd never allowed himself to be tied down to one woman in the past, especially a woman who claimed to have no interest whatsoever in him. Playing the field, choosing women who were sophisticated and undemanding, made it easier to keep his career as his number-one priority.

He'd already told Jeanette that Serenity was not where he intended to spend the rest of his life. It was too small and provincial for him, but the town manager's job was two steps up from the building and zoning job he'd had in a town barely big enough for a traffic light and one significant step above the chief financial officer's role he'd had in another tiny community. Serenity was just one more stepping stone.

Two years here, three at the outside, and he'd be ready for a bigger city, maybe even Charleston, which would probably drive his parents straight into an early grave. They were still reeling from his decision to work in local government. If he insisted on working right under their noses, they would probably die from the supposed humiliation of having their son employed as a public servant, no matter how lofty the capacity. His father especially wanted him to have the perceived power that came with elected office.

"No McDonald has ever worked for low wages and at the whim of some half-assed council of yokels," his father had said on more than one occasion. His derision had been unyielding.

"Then I'll be the first," Tom had retorted, unwilling to bend. "My life. My choice."

"Well, don't come running to me when you're getting on in years and don't have two dimes to rub together," his father had replied.

"Wouldn't dream of it," Tom had said, feeling triumphant about sticking to his guns, when it would have been easier to cave in to his father's demands.

It was at times like those that he really did wonder if he hadn't chosen his career just to spite his family. The truth, though, was that he enjoyed helping a town define or re-invent itself. He had clear visions of what communities ought to be and how to manage growth and development in a responsible way.

Serenity had appealed to him because it was on the cusp of huge change. So far, it had retained its small-town charm. Thanks to a few business visionaries like the women who'd opened The Corner Spa, and Ronnie Sullivan who'd helped to revitalize downtown with his hardware store and con-struction-supply company, Serenity was trying new things. It had avoided sinking into despair the way so many small towns did when they let growth get out of hand and allowed big-box stores to ruin local businesses.

He didn't miss the irony that one of the charms of small-town life in Serenity—the Christmas festival—was cur-rently the biggest annoyance in his life. And that a woman who seemed almost as uninterested in it as he was had the potential to derail all his well-laid plans.

"Damn," he muttered, tossing his pen across the room. He was overanalyzing things as usual. If he wanted to spend the evening with Jeanette, then he was wasting time holed up in his office. By now she'd probably concluded that he'd had second thoughts and decided to back his mother. He knew that would not sit well with her.

Unfortunately, when he called The Corner Spa, she'd already left for the day. A check of the phone book didn't reveal a home phone number, which meant she'd deliberately kept it unlisted. He could call any of her friends and get it, but it would probably come with a whole passel of unsolicited advice from the women Cal and everyone else in town referred to as the Sweet Magnolias. *Sweet,* he thought. *Meddling* was more like it.

He was still determined to find Jeanette and spend the evening with her. One of the advantages of being at Town Hall was that he had access to computerized property records. He typed in her name, but nothing came up. That must mean she was living in a rented home or apartment. Apartment complexes were few and far between in Serenity, but a rental home could be anywhere. He clicked off the computer with frustration. Now what?

There was only a handful of places where people hung out on a Friday night. Sullivan's was one. Rosalina's was another. It would be easy enough to check out both of those.

But as he walked outside, he heard what sounded like a low roar. Glancing up at the October sky, he saw bright lights in the distance. Football! There must be a game at the high school. With Cal's involvement in high-school sports, even though he coached baseball, not football, Tom suspected that's where he'd find not only Cal and Maddie, but their friends, Jeanette included.

He drove across town to the high school, but had to circle several blocks before he found a parking place. Cheers and groans greeted him as he hurried back to the stadium. Inside the gates, he bought a hot dog and a soft drink, then scanned the bleachers for familiar faces.

"Hey, Tom, up here!"

He looked up and saw Cal waving. Maddie was beside him, along with all their kids, even the baby. Jeanette was at the end of the row, holding Jessica Lynn on her lap. She didn't even glance his way. He almost smiled at the deliberate snub. It proved she'd noticed his absence and drawn the wrong conclusion about it. That meant he must matter to her, at least a little. He'd take it.

Tom sprinted up the steps, then squeezed past Cal and Maddie and the kids to sit beside Jeanette.

"I thought I might find you here," he said just as Jessica Lynn reached for his hot dog, grabbing it in her tiny fists and then covering herself in mustard.

Jeanette retrieved the hot dog and laid it back in his bun. "You may want to reconsider eating that," she said as she wiped off the little girl's hands and face. There was nothing to be done about the mustard all over her pink T-shirt.

Tom shrugged, wrapped up the hot dog and set it at his feet.

"I'll get another one later. Are we winning?"

"The scoreboard's over there," she said, nodding toward the end of the field.

"You mad at me?"

"Why would I be mad at you?" she asked, still avoiding his gaze.

"Because I told you I'd call and I haven't."

"I haven't been sitting by the phone, if that's what you're thinking," she said.

"Oh, I'm sure of that," he said. "Still, I'm sorry. I've had a lot on my mind."

"Such as whether you want to be seen with a woman who'd insult your mother right to her face?"

He grinned. "Nope, that had nothing to do with it."

She met his gaze at last. "What was it, then?"

"I was wondering whether you're starting to matter too much to me," he said. There, he thought as heat zinged through him, that was the problem. One look and he was completely off-kilter. He hated the sensation, but he couldn't seem to stop himself from coming back for more. "Could we go somewhere and talk?"

"I'm at a football game with friends," she said, pointing out the obvious.

"Yet you didn't even know the score," he said, barely containing a chuckle. She was going to fight him every step of the way. He was counting on the attraction being mutual. In the end, she would succumb to it, just as he had.

"I knew the score," she contradicted. "I just didn't want to tell you. I wasn't entirely sure I wanted to speak to you at all."

"And now?"

"You've almost redeemed yourself with that comment about me maybe mattering too much."

"Almost? What else do you need to hear?"

"That your mother's been banished to Siberia," she suggested.

He grinned. "It hasn't come to that, but I did tell her that I wouldn't listen to another word said against you."

She looked surprised. "Really? Did you mean it?"

"I walked off and left her sitting in Sullivan's parking lot when she tried to get in the last word."

Her expression brightened. "Thank you."

"Anytime. Now can we go someplace and talk?"

A worrisome glint sparked in her eyes. "Sure, but there's one thing I need to do first."

"Oh?"

To his shock, she looped a hand behind his neck and laid a kiss on his mouth that sent his pulse scrambling and set off more fireworks than a Serenity High victory.

When she finally pulled back, he stared at her, dazed. "What was that for?"

She regarded him with a self-satisfied smile. "One of these days I'll explain," she promised, then gave him an impish grin. "Or not."

Just then Tom realized that Cal, Maddie and half the people in the bleachers were staring at them with fascination. Given the speed of the Serenity rumor mill, the whole town would be talking about that kiss by morning, how she'd staked her claim on him right out there in public. He was stunned that Jeanette had been willing to do that.

"I think more people are watching us than the game," he told her, watching closely for her reaction.

"Precisely," she said with surprising satisfaction. "We can go now."

Tom still had no clue what she'd been up to, but maybe it didn't matter. Why question a kiss that had pretty much rocked his world? He stood up and followed her.

She handed Jessica Lynn off to Cal as they passed. "Good night," she told them. "Thanks for inviting me along."

"Glad you could come," Cal said, a wide grin on his face.

Maddie just stared at her in a way that suggested she

was going to have a whole lot of questions for Jeanette first thing Saturday morning.

Tom didn't know what the heck had just happened here tonight, but whatever was going on in Jeanette's head was more promising than anything she'd said or done to date. In the past that small victory might have been enough to satisfy him, to restore his ego and have him moving on. Instead, he could hardly wait to see where that kiss might lead.

Though it had probably been wildly misguided, Jeanette took great satisfaction in her public display of affection for Tom. That ought to take the wind right out of Mary Vaughn's sails and squelch any rumors about Tom's sexuality she might consider spreading. It was the least Jeanette could do for a man who'd taken her side over his own mother's. She was still a little overwhelmed by that. It couldn't have been easy.

"Where would you like to go?" he asked as he led the way toward his car.

"I don't know about you, but I'm starved," she said.

"Sullivan's?"

She shook her head. "Dana Sue and Erik," she said meaningfully.

"Of course," he said at once. "Meddling."

"Exactly."

"How about Rosalina's?"

"Much better. And we'll be ahead of the game crowd, so we should pretty much have the place to ourselves."

"Oh? You looking for privacy because you're planning on kissing me again?"

"No, because you said you wanted to talk."

"Kissing sounds more interesting."

"I was afraid I might be giving you the wrong idea about that," she said.

"What exactly would be the wrong idea about a kiss that could have heated an entire village in Alaska?"

She fought to hide how pleased she was by his assessment. "The wrong idea would be that there're going to be more of them on a regular basis."

He sighed dramatically. "I had a feeling that's what you meant. Of course, that does raise the question of why you did it in the first place, given all the potential negatives, such as me getting ideas, people talking and so on."

"It's probably best if we don't get into that," she said, still thinking of Mary Vaughn's ill-informed opinion. He might find it as laughable as she did, but then again, he might not. She didn't want to be responsible for stirring up ill will between those two. If nothing else, in their capacities as town manager and president of the chamber of commerce, they were bound to have to work together.

When she and Tom arrived at Rosalina's, they did, indeed, have the small, family-run Italian restaurant to themselves. Jeanette loved the smells—garlic, tomato, baking dough. The aromas were as comforting as some of the herbal scents she used at the spa.

"A large pizza with mushrooms, olives and green peppers?" Tom asked after they'd been seated.

She regarded him with surprise. "You remembered that from when we were here with Maddie and Cal?"

"I pay attention to the important things, Jeanette," he said solemnly.

She was impressed. "What else do you think you know about me?"

"Let's get our order in and then I'll tell you," he suggested, beckoning the waitress and ordering the pizza and soft drinks. He glanced at Jeanette. "No salad, right?"

"The veggies on the pizza count," she said.

"I'll be back with your drinks in a sec," Kristi Marcella, the pretty, dark-haired daughter of the owners, told them. Kristi was going to community college now, but she still helped out at the restaurant on weekends. "About fifteen minutes on the pizza."

"Thanks," Jeanette said, then regarded Tom quizzically. "Okay, shoot."

His expression turned thoughtful. "Let's see now... You smell like lavender. You're crazy about orange-cranberry scones and Sullivan's apple bread pudding. You're low-key and easygoing most of the time, but you have a fiery temper when someone does you wrong. And there's something keeping you from getting involved with me that you haven't explained, even to your best friends."

She was about to correct that last impression, but he touched a finger to her lips.

"I know what you've said, but it's not the fact that I told you I'd leave here eventually," he said. "It goes deeper than that."

She sat back in her chair, shaken by his insight.

"How'd I do?" he asked.

"Pretty good," she admitted. "Especially for someone who hardly knows me."

"That's what I find intriguing," he said. "Even people who are close to you, who've known you far longer than I have, don't know any more than what you've allowed them to see. There's a part of your past you're hiding and it's something that's obviously significant. It's shaped who you are."

She wasn't sure how she felt about his ability to read her

so well. "Not the way you mean," she argued. "There are just some things I don't like to talk about, things I don't like remembering."

"If they're too difficult to talk about, too disturbing to remember, then they're important," he said. "I'm not sure it's healthy to keep such things bottled up inside. Burdens are eased when they're shared with friends, and you have some good friends."

"Where's your couch, Dr. McDonald?" she inquired testily. "I had no idea I was going to be psychoanalyzed tonight."

To her relief, he instantly backed down, his lips curving into a smile.

"No couch," he said with exaggerated sorrow. "And no house to put it in, anyway."

Grateful for the change of topic and for the arrival of the waitress with their food, she took advantage of the moment to gather her thoughts before asking, "Where are you living? Are you still at the Serenity Inn?"

He nodded.

"Those rooms are tiny. I stayed there when I first moved here, but I couldn't wait to find someplace bigger." She put a slice of the steaming pizza on her plate, drew in a deep, appreciative breath, then blew on it to cool it down.

Tom's gaze seemed to be fixed on her mouth. The intensity of his fascination was disconcerting.

"Tom," she said quietly, then more emphatically, "Tom!"

"Hmm?" He shook his head. "Sorry. I got distracted."

"I noticed," she said with amusement.

"What were we talking about?"

"You said you were living at the inn and I said that I'd lived there when I first got to town," she reminded him. "Do you plan on staying there? After all, you've made it clear you don't plan to stick around Serenity that long, so why bother with a home?"

He frowned. "Actually, I've been looking for a house."

"I'm sure Mary Vaughn would be delighted to help with that," she said.

"She's offered," he said in a tone that suggested he didn't like what else she was offering. "I think I can handle the house hunting on my own." He paused, then added, "Unless you'd like to help."

To her surprise, she found herself saying, "I could spare a couple of hours late tomorrow afternoon if you really want another opinion."

He seemed as startled by the offer as she had been. "You're sure?"

"Yes. Why not?" she said breezily. What was a couple of hours? They'd be driving around Serenity, not parking someplace for a long, intimate chat. And she'd been considering moving out of her own rental apartment and buying a house. This would be the perfect opportunity to see what was available.

"Should I pick you up at the spa?" he asked.

"Yes. It'll save time if I don't have to go home after work."

"When should I be there?"

"My last client will be finished at quarter to four. I can be ready by four. That won't give us a lot of time, but we should be able to check out a couple of the open houses anyway."

"I'll get the paper and map out the ones that seem most interesting," he said. "That'll save time."

"Great idea."

"Okay, then, it's a date," he said.

She had a hunch he'd chosen the word deliberately, but she let it pass.

"Since we're discussing living arrangements," he continued, "I realized earlier tonight that I have no idea where you live or how to get in touch with you except at the spa. When I couldn't find a number in the phone book, I took a chance you'd be at the football game."

She ignored the unspoken request for her address and phone number. "You were actually there looking for me? I thought maybe Cal had invited you because Maddie made him. She's sneaky that way."

"So I've gathered, but no. It was just a spur-of-the-moment decision after I struck out on my attempt to reach you at work." He studied her. "You going to give me a home number or a cell-phone number, or do you intend to do everything possible to keep the mystery alive?"

She weighed his question, then grinned. "Actually, the mystery thing seems to be working well for me, if it has you chasing around town trying to find me," she said.

"A phone call would be quicker and more rewarding," he suggested.

"Maybe for you, but I kind of like knowing you'll have to try harder."

"That perverse streak of yours is a challenge," he said.

"You'd be bored in no time without a few challenges in your life," she guessed. "I suspect most women fall for you the second you meet. You're handsome, funny, rich. That makes you quite a catch."

"But you're not interested?" he concluded, his eyes sparkling with mischief.

"Interested, yes," she conceded. "Hooked? Nope. You'll have to work harder to reel me in."

"Careful, Jeanette," he warned. "I've already warned

you that I get a little crazy when it comes to challenges and dares. You sure you're ready for that?"

There was something in his tone, something in the electricity sizzling all around them that made her reckless. She lifted her gaze to his. "Bring it on."

As soon as the words were out of her mouth, as soon as she saw the dangerous sparks in his eyes, she knew she'd crossed a line from living safely within her comfort zone to a situation filled with risks. Somehow, though, she couldn't dredge up any regret.

She'd missed this giddy sensation in her head, this off-kilter sensation in the pit of her stomach. She wanted it to last a little longer. Dana Sue was right. Caution might keep her safe, but it wasn't really living. It had been far too long since she'd felt this way, far too long since a man had looked at her the way Tom was looking at her now. So what if it didn't last forever? She'd survived a broken heart more times than she could count. She knew she could do it.

As Tom reached for her hand, lifted it to his lips and kissed her knuckles in a gesture straight out of the old black-and-white movies she loved, she sighed and let herself fall just a little bit in love. She ignored all the warning signs of disaster ahead—including the troubling image of his harridan of a mother—and uttered a silent prayer that this time things would work out and her heart would remain intact.

CHAPTER ELEVEN

———◆———

The very last thing Mary Vaughn wanted to do was ask her ex-husband for anything, but Sonny was necessary if she was to make this traditional-Christmas thing work for Rory Sue. Her daughter was still grumbling about not being allowed to go to Aspen for Christmas, so Mary Vaughn knew she had to make good on her promise that the holiday would be magical, the way it had been when Rory Sue was a child. She also needed to make it very clear to Sonny that Rory Sue could not be allowed to play them off against each other, that they had to work as a team. Howard had promised to leave it to her to work this out with Sonny, but if she put this conversation off for too long, he was bound to stick his nose in it. Her former father-in-law was incapable of butting out.

She might as well make the call while she was sitting around waiting for prospective buyers to check out the open house she was holding today. Even talking to Sonny was preferable to sitting around here being bored to tears. Only a half-dozen people had wandered through all day and not one of them had expressed much interest. She'd shown the house to a young couple the night before, but they hadn't come back as they'd said they would.

She dialed Sonny's direct line. To her surprise the sound of his voice gave her a little jolt. Puzzling. She and Sonny hadn't had that much chemistry when they were married. It was unlikely that had changed at this late date.

Like his daddy, Sonny was basically a jovial guy. The divorce had been amicable, even if she made it her business not to set eyes on him any more than necessary. She was still humiliated by the fact that Sonny was the one who'd cut her loose and not the other way around.

"What's up, darlin'?" he asked now. "That little girl of ours having problems?"

"Rory Sue is fine," she assured him. "But I am calling because of her."

"Oh? Why's that?" Sonny asked, then murmured something to someone else. "Sorry, darlin'. Just give me a minute, okay?"

Mary Vaughn tapped her foot as she waited for his undivided attention. He'd once been very good at giving her that. It was why she'd turned to him way back in high school when Ronnie Sullivan had rejected her. Sonny had been there and waiting, like an eager puppy. It was a shock to realize that was no longer the case. Even though they'd been divorced for nine years now, she'd always believed she could get him back with the snap of her fingers. Now, it seemed, she couldn't even keep his attention for the length of a phone call. The discovery made her even edgier.

"Sorry," he said again when he finally came back on the line. "It's been crazy around here today. Everybody and their brother has decided they need a new pickup and they all need it right this second. I swear I haven't had this much business since I opened the dealership twenty-five years ago. So, tell me quick, what's going on?"

"We need to talk," she said.

"We are talking."

"In person," she said, growing exasperated.

"Is this about that ski-trip business? I told Rory Sue it was up to you."

"And I'd already told her she couldn't go. Thanks for backing me up," she said sarcastically.

"Hey, darlin', don't bite my head off," he replied testily. "Rory Sue never mentioned that she'd already discussed it with you."

"Well, of course she didn't," Mary Vaughn said. "Sonny Lewis, aren't you onto her by now? From the time she was a baby, she's always come to you after I've told her no. The other day she even tried going to your daddy, but I put a stop to that. For once, Howard is actually on my side. Christmas without Rory Sue here is just not acceptable. I'm surprised you would even consider such a thing."

"To tell you the truth, she caught me at a bad time and I was only half listening to her," he admitted. "Once I'd said okay, I could hardly change my mind just because I'd had time for regrets."

It was just as Mary Vaughn had thought, though for once it gave her little satisfaction. "I'll just bet she deliberately called in the middle of your weekly sales meeting, am I right? It would be just like her."

"As a matter of fact, that's exactly when it was," he said. "That girl is a whole lot sneakier than I thought. I'll have to watch that from here on out."

"In the meantime, can you meet me at Sullivan's for dinner Tuesday night so we can figure out what we're going to do over the holidays? My treat, of course." It was a point of pride to her that she was every bit as successful as he was, that she hadn't taken one dime of alimony from him, only support for Rory Sue and half of her college tuition.

"You want to have dinner with me?" he said.

She found his shocked tone annoying. "I'm not going to jump your bones, for goodness' sake."

He laughed. "Never thought you were. Okay, I can have dinner on Tuesday if you want. Name the time and I'll be there."

"Seven okay? I have to show a client a house at six."

"Which means it'll be seven-thirty," he responded dryly. "But I'll be there at seven on the dot, just the same."

"If it won't put you out too much," she snapped, losing patience.

What ever made her think that she and Sonny could cooperate long enough to have dinner, much less an entire holiday season of peace and good will for the sake of their daughter?

As exasperated as she was with Sonny, it was nothing compared to the way she felt when she happened to glance out the window and spotted Tom and Jeanette coming up the walk toward the house she was showing.

She hadn't believed it even after three different people had told her that they'd seen the two of them in a lip-lock at last night's football game. Now here they were, Saturday afternoon, looking at houses together. No wonder Jeanette had been so quiet when Mary Vaughn had suggested Tom might be gay. She knew otherwise. She'd apparently been seeing him on the sly, which just proved that even a woman as savvy as *she* was couldn't always predict who might turn out to be a backstabbing little witch.

* * *

Jeanette recognized Mary Vaughn's car outside the little bungalow that was on Tom's list of available properties. The front door was ajar and there were colorful balloons tied to the Open House sign in the front yard. Every attempt had been made to give the house curb appeal. Fall flowers in yellow and gold bloomed in pots beside the steps, the grass was thick and green and the shutters had been recently painted a glossy white that contrasted nicely with the gray vinyl siding.

As attractive as the house was, though, it didn't stop her from feeling a knot of dread form in her stomach.

"This is Mary Vaughn's listing," she told Tom. "She's inside."

"Is that a problem?"

"Not for me, but you and I both know she has a thing for you. She may not handle it well seeing the two of us together." Especially if she'd heard about their kiss at last night's game.

He grinned. "You worried, sugar?"

"No, but you probably should be. She doesn't take rejection well."

As if to prove her wrong, Mary Vaughn appeared just then, a smile plastered on her face. "Well, look who's here!" she chirped. "I certainly wasn't expecting to see the two of you together, especially at one of my open houses."

"Spur of the moment," Tom said, which wasn't exactly true. "Jeanette agreed to come along with me while I looked at a few properties."

Right in front of their eyes, Mary Vaughn transformed herself into full real-estate-agent mode, whipping out a spec sheet on the house and handing it to Tom. "I think you're going to love this house. It's perfect for a single man," she said briskly, then added with a pointed look at Jeanette, "or for a young couple anticipating starting a family. The rooms are cozy and inviting."

Her spiel remained bright and cheery as she took them through the downstairs rooms—two bedrooms, a bath and a large kitchen, plus a living room that had been crammed with too much furniture. It was currently decorated with enough chintz to make Tom cringe, but Jeanette saw something else—the potential for something every bit as cozy and warm as Mary Vaughn had suggested.

"There's another bedroom and bath upstairs. Right now it's not much, but with a little work it could become a lovely master suite," she said, leading the way up a narrow staircase.

Jeanette trailed along behind. Clearly, she thought, Mary Vaughn had concluded that if she couldn't have Tom, then at least she might come away from the awkward encounter with a sale.

"It's not bad," Tom said, after giving the upstairs bedroom suite little more than a cursory glance around. "The price seems a little steep to me. Is it negotiable?"

Mary Vaughn gave him a conspiratorial look. "You know I work for the seller, Tom, but just between you and me, this house is a steal at that price."

"Maybe so," Jeanette said. "But I know Nancy Yates and she's anxious to sell and make a permanent move to Florida to be near her kids. I'll bet she'd accept a reasonable offer."

Mary Vaughn shot an annoyed look at her.

Jeanette shrugged. "Sorry. I just happen to know that."

Mary Vaughn rallied quickly. "Well, of course Tom wants to get the best possible deal, but I need to look out for Nancy, too."

After they'd seen the bedroom upstairs, she led them

downstairs and into a backyard that was filled with flowers and even had a small waterfall in one corner. That was when Jeanette fell in love with the house. The peace and serenity of that garden called to her in a way that she'd never dreamed possible. If Tom wanted this house, he was going to have to fight her for it.

"Nancy was into gardening," Mary Vaughn explained. "She spent a lot of her time out here after she retired. You won't find a lovelier space anywhere in Serenity." She beamed at Tom. "I'll bet you're a barbecue man, though, aren't you?"

"On occasion," he said. "But I like the atmosphere out here. It's really peaceful." He glanced at Jeanette. "What do you think?"

She hesitated. The last thing she wanted to do was say something that would sell him on having this particular house. Still, she couldn't lie. "I love it. It reminds me of the patio area at the spa."

"I'm not sure I have enough of a green thumb to keep it up," Tom said.

"That's why people hire gardeners," Mary Vaughn told him. "I have several I can recommend. You won't have to lift a finger. You can just come out here in the evening and relax with a drink."

Tom turned to Jeanette. "And a friend," he suggested.

Jeanette saw Mary Vaughn's eyes narrow at the innuendo. She might be handling the situation with aplomb, but she wasn't overjoyed about it.

Though Mary Vaughn looked as if she desperately wanted to make some comment, she was prevented from it by the arrival of another couple. "Ah, you've come back," she called to them, her expression filled with delight.

Though she looked eager to escape, she turned to Tom. "You'll be okay on your own for a bit?"

"We'll be fine," Tom assured her.

After she'd walked away to greet the young couple, Tom turned to Jeanette. "Okay, tell me the truth. What do you really think?"

"I think it's cozy, just the way she said," she admitted cautiously.

"What aren't you saying?" he asked. "Did you spot mold somewhere? Stains on the ceiling that suggest the roof leaks?"

She shook her head. "It's perfect."

"Then why don't you sound more enthusiastic? What's the problem?"

She lifted her gaze to his and opted for honesty. "I want this house. I fell in love with it the second we walked into the garden. The house is just the right size for me, too. I'd turn one of the downstairs bedrooms into a study, then use the other one temporarily while I had the upstairs made into a master suite, just the way Mary Vaughn suggested. There's room for a huge tub, a walk-in shower. I'd put in a skylight, too." She let her imagination run wild. "And a king-size bed with mounds of pillows, a sofa I could curl up on to read." She sighed. "It would be amazing."

When she risked a look at Tom, he was studying her intently. "Any room in there for me? Especially in that king-size bed?"

She swallowed hard. "Are we talking hypothetically?"

His lips curved slightly. "If we must."

"Then hypothetically there might be room in there for you."

"Why didn't you mention you were looking for a house for yourself?"

"I didn't really intend to do that today. It's just been in the back of my mind for a while now that I'd like something permanent. I thought I might get a few ideas while we were looking around, but I didn't expect to find the ideal place. Then I walked out here and knew this was the house I wanted." She regarded him with regret. "Sorry."

"Don't be sorry," he said, touching her cheek. "I can see how much it means to you. And to be honest, I can see you out here." He grinned. "Of course, I can also see me with you."

"What do we do now? Are we going to have a bidding war?"

He laughed. "I'm sure that would make Mary Vaughn extremely happy, but no. Since you think the owner might negotiate on the asking price, do you have a number in mind? Are you ready to make an offer?"

Her palms turned damp at the thought of actually committing to a mortgage for the next thirty years, but then she envisioned sitting outside with the Sweet Magnolias and a pitcher of margaritas and she was instantly calmer.

"Are you sure?" she asked. "You're the one who needs a place sooner rather than later. You can't stay at the inn forever."

"If you're really all that worried about my well-being, you could agree to share this house with me."

She laughed. "Do you always have an angle? You are such a guy."

"I'm not joking," he assured her. "At least not entirely. I could help out with the renovations, and that room you're intending to use as a study could be mine for the short term. I'll pay rent, which will help with your mortgage. Seems like a win-win to me."

She wasn't sure if he was serious or merely testing the waters, but she shook her head. "I don't think so."

"Don't be so quick to turn me down. I'm very good with a hammer."

"Do you know the kind of talk that would stir up? Your job would be on the line within a month."

"Just because you and I have a legitimate landlord-tenant business arrangement?"

She rolled her eyes. "How long do you honestly think it would stay that way?"

He shrugged, his expression all innocence. "Up to you."

"If I thought you could really live by that, I might consider the idea, but we both know otherwise. You'd spend every spare second trying to seduce me."

He didn't even try to deny it, just grinned and said, "But you're not easy to seduce, are you?"

"Not usually," she said. "But I don't trust myself around you. You have an unpredictable effect on me. I think you can persuade me to do all sorts of things I don't plan on doing."

He tried and failed to hide a self-satisfied smile. "That's the most encouraging thing I've heard in a while. Go make an offer on the house. We'll deal with the details of our arrangement later."

"We don't have an arrangement," she insisted.

"Later," he said, waving her off. "Go, before that other couple puts in a bid and all of this becomes moot."

Jeanette hesitated. Could she really do this? Could she impulsively make an offer on a house she'd seen for the very first time just minutes ago? She'd been frugal with her money. The down payment was tucked away in her savings account. She wasn't a hundred percent certain what the mortgage and taxes would be, but she knew she could swing it. She was making good money at the spa and she spent very little beyond groceries and rent.

"Do you want me to run numbers for you?" Tom asked, evidently guessing the source of her hesitation. "I have a calculator with me."

"No. I'm just nervous. This would be a huge commitment."

"Okay, let's break it down. You planning on leaving your job and moving somewhere else anytime soon?"

She shook her head. "No. I love it here."

"You have enough for a down payment so that the mortgage won't strap you?"

"Yes."

"Then this makes financial sense and, if that gleam in your eye is anything to judge by, it makes emotional sense, too."

A smile began to tug at her lips, then spread. "It does, doesn't it?"

"From every angle I can think of."

Impulsively, she reached out and gave his hand a squeeze. "Thanks." She slid open the sliding door to the kitchen and stepped inside. "Mary Vaughn!"

"In the living room," she called.

Jeanette walked in and found her sitting across the table from the couple who'd arrived just moments before. There were papers spread out on the table that suggested they were about to enter their own offer.

"Mary Vaughn, could I speak to you for a moment?" Jeanette said. "Alone." She smiled at the couple. "I'm sorry for the interruption."

Apparently sensing that she might have a bidding war on her hands, Mary Vaughn excused herself and followed Jeanette into the kitchen. "What's up? Did Tom decide he wants to make an offer? Because that young couple is about to do the same."

Jeanette took a piece of paper from her purse and scribbled a number. "That's my offer. If you need me to fill out a formal bid, I can do that."

Mary Vaughn stared at her without even glancing at the paper. "This is *your* offer?"

"Mine," Jeanette confirmed.

"And Tom?"

"We've worked this out. He'll keep looking." Or he'd keep pestering her about moving in here, but she didn't think she should share that with Mary Vaughn, not if she was to have a chance at getting this house. Mary Vaughn might be forced to go with the high bidder for the sake of the seller, but she might not be above seeing to it that the other bid was little more than pennies higher just to keep Jeanette and Tom from moving in here together.

Now Mary Vaughn glanced at the bid Jeanette had written down, then shrugged. "I'll get you the paperwork to make the offer formal."

"Is it high enough to beat what they're going to offer?" Jeanette asked.

"I'll take your offer and theirs to Nancy," Mary Vaughn said evasively. "She'll make the decision."

"Are we in the same ballpark?" Jeanette persisted. "I want this house, Mary Vaughn."

She knew it was a mistake the second the words were out of her mouth. Mary Vaughn now knew Jeanette would up her offer, if need be.

"I'll call Nancy as soon as I have your paperwork and theirs."

She went inside, returned with several forms and waited while Jeanette filled them out.

"I'm going to try to reach Nancy now," Mary Vaughn told her. "She told me she'd stick close to home today during the hours of the open house, just in case someone made an offer. If you want to wait, you can, though she may need time to think this over."

Jeanette nodded. "I'll wait. I'll be in the garden with Tom."

She found him sitting on the steps that led from the French doors in the dining room to the patio. He stood as she approached. "Well?"

"I gave her an offer. So did that couple who just arrived. Apparently this is their second visit."

"Mary Vaughn's taking both offers to the seller?"

She nodded, her expression glum. "If there's any way to justify it, I think she'll see to it that Nancy takes *their* bid."

"Why?"

"Because she's ticked off about me being here with you."

"Oh, come on, she's a professional. She won't let her personal feelings interfere with doing the best job she can for her client."

"You're not really that naive, are you? Or is it just that you don't know Mary Vaughn that well?"

"Okay, it's true I don't know her well at all, but come on, she wouldn't be as successful as I'm told she is without being thoroughly ethical and above reproach."

Jeanette thought of the way the woman had gone after Ronnie, but that wasn't business. It was personal. "I suppose she has standards about this kind of thing," she conceded.

"Not exactly a ringing endorsement," Tom noted. "Do the two of you have a history?"

"Not us. The history's between her and Dana Sue. When Ronnie first got back to town, Mary Vaughn was all over him, despite the fact that he was trying to work things out with Dana Sue. She made no bones about wanting him. It got a little sticky. There's no love lost between her and Dana Sue."

"And by extension, you?" he asked.

"Oddly enough, no. We've always gotten along okay. She's a client and she encouraged me to join the Christmas festival committee, but that was before she set eyes on you. Something tells me she now considers me a rival."

He gazed into her eyes and smiled as he touched her cheek. "There can't be a rivalry when there's no contest. You're the one I want, Jeanette. The only one."

She shivered at the intensity in his voice, then forced her gaze away. "Stop saying things like that."

"Even if it's true?"

"It can't be true. You've only gotten this crazy idea because I'm unattainable. Some men are like that. They only want what they can't have."

"But I can have you," he said with so much confidence she was tempted to smack him.

"I don't think so," she insisted, backing out of reach. There were a dozen different ways he could prove her wrong just by a touch and they both knew it. She just didn't intend to admit it.

The kitchen door slid open a few feet away and Mary Vaughn stepped out. "Jeanette, could you come inside?"

Nervously, Jeanette went into the kitchen. She glanced around and saw that the other couple was gone. Did that mean what she hoped it did? Or was Mary Vaughn about to tell her that her bid had been rejected?

Mary Vaughn gave her a halfhearted smile and held out the portable phone. "I have Nancy here and she'd like to speak to you."

With her pulse scrambling, Jeanette accepted the phone. "Hi, Nancy, how are you?" she said. "How's Florida?"

"Just wonderful," Nancy said, sounding happier than she had in months. "I love being so close to the beach and the kids."

"I'm glad," Jeanette said sincerely. "I know it was lonely for you here after Garrett died."

"It was, but until a few minutes ago, I wasn't sure how I'd feel about letting go of that house and all my memories, so *I* could stay down here. Then Mary Vaughn called with two offers. She mentioned one of them was yours. That was all I needed to hear to be content with my decision." She laughed. "Thank goodness, yours was the highest bid and more than I'd hoped to get, as well. My kids would never have let me hear the end of it if I'd let sentiment overrule common sense."

"I fell in love with the house the second I walked into the garden," Jeanette said honestly, barely able to contain her excitement.

"You and I talked a few times about gardening when we had a chance to visit on the patio at the spa," Nancy recalled. "That's how I know you'll take good care of it. As far as I'm concerned we have a deal, Jeanette. You, Mary Vaughn and the bank can take care of the details, and assuming everything goes smoothly, the house is yours. I want you to make me a promise, though."

"Anything," Jeanette said at once.

"Will you let me stop by for a visit if I get back up that way?"

"You'd be welcome anytime," Jeanette told her, trying to contain her urge to give a shout that would shatter Nancy's eardrums. "Thank you so much. I can't tell you what this means to me. I'm so excited, I'm shaking."

"I just hope you'll be as happy there as I've been."

"I'm sure I will be. Goodbye, Nancy, and thank you again."

As she disconnected the call, she turned to see Tom regarding her with a grin.

"It's yours?"

"It's mine, or it will be once the bank approves my loan and we can close on it," she said as he scooped her up and whirled her around. When he set her back on her feet, she caught a quick glimpse of—what? sadness?—in Mary Vaughn's eyes. But then she forced her trademark smile.

"Congratulations," Mary Vaughn told her. "How would you two like to go out for dinner and some champagne to celebrate? I'll take you to Sullivan's."

Tom gave Jeanette a questioning look. "What do you think? Are you free?"

Jeanette thought Mary Vaughn was being extremely gracious under the circumstances. Maybe she was also just a little anxious to show the world that she wasn't the sore loser she'd been when Dana Sue won Ronnie for a second time. After considering the invitation for a moment, she nodded. Why not let the other woman have a chance to save face.

"We'd love to, Mary Vaughn," she said. "And thank you for whatever you said to Nancy to persuade her to take my offer."

"Oh, sweetie, there was no persuasion involved. It was all about dollars and cents—that and the fact that you took the time to be nice to her when she was hurting after Garrett died. That's just more proof that what goes around comes around." She sighed audibly, then murmured half to herself, "Probably a lesson I need to learn."

Jeanette caught her words. "Mary Vaughn, are you okay?"

That fake smile she'd perfected was back in place so fast, Jeanette almost thought she'd imagined the weary resignation she'd heard in her voice. "I'm just peachy, sugar, but I sure could use a glass of champagne. Why don't I meet you at Sullivan's in fifteen minutes. I'll close up here and put a Sale Pending sign out front."

"Okay, we'll see you there," Jeanette said.

She had the distinct impression that Mary Vaughn needed that time to compose herself for the performance she was about to give to the whole town, the one to prove she was still on top and unfazed by whatever was going on between Jeanette and Tom. Jeanette couldn't help admiring her. If they'd switched places, she'd be heading home to comfort herself with a half gallon of strawberry-cheesecake ice cream.

CHAPTER TWELVE

Tom couldn't think of a single time in his life when an evening promised to be more awkward. He had a hunch that all eyes were going to be on the three of them when they walked into Sullivan's, as the locals tried to figure out when the hair-pulling was likely to start between Mary Vaughn and Jeanette.

After all, Mary Vaughn had hardly made a secret of her interest in him. And Jeanette had publicly claimed him in the stands at last night's football game, even though she said she didn't really want him, at least not the way he wanted her. He thought she might be a trifle delusional about her own feelings, but he couldn't prove it. Not yet, anyway.

Of course, he could always hope that people in Serenity kept their noses out of everyone else's business, but from what he'd observed that was most definitely not the case. He had only to look at the Sweet Magnolias, their husbands and his own secretary for proof of that.

"You don't seem to be looking forward to this dinner," Jeanette commented as they drove to Sullivan's.

"What was your first clue?" he asked.

"The fact that you haven't said two words since we left Mary Vaughn."

"Don't you think this is going to be incredibly weird?"

"Yes," she said without hesitation. "But we owe it to her."

He stared at her in confusion. The workings of this woman's mind were a mystery to him. "Why is that?"

"She's trying to save face, prove it doesn't matter that you rejected her and chose me. Not that you have, of course."

"I have," he said flatly so there could be no mistake about it. "And whatever your intentions last night, that kiss you laid on me at the stadium told the world that you chose me back."

She flushed slightly. "I had my reasons for that kiss. Don't make too much of it."

He glanced at her with undisguised skepticism, then focused on the road again. "Want to explain that?"

"Not really."

"In that case, I prefer to think that you were staking your own claim."

"Yes, that would suit your ego, I'm sure."

"Without evidence to the contrary, why shouldn't I come to that conclusion?"

"Because I've told you otherwise."

"Words," he said, his tone dismissive. "Nothing but words."

She frowned at him. "You don't have to have dinner with us, you know. You can drop me off. Mary Vaughn and I can celebrate without you."

"But that would hardly prove whatever cockamamie thing she's trying to prove, would it?"

"Not as effectively, no. Seeing all three of us together will show Serenity that there are no hard feelings."

"Then it's my duty to play this out," he said solemnly. "Never let it be said that my mother didn't raise me to be a true Southern gentleman. I'm willing to do whatever it takes to protect a woman's honor."

"You don't have to get carried away," Jeanette said.

"Apparently I do." And something told him, he was going to regret it.

Inside Sullivan's, Jeanette abandoned him the second they'd been shown to a table. He stared after her in bemusement as she headed directly for the kitchen. Maybe she was going to share the news that she'd contracted to buy a house, but he suspected she had a few other tidbits she wanted to share with her friends, as well.

Something told him he could spend the next fifty years with her and never entirely understand her. Of course, unraveling her secrets would definitely give him something to look forward to. And his anticipation of that prospect was something refreshingly new to him. Never before had he found a woman so intriguing that he could envision growing old with her.

Mary Vaughn sat in her car in the parking lot at Sullivan's retouching her already flawless makeup and trying to work up the courage to go inside. The instant she'd uttered the invitation to Jeanette and Tom, she'd regretted it. She had considerable experience pretending all was right with her world when it was crumbling around her, but she wasn't sure she was capable of putting on such a display tonight. This latest setback was still a little too fresh.

"Nothing for it," she muttered, and exited the car. She would not let one single soul in Serenity know how she felt about having yet another man stolen right out from under her. Not that Tom had ever been hers, but she'd wanted him. The whole darn town probably knew that, just the way they'd always known what was going on with her folks and had never said a single word, much less stepped in to protect her or her mother.

As an only child, Mary Vaughn had learned to keep silent about her problems from a master. Her mother had endured years of abuse—verbal and physical—from her alcoholic husband without asking for help. When Mary Vaughn had been old enough to ask her about it, she'd denied that there was a problem. She had bruises because she was clumsy. The raised voices were nothing more than "discussions." Because her mother had refused to acknowledge what was happening, Mary Vaughn had been forced into silence, as well.

She'd always told herself that things would be different if her father had ever attacked her, that her mother would leap to her defense and take them away from the whole awful situation, but she'd harbored her doubts about that. Thankfully her theory had never been tested. Her father had been content to take out his anger on her mother.

She'd gone to school with her chin up and ignored the whispers from neighborhood kids who'd seen her father weaving his way home from Serenity's most notorious bar, who'd heard the inevitable shouting that followed his arrival. She'd denied the abuse when compassionate, concerned counselors had sought to help. She'd become as masterful as her mother at living a lie.

She'd fallen for Ronnie Sullivan in part because he'd been new in town and hadn't looked at her with pity the way others at school did. She'd married Sonny because he'd loved her in spite of her troubled background. He'd even claimed to admire her for rising above the situation and striving to make her own way in the world.

By then her father and mother were both dead, her father from complications from cirrhosis of the liver, her mother from a heart attack. Mary Vaughn hadn't truly mourned either one of them. What she'd mourned was the family she'd never had.

Sonny—son of the town's most respected citizen—had become her whole family, and then Rory Sue. She'd known from the beginning that whatever her marriage to Sonny might lack in passion, she would always be safe and she would always have his respect. And because of his family, she'd have the *town's* respect, as well, though she'd worked darn hard to earn that for herself. She'd told herself that safety and mutual respect were more than enough, and they had been for her. It was Sonny who'd eventually wanted more.

When he'd left her, she'd been forced once again to keep her chin up and ignore the whispers. She drew on that experience now to walk into Sullivan's without letting anyone see how her heart was aching. She was here to celebrate the sale of a property and, by gosh, no one was going to think otherwise.

There wasn't a false note in her voice or a wavering of her smile to suggest that she was anything other than thrilled for Jeanette for getting the house of her dreams… and maybe the man that Mary Vaughn had wanted, as well.

When the champagne came, she lifted her glass. "To a wonderful future in your new home," she said, then clinked glasses with Jeanette and with Tom. "I hope you'll be happy there."

"You do know this is my house, right?" Jeanette said wryly. "Tom is still looking. Maybe you can think of something he would like."

"Well, of course I can," Mary Vaughn said, cheered

to know that whatever was heating up between these two hadn't reached a stage where they'd be moving in together. She beamed at Tom. "Did you like the style of the house you saw today, or would you like something newer and a little more modern? Maybe something more impressive that befits your stature as town manager and as a McDonald? I'm sure you're used to a large house."

"Actually, what I'm used to is something not much bigger than my room at the Serenity Inn," Tom said. "I spend so much time on the job that all I need at home is one room where I can relax, a refrigerator to hold a few necessities and a bedroom."

"I think we can do better than that," she said. "You know, I didn't want to mention this earlier, but I had a call from your mother the other day."

Tom's expression turned dark. "Oh?" he said, his voice like ice.

"She'd apparently picked up one of my brochures on her last visit and saw a few houses she thought might be appropriate for you. She said she'd call next week and schedule an appointment to look at them."

"I don't think so," Tom said. "If she calls back, tell her that you're working for me, not her."

Mary Vaughn winced. She'd already gathered that Clarisse McDonald had a mind of her own and would not take kindly to being dismissed. "I think she's just trying to take some of the burden off your shoulders," she said, hoping to pacify him. "After all, you're incredibly busy getting settled into your new job, plus the Christmas festival takes a lot of your time."

He leaned forward. "Mary Vaughn, I would greatly appreciate it if you did not show my mother any houses in Serenity, unless she's planning to live in one of them herself.

I'll make my own choice when the time comes. If that's a problem for you, then I'll work with another agent and you and my mother can look to your heart's content."

Obviously she'd stepped into the middle of some family dynamic she didn't understand. "Of course it's not a problem, Tom," she said, backing down at once. It would have been a coup to have someone of Clarisse McDonald's stature as a client, but a good relationship with Tom was more important. "Don't worry. If she calls again, I'll make some excuse to put her off."

"Thanks."

Mary Vaughn turned to Jeanette. "Do you have a contractor in mind for any renovations once the house is officially yours?"

Jeanette shrugged. "I'm still a little dazed that I actually signed a deal to buy a house today. I suppose I'll talk to Ronnie. He knows most of the contractors in town."

"And, of course, she has my promise to help," Tom added, giving Jeanette a meaningful look.

"I thought I'd declined your offer," she said, regarding him with amusement. "It came with too many strings."

"We can always negotiate," Tom said. "That could be fun."

Mary Vaughn sat back, barely containing a sigh. Okay, they might not be moving in together, but there was definitely something there. She was practically being singed by the sizzle in the air.

What was wrong with her? She was much more suited to a man like Tom McDonald than Jeanette was. She understood style. She had money and social graces. She'd worked hard to create a polished, well-educated, successful life so she would never be trapped in a lousy marriage as her mother had been. She'd been determined to have options.

Sonny might not have been her first choice, but he'd been a decent guy from a good family. He'd adored her, and yet he'd left her. In some ways, that had been harder to take than losing Ronnie Sullivan the first time.

Obviously she had some kind of fatal flaw when it came to men, but for the life of her she couldn't figure out what it was. Was she too aggressive, too self-confident, too independent? Or was it the exact opposite? Was she too needy?

Ironically she'd always been so focused on her relationships with men that she'd done little to cultivate friendships with women, so there was no one she could ask where she was going wrong. Up until today, she would have considered asking Jeanette, but that was out of the question now. It would be too humiliating to ask the woman Tom was clearly infatuated with.

One of these days, though, she needed to figure it out, because she was tired of going home alone at the end of the day. All the money and success in the world couldn't compensate for having no one special in her life beyond a daughter who was mad at her half the time.

She took one more sip of champagne, then cut herself off. The last thing she needed was alcohol to deepen the funk she was already in. The only thing less attractive than a sore loser was one who was throwing herself a pity party. Mary Vaughn was not going to be that woman. She was a survivor, dammit! No matter what else happened, she wouldn't ever let herself forget that.

Jeanette, Tom and Mary Vaughn were just finishing up a shared slice of chocolate-decadence cake, when Helen and Maddie arrived, along with their husbands and kids. At the same time, Dana Sue emerged from the kitchen with another bottle of champagne, a bottle of sparkling cider for the kids and glasses for everyone. Erik and Karen were on her heels. Elliot arrived just minutes later with Karen's kids.

"What's going on?" Jeanette asked, staring at them in amazement. "What are you doing here?"

"You bought a house!" Maddie exclaimed. "That deserves a celebration. Not just for you, but for us. It means you won't be leaving us."

"How did you know about the house?" Jeanette asked.

"Did you really think Dana Sue wouldn't call us the second you told her about making an offer that Nancy Yates accepted?" Helen scoffed. "She, Maddie and I have been terrified you'd pack it in one of these days and leave Serenity. After all, you've lived in Charleston and even Paris. We figured Serenity couldn't keep you forever."

"Still, it's not as if anything's final," Jeanette protested. "I haven't even applied for the loan yet. I can't do that until Monday."

"Oh, please, you'll get the loan," Helen said. "Just use all of us as references. I'm telling you, it's a done deal."

"So, this definitely qualifies as big news," Dana Sue said in her own defense. "It's something you share with friends." The last was said with a look at Mary Vaughn that came very close to suggesting she was an unwelcome interloper.

Jeanette saw the quick flash of hurt in Mary Vaughn's eyes, but doubted anyone else did—she'd covered it too quickly. In an instant, the Realtor was on her feet, a smile firmly in place.

"I'll leave you to your celebration," Mary Vaughn said, reaching for her purse.

"No," Jeanette said, sending a warning look toward Dana Sue. "You have to stay. At least for one glass of champagne."

"I don't know," Mary Vaughn said, glancing warily at Dana Sue.

"Stay," Dana Sue said, clearly taking her cue from Jeanette. The single word might not have been uttered with much warmth or graciousness, but it was enough to have Mary Vaughn sitting down again, albeit on the edge of her chair, clearly prepared to flee.

Most of the other diners had left, so Ronnie helped Dana Sue pull some tables together. Maddie's Kyle and Katie were instructed to keep Jessica Lynn and Karen's son and daughter from destroying the place, while the babies slept quietly in their carriers.

"Okay, tell us how this happened," Maddie instructed Jeanette. "I had no idea you were even looking at houses."

"I wasn't," Jeanette admitted. "Tom was. I went along with him after work today. I stole this one right out from under his nose."

"Broke my heart, too," he claimed with a heavy sigh. "I loved this house."

Jeanette frowned at him. "Oh, you did not. I saw the expression on your face when you saw all that chintz in the living room."

He grinned. "Well, all those flowers were a little overwhelming, but the furniture's going." He turned to Mary Vaughn. "It *is* going, isn't it?"

"What difference does it make to you?" Jeanette inquired. "You're not the one who has to live with it."

"Hey," he protested. "I thought we had a deal."

Helen regarded him with a withering look. "What deal?" She turned to Jeanette. "Tell me you did not make some kind of deal with him without letting me look over the paperwork. I'm still a little miffed that you didn't discuss the contract for the house with me before you signed it."

"I had to act quickly to get the house," Jeanette told her. "There was another bidder. You can handle the closing for me, I promise. In fact, you can handle every detail from now on. I'm clueless about this kind of thing."

"But what about this deal Tom mentioned?" Helen persisted. "What's that about?"

Jeanette scowled at him. "He thinks he's being amusing. He got some crazy idea about renting a room from me in exchange for his help with some of the renovations."

"It's a good deal," Tom insisted.

Ronnie regarded him with amusement and maybe just a hint of admiration for his ingenuity. "Nice plan, but I have to ask. Do you know one end of a hammer from another?"

"I have plenty of skills that are useful around the house," Tom said.

"But do any of them have anything to do with renovations?" Cal asked, then got a sharp nudge in the ribs from Maddie. He frowned at her. "Hey, what did I do?"

"You're embarrassing Tom and Jeanette," Maddie told him.

"It was a fair question," he protested, looking to Ronnie, Elliot and Erik for support. "Wasn't it fair?"

"Definitely fair," Ronnie agreed. "Just not smart."

Tom turned to Ronnie. "You can check me out yourself. Turn me loose with a few tools."

Jeanette rolled her eyes. "I don't care if you receive a stamp of approval from these guys and show me a diploma from trade school, you are not moving in with me. I intend to hire a qualified contractor. Ronnie, can you recommend someone?"

"You name the time and I'll look over what you need done and help you find the right guy," Ronnie told her.

"Traitor," Tom murmured.

Ronnie grinned. "I go home with one of these women. When push comes to shove, I take my cues from them."

"Whatever happened to men sticking together?" Tom lamented.

"Obviously those men are not married to Sweet Magnolias," Cal said, still rubbing his side where Maddie had poked him.

Jeanette glanced at Mary Vaughn during this exchange and saw the wistful look in her eyes. For once it didn't seem to be directed toward Ronnie in particular, but rather the whole group. She was glad she'd included her. This wasn't the first time she'd sensed that despite her success, Mary Vaughn was lonely. Jeanette had a feeling she wanted desperately to be included, but didn't know how, especially with her history with Dana Sue and Ronnie.

Jeanette looked around at those gathered. "This is so nice of you guys. I think one of the things I like most about living in Serenity is that I found such good friends here. It's like being surrounded by family."

"Family isn't always all it's cracked up to be," Mary Vaughn said bitterly, then looked surprised and embarrassed at having spoken.

"Amen to that," Tom said, giving her a commiserating look. "What is it they say? You get to choose your friends, not your family."

"Which is exactly why I count myself lucky to have found all of you," Jeanette said. "I think we should have another toast, this time to friendship."

"I can certainly drink to that," Maddie said.

"Absolutely," Helen chimed in, as did Dana Sue, Karen and even the men.

Karen's eyes were misty. "I can testify to how important

all of you are in my life. You turned it around." Her gaze held Elliot's. "You and Elliot, of course."

"Of course," Maddie said dryly. "Have you two set a wedding date yet?"

"I'm pushing for an elopement," Elliot said. "But Karen and my family seem to have their hearts set on a huge church ceremony. For that we have to wait until Karen's annulment comes through. The priest says that could take a few more months. I'm trying to be patient."

"Which is not his strength," Karen said, linking her fingers through his. "But I want to do everything right this time. It's going to last forever."

Jeanette barely contained a sigh. Watching the romance blossom between those two had been amazing. Elliot had been fully committed practically from their first meeting, but Karen's past with a man who'd abandoned her and their children, along with Elliot's family's disapproval of him marrying a divorced woman had complicated the situation. But he'd remained steadfast despite the obstacles. They were finally finding the happiness they both deserved.

As if he sensed Jeanette's envy, Tom reached for her hand beneath the table and gave it a squeeze. She looked into his eyes and saw a depth of understanding there that sent another jolt of electricity through her. She jerked away in dismay. It was the second time he'd made her feel this way, all warm and fuzzy inside. Attraction was one thing, but she could not be falling for him, not even a little bit. She wouldn't allow it. Despite his flirting, despite the undeniable sizzle between them—or maybe *because* of them— she couldn't trust him or herself.

It didn't matter how well he fit in with her friends. It didn't matter that he was sensitive and kind. All that mattered was that eventually he would choose his career over her and leave. He'd said so himself.

As if he sensed that her withdrawal ran deeper than removing her hand from his, he met her gaze. "Everything okay?"

Jeanette forced a smile. "Just a close call," she said. "But I'm fine now."

"Am I supposed to know what that means?"

She shook her head, then got to her feet. "Thank you all so much for coming here tonight," she said, deliberately avoiding Tom's gaze. "I think I've hit a wall. I'm exhausted. Mary Vaughn, how about it? Can you give me a lift home?"

Tom frowned. "I can drive you."

To Jeanette's relief Mary Vaughn was immediately on her feet. "I'll do it. We can go over a few things on the way, okay, Jeanette?"

"Sure. Good night, everyone."

She all but raced out of Sullivan's and beat Mary Vaughn to her car by a full minute.

"Want to tell me what that was about?" Mary Vaughn asked as she unlocked the car.

Jeanette shook her head.

"There are a whole bunch of people in there who would have been happy to drive you home. Why me?"

"Because I thought you might be the only one who wouldn't have a million questions," Jeanette said ruefully. "Was I wrong?"

Mary Vaughn chuckled. "Oh, I have questions," she said. "But I can keep them to myself."

"I'd appreciate that," Jeanette said, leaning back against the seat with a sigh. "By the way, how are you doing? That wasn't too uncomfortable for you, was it? Not just dinner, but the whole evening?"

"Actually it wasn't half as awful as I was anticipating," Mary Vaughn said. "Do you know how lucky you are to have friends like that?"

Jeanette nodded. "I do. I thank God for them every single day."

As they pulled up in front of her small apartment complex, which Mary Vaughn had visited once before to pick up an order of skin cream after spa hours, she turned to face Jeanette. "Do you think...could we maybe grab lunch sometime? Or go to a movie? I know it probably seems weird since you know I was interested in Tom, but that ship has clearly sailed. I just want you to know there are no hard feelings. I'd like us to be friends, at least if it won't put you in an awkward position with Dana Sue and the others."

Jeanette remembered the wistful expression in Mary Vaughn's eyes earlier. She understood loneliness all too well. "I can't imagine they'd object to us having lunch sometime. I don't have my schedule in my purse. Why don't we set it up next time you come into the spa."

"That would be great," Mary Vaughn said. "Thanks for the sale today. If you have any questions when you go to the bank for the loan, let me know. Otherwise, I'll see you at the spa later in the week. And I'll do everything I can to push this paperwork through so you can close on the house as soon as possible."

Impulsively, Jeanette leaned across and gave her a quick hug. "Good night. See you soon."

The faint sheen of tears she spotted in Mary Vaughn's eyes caught her off guard. It told her she'd done exactly the right thing by including her tonight. Underneath all her polish, beneath her aggressive attempts to go after whatever she wanted with single-minded determination, Jeanette sensed that Mary Vaughn had as many insecurities as the rest of them. It was something she never would have guessed before tonight.

CHAPTER THIRTEEN

Jeanette's phone rang off and on all day Sunday, but she did her best to ignore it. Eventually she went for a long walk just to escape the temptation to pick it up. She knew from caller ID that most of the calls were from Tom, but a few had been from Maddie, Helen and Dana Sue, all of whom were no doubt increasingly frustrated at not being able to figure out why she'd walked out on Tom the night before.

It wasn't until late Sunday night, when the calls finally ended, that she realized she'd only postponed the inevitable. She had to face Tom first thing in the morning at the Christmas festival meeting. She couldn't skip it again. It would show a level of cowardice that even she found unacceptable.

Before she went to bed, she laid out one of her favorite outfits as a confidence booster. She told herself the bright red sweater seemed appropriate, but the truth was, she'd chosen it because it flattered her coloring. She teamed it with gray slacks and a pair of red shoes that Helen had talked her into buying. While these weren't the outrageously expensive high heels Helen preferred, they had cost more than Jeanette usually spent on an entire outfit. Buying the matching purse had given her heartburn.

When she walked into the meeting room at Town Hall, she felt confident and sexy. As soon as she saw the appreciative gleam in Tom's eyes, she realized she probably should have opted for dowdy. This selection was clearly giving him ideas. She swallowed hard, forced a smile for Tom, then chose a seat on the other side of Ronnie.

"You can't hide from him forever, sugar," Ronnie whispered in her ear. "The man has it bad."

"No, he doesn't," she insisted. "I'm a challenge, nothing more."

Ronnie chuckled. "Wishful thinking. You got something against handsome and rich?"

"Nothing at all," she assured him.

"Then why are you avoiding him?" he asked, still in an undertone.

"I'm not," she said.

"That's not what his half-dozen, increasingly worried calls to my house yesterday suggested."

"He called there?" she said, dismayed. "I'm so sorry."

"He was freaking out because he couldn't reach you. It didn't help that Dana Sue hadn't been able to reach you, either. It took some serious persuasion on my part to keep the two of them from racing over to check on you. I swear, if you hadn't walked in here just now, there'd be a posse out looking for you before lunchtime."

"I'm sorry," she said again. "I never meant to involve everyone else in my drama." Not that there was much drama involved. In fact, she was trying very hard to *prevent* drama.

"Nothing to be sorry about," Ronnie assured her. "I told 'em you probably needed a little space to absorb the fact that you'd taken such a big step. Buying your first house is scary business. It is your first, isn't it?"

Jeanette nodded. "And it all happened so fast that I'm absolutely terrified I might have made a mistake. I called the bank this morning to make an appointment to apply for the loan and hung up before anyone said hello."

"Buyer's remorse, cold feet, whatever you want to call it, is perfectly normal," Ronnie assured her. "You'll get over it. And you need anything, you have all of us as backup."

"Thanks."

He studied her closely. "Other than being scared silly over committing to apply for a thirty-year mortgage, everything else is okay?"

She gave him her brightest smile. "I'm fine."

"Okay, then, that's good enough for me." He grinned. "Word of warning, though. Just your assurance about that might not be enough to satisfy Tom or my wife."

She glanced at Tom, who was watching her exchange with Ronnie intently. "Yeah, I get that."

A moment later Tom called the meeting to order and then ran through the agenda in record time. It was obvious he wanted this meeting over with, much to Howard's annoyance.

"Where's the fire, son?" Howard demanded when Tom cut his report short and called for adjournment. "I thought we could discuss where we're going to get the town Christmas tree this year."

Tom barely contained a sigh. "Where do you usually get it?"

"We've found most of 'em on the outskirts of town," Howard said. "Up until recently there was a lot of heavily wooded property nearby, but development's had an impact on that." He cast a hard look at Ronnie as if the construction boom was all his fault. "I think we're going to have to go a different direction this year. There's a farm that raises Christmas trees just outside of Columbia. I think we should go up there and take a look around. It'll probably cost us a little more, but I think we'll find a better selection."

"Okay, I designate you to go," Tom said. He was about to gavel the meeting to a close, when Howard spoke again.

"This is a committee decision," Howard protested, then added with enthusiasm, "I say we all go next weekend. There may not be a chill in the air yet, but we'll play some Christmas music in the car, take along some hot chocolate, really get into the spirit of things." He beamed at them. "We can make a day of it."

Jeanette and Tom groaned almost simultaneously.

"I can't go on Saturday," she said. "It's one of my busiest days at the spa."

"Saturday's no good for me, either," Mary Vaughn said. "I usually have an open house going that day or, if I don't, I'm out showing properties. Same with Sunday."

Howard frowned at Ronnie. "I suppose you're going to tell me that the hardware store does too much business on Saturday for you to get away, too."

Ronnie shrugged. "As a matter of fact, yes."

Howard shook his head. "Okay, then, we'll make it a weekday. Tuesday suit everyone? That's a week from tomorrow, so you have plenty of advance notice. Jeanette, can you make that work?"

Knowing that one day was no better than another for doing something she absolutely did not want to do, she nodded. "I'll reschedule my appointments. Tuesdays are usually pretty light."

"Good," Howard said approvingly. He turned to Tom.

"And nothing much happens on a Tuesday around here, am I right? No big meetings."

"None," Tom conceded with obvious reluctance.

"Tuesday, it is, then," Howard said with satisfaction. "We'll leave from here at 7:00 a.m. We can even skip our regular Monday meeting. That ought to make everyone happy." He turned to Tom. "Now you can end the meeting if you want to."

"Thank you," Tom said. "Meeting adjourned. Jeanette, could you stay for a few minutes so we can discuss the vendor situation?"

"I need to get to the spa," she said, not anxious to be alone with him.

"Ten minutes," he said.

"Okay," she agreed reluctantly and followed him into his office.

Tom closed the door behind them and clicked the lock. He gestured toward a chair, but Jeanette remained standing. He shrugged.

"Everything okay with you?" he inquired mildly.

"Fine."

"You're not mad at me for some reason?"

"Not at all."

He regarded her with bewilderment. "Then could you explain what happened Saturday night and why you wouldn't answer any of my calls yesterday?"

Jeanette immediately went on the defensive. "I left Saturday night because I was tired. I didn't answer the phone yesterday because I didn't want to talk to anyone. I had a lot on my mind."

"Was this about buying the house?"

"Mostly."

"And the rest? Did that have anything to do with me?"

"Why do you automatically assume that I think about you at all?"

He lifted a brow.

"Okay, yes," she conceded grudgingly. "You were part of it." She met his gaze. "Tom, you seem to want a whole lot more than I have to give. We hardly know each other and you want to share a house with me. Maybe you're just joking—"

"I'm not," he said evenly.

She shuddered. When he said stuff like that, she almost lost what little resolve she still had to keep her distance from him. She held up a hand as if to hold him back. "That's what I mean. It's too much, too soon."

He frowned at that. "Will you sit down so we can actually have a conversation? I feel as if you already have one foot out the door."

"I told you I need to get to work."

He sighed with frustration. "Have lunch with me, then. Let's talk this through. I don't want to make you uncomfortable. It's just that I'm a decisive man. I don't see the point in wasting time when I know what I want."

"And what you want is me?" she asked incredulously. "Come on. That's crazy."

He nodded. "I'm a little thrown by it myself."

"Yet that hasn't slowed you down."

He shrugged. "I don't see any reason to slow down. I've always set goals for myself, then gone about achieving them. I don't let obstacles stand in my way."

"Are my feelings just one more obstacle for you to overcome?"

He winced. "In a way."

"Well, let me know when you recognize that my feelings might have validity, that when I tell you I need time, you get that I mean it. Maybe then we'll have something to talk about."

She went to the unlocked door between his office and Teresa's and yanked it open. She'd almost made it to the outer office, when Tom whirled her around and kissed her, a sizzling, lengthy kiss designed to leave her weak-kneed and breathless. Which it did.

"I'll pick you up at the spa at noon," he said quietly, ignoring Teresa's openmouthed stare. "We'll talk more over lunch."

Jeanette regarded him with exasperation. "Did you not hear one word I just said?"

"Every one," he assured her. "And that kiss just contradicted most of them. We'll discuss the rest when I see you later. And don't even think about standing me up, because I will find you and we will have this conversation."

Before Jeanette could gather her wits, he walked back into his office and closed the door.

"Whew!" Teresa murmured, fanning herself with the minutes of the last council meeting. "I'd heard all about the fireworks between you two at the game Friday night— that was all over town by Saturday morning—but I had no idea..." She shook her head.

"Teresa, I'm begging you, please do not tell Grace Wharton about this," Jeanette said, knowing that was exactly where Teresa would be headed in a couple of hours, sooner if she took a coffee break. "It will just add fuel to the fire. I know I started it by kissing him at the game Friday night, but that, well, it was impulsive. I don't usually do things like that."

"Honey, nobody's holding it against you," Teresa soothed.

Jeanette scowled. "That's not what I meant. I had my

reasons for that kiss, but it was a mistake. A *huge* mistake! I realize now that I don't want to be the subject of town gossip, and even though he doesn't seem to give two hoots about it, it won't be good for Tom, either."

Teresa regarded her with disappointment. "You want me to keep the kiss I saw just now to myself?"

Jeanette nodded. "Please. I'll give you a free facial," she said.

"You must want my silence a whole lot," Teresa said with increasing amusement.

"I'll throw in a massage, too," Jeanette added, unable to keep a hint of desperation out of her voice.

Teresa couldn't seem to stop grinning, which suggested Jeanette was compounding her mistake by making such a big deal of this latest kiss.

"To tell you the truth, Tom would have my hide if I accepted what amounts to a very generous bribe from you, so I'll decline the facial and the massage, but the fact that you offered…" Her grin spread. "What that proves is that this relationship the two of you have is getting downright interesting. I'll keep what I saw just now to myself, but something tells me it won't take long before the whole town knows your business, anyway. It's impossible to hide that kind of heat."

That was exactly what Jeanette was afraid of. It was getting more and more difficult to keep denying it to herself, as well.

Tom was feeling rather pleased with himself when there was a tap on the door to the conference room. He opened it to find Ronnie on the other side.

"You and Jeanette finish your conversation?" Ronnie asked.

Tom nodded.

"Then maybe you have time to listen to a piece of advice from a man's who made more than his share of mistakes when it comes to women."

Since his current plan seemed to be having less success than he'd anticipated, Tom waved Ronnie to a chair. "I'd welcome another viewpoint."

"Back off," Ronnie said succinctly. "I talked to Jeanette before the meeting. She didn't say much about what was going on with the two of you, but I picked up on one thing."

"Oh?"

"She's scared to death of what she's feeling for you."

"If I give her space, she'll just think it to death," Tom argued.

"If you don't, you'll lose her," Ronnie said. "She's feeling pressured. When I wanted Dana Sue back, I was in her face a lot. All that accomplished was to solidify her defenses. Once I got busy with opening my business, she had time to start missing me. She got her feet back under her, felt in control again. Some women, they need to feel like they're in charge. It terrifies them when they think they're not, especially if they've been hurt in the past."

Tom could see the wisdom in that. Of course, backing off meant losing time, when he only had a finite amount of time to convince Jeanette that they had something special. A part of him didn't want to waste a minute of that.

"How long?" he asked Ronnie.

Ron chuckled at his obvious impatience. "As long as it takes."

"Does it have to start right this second? I'm supposed to pick her up for lunch in a couple of hours."

"Up to you," Ronnie told him. "But canceling could be a good thing."

Tom shook his head. "And you had to work this hard to get Dana Sue?"

"Harder," Ronnie said. "I had a whole lot to make up for and, believe me, she didn't make it easy. I assure you that I have some firsthand experience with the value of patience and persistence."

"Patience and persistence?" Tom echoed thoughtfully. Persistence he could handle. Patience? Not his strong suit. "I'll give it some thought."

"Hope you don't mind me interfering," Ronnie said. "And if the situation starts getting to you, you can always call me or Cal and schedule a football game to work off some frustration. Nothing like a little sweat and a few beers to take the edge off."

"Yeah, nothing like it," Tom agreed. Unless it was some energetic sex with the woman who'd gotten under his skin.

Mary Vaughn was surprisingly nervous about her upcoming dinner with Sonny. A lot was riding on how this evening went. If they couldn't come up with a really good plan, it was going to be hard for her to keep saying no to Rory Sue's pleas to go to Aspen for the holidays. The only thing worse than having her daughter gone would be having her underfoot and moping around the house as if her life was ruined and it was all her mother's fault.

She'd taken to heart Sonny's comment about her penchant for getting caught up with business and showing up late. Determined to prove she could be on time, she'd canceled her appointment and was waiting at Sullivan's fifteen minutes early. It gave her a great deal of satisfaction to see the shock on his face when he walked in and saw she was already seated.

He leaned down and dropped a casual peck on her cheek.

"Well, this is a pleasant surprise," he said. "Did your appointment cancel?"

She bristled at the suggestion that she wouldn't have been on time otherwise, then shrugged ruefully. "I canceled it myself. I wanted to prove something to you."

"Darlin', there's nothing you need to prove to me. You are who you are. I accepted that a long time ago."

She listened closely for any undercurrent of nastiness in his tone, but he sounded more amused or resigned than anything.

"Well, I'm turning over a new leaf," she swore to him. "I'm going to be more considerate of other people's time."

Sonny didn't look entirely convinced. Instead, he glanced around in search of the waitress. "You want a drink, Mary Vaughn? Maybe some wine?"

"Just a glass," she said. "They have a nice red zinfandel."

When the waitress arrived, he ordered that, then a beer for himself. Mary Vaughn shook her head. No matter how hard she'd tried to cultivate his taste for wine, Sonny had always preferred beer. In a way it was admirable that he stuck to what he liked, rather than setting out to impress people by buying fancy wines the way she did. Though she'd tried her share of beer way back, just like all the other kids, she'd cut herself off years ago. Her aversion to it had come from having a father who indulged in way too much of it.

She studied Sonny closely as he chatted with the waitress, the daughter of one of his salesmen. He was tanned, fine lines fanned out from the corners of his dark blue eyes, and his light brown hair had more threads of silver in it than the last time she'd seen him. He was wearing navy blue slacks, a pale blue silk-blend shirt with the sleeves rolled up and a designer tie that had been loosened. She recognized the tie because she'd helped Rory Sue pick it out last Christmas. She wondered if he'd chosen it deliberately because of that, or if he even remembered where it came from. Either way, he looked good. Better than he had during the last year of their marriage when the tension had left him looking harried and unhappy most of the time. She'd recognized his unhappiness way too late.

"Give us a few minutes," he told the waitress. "We haven't even looked at the menu yet." He turned to Mary Vaughn. "Or are you in a hurry?"

"I'm in no rush," she said, finally letting herself relax. She'd been half-afraid that he was going to insist that she get to the point so he could bolt back to the dealership. She smiled at him. "You look good, Sonny. Rested. Are you playing a lot of golf?"

"A couple of times a week," he said. He looked her over. "How about you? Still working too hard?"

"Most of the time, especially with Rory Sue gone."

"New man in your life?" he asked.

She shook her head.

"I thought there might be something brewing with you and the new town manager," he said. "At least that was the hot rumor at Wharton's a couple of weeks back."

"Bad information," she said succinctly. "What about you? Have you been dating?"

He chuckled. "Aren't we a pair? Asking all these civilized questions about each other's love life. Who would have thought we'd ever get to that point?"

She met his gaze. "We were friends before we were anything else," she reminded him, then added wistfully, "Sometimes I miss that more than anything, the way we used to talk for hours about everything going on in our lives."

He regarded her with surprise. "You do?"

She nodded. "Weird, isn't it?"

He covered her hand with his. "Not so weird. I miss that, too, Mary Vaughn. Only trouble is, there's a whole lot of baggage that goes along with that. Most of the time it's hard to see past the way things ended."

"I know," she admitted. Because there was nothing to be gained by looking back, she said, "What are we going to do about Christmas?"

"Celebrate it?" he asked, looking bewildered.

She shook her head, exasperated. "Why did I think you'd be any help with this?"

"Come on, Mary Vaughn. I'm no good at planning this kind of thing. You were always in charge of the holidays. I just went along for the ride. What do you think it's going to take to make Rory Sue happy? I could finally give her that new convertible she's been wanting."

"Absolutely not," Mary Vaughn said at once. "This isn't about buying her off. We'd agreed that you'd give her the convertible when she graduates from college. The car she has will do just fine until then."

He shrugged, but didn't argue. "Then I'm at a loss."

"I know what she wants more than anything," Mary Vaughn ventured at last. "She wants us to be together the way we used to be."

Sonny frowned. "What the devil are you suggesting, Mary Vaughn? That we get married again just to make our daughter happy even if it makes us miserable?"

She flushed at his immediate and insulting reaction. "No, of course not," she said defensively. "I'm just saying that maybe we could all put aside our differences and do things together for the holidays."

His expression relaxed. "What kind of things?"

She thought of the committee's plan to go hunting for

the town tree. "We could go out and chop down a Christmas tree together," she suggested. "Remember how much Rory Sue always loved that? She said it was the best part of Christmas."

"I suppose," he said doubtfully. "You think that'll do it?"

"No, of course not," she said impatiently. "But it's a start. Maybe we can go to Charleston shopping one day. The stores will be all decorated and festive."

"And crowded," Sonny predicted direly.

"Oh, stop being such a grouch. That's part of the fun. We can stop at Lydia's Bakery on the way home and have hot chocolate and sugar cookies the way we used to when Rory Sue was little." She gave him a wistful look. "Don't you wish she was still young enough to want to see Santa? Sometimes I take out all those pictures we have of her back then. She was the prettiest little girl in the whole wide world, wasn't she?"

"She was," Sonny agreed. "Still is, for that matter."

Since he was starting to sound more nostalgic and agreeable, she smiled at him. "If you'll go along with the shopping trip, you can carry all the packages and I'll pay for them. How's that for fair?"

He shook his head. "You have a strange notion about what's fair, you know that, don't you?" he said, but there was a hint of tolerant amusement in his eyes. "Any other big ideas?"

She thought back to the holiday celebrations in the past and what had made them special. "We should go to church together on Christmas Eve, have a big Christmas dinner at my place, then go caroling over at the nursing home the way we used to. Would that interfere with anything you have planned?"

"No," he admitted, though he didn't seem all that enthralled by the plan. "You including my dad in this?"

"Of course. Rory Sue would expect him to be with us. With your mom gone and your brothers scattered across the country, it'll be good for him to have a real family Christmas again, too. Don't you think so?"

"I suppose," Sonny said. He gave her a skeptical look. "And you honestly think that a few days of faking it will make Rory Sue happy?"

"We don't have to fake it," she said. "We used to have fun together, Sonny. I can remember when we laughed all the time. Surely we can make an effort to get along for a few days."

"I don't know, Mary Vaughn," he said, looking worried. "What if it gives Rory Sue the wrong idea? You know how she is. Every time I see her she asks me when I'm going to give you another chance. What if she thinks I'm doing that and gets her hopes up?"

"I'll make sure she knows this is something we're doing to make sure she has a good Christmas," Mary Vaughn promised. "Maybe we should plan an open house, too. That was one of our traditions." Suddenly she was filled with nostalgia. "I loved those, the house smelling like pine and cookies, lights glittering inside and out, and everyone we knew stopping by. I miss that."

He regarded her with surprise. "Why'd you stop doing it?"

"It wouldn't have been the same without you there," she admitted. Moreover, she'd been scared to death that no one would come, that most of the people who'd chosen sides after the divorce had taken Sonny's. A lot of people had thought that she was the one who'd ended their marriage and Sonny had let them believe that. She supposed it had been his gallant way of letting her save face. Ironically, though, it had turned a lot of people who adored Sonny against her. She wondered if it would have been any different if they'd known the truth—that he was the one who'd walked out.

She looked up to see Sonny studying her with a frown.

"Mary Vaughn, you're happy, aren't you?"

"Well, of course I am," she lied. Because she didn't want to dwell on the depressingly lonely state of her life, she beamed at him. "I am starved, though. Let's order. I'm thinking about the pork chops. What about you?"

"Pork chops sound good," he said, though he sounded oddly distracted. "I'll get Becky back over here." He waved to their waitress, then placed the order. "I'll have another beer, too." He glanced at Mary Vaughn's half-full glass of wine. "You want another one?"

She shook her head and decided to skip all pretenses for once. "Actually, you can bring me a beer, too."

Sonny stared at her when Becky moved off. "You want a beer?"

She nodded, then leaned forward. "Can I tell you a secret?"

"Sure," he said, looking intrigued.

"I never have liked wine."

He regarded her with astonishment. "Then why on earth have you always made such a production about drinking it?"

She shrugged. "Because I thought I should," she admitted. "I thought it made me seem more sophisticated and worldly."

Sonny shook his head. "Sugar, you've always been the most sophisticated woman I know. It didn't take wine to make you seem that way." His expression turned thoughtful. "It was because of your daddy, wasn't it? He drank beer, and you never wanted to do anything to make anyone think the two of you were alike."

Her eyes misted over at his insight. "Damn you, Sonny Lewis," she whispered in a choked voice. "You always did know me better than anyone."

She stood up and hurried toward the ladies' room before anyone could catch her bawling her eyes out.

She spent ten minutes composing herself and repairing the damage from her tears. When she walked out of the restroom, Sonny was standing right there waiting for her.

"Another minute and I was coming in after you," he said. "You okay? I didn't mean to upset you."

"What upset me wasn't what you said," she told him candidly. "It was you knowing what goes on inside me." She met his gaze. "I miss that, Sonny. I honest to God do."

For an instant, he seemed to go perfectly still. Then he warned, "You shouldn't say things like that, sugar. You'll turn my head."

"Would that be so awful?" she asked before she could stop herself.

He took her hand in his and gave it a squeeze. "You know the answer to that," he chided lightly, but when she looked into his eyes, what she saw was regret.

Seeing that filled her with sorrow that she'd once been so careless with this man's heart. It also made her resolve to do everything in her power to make amends. It might be too late for their marriage, but maybe they could somehow salvage the friendship that they'd shared.

CHAPTER FOURTEEN

Jeanette had been just going through the motions at the spa for nearly a week. She'd been irritable for days, snapping at her friends and barely civil with her clients. The worst part of her uncharacteristic mood was that she had no idea what had started it. She was usually the most even-tempered person she knew.

She was on the patio at the spa, wrapped in a sweater to ward off the chill in the air, staring morosely into a glass of tea she didn't really want, when Maddie, Helen and Dana Sue descended on her.

"Uh-oh," she murmured, regarding the threesome worriedly. "Am I in trouble?"

"You tell us," Maddie said. "You haven't been yourself all week. Today you insulted Emily Blanton."

Jeanette stared at Maddie in horror. "No, I didn't." She tried to remember the conversation she'd had with Emily. Nothing even remotely insulting stuck out. "Honestly, Maddie, I'm sure I didn't."

"You told her it didn't make a bit of difference which product she bought," Maddie said, her lips twitching with amusement.

"That's not an insult," Jeanette said, looking to the others for support. "Is it?"

Dana Sue giggled. "It is when the implication is that absolutely nothing could help her."

"And naturally that is exactly the way she took it," Maddie said, breaking into a full-fledged grin.

Helen regarded Jeanette with sympathy. "Of course, the truth is probably your best defense. *Nothing* is going to help that woman's skin. She spent the last fifty years baking herself in the sun and now she's hoping some cream will enact a miracle."

"But Emily is a sweetheart," Jeanette said. "I would never intentionally hurt her feelings." She buried her face in her hands. "I don't know what's happening to me. I really don't."

"When was the last time you saw Tom?" Dana Sue inquired, her expression innocent.

"A week ago today," Jeanette said, not sure what her friend was driving at. "At the Christmas festival committee meeting. We were supposed to have lunch, but Teresa called and canceled."

"And you haven't seen him or spoken to him since then?" Dana Sue persisted.

Jeanette shook her head.

"Well, there you go," Maddie said. "Tom's got you all confused and twisted up inside."

"I am not twisted up inside about Tom McDonald," Jeanette protested, annoyed by the suggestion that any man, especially Tom, could affect her mood. "I can't be."

Helen regarded her with a mystified look. "Why can't you be?"

"I just can't be, that's all," she said stubbornly.

"We've all been there," Helen said. "Even me. It's nothing to be embarrassed about."

"I'm not embarrassed and I am not twisted into knots just because some man hasn't called me," Jeanette retorted.

"Okay, let's back up," Maddie suggested. "Why would it be such a big deal if Tom is getting to you? From what we've seen, he's a great guy." She turned to the others. "Right?"

"Absolutely," Dana Sue said. "Ronnie likes him, too. Thinks he's a stand-up guy."

"So does Cal," Maddie added.

"Well, there you go," Helen said. "A Sweet Magnolias' and friends' stamp of approval!"

"Isn't my opinion the one that counts?" Jeanette inquired testily.

"Well, of course," Maddie said. "But you need to explain what the problem is so we'll understand. You know we'll provide backup."

Jeanette really didn't think she had any obligation to explain herself, but because these were her friends, she tried. "In a nutshell, it's because I'll wind up taking a backseat to his career. The second he gets a chance at a better job in a bigger city, he'll be gone. Obviously he's finally seen the light and agrees with me that it's pointless to start something with absolutely no future." She frowned, then added, "Then, of course, there's the little fact that his mother hates my guts."

Maddie chuckled. "Tom doesn't strike me as the kind of man who let's his mama decide whom he can and can't date."

"Yeah, that's what I thought," Jeanette said grimly. "Until he canceled a lunch he'd practically begged me to agree to."

"Call him," Helen advised. "Ask him out."

"Absolutely not," Jeanette said. "It's for the best."

"Then tell us why you're so miserable," Dana Sue said.

Jeanette hesitated, then said, "It's the new house. The paperwork for the loan is overwhelming. I feel as if I'm locking myself into something without having any idea if it's going to work out."

"Sort of like marriage," Maddie commented. "Life doesn't come with guarantees, sweetie, not when it comes to relationships or houses. All you can do is make an informed decision."

Jeanette leaned forward, facing them intently. "Don't you see? That's just it. I didn't make an informed decision. I walked into that garden and decided I had to have it. The house itself was almost secondary. Putting in that offer was pure impulse. I *never* do anything on impulse."

"Then you're way past due to cut loose," Maddie told her. "Look, we all know the house. We were in and out of it as kids. Not one of us thinks you made a mistake. If you can't trust your own instincts, then trust ours. That house is perfect for you."

"You just want a sign that I'm not going to bail on the spa," Jeanette countered. "You may not be entirely trustworthy when it comes to this."

"Hey," Helen said, clearly offended. "When have we ever not been straight with you, even when it wasn't in our own best interests?"

Jeanette winced. "Sorry. There I go again. I just blurt out whatever comes to mind these days. You guys are wonderful, the best friends I could possibly hope for. Really."

"Okay, then," Helen said. "Let's cut to the chase. My recommendation is that you call Tom and see him as soon as possible. Have sex. It will improve your mood, to say nothing of giving you this amazing glow."

Jeanette chuckled despite her sour mood. "Sex as therapy? You spread that around, it will cut into business here. Right now, women rely on us to provide their skin with a youthful, dewy glow. If they find out they can achieve the same effect with sex, who knows when they'll come back again."

Helen laughed. "Okay, then, we keep that just among us. My recommendation to you stands. And now I have to go home to my husband. All this talk about sex has given me ideas."

"Me, too," Dana Sue said, standing up. "Maybe I'll try to catch Ronnie in the supply room at the store. Leaving the door unlocked adds an element of risk that's a real turn-on."

Maddie sighed. "Cal and I have to make an appointment to have sex these days. There are way too many kids underfoot." She blushed. "We've been sneaking off to the Serenity Inn in the afternoon."

Helen, Dana Sue and Jeanette stared at her, then Helen's expression turned thoughtful.

"I wonder how Erik could feel about that," she said. She glanced at Dana Sue. "He has, what, maybe an hour between the end of the lunch rush and the start of dinner prep at the restaurant?"

Dana Sue nodded, clearly amused.

"Okay, then," she said. "That ought to liven up tomorrow afternoon."

Maddie winced. "We'll have to work out a schedule. Cal will freak if we start running into everyone we know in the parking lot at the inn!"

"Just so you don't run into Tom and start giving him ideas," Jeanette said. "He already has plenty of ideas of his own. Or he did."

"Call him," Helen repeated.

"Before tomorrow," Maddie added. "And apologize to Emily Blanton."

Jeanette nodded without speaking. It was probably best if the rest of them didn't know exactly what she was agreeing to do. Talking to Emily Blanton she could handle. Talking to Tom was out of the question. Besides, she'd see him first thing in the morning for the outing to pick out the town Christmas tree. Then maybe she could figure out what was going on with him without putting her heart on the line.

Tom was going just a little bit crazy wondering whether Jeanette had even noticed his absence. He'd decided to give Ronnie's advice a try for one week. That week was up yesterday.

Now he was pacing in the parking lot outside of Town Hall waiting for the arrival of the rest of the committee members. Howard had shown up a few minutes earlier with a brand-new minivan with dealer tags still on it for the trip to the tree farm. He'd had the windows rolled down and a Christmas CD blasting away. Tom had shuddered at the thought of being cooped up with all that holiday cheer for several hours.

"Climb on in," Howard said jovially. "You can ride up front with me. Make sure the CD player has music going. I brought along a dozen Christmas discs. Those should hold us. And there are a couple of Thermoses of hot chocolate and some cups. Help yourself."

Tom held up the cup of coffee he'd gotten earlier at Wharton's. "I'm not much for hot chocolate. I have coffee."

Howard looked disappointed, but he didn't push. When he spotted Mary Vaughn turning into the parking lot, he beamed. "One more accounted for. Hopefully Ronnie and

Jeanette will be here soon and we can get on the road. I'm really looking forward to this."

Tom spotted Jeanette strolling in their direction, her feet dragging. She clearly wasn't looking forward to the outing any more than he was. Ronnie caught up with her and said something that made her laugh. Jealousy shot through Tom with a force that stunned him. For the space of one tiny second, he wondered if Ronnie had had an ulterior motive for warning him off, then dismissed the idea as insane. Ronnie was madly in love with his wife. It was plain to anyone who saw them together.

"Mary Vaughn, why don't you sit up front with Howard," Tom suggested, even as he turned to assist Jeanette into the back. He gestured for Ronnie to get into the far backseat, then climbed in to sit beside Jeanette, who was regarding him warily.

He waited until they were under way and the Christmas music was blasting again before turning to her. "How've you been?"

"Okay. You?"

"Good. It's been a crazy week."

"Yes, for me, too."

Tom barely contained a sigh. This wasn't going well. She didn't show the slightest sign of having missed him. If anything, she was more distant than ever. He decided then and there to scrap Ronnie's advice.

He leaned over. "I missed you," he said in a low voice.

Color bloomed in her cheeks, but she continued to stare straight ahead.

"Did you miss me?" he asked.

That drew a glance. "Not especially," she said, but the increasing stain on her cheeks suggested otherwise.

Behind him, he heard a barely contained chuckle. He turned and glowered at Ronnie. "You said something?"

"Not a word," Ronnie claimed, his expression innocent. "But I was thinking the time might go faster if we sang a few carols."

Jeanette twisted around awkwardly, constrained by her seat belt. "Are you crazy?" she demanded in an undertone.

"Great idea!" Howard said. "That's just what we need to get in the mood. Mary Vaughn, darlin', check out the cover of that CD and tell us which song is coming up next so we can be ready."

Tom groaned.

"It's 'White Christmas,'" Mary Vaughn announced in an upbeat tone.

"Now, we all know the words to that, I'm sure," Howard said. When the song started, he chimed in. After a pause Mary Vaughn joined him, as did Ronnie.

Tom and Jeanette exchanged a commiserating look.

"Come on, you two," Howard said, glancing at them in the rearview mirror. "Let's hear it. I think we've got the makings of a nice little choir right here in this car. Mary Vaughn tells me we're going to revive our family tradition of going to a nursing home to sing on Christmas Day. Maybe you all would like to join us."

"Not if hell froze over," Tom muttered.

"And Serenity, too," Jeanette added with such feeling that he laughed out loud.

"Great idea, Howard," Ronnie said with enthusiasm, just to spite the two of them. "And don't forget we're expecting all of you at Sullivan's for Christmas dinner. Howard, are you up for playing Santa again this year?"

"You bet," he said. "It's at the top of my list for the holidays, right after being Santa on the opening night of the festival."

Jeanette slid down in her seat. Tom reached for her hand, partly because he just plain needed to touch her and that was the only appropriate gesture and partly to show solidarity. To his relief, she didn't pull away. Instead, she released a barely audible sigh and met his gaze. He felt his heart drop at the longing he read in her eyes.

Maybe Ronnie's stupid scheme had worked, after all, he decided. If it had made Jeanette miss him, even for a minute, made her question, even once, if he'd lost interest, then the solid week of torture had been worth it.

The Christmas-tree farm should have been Jeanette's worst nightmare, but after the first few minutes, she drew in a deep breath of pine-scented air and suddenly recalled all the wonderful Christmases of her childhood, the ones that had been filled with cookies and candy canes, a brightly lit tree decorated with ornaments she and her brother had made and popcorn they'd strung.

There was some chill in the air, after all, just enough to make it feel like Christmas, and every step over the carpet of pine needles released their fresh, wintry scent.

"Are you cold?" Tom asked, walking up behind her and circling her waist with his arms.

Jeanette allowed herself to lean back against him for just an instant before pulling away. "No, this is invigorating." She gazed up at him. "Doesn't it smell wonderful out here?"

"It smells like the cleaning solution they use at Town Hall," he said.

"It does not. It smells exactly the way Christmas morning is supposed to smell."

Tom shrugged. "In my family, our trees were always artificial. They had to stay up for weeks. Live trees were too messy, to say nothing of being a fire risk."

She regarded him incredulously. "You never had a live tree?"

He shook his head. "Not that I recall. The decorators insisted that artificial was much more practical."

"Decorators? You didn't put the tree up yourselves?"

"Trees," he corrected. "We usually had half a dozen, one in each of the downstairs rooms, along with boughs of evergreens, also artificial. It took several weeks for the decorators to do their job and turn our house into some kind of holiday theme park."

"I can't imagine. What about the decorations? Did you make some?"

"I made a few in school, but they were never on our trees. I think the housekeeper might have held on to some of them, but my mother insisted that the formal trees had to have a theme. It changed every year. My sisters and I were warned not to break any of the glass ornaments or we'd have to pay for them out of our allowances."

"How awful," she said. It just reconfirmed everything she'd thought about Mrs. McDonald being a difficult, demanding woman and a snob. "Didn't you have any special family traditions?"

"Not much beyond going to the Christmas Eve service at the church. Oh, and the round of parties that began right after Thanksgiving. My sisters and I were banished from most of those until we were older and could be counted on to be civilized in company."

"But Christmas should be magical, especially for kids," she protested, feeling bad for him. She understood his bah-humbug attitude a whole lot better now. Hers came from having a tragedy rip away a tradition she'd loved. And Tom, he'd never even known how joyous the holidays could be. She wasn't sure which was worse.

Tom shrugged off her sympathy. "It was just the way we did things. I never knew anything different."

"But I can see why the holidays don't matter much to you," she told him.

"What about you? Were your holidays always idyllic?"

She hesitated before answering, then, almost overcome with nostalgia, she said quietly, "They were when I was little."

Tom picked up on her phrasing at once. "What happened to change that?"

She opened her mouth, then closed it again. If she said the words, the enjoyment she'd been feeling amidst all these beautiful trees would be lost.

"Jeanette, what happened?" Tom pressed.

She sighed and began slowly, "I had an older brother— Benjamin. He was the best." She closed her eyes and pictured him, standing tall and proud in his football uniform, an adoring girl on each arm. The words flowed more quickly. "He'd won an athletic scholarship to the University of South Carolina. My parents were so proud of him. Neither of them had been able to go to college. My dad's a farmer. He works the same farm today that his father and grandfather did before him. He wanted more for Ben."

Tom just nodded and waited without interrupting.

Tears welled up and slid down her cheeks. "It was Christmas Eve," she said, lost in the memory that had changed her life. "I was fifteen and Ben had just turned eighteen. We'd all gone to church, but Ben had driven his own car. He'd picked up his girlfriend on the way to the midnight service. When they left after the service, he said he'd see us at home..." Her voice trailed off and she swallowed hard against the flood of memories of that awful night.

Tom touched her cheek, his eyes soft with compassion. "What happened?"

"He never made it," she said. She paused for breath and it was a moment before she could go on. "After he dropped off his girlfriend, his car hit a patch of black ice. The police said he was probably going too fast. The car spun out of control and slammed into a tree. They said he died instantly."

"Oh my God, Jeanette, I am so sorry," Tom said, brushing the tears from her cheeks. "I can't imagine what that must have done to all of you."

"We never celebrated Christmas again," she told him, regrets washing through her anew. "When I wanted to get out the decorations the next year, my mother fell apart. My dad put them back in the attic. I never tried again."

"No wonder you hate the holidays," he said. "You have such terrible memories associated with the season."

"Ironically, I don't hate the holidays because I'm sad," she said, trying to explain. "Not exactly, anyway. I hate them because of the way Ben's death changed my parents. They'd been warm and generous and outgoing. My dad had high expectations for my brother, but he doted on me. After that, though, it was as if I didn't even exist. I might as well have died right along with Ben, because nothing I did seemed to make any difference to them." She met Tom's gaze. "You have no idea how lonely and isolated that can make you feel, not mattering to the people you're supposed to matter to."

"My parents always involved themselves too *much* in my life. I felt smothered. They laid out all these expectations that had nothing to do with what I wanted. It wasn't enough that I excelled at school, I had to excel at the classes my father thought I ought to be taking. I had to spend time with girls my mother thought were appropriate. I went along with it until I graduated from law school, but then I did things my own way. That's when the real battles started."

He shook his head. "So, no, I don't know how it feels to be ignored, but it must have hurt terribly."

"It still does."

Shock spread across his face. "You haven't made peace? It's been how many years now?"

"Almost twenty, and nothing's changed. I called home a few weeks ago and my mother hardly recognized my voice. When I asked to speak to my father, she gave me an excuse about him being outside. She didn't offer to have him call me back. I don't even know if she told him I called. That's the way it happens every time I reach out to them, but I keep trying, anyway. I keep hoping that someday they'll remember that they have another child, one who's still living, who still needs them."

She shivered. Tom took off his jacket and wrapped it around her. She didn't even try to tell him that nothing could ward off a chill that originated deep inside. Instead, she let his warmth seep into her, breathed in the citrus scent of his aftershave. It wasn't enough to take away the memories, but it was comforting just the same.

Tom wanted to seek out Jeanette's parents and knock some sense into them. Even in their grief, they should have seen how much she needed them.

As flawed as his relationship with his own parents might be, at least they had contact. Even when they were at odds, he knew they loved him. And even when he was most annoyed with them, as he had been with his mother over her attitude toward Jeanette, he couldn't imagine cutting her out of his life permanently.

How could Jeanette's parents live with themselves, abandoning her as they had? Because he had no answers, he settled for keeping a close eye on her the rest of the day, trying to let her know with a gesture or a touch that there was someone who cared about her, who valued her.

He thought he understood her a whole lot better now. He got why she was so touchy at any suggestion that she might not be first with him, why he might not make her a priority in his life. He had no idea, though, how to change the impression he'd given her. He *would* leave here someday. That was his plan and he'd determinedly adhered to his plan from the day he'd made it. Falling in love hadn't been on the plan, not for a few years, anyway. He'd envisioned finding a wife after he'd reached his goal of running a large city. That's when he'd make time for more than work, though how he intended to carve out enough time wasn't something he'd figured out.

In the meantime, though, out of the blue, here was Jeanette, a woman who captivated him, who filled him with a desire to protect her, who made him just a little bit crazy with lust. What the heck was he supposed to do about that, especially given her issues?

Right now, she was standing beside the tree Howard had picked out for the town green. The towering pine dwarfed her. She gazed toward the top, her expression awed, as if it was the first Christmas tree she'd ever seen. Maybe, in a way, it was. Not the very first, but the first since that terrible Christmas when her world had died right along with her brother.

He moved to stand beside her and clasped her hand in his. "It's awfully big," he said critically.

"No, it's perfect," she said. "Howard's right. This is the one. I've never seen anything like it. I can just see it with hundreds and hundreds of twinkling lights. It will be amazing."

"It's bound to cost a fortune," he said, still playing devil's advocate.

She frowned at him. "So find the money," she said in a tone oddly reminiscent of Howard's. "Tom, we *have* to have this tree."

He gazed into her eyes. "It means that much to you?"

She reached out and reverently touched the thick branches. "It does."

"Then we'll find the money somewhere, but if anyone complains about potholes not being filled, I'm sending them to talk to you and Howard."

Just then Howard returned, trailed by Ronnie and Mary Vaughn. Howard's expression was glum. "The man wants an arm and a leg for this one," he said. "We might have to settle for something smaller."

"No," Jeanette protested. "Did you tell him it was for the town square?"

"Of course I did," Howard said. "Told him all about the choirs and the kids and Santa. Bottom line, he's a hardheaded businessman. Can't say I blame him, but it's still a disappointment."

"We're getting this tree," Tom said decisively.

Howard regarded him incredulously. "You're the one who set the price limit."

Tom shrugged. "I'll find a few more dollars somewhere."

"It's not just a few bucks," Ronnie reported. "More like a few hundred."

Tom glanced around at the circle of grim expressions. "Is everyone agreed that this is the tree we want?"

"Yes," Mary Vaughn said, her eyes sparkling much as Jeanette's did. "We've never had one this magnificent."

"Then I'll authorize purchasing it," Tom said. "Mr. Mayor, are we in agreement?"

"You can find the money in the budget?"

"I'll come up with the money," Tom said. Out of his own pocket, if need be. Anything that put that shine back into Jeanette's eyes was worth every penny. To keep it there, he might even be persuaded to help decorate the monstrous thing, though he vowed to grumble about doing it just on principle.

Jeanette threw her arms around him and planted an enthusiastic kiss on his cheek.

Tom grinned. As incentives went, that wasn't a bad one, either. "Where's the farmer?" he asked. "Let's get a tag on this tree and arrange for it to be delivered."

"I'll take care of that," Howard said, beaming. "Knew you weren't the grinch you've been pretending to be."

"Yes, I am!" Tom called after him.

"Oh, give it up," Jeanette said. "None of us are going to buy that act anymore. You caved in and bought the perfect tree."

"No tree's perfect. It's probably lopsided," he grumbled, trying to restake his claim to being a bah-humbug kind of guy. "Probably has a trunk that's crooked as an old walking stick. Did anybody check that?"

Ronnie laughed. "Too late, pal. You're today's hero, whether you like it or not."

"Mine, anyway," Jeanette said, regarding him with surprising heat.

Well, damn, Tom thought. He'd been relying on stolen kisses to get her attention, when all it had taken was a thousand-dollar Christmas tree.

CHAPTER FIFTEEN

After two months on the job, Tom had established a routine of sorts. He stopped by Wharton's every morning for coffee and gossip on the way to the office, he had lunch at his desk and at the end of the day he went jogging to work off some of the restless energy from being confined all day. He'd joined Dexter's Gym, but as everyone had warned him, he found the atmosphere so depressing, he rarely did more than one or two workouts a week there.

His job was surprisingly challenging. With development in and around Serenity booming, there were plenty of plans being submitted that required detailed scrutiny. No one else on staff had his expertise when it came to looking for potential problems and the impact new development would have on Serenity's schools and other institutions.

He'd been actively seeking new business for downtown and working with owners of the vacant properties on Main Street to give one-year rent concessions to people willing to open shops. He hoped that a lower overhead to start would encourage people to take a risk on the town and give them a chance to get their businesses established. So far he'd had two people commit to opening shops after the first of the year and three more considering leases for spring. He'd be reporting that at the next council meeting.

He'd also ordered a methodical and thorough check of the town's infrastructure, something that had been ignored for too long. There was a narrow bridge over a tributary to the Great Pee Dee River that worried him, but the engineering reports indicated it was structurally sound for now. He wanted to get a jump on making sure it stayed that way. Water and sewer lines needed updating. In fact, the entire water-treatment system needed to be overhauled because of the demand from all the new development. He had a proposal for defraying much of that cost with hookup charges and other fees to the developers.

And he'd committed the start-up money for Cal's Little League proposal. He put it into the Parks and Recreation Department budget with the council's blessing. He'd promised to coach that second team, too.

All in all, despite his short time here, he felt as if he'd already made a contribution to Serenity. With so many irons in the fire, though, he'd had little time to hunt for a house or to pursue Jeanette the way he'd wanted to. That only added to his stress, which increased the necessity for these nightly runs. He usually made his way through town, then looped around the lake, which was surrounded by azalea bushes that he suspected filled the landscape with vivid color in the spring. There was usually a group of women sitting in the gazebo chatting in the fading evening light. He'd grown so accustomed to seeing them there that he always greeted them, even though he recognized none of them. He knew they'd be gone as soon as darkness fell, as would the last stray couples who'd been enjoying an evening walk.

He was pushing himself on a final lap around the lake when his cell phone rang. He was tempted to ignore it, but the police and fire departments had the number in case they needed to reach him in an emergency, so he stopped and bent over to catch his breath as he glanced at caller ID. His mother. It was her fifth call today. He'd managed to evade the others, but clearly she didn't intend to give up.

"Hello, Mother," he said, giving in finally.

"What's wrong with you?" she demanded. "It sounds as if you're out of breath." She sounded more irritated than worried.

"You caught me in the middle of my run. What's on your mind?"

"Have you found a house yet?"

"I haven't had time to look," he told her.

"Which is exactly why I wanted to do it for you," she said, clearly miffed. "But I was told in no uncertain terms to butt out."

"I seriously doubt Mary Vaughn phrased it that way," he said.

"Well, of course not. She's a lovely woman. She's available, too, I believe."

Subtlety was not his mother's strong suit. "I'm aware of that," he told her.

"Have you asked her out?"

"Mother!" he said, a warning note in his voice.

"Well, surely you're not considering going out with that little strumpet, Jeanette whatever-her-name-is."

"Okay, that's enough," he said. "I'll talk to you later."

He was about to cut off the connection when he heard her call his name insistently. He relented and put the phone back to his ear. "Yes?"

"Okay, I didn't mean to get your dander up. I know that's exactly the wrong thing to do. After all these years of watching you and your father, you'd think I'd know better. You're like a child. You'll do exactly the opposite of whatever I suggest just to spite me."

"Was that supposed to be an apology?"

She sighed dramatically. "I'm sorry," she said without much sincerity. "I didn't call about any of this."

"Then why did you call?"

"The drapes for your office are ready. I'd like to bring them over tomorrow. I thought afterward we might have time to look at a few houses."

This time his sigh was as dramatic as hers. "Bring the drapes if you want, but I don't have time to go house hunting tomorrow," he said.

"Well, surely you'll at least be able to find the time to have lunch," she said.

He thought about that. Sooner or later he and his mother were going to have to spend some time together. She was not the sort of woman to let anyone push her aside forever, especially one of her own children. Though she was sometimes her own worst enemy in those relationships, she tried her best to be a good mother in the only way she knew how. It had taken him thirty-five years to recognize that.

"We can have lunch," he said. "On one condition."

"What?" she asked warily.

"That we include Jeanette and you promise to be civil to her."

"Absolutely not," she said at once.

"Okay, then, no deal."

"Thomas McDonald, I do not appreciate your attempt to blackmail me into spending time with a woman I can't abide."

"You barely know her."

"Just the same, I have no desire to know her any better," she said stubbornly.

He knew it was vanity and pride more than snobbery that made her so determined to keep Jeanette at arm's length. Surely she was embarrassed over the fiasco she'd created at Chez Bella's. At least that's what he wanted to believe.

"And it doesn't matter to you that she's important to me?" he asked quietly.

She gasped. "How important?"

"I'm not one hundred percent certain yet, but right now I'd have to say very important. And I would very much appreciate it if you would at least give her a chance. Come on, Mother, it won't be the first time in your life you've had to be polite to someone you're not fond of. You do it all the time for the sake of one charity or another. Can't you do at least as much for me?"

"Well, when you put it that way, I suppose I have no choice," she said grudgingly. "I'll be at your office at eleven-thirty to drop off the drapes. Make a reservation for lunch at noon. Tell your little friend not to be late."

"Yes, ma'am," he said, hiding his amusement at her dictatorial attitude. He recognized it as an attempt to have *some* control over the situation.

He hung up, pleased with himself for setting in motion a truce between Jeanette and his mother. Unfortunately, though, only one side had agreed to a meeting. Something told him Jeanette was going to be a much tougher sell.

"Oh no, no way!" Jeanette said, staring at Tom as if he'd grown two heads or, at the very least, lost his otherwise intelligent mind. "I will not have lunch with your mother! Not for a million dollars."

"Not even to thank me for making sure the town got the Christmas tree you wanted?" he cajoled.

"Not even for that," she said flatly.

If she'd known why he'd suddenly appeared at her apartment bearing pizza and a bottle of expensive wine, she'd have tossed him right back out on his sexy backside. Now, with the aroma of the pizza teasing her taste buds, it was a little late to send him on his way. That didn't mean she had to agree to this absurd plan of his.

"Your mother will take one look at me and dump a glass of ice water over my head," she predicted.

"I already have her word that she won't do that," he said.

"What did you do? Make a list of rules for her to abide by?"

"It wasn't a list. I just reminded her that she is perfectly capable of being civil, even under the most awkward circumstances, and that I expected nothing less of her under these."

"Gee, that makes me feel all warm and fuzzy," Jeanette said sourly, reaching for a slice of pizza with black olives and mushrooms, just the way she liked it. She was getting at least one slice before this conversation deteriorated—as it was bound to do.

"Have some wine," Tom said, filling her glass to the brim.

"I'm not going to go along with this, no matter how drunk you try to get me," she said, but she did take a sip of the wine. It was excellent. He hadn't bought it in Serenity, unless he'd managed to wheedle it out of Dana Sue from Sullivan's wine cellar.

"Look, I know my mother made a mess of things when the two of you first met, but she's basically a nice woman."

"Nice?" she repeated skeptically. "Is this the same woman who behaved so badly last time we ran into each other that you walked out on her?"

He looked chagrined. "The same one."

"Yet you think the three of us having lunch is a good idea," she mused, then gave him a piercing look. "Are you delusional?"

"More than likely," he admitted. "But we could try. I have her commitment that she'll behave. If you'll go at least that far, it shouldn't be awful."

She shook her head. "Can you even hear yourself? You're inviting me to a lunch that 'shouldn't be awful.' That is not a great recommendation. Why do you even want to try this?"

"Because she is, for all of her flaws, my mother. And you matter to me. I'd really like it if the two of you got along."

"You mean better than the two of *you* do?" she asked.

He winced. Then, as if he sensed she might be wavering, he leaned closer. "I would be really, really grateful."

She studied him with a narrowed gaze. "How grateful?"

"Very."

"Grateful enough to help me move when the time comes?"

He grinned. "I was planning to do that anyway."

"Really? That's great. Would you be grateful enough to help me paint the living room and bedrooms downstairs?"

His smile spread. "I could be persuaded to do that."

"Would you fix every leaky faucet in the house?"

He looked hesitant. "I can try, but you might be better off asking Ronnie to do that. Or hiring a plumber." He brightened. "Yes, definitely a plumber. I'll hire a plumber for you."

"And an electrician? I'm thinking there should be a lot of ceiling fans."

"Done," he said.

"A new roof?"

His mouth gaped a little at that, which made her laugh.

"Just kidding. The roof's in great shape. I just wanted to see how far you'd go."

He shrugged. "Pretty far. Look, nobody knows better than I do how impossible my mother can be, but if it makes you feel any better, she was just as difficult with the men my sisters chose to marry and every one of them had trust funds and family trees she could trace back to the *Mayflower*. It's just a mother-hen thing."

"Except you and I aren't planning to get married," Jeanette reminded him.

"Speak for yourself," he said.

Well, that certainly upped the stakes in an unexpected way, she thought, waiting for a panic that never came.

Eventually, she allowed herself to meet Tom's gaze and the earnest entreaty she found there. She struggled against the tide of emotions it stirred in her, but predictably, she lost the battle. "Okay, but don't say I didn't warn you. This is a bad idea."

"No, it's not," he said confidently. "You'll charm the socks off her."

Jeanette would settle for getting through the meal without strangling her.

Mary Vaughn's car sputtered to a stop on the side of the highway ten miles outside of Serenity. She'd bought the stupid gas guzzler because it was supposed to be reliable, and also to stick it to Sonny who didn't approve of any car that didn't come off the lot at his dealership.

Unfortunately the closest dealership for this car was an hour away at best; most of the mechanics at the garages in Serenity wouldn't touch it. She needed a tow truck and a ride home.

Gritting her teeth, she punched in Sonny's number, prepared to listen to a diatribe about what a mistake she'd made in getting the car in the first place.

When Sonny picked up, she announced, "I'm stranded on the highway. I don't need a lecture. I need help."

"Flat tire?"

"No, the stupid thing just died on me. I'm lucky there was no traffic and I could get to the shoulder without anyone hitting me."

"Where are you exactly?"

She told him.

"Whatever you do, don't stand on the side of the road," he instructed. "Stay in the car. Help's on the way."

For once she was grateful for his brisk, no-nonsense approach to a crisis. She could recall many times when she'd wanted and needed sympathy, only to get practical advice and concrete solutions. At the time it had seemed like a flaw. Today it was reassuring.

"Thanks, Sonny."

"No problem, sugar. You stay put."

Twenty minutes later, a tow truck pulled up, followed by Sonny.

"I figured you'd want the car towed to the dealership," he said. "And that would leave you without a way to get home."

She eyed him warily as he actually got out and held the door for her, something few other men she'd met bothered to do anymore.

"It'll also give you plenty of time to gloat," she said as she settled onto the luxurious leather seat, which she was forced to admit was more comfortable than her own.

He grinned. "I hadn't planned to, but I can if it'll make you feel better."

"No, please don't," she said.

Once he'd spoken to the driver of the tow truck, he climbed back behind the wheel of his car. "You okay?"

"Just annoyed," she said. "There's no telling how long it'll take to get the car fixed."

"I'll give you a loaner, no problem," Sonny said.

She frowned at him. "Why are you being so nice?"

He frowned at the question. "Why wouldn't I be?"

"It just seems weird, given all the water under the bridge. I mean, I know we agreed to get along when Rory Sue's home for Christmas, but this is above and beyond."

His gaze leveled with hers. "Why'd you call me if you were anticipating nothing but grief?"

She fidgeted for a minute before admitting, "Because I knew I could count on you."

"Well, there you go," he said. "Good ol' Sonny Lewis to the rescue, as always."

Mary Vaughn heard an unexpectedly bitter note in his voice. She'd upset him, which was the very last thing she'd intended. She'd thought she was paying him a compliment. She reached over and covered his hand, which was gripping the steering wheel too tightly. "I'm sorry."

"For what?"

She thought about it. "I don't know. Maybe for everything I put you through."

"Don't," he said harshly, shaking off her hand. "Don't apologize when you don't really even know what it's for."

She sat back and stared straight ahead, her stomach churning at the realization that she'd inadvertently hurt him yet again. Every few minutes, she stole a glance at him. His jaw was set, his mouth turned down.

"I really am sorry," she whispered.

He muttered an oath, then glanced her way. "Don't beat yourself up. You know, I go along thinking I've put all the pieces of my life back together, that my life is really good. Then it hits me that you still have the power to cut right through me. I don't like it, Mary Vaughn. I don't like what that says about me."

"It says more about me," she returned mildly. "That I would keep doing things to hurt you when you've been nothing but wonderful to me our whole lives. I don't like feeling that thoughtless and selfish, either."

He didn't respond, didn't jump in to tell her that she wasn't either thoughtless or selfish, as he might have done in the past. He let the words just hang there, undisputed. It hurt, but she couldn't deny the truth of what she'd said and obviously he wasn't willing to do it anymore, either.

"Do you think it's possible to change?" she asked. "I mean, old as we are, do you really think a person can stop bad habits?"

"Sure," he said at once. "At least, I want to believe it's possible."

"Me, too."

He turned into the lot at his dealership. The anger and vulnerability vanished behind his more familiar smiling mask, no doubt for the benefit of his employees and any customers who might be around. "Come inside and I'll get you set up with that loaner."

"You don't have to do that," she said.

His scowl returned. "Don't be an idiot. You need a car. I have cars. It's as simple as that. It doesn't have to get complicated."

"Okay, then," she said briskly. "I'll pay you, of course."

His scowl deepened. "You're testing my patience, Mary Vaughn."

"Lunch?" she suggested, instead. "Dinner? Can I at least do that?"

He looked as if he was waging an internal war with himself, but he finally sighed and nodded. "Lunch would be great."

"Tomorrow?"

"Sure, why not?"

She grinned at his evident reluctance. "I promise to make it painless," she said lightly.

"Don't go making promises you can't keep, sugar. I'll see you tomorrow at noon. Sullivan's? Or do you feel like driving over to that diner you used to like for some real Southern cooking?"

"You'd probably rather have a burger at Wharton's," she said.

"Under other circumstances, yes," he agreed.

"You mean with anyone other than me."

"You have to admit, the whole town will be speculating if we walk into Wharton's together, including my father."

"It won't be the first time I've stirred up gossip," she reminded him. "I can handle it if you can."

He regarded her speculatively, then shrugged. "Okay, then. Wharton's it is."

Satisfied, Mary Vaughn gave him an impulsive peck on the cheek, then walked out. She wasn't entirely sure what had just happened between her and Sonny, but suddenly it felt like a whole lot more than agreeing to some kind of thank-you lunch.

The next day Mary Vaughn sucked in a deep breath, then walked into Wharton's and marched straight to a prime booth right in front of the window. If she and Sonny were going to have this little get-together in gossip central, they might as well be in plain view. Hiding in back would only stir up more speculation.

Grace Wharton arrived before Mary Vaughn could slide all the way into her seat and studied her with undisguised curiosity. "Don't see much of you in here at lunchtime, at least not all by yourself," she said as she set a menu on the Formica-topped table.

"Someone's joining me," Mary Vaughn said, oddly reluctant to admit that it was Sonny. She was the one who'd claimed not to give two figs about stirring up gossip, but all of a sudden she wondered if it wasn't a bad idea. For one thing, as Sonny had reminded her, Howard was a regular here at lunchtime, along with several of his cronies. At least at Sullivan's most of the lunch customers were daytrippers who'd read about the restaurant in one of the regional magazines. And if they'd driven to that diner, it was doubtful they'd have seen anyone they knew.

"A client, I imagine," Grace said, setting another menu at the place across from her.

Mary Vaughn lifted her chin and met Grace's gaze. Grace was a wonderful woman who prided herself on knowing everything that was going on in town. She knew it because she paid attention and asked intrusive questions. Amazingly, no one in town held it against her. That didn't mean Mary Vaughn had to cooperate.

"I'd like a glass of sweet tea, please," she told Grace. "And you can go ahead and bring a diet soda for my friend."

Normally her deliberate evasiveness would have piqued Grace's curiosity to the point that she'd try a few more questions, but for some reason today, she just hurried away to fill the order.

Not two minutes later, just as Grace was putting the drinks on the table, Sonny walked in, removed his sunglasses and took a minute to allow his eyes to adjust. His hair was a little windblown, which told Mary Vaughn that he'd borrowed a convertible from the lot for the drive. She'd always thought he looked sexy as the dickens when his hair was mussed, his sleeves rolled up and his shirt open at the collar as it was now. Once again, she felt that funny little jolt of awareness that made her feel suddenly self-conscious with a man she'd known almost all her life.

"Well, will you look at what the cat dragged in," Grace said, glancing from him to Mary Vaughn. "He's probably here to meet his daddy."

Mary Vaughn didn't reply, in part because she couldn't seem to get a word past the unexpected lump in her throat. Damn, he was good-looking. She'd always known that, but it had never kicked her pulse into gear the way it seemed to be doing today.

When Sonny headed straight for Mary Vaughn's booth right by the front window, Grace inhaled sharply and murmured, "Well, I'll be," then whirled around and rushed away, no doubt to spread the word far and wide that Mary Vaughn and Sonny Lewis were about to break bread together, and that they were acting perfectly civilized. Wharton's would be packed within the next half hour with people wanting a glimpse of the two of them. Bets would be wagered before the end of the day on what it all meant. Mary Vaughn sighed.

"You were right. This was probably a bad idea," she told Sonny.

He shrugged, as unconcerned today as she'd been the night before. "It's Serenity, sugar. Talkin' is what people do."

"Do you really want them talking about us?"

"Nothing new in that," he reminded her. "Are you ready to order? I need to get back for my sales meeting."

Mary Vaughn was feeling too uncomfortable to even

glance at the chalkboard with the day's specials on it. "I'll have whatever you're having."

"Cheeseburger with fries?" he asked, sounding surprised.

Normally she ate a container of yogurt or a salad for lunch unless she was dining with a client. She hadn't had a burger in a year.

"A burger sounds perfect," she said, throwing caution to the wind. Today seemed the day for it.

"And fries?" Sonny asked again, as if he still couldn't quite believe his ears.

"And fries."

A smile spread across his face. "You remember what we were talking about last night, about people being able to change?"

"Of course."

"Sugar, if you'll order a milk shake with that, then you'll make a true believer out of me."

She frowned at his teasing. "It's lunch, not a conversion."

"After watching you nibble on lettuce leaves most of our adult lives, this is noteworthy," he insisted.

"You won't be so pleased by that when my hips start looking like two watermelons stuffed into a pair of pants."

"You know, Mary Vaughn, that's just one more thing you never understood about me. You're a beautiful woman, no doubt about it, but I always loved who you were, not how you looked."

She regarded him with skepticism. Before she could argue with him, though, Howard walked into Wharton's took one look at them and gaped.

"Never expected to find you two sitting here all cozy," he said. "You here to talk about our Christmas plans with Rory Sue?"

Mary Vaughn left the explanation to Sonny.

"Nope," he told his father. "We're on a date."

Even though her heart took an unexpected lurch at his ridiculous claim, Mary Vaughn scowled at her ex-husband. "We are not."

He grinned. "What would you call it?"

"A mistake," she suggested dryly.

Howard beamed at them. "Well, whatever it is, it's good to see the two of you together. Rory Sue would be mighty pleased if she could see you."

"Don't you say a word to Rory Sue about this," Mary Vaughn said.

"That's right, Daddy," Sonny admonished. "You keep this to yourself. We don't want her getting ideas. She'll just wind up being disappointed."

Howard gave his son a penetrating look. "You so sure about that? I never did understand why the two of you split up in the first place. You never gave me an explanation that made a lick of sense."

"Because it was none of your business," Sonny said flatly. "Go on and meet your friends, Daddy. Their eyes are practically bugging out from staring over here. You might as well fill them in on what the two of us are doing here together."

Howard regarded him with obvious frustration. "I don't *know* why you're here together."

Mary Vaughn gave him her sweetest smile. "Then you won't have too much to say, will you? You can move right on to other, more interesting topics."

"You're still full of sass and vinegar, aren't you?" For once, Howard's tone was almost admiring.

"I do try to be," she told him.

"Well, whatever you're doing here, enjoy yourselves," Howard said and walked away to join his friends.

"Well, that was awkward," Mary Vaughn said.

Sonny's eyes, however, were glinting with humor. "But you have to admit it was kind of fun to get him all riled up. Daddy hates being out of the loop when it comes to family, and now he's convinced we're keeping something from him."

"An interesting perspective," Mary Vaughn agreed. "After all the times your daddy was on my case about one thing or another, including all his objections to the two of us getting married in the first place, I have to admit it's downright rewarding to see him hoping we'll get back together. I figured he'd go to his grave still thanking God we'd gotten a divorce."

For an instant, Sonny looked stunned. "You think that's what he wants? For us to get back together?"

"I think he wants his granddaughter to be happy, and us getting back together is what *she* wants."

"Uh-oh," Sonny said, looking disconcerted.

Mary Vaughn laughed at his expression. "You scared your daddy's going to start meddling?"

"He's not above it," Sonny predicted direly. "And if I were you, I wouldn't be so amused. My father almost always gets what he sets his mind to."

Mary Vaughn felt a tiny shiver go through her. She couldn't be sure if it was out of fear...or anticipation.

CHAPTER SIXTEEN

Jeanette slipped into Sullivan's through the kitchen door, made a dash across the room and peeked into the dining room to see if Tom and his awful mother had been seated yet.

"Not that I don't love to see you under any circumstances," Erik commented. "But do you want to tell me why you're in my kitchen, instead of out there with the other diners?"

"Tom's mother," she said in a low voice.

"You checking her out?" he asked, his expression bewildered.

"No need for that," Jeanette said. "I already know the old harridan."

Erik's lips twitched. "Does Tom have any idea what a high opinion you have of his mother?"

"He does," she said, then pulled out a stool and sat down. "And can you believe he wants us to have lunch together, anyway?"

Erik didn't even try to contain a chuckle. He pointed toward the dining room. "Out of my kitchen. I'm not getting in the middle of this."

"Dana Sue would let me stay," she said.

"Dana Sue's not here. I'm in charge."

She frowned at him. "Does being in charge always make you mean?"

"You'll have to ask Karen or Dana Sue about that. Or maybe Helen. Of course, this kitchen is the one place she never seemed to mind taking orders from me." He sighed dramatically. "Now that we're married she never listens to me at all."

"If I could spare the time, I'd feel real sorry for you," she said. "But I'm having my own pity party here."

"No," he corrected, "you're having it out there. My kitchen's off-limits. Go."

"If you say so, but I'm warning you not to serve us with the good china or crystal. Some of it's likely to end up broken before we're through today."

"Be sure you give me a heads-up before you start throwing things. I'd like to evacuate the other customers." His expression turned wicked. "Or charge 'em extra for the floor show. Now, go."

"You are not a very sympathetic man," Jeanette told him, but she reluctantly left the kitchen and headed toward the table where Tom and his mother were just being seated.

Tom's expression brightened the instant he saw her, which she figured was going to be the high point of the meal. After his mother caught sight of her, things were likely to slide downhill.

"Where'd you come from?" Tom asked, pulling out a chair for her.

"I stopped in the kitchen to speak to Erik," she fibbed.

Mrs. McDonald gave her a sour look. "Probably told him to lace my food with arsenic," she murmured.

"Mother!" Tom chided.

Jeanette gave her a cheery smile. "Now, why didn't I think of that?"

Tom frowned at her. "Jeanette!"

To Jeanette's surprise, his mother's lips almost curved into a smile, though she quickly hid it by taking a sip of water. That tiny hint of approval, though, gave Jeanette hope. Maybe Mrs. McDonald was one of those perverse women who liked stirring the pot, but liked it even better if someone else responded by adding a little spice instead of backing down. It was entirely possible she admired a woman with spunk. Well, *she* had spunk to spare.

"Erik's made a wonderful broccoli quiche today," she told them. "He was just taking one out of the oven when I was in there."

"I've never understood the appeal of quiche," Mrs. McDonald said.

"The meat loaf is a favorite," Jeanette said, doing her best to remain upbeat. "And, of course, no one does a better job with fish."

"She's right," Tom said. "I've had both and can highly recommend either one. I think today's special is steamed sea bass with julienne vegetables. I'm having that. Mother, what looks good to you?"

"I'll just have a bowl of soup," she said without glancing at the menu.

"The gazpacho is excellent," Jeanette said.

"Too spicy," his mother said.

"They put homemade noodles in their chicken soup," Tom said, starting to sound a little desperate.

"I'm not ill," his mother replied tartly. "I believe I'll try the lentil soup."

Tom regarded her with relief. "I'll get the waitress," he said eagerly. Apparently his enthusiasm for this adventure had died and he was now as anxious to have this meal over and done with as Jeanette was.

He placed their orders. Jeanette placed her own and then Tom sat back and regarded the two of them expectantly. When his mother remained grimly silent, so did Jeanette. Under the table he placed a hand on her thigh and then gave her an imploring look. She relented. She could at least make an effort. If it blew up in her face, well, she'd warned Tom his expectations were too high.

"Mrs. McDonald, I understand you're involved with a number of charity functions. Are you working on anything now?"

Tom beamed at her gratefully. His mother looked as if she wanted to ignore the question, but when he scowled at her, she gave in.

"The ball for the cancer society is coming up," she said grudgingly.

"That's always been one of the most successful events in Charleston," Jeanette said, then added, "We used to get a lot of clients in the days leading up to that. Everyone wanted to look their absolute best."

The second the words were out of her mouth, she knew she'd said exactly the wrong thing. She'd just reminded Mrs. McDonald what she did for a living and where she'd previously worked. Worse, if she wasn't mistaken, Mrs. McDonald had come into Chez Bella's prior to the cancer ball for the treatment that had resulted in so much misplaced animosity.

The older woman gave her a smug look. "You see, Tom, it's just as I've always told you. These events aren't a frivolous waste of time for the rich. A lot of people rely on them to make money." She turned to Jeanette. "I'm sure you counted on those tips to make ends meet, didn't you?

Even in Charleston's less established neighborhoods, housing is expensive."

Jeanette refused to be baited. "Actually, Bella paid me handsomely, but my clients were always very generous, as well. They are here, too. I like to think it's because I give them excellent service." And not because they wanted to be sure she could afford to keep a roof over her head, which was what Mrs. McDonald was trying so hard to imply. She forced a smile. "But it's never been about the money for me. I love what I do. And it's been very rewarding to build a new spa from the ground up, to be in demand with a whole new clientele, many of whom never thought of getting a spa treatment before we opened here."

"Then you've priced these treatments for the masses?" Mrs. McDonald said derisively. "I've always held the belief that people get what they pay for."

Jeanette was rapidly losing patience. Her hold on her temper was one fragile thread away from snapping. Apparently Tom sensed it.

"Mother, why don't you tell Jeanette about the cruise you and Dad are planning in January."

His mother smiled at him, her expression doting. Even Jeanette, as biased as she was, could see her love for her son shining in her eyes. Maybe she wasn't all bad. If Jeanette really set her mind to it, maybe she could give Mrs. McDonald the benefit of the doubt. She owed that much to Tom.

"I'm surprised you remembered we were going with all you have to do," Mrs. McDonald said.

Jeanette figured he was probably looking forward to her absence, but of course she couldn't say that, not with her resolution to be more open-minded so fresh.

Mrs. McDonald turned to Jeanette. "We're taking a two-week cruise in the Caribbean," she said, then added pointedly, "All of it first-class, including a magnificent spa."

"Which cruise line?" Jeanette inquired.

When Mrs. McDonald named it, her tone superior, Jeanette nodded. "Of course, I know Laine Walker very well. She's in charge of their spa services."

Mrs. McDonald looked taken aback. "You know Laine?"

Jeanette nodded. "She trained with me in Paris."

To her satisfaction, Mrs. McDonald's mouth gaped. "*You* trained in Paris?" she repeated incredulously.

"For several years," she told her, triumphant at having thrown her so completely. "That's where Bella found me. I was working at one of the most exclusive spas in the city when she convinced me to come to Charleston. I'd missed home, so I accepted her very generous offer."

"I had no idea," Mrs. McDonald murmured and fell silent.

The rest of the meal went smoothly enough with Tom leading the conversation and doing his best to make sure he included both of them. He stuck to safe, neutral topics— the food, the weather, favorite restaurants in Charleston.

When those topics were exhausted, Jeanette glanced at her watch and stood. "I'm sorry to have to run, but I need to get back to work. I have a full schedule of clients this afternoon."

"I'll walk you out," Tom said. "Mother, why don't you take a look at the dessert menu."

"Goodbye, Mrs. McDonald," Jeanette said, unable to add that it had been a pleasure to see her, when it had been stiff and awkward.

Outside, Tom uttered an audible sigh of relief. "That wasn't so bad, was it?"

"Compared to torture?"

"Come on," he coaxed. "At least she tried."

"No, at least she didn't dump her meal in my lap," Jeanette corrected. "She wanted to, though. I could see it in her eyes."

"That was before you mentioned training in Paris. You took the wind right out of her sails with that one. Why didn't I know about Paris?"

"You never asked," she said simply. "As for your mother, she'll probably never look at Paris quite the same way again, now that it's been tainted by the likes of me."

"Can't you please give her a break?"

"I just did," she reminded him. "I didn't walk out on both of you."

"You really don't think it went well?"

She regarded him with astonishment. "Were you there?"

"Of course I was. There was no water dumped, no food thrown, no bloodshed. I consider it a success."

"Then obviously you had very low expectations," she told him.

He shrugged. "Can you blame me? The two of you got off on a bad foot back in Charleston. Her fault," he hastened to add. "Peace isn't going to happen overnight. Eventually the two of you will be able to laugh about what happened."

She shook her head. "Please, please, please, do not ever ask me to do this again. She's your mother and I don't mean to insult her or you, but I don't like her. She doesn't like me. Let's just call it a draw and be done with it."

"I don't think I can do that," Tom said.

"Why not?"

"It'll be damn awkward at the wedding," he said, then kissed her hard and walked away.

Jeanette stared after him, openmouthed with shock. Wedding? Was he crazy? It was the second time he'd said something like that, and while she was flattered, maybe even a little tempted, she knew with one hundred percent certainty that she couldn't marry into a family like his. She couldn't marry *him*. She hadn't even reached the point where she was willing to date him.

She rubbed her still-tingling lips. Sex with him, on the other hand, might be a distinct possibility.

Tom whistled as he returned to his office, which had Teresa regarding him with undisguised curiosity.

"You're in a good mood," she said. "Does it have something to do with the lunch you just had with Jeanette at Sullivan's?"

"Jeanette *and* my mother, which you already knew," he reminded her. "I know you check the calendar I keep every day now to be sure I'm not scheduling things you don't know about."

"Wouldn't be doing my job if I didn't know what you were up to during office hours." She smiled. "So, lunch went well?" She sounded incredulous.

"Truthfully, lunch was a little tense," he admitted. "But I have high hopes for later tonight."

"I assume you're referring to an evening with Jeanette and not your mother," she said.

"Of course. Hold my calls. I need to make some plans."

Teresa followed him into his office. "What are you up to?"

"None of your business," he said.

"If you don't mind me saying so, you have a very strange way of courting a woman."

"I repeat, none of your business."

Teresa was undeterred. "Do you want Jeanette or not?"

He sighed, sat down behind his desk and looked up at

her. He should have known his secretary would have an opinion about this. "Obviously you think I'm going about it all wrong."

"Well, duh! You took her to lunch with your *mother,* a woman she despises, from everything I hear." She gave him a wry look. "And we both know I hear quite a lot."

"Agreed," he conceded.

"Yet you think Jeanette's going to be eager to spend a romantic evening with you?" She shook her head. "I don't think so. She's probably hightailing it out of town, as we speak."

"Why would she do that?"

"Read my lips. Because you subjected her to an hour with your mother, whom she hates. And based on my experience over the whole drapery project, I don't blame her," she said. "If you'll pardon me for saying so."

He waved off the apology. He could hardly argue the point.

"Look, I was trying to bridge the gap between them, make peace, open the lines of communication."

"Ha! I imagine all you did was remind both of them that they don't like each other. Trust me, that does not work in your favor."

"What am I doing having this conversation with you?" he muttered. "It's completely inappropriate."

"You need my help," Teresa replied. "Like most men, you are clueless when it comes to women, especially Jeanette, who has not dated anyone since she moved to Serenity three years ago. She has a hard-and-fast rule about dating. If you expect her to break that rule, you need to be offering more than a guaranteed conflict with your mother."

"Some people consider me a good catch," he told Teresa.

"Maybe you are. The jury's still out on that around here.

All I'm saying is you're going to have to strut your stuff if you want Jeanette."

He stared at her. "Strut my stuff? What the hell does that mean?"

"Show her the kind of man you are. Treat her with dignity and respect. Woo her. And for goodness' sake, leave your mother out of it."

He would dearly love to leave his mother out of it, but she was already a bone of contention. He seriously doubted any of them could pretend otherwise.

"Okay, Ms. Lonely Hearts, what should I do next? I can't keep sending Jeanette scones and bread pudding or dropping by with her favorite pizza."

Teresa sat down, her expression thoughtful. "Just how much money do you have?"

Tom nearly choked at the question. "Excuse me?"

"I'm not asking to see your bank statement," she said. "I'm just wondering if you have enough to do something completely over the top."

"Such as?"

"Flying her to Paris for dinner," she said, her expression dreamy. "Jeanette wouldn't be able to resist a man who did something like that. She loved living in Paris."

For a moment, Tom actually considered the idea, then dismissed it. He doubted he could convince Jeanette to take a day trip to Savannah with him, much less an excursion to Paris.

"I think we'd better forget about Paris for the time being," he told her.

"Well, taking her bowling's not going to do it," Teresa said.

Tom's head was starting to reel. "Who said anything about bowling?"

"There's not a lot else to do in Serenity."

"I don't think Jeanette moved here for the exciting night-life," Tom said. "Teresa, I appreciate your input, I really do, but I think I'd better follow my own instincts about this." He met her gaze. "And let's make this the very last conversation we have about my love life, okay?"

"Suits me," she said, standing up and heading toward her own office. She glanced back over her shoulder. "But just to be clear, from what I can tell, you don't actually *have* a love life."

Clearly miffed, she walked out and shut the door behind her with a little more force than necessary.

"Thanks for pointing that out!" Tom called after her.

"My pleasure!" she shouted back.

Tom shook his head. Only several weeks ago his life had been on track, serene even. Yet in such a short time, he'd managed to get himself caught up with a disapproving mother, a meddling secretary and a fascinating woman who claimed to want nothing to do with him. Apparently fate really did enjoy having its little laughs.

Jeanette gave herself a stern lecture as she changed back into her work clothes. She was not going to let that ridiculous lunch with Mrs. McDonald get under her skin. She was not going to take out her frustration on her clients. She was going to be pleasant for the rest of the afternoon if it killed her. And she absolutely, positively was not going to think about that kiss Tom had laid on her on the sidewalk in front of Sullivan's and yet another mention of marriage.

Half the town had probably heard about that kiss by now. Maddie knew, Jeanette was sure of it. She'd caught the glint of amusement in Maddie's eyes when she'd walked into the spa. She'd ducked into a stall in the ladies' room just to keep Maddie from cross-examining her about that kiss.

Avoiding Maddie, however, turned out to be the easy part. She'd forgotten how quickly the Serenity grapevine worked with the general population.

"What's going on with you and the new town manager?" Drew Ann Smith inquired just as Jeanette began her facial. "Everybody's talking about it."

"I can't imagine why," Jeanette said evasively.

Her response made Drew Ann laugh. "You kissed the man in the stands at the football game. Everyone was amazed the girders holding up the bleachers didn't melt."

"Just trying to prove a point," Jeanette said blithely.

"And did you?" Drew Ann asked. "Prove the point?"

Jeanette thought about it. "Oh, I'm pretty sure I did." Unfortunately, she'd also stirred up a hornet's nest with the discovery that kissing Tom and being kissed by him were addictive.

"Heard you two were going at it again in front of Sullivan's today," Drew Ann said, her voice muffled by the towel that Jeanette had deliberately draped over her mouth in a futile attempt to silence her.

"Why is everyone so interested in what's going on between Tom and me?" she asked plaintively.

Drew Ann chuckled. "This is Serenity. Most of our lives are fairly routine and boring. Keeping up a steady play-by-play on the hot romances in town is what we do."

"Tom and I are not having a hot romance."

Drew Ann yanked away the towel and stared at her. "Are you crazy? If a man who looks like that and kisses like that wanted me, he wouldn't have to ask twice."

"I imagine Wendell would have something to say about

that." Jeanette was referring to Drew Ann's husband, who ran one of the town's two insurance agencies.

Drew Ann chuckled. "Wendell would probably be relieved to have a break."

Jeanette's gaped. "Drew Ann!"

"Well, it's true. Ever since I hit menopause, sex is on my mind all the time. I guess it's because I don't have to worry anymore about getting pregnant."

Jeanette wasn't sure which made her more uncomfortable, discussing her own relationship or Drew Ann's. Listening, though, came with the territory, so she let Drew Ann chatter on, murmuring appropriate comments on cue and trying to keep the image of Drew Ann and Wendell going at it like rabbits out of her head.

By the time she got back to her office, though, she had to fan herself to cool down from all that talk about sex. She sipped from her glass of tea and was about to get to her next client when the phone rang. She grabbed it because she knew the receptionist wouldn't have put it through if it wasn't important.

"Jeanette?" The quavery voice was her mother's.

"Mom? Is everything okay?" Jeanette asked, a knot of dread forming in her stomach. Of course everything wasn't okay. Her mother never called her. Only an emergency would have her doing so now.

"It's your father," she said. "He's in the hospital. I just thought I should let you know."

Jeanette sat down hard. "What happened?"

"He had an accident on the tractor. He ran it into a ditch and it fell over on top of him. That was about a week ago and—"

"A week ago? And you're just now calling to tell me?"

"We didn't want to worry you," her mother said. "Now,

though, he's got pneumonia and one of those staph infections that people get in the hospital. The doctor said it could be serious and that maybe I should call you."

"Which hospital, Mom?"

She named a Charleston hospital that Jeanette was familiar with. He wouldn't have been transferred from the small regional hospital if it wasn't very serious.

"I'll be there as soon as I can get away."

"You don't need to rush," her mother protested.

"If Dad's sick, I need to see him," Jeanette said, trying hard not to scream at her in frustration. A week? He'd been in a tractor accident a week ago and she was just now finding out about it. What did that say about their family? "I'll be there in an hour. Two, at the most."

She hung up and bit back a curse. Once again, she'd been an afterthought. If her dad hadn't developed complications, if the doctor hadn't suggested that her mother call, she might never have known he was injured in the first place. Her mom was probably already regretting having called.

She hurried down the hall to Maddie's office and quickly explained the situation. "I can do Maxine's treatment, but then I really need to go. Can someone call and cancel the last two appointments on the schedule?"

"I'll do it," Maddie said. "If you want to cancel Maxine, just tell her you have a family emergency."

"She's already here. She has to drive nearly an hour to get here. I can do it," Jeanette said, then realized she was shaking and that her eyes were welling up with tears. Maddie was around her desk in a heartbeat.

"Sit down," she ordered. "Don't even think about going anywhere till I get back. I'll talk to Maxine and see that those calls are made. When you're back you can give Maxine a free facial if you want to, to make up for the inconvenience of her driving all this way."

"Yes, please. Do that," Jeanette said.

After Maddie left, Jeanette let the tears flow unchecked. Some were for her father. Given her mother's tendency to downplay everything, who knew how serious his condition really was? Mostly, though, her tears were for a family that no longer seemed to exist, the one of her childhood that had been loving and close and filled with laughter.

When the door to Maddie's office opened, she mopped her eyes with a tissue and looked up to find Tom there.

"Maddie called me," he said. "I'm driving you to Charleston."

"No," she said fiercely. She could not deal with him right now.

"You're in no condition to drive yourself. Everyone else is tied up, so I'm a last resort. Don't argue. You know you won't win, not against me and certainly not against Maddie."

"Okay, fine, whatever," she muttered, choking back a sob. "What is wrong with me? I can't seem to stop crying."

"You're scared for your father," he said. "You'll feel better once you've seen him for yourself and know exactly how he's doing. Let's go."

"I'm not just scared for my father," she said. "I'm furious with my mother. She kept this from me. She didn't think I needed to know that he'd been in an accident, that the tractor had rolled on top of him. He could have been killed!" Her voice escalated, but she couldn't seem to help it. "And letting me know was some kind of afterthought."

Tom hunkered down beside her and clasped her hands in his. "He wasn't killed. Concentrate on that. As for the infection and the pneumonia, those are setbacks, nothing more."

She shook her head. "And here I thought your mother was terrible," she said wearily. "Mine takes the prize."

"Do you really want to debate about which of our mothers is more dysfunctional?" he asked. "Let's just get to the hospital."

"He'd better not die before I get there," she said angrily. "If he does, I swear I'm never speaking to either one of them again."

Tom didn't say a word. He just met her gaze, one brow lifted. Jeanette giggled. "Okay, now you must think I've really lost it," she said, her fury easing slightly.

He tugged her gently from the chair. "No, I don't. Your reaction is understandable," he told her, sliding a comforting arm over her shoulders and guiding her out of the spa through the back door.

"I don't want to do this," she said, dragging her feet.

He grinned. "Also understandable."

He continued to propel her forward until they reached his car, a nifty little two-seater she'd never seen before except in ads in luxury magazines. It was not the car she'd ridden in before. "You really are rich, aren't you?"

"My parents are," he corrected. "This car was a present when I graduated from college and they still had high hopes for me."

"Can I drive it?"

"Not in your present state of mind," he said, opening the passenger door.

"How fast does it go?"

"Pretty fast," he said, regarding her with amusement. "Planning on running away from home?"

She smiled again. "Could we?"

Tom grinned. "Ask me again after you've seen your father. I might be all for it."

Jeanette's smile faded. "Tom, do you think you can really run away from home, when you don't even know where home is anymore?"

Tom's expression sobered, too. "I honestly don't know," he told her. "I think that's a discussion best left for another day."

"Yeah, I suppose," she said.

She leaned back in the seat and closed her eyes. What she really wanted was to shut off her mind, but unfortunately that seemed impossible. All the way to Charleston, a steady reel of memories played in her head. In most of them, her dad was the way she liked remembering him—doting on her, always ready to comfort her or read her a story or to make her laugh. He'd been so proud of her accomplishments and of Ben's. He'd been steady and sure, the glue that held them all together. She'd never been able to reconcile that man with the one who'd withdrawn from everyone, from life itself after Ben's death.

Tonight she wanted to throw her arms around the dad she remembered from her childhood. Her greatest fear, though, was that she'd find that other man, the one who barely acknowledged her, lying in that hospital bed.

CHAPTER SEVENTEEN

———◆◆◆———

Jeanette hated the antiseptic smell of the hospital. She hated the squishy sound of the nurses' shoes as they hurried up and down the hallways. The sounds of the machines, the steady beeping that monitored breathing and heartbeats, made her cringe. If Tom hadn't maintained a firm grip on her hand, she might have made a run for it.

Outside the door of the intensive care unit, she hesitated. "Maybe I should find my mother first. She's probably in the waiting room."

"If that's what you want to do," Tom said. "I think it's right down the hall."

She stood there, wavering between two equally distasteful choices. "I'm still too mad at my mom," she said at last. "I don't want to start a fight with her first thing."

"Okay, then go on in and spend a few minutes with your dad. I'll find us some coffee." He studied her worriedly. "Or do you want me to come in with you? I can stay in the background. Your dad wouldn't even know I'm there."

"The sign says family members only," she said, pointing out the detailed list of rules posted on the door.

She watched him walk away and had to fight the urge

to run after him. How had he suddenly turned into someone she knew she could count on? Someone she trusted
completely to get her through this crisis? She had no idea.

Finally, she drew in a deep breath, pushed the button
that allowed the doors to whoosh open and stepped into
the high-tech unit with a half-dozen or so small rooms circling a central nurses' station. She stopped a passing nurse.

"I'm looking for Michael Brioche."

"You're family?"

"I'm his daughter."

"Right this way," the nurse said, regarding her with compassion. Her name tag read Patsy Lou. "He's having a tough
time of it, but we're hoping the antibiotics will work. Don't
be too alarmed by all the tubes or the respirator. Everything's there to help him get well."

Jeanette swallowed hard. "He's not breathing on his
own?"

"Don't panic," Patsy Lou soothed. "We're already wean-
ing him off it. It was just temporary while his lungs were
having to struggle to get enough oxygen."

"Is he awake?"

"From time to time, but we're keeping him pretty heavily
sedated most of the time so he doesn't fight the respirator."

Jeanette walked into the small, glassed-in room and
gasped. Both of her father's legs were in casts, one to his
knee, the other to his hip. His skin was pale and waxy. His
thick hair, once as dark as her own, was almost completely
white now. She could hardly recognize the strapping, hardy
man she'd seen a year ago on her last awkward visit home.

She approached the bed slowly, then pulled a chair up
beside it. She was so focused on adjusting to the sight of
this immobilized man and reconciling it with the always-

on-the-go man her father had once been that she was barely aware of the nurse leaving her alone in the room.

"Daddy," she whispered, reaching out to touch his hand, which was lying on top of the sheet. It seemed like the only part of him not attached to some sort of wire or tube. It was warm and callused, the way she remembered. His forearm and hand were tan from working outside, but there was a band of white skin where his wedding band had been. The absence of that ring made him seem even more vulnerable. She linked her fingers with his.

"Oh, Daddy, what have you gone and done?" she asked, tears gathering in her eyes.

To her shock, he stirred slightly, almost as if he'd heard her.

"Don't move," she told him. "Just rest and get your strength back. I'm going to stay right here until you're on the mend."

Maybe it was only the respirator doing its job, but a sigh seemed to shudder through him at her words. She wanted to believe that he knew she was here, that he was glad she was here, but that was probably nothing more than wishful thinking.

It didn't matter, though, because she had no intention of leaving until he was out of danger and could tell her himself to leave, if that was what he wanted. Maybe, though, maybe for once, he would ask her to stay.

When he came back from the cafeteria with three cups of coffee, Tom spotted Jeanette's mother in the waiting room. There was no mistaking her. She had the same dark eyes, though hers were sunken and filled with worry. Her face had the same gamine shape, though on her it appeared gaunt. Her flowered cotton dress was faded from too many washings, but it had been neatly pressed and she still had the lithe figure of her daughter. She was working a rosary through her fingers, her lips moving silently.

Tom approached, but didn't interrupt her. He took a seat nearby and waited until she looked up.

"Mrs. Brioche?"

Confusion filled her eyes, then alarm. "Is it Michael? Is he okay? Has something happened?"

"Everything's okay, as far as I know. I'm sorry if I scared you. I'm not a doctor. I'm a friend of Jeanette's. I drove her to the hospital."

She glanced around the waiting room. "She's here?"

"She's in with your husband now. I went to get coffee. Would you like some?" He offered her a take-out cup. She accepted it, but didn't drink. Instead, she held the cup in both hands, as if absorbing the warmth.

"I'm Tom McDonald, by the way," he told her. "I'm the town manager in Serenity."

"I see," she said distractedly, then stood up. "I should probably get Jeanette. They don't want us staying in there too long."

"I'm sure she'll be out soon," he said. "Why don't you take a break while you can. Would you like something to eat? I can go down to the cafeteria again and bring back some soup or a sandwich."

She shook her head. "You're very kind, but no. I'm not hungry." She glanced toward the intensive care unit. "Since Jeanette is in with her father, I believe I'll go to the chapel. I didn't want to be that far away when no one else was here, you know, in case something happened."

"Then go now," Tom encouraged. "I'll tell Jeanette where to find you."

"You won't be leaving as soon as she's visited with her father?"

"I don't think so."

"Okay, then."

Tom watched her go, then took a sip of his own coffee. It was bitter, but hot. He thought about the encounter with Mrs. Brioche, but couldn't quite decide what to make of it. Obviously she was worried about her husband, but she'd hardly spared a thought for Jeanette and what she might be feeling. He was beginning to grasp what Jeanette had meant about her family being disconnected. By comparison, his own family was a role model. For all of the ridiculous emphasis on social stature, the frequent and volatile disagreements over the choices their son and daughters were making, and the unwelcome intrusiveness, he'd never once doubted that he and his sisters were loved. If anything, they were loved too much. When he'd had that injury playing college baseball, the entire family had gathered at the hospital within hours, driving the doctors and nurses crazy with their questions. His father had wanted to fly in specialists. His mother, predictably, had wanted to bringing in a caterer to be sure he was well-fed. Like so many Southern women of her generation, she equated food with both hospitality and crises.

He looked up and saw Jeanette walking slowly toward him, her cheeks damp with tears. He was on his feet in an instant. "You okay?"

She nodded, her eyes dull. "He's not even breathing on his own," she said, her voice choked. "They have him on a respirator and both legs are in casts. It's awful." She glanced around the waiting room. "I thought my mother would be in here."

"She was. I spoke to her for a few minutes. She went to

the chapel. She should be back shortly or you can go there if you'd like to, maybe say a prayer for your father."

"Let me guess. She was working her rosary beads."

"She was."

Jeanette sighed. "Before Ben died, we hardly ever went to church except on holidays like Christmas and Easter. It wasn't that we weren't religious, I don't think. It was just that most of the year, my dad worked seven days a week trying to keep the farm afloat. My mother worked the fields with him, and when we were old enough, so did Ben and I."

She took a sip of her coffee and closed her eyes. A smile played across her lips. "As hard as we worked, as exhausted as we all were, those were the good days," she said quietly. "After Ben died, everything fell apart. My dad stayed in the fields even longer. When he came inside, he ate, then went to bed without saying a word to my mother or me. My mom suddenly turned to the church. She went every single day. She baked cakes for the bazaars and for the Sunday social hour. I'm not sure if she was trying to save Ben's soul or her own or just escape the dismal atmosphere at home."

"If it gave her comfort..." Tom began.

"But it didn't," Jeanette said. "If something gives you comfort, it should uplift you, don't you think? Instead, it was her way of withdrawing from everything. My dad worked. She went to church. Obviously she's still doing it." She blinked back fresh tears. "I just realized, with his injuries, my dad won't be able to work for a long time. How will he cope without that?"

"One worry at a time," Tom advised. "Let's make sure he recovers first."

As he spoke, he glanced across the waiting room and spotted Jeanette's mother standing hesitantly in the doorway. As much as he hated the way she'd apparently shut

Jeanette out of her life, he couldn't help feeling sorry for her. She looked so terribly lost and alone. His good manners kicked in.

"Mrs. Brioche," he said, standing.

Jeanette's head snapped up. "Mom!"

"Hello, Jeanette," she said, her tone hesitant.

Tom looked from one to the other, saw the longing and anxiety in Jeanette's face, the uncertainty in her mother's. And something else… He leaned down and whispered into Jeanette's ear, "She needs you as much as you need her. I'll go for a walk and give the two of you some time." He touched her cheek. "Okay?"

For a moment he thought she might argue, but then she nodded. "Don't be long, though, please."

"Just a few minutes, I promise."

As he walked past Mrs. Brioche, he gave her hand a reassuring squeeze, then left them. He couldn't help wondering if a few minutes—or even a few days—would give them the time they needed to find their way back to each other.

Despite her earlier anger, Jeanette felt a stirring of sympathy for her mom. She looked so scared, so lost. It reminded her all too vividly of the way she'd looked for months after Ben's death, as if nothing made sense anymore.

"Mom, please sit down," she said at last, when her mother continued to hover in the doorway. "Unless you want to go right in to see Dad."

"No, it's too soon. You just came out. He needs to rest between visits."

"Then sit." She studied the exhaustion in her mother's eyes. "Have you been getting any rest at all?"

Her mother shrugged as she took the seat next to Jeanette. "I was going home at night, but since they moved him into intensive care with the pneumonia and all, I've been staying right here. I manage to close my eyes off and on."

"Why don't you visit with Dad for a little while now and then go home for a few hours and sleep? You'll feel better if you shower and change your clothes, too. I'll stay right here until you get back."

"Your friend, Mr. McDonald, said he drove you. Won't he have to go back?"

"He can leave. Someone will pick me up whenever I'm ready to go." Even though she knew Maddie, Helen or Dana Sue would come in an instant, she also knew it wouldn't be necessary. Tom wasn't going anywhere. She'd seen the stubborn set of his jaw earlier when he'd announced he was driving her over here in the first place. He was the only man she'd ever known who hadn't taken off at the first sign of emotional upheaval. One of these days, when this crisis had passed, she'd have to think about that.

"Are you...? Is he important to you?" her mother inquired, hesitating as if she wasn't sure she had the right to ask.

"He's a friend," Jeanette said.

For just an instant, there was a spark of animation in her mother's eyes. "These days that can mean a lot of different things," she said. "I watch TV. I know all about 'friends with benefits.'"

Taken aback, Jeanette chuckled. "Mom!"

"Well, I do," she said, her lips curving in a way that reminded Jeanette that at one time her mother had had a wicked sense of humor.

"Tom is not that kind of friend," Jeanette said, blushing furiously. "There are no benefits." Though it certainly wasn't for lack of desire, she thought. She knew it could change in a heartbeat if she allowed it.

"Still, I'm glad to know there's someone in your life you can count on," her mother said. She looked as if she might have more to say about that, but instead, she fell silent and stared at her hands. Jeanette had the sensation that an important and rare moment of understanding between them had just slipped away.

When her mother finally met Jeanette's gaze again, she asked, "How did your father seem when you were with him?"

"He was so still," she said. "Not like Dad at all."

"I know. I can barely stand to sit there beside him," her mother admitted. "Even these last years, when he's been so quiet and withdrawn, there was such strength and vitality about him." Her lips curved slightly and her expression turned nostalgic. "Did I ever tell you about the first time I saw him?"

"I don't think so," Jeanette said. Just when she'd reached an age when her mother might have started confiding all sorts of things to her—and she'd been old enough to finally listen—Ben had died and, along with him, any possibility of intimate, revealing conversations.

"It was a summer day, hot as the dickens, and I'd ridden over to the farm with my father. The drive took an hour or more. He wanted to talk to Michael's father about something or other and I just wanted to get out of doing chores at home. Michael rode up on a big ol' tractor wearing these faded jeans and a tight white T-shirt and I thought my heart would stop. He looked right into my eyes as he jumped down, then walked straight up to me and smiled. There was this cocky air about him, but that smile was so slow and sweet it darn near took my breath away. And then, do you know what he said? He told me I was the prettiest girl he'd ever seen and he was going to marry me. Right then and there, just like that. Can you imagine such a thing?"

"Actually, I can," Jeanette said, smiling. She thought of how often Tom had said something equally outrageous to her. "What did you tell him?"

"That he was going to need a whole lot more than pretty words if he expected me to have anything to do with him," her mother responded. "But the truth was, I was a goner and we both knew it."

"How long before you gave in and married him?" Jeanette asked, wondering if she could compare what happened back then to her own situation and learn anything about what might lie ahead.

"Now, there are two parts to that answer," her mother said. "I gave in a whole lot sooner than I said yes to marrying him."

Jeanette couldn't help it. She gaped. "Mother!"

"Well, the marrying had to wait. I was barely eighteen and my parents weren't about to let me marry a man on a whim. We could have eloped, of course, but I wanted a real wedding and your daddy couldn't deny me anything I had my heart set on, so we waited. We got married one year to the day after we met. Your father picked the date, which proved to me just how romantic he was. He'd remembered the significance of it."

"Have you ever regretted it?"

"Not for one single minute," her mother said. "You know, to this day, I climb up on that tractor with him on our anniversary and we take a ride around the farm."

Jeanette thought back. "I remember that," she said with a sense of amazement. "I never understood the significance of it. The rest of the year Daddy couldn't get you anywhere near that tractor."

"I've always had a healthy respect for farm equipment. It's big and dangerous if it's not handled properly. Just look at what happened to your daddy. I count my blessings that it wasn't any worse."

"Mom, why didn't you let me know last week when it happened?" Jeanette asked, unable to keep an accusatory note out of her voice.

A long pause greeted the question. "You've been away so long," her mother said finally. "I suppose your father and I got used to handling things on our own."

Jeanette felt her temper stir. "You say that as if I abandoned you," she said heatedly, unable to stop now that she'd started. "You and Dad shut me out. That's why I left. There didn't seem to be any reason to stay. Even when I mentioned coming home for a visit two months ago, you acted as if you didn't really want me there."

Her mother dropped her head. After a moment, she looked up and met Jeanette's eyes. "I'm sorry. I honestly don't know how things got so mixed up. After Ben died, it seemed like I was lost. I couldn't cope with anything. And what little strength I did have…" She shrugged. "Well, your father needed me."

"*I* needed you, too," Jeanette said.

There was genuine dismay in her mother's expression as she reached for Jeanette's hand. "I know you did. Every time I looked at you, I could see the pain in your eyes, but I had no idea what to do about it. After Ben died, your father and I failed you. There's no question in my mind about that. I don't know that either of us could have done anything differently, but I am sorry. I regret the way we handled things, I truly do."

This hint that her mother had at least *recognized* her pain allowed Jeanette to be more generous than she had been. "You and Dad were grieving. I understood that."

"So were you," her mother said, not cutting herself any slack. "I don't know how we let ourselves pretend otherwise. You'd always been so self-sufficient, I suppose—" She stopped herself, then, "No, that's no excuse. What we did was wrong."

Her mother's words, even though such a long time coming, eased the ache in Jeanette's heart. Healing was still a long way off, but it was a start.

"Maybe I should have tried harder, come home more often, instead of just giving up," Jeanette said, willing to shoulder at least a little of the blame for how things had deteriorated between them.

Her mother squeezed her hand. "You're here now. Your daddy is going to be so pleased when he wakes up and sees you. He's missed you. He's too proud to let you know that, but I know he has." She sighed. "Maybe things will be different now. Maybe us finding our way back to each other is the silver lining to this cloud."

Jeanette wanted that. She really did. She just wasn't sure things could change so easily.

Jeanette spent most of the next week at the hospital. Her father improved quickly and, as her mother predicted, he was clearly happy to find her at his bedside. Sadly, though, after an initially tearful exchange, he retreated once more into silence.

"I think it's depression," Maddie said when Jeanette described it to her. Maddie and the Sweet Magnolias had taken turns coming to the hospital to sit with her on the rare occasions when Tom wasn't by her side.

"You should speak to his doctor about it," Maddie continued. "Or get him into counseling."

"Not going to happen," Jeanette said wearily. "He thinks psychiatrists and psychologists are a waste of time and money. As for drugs, he doesn't have much use for those, either."

"That's just plain crazy," Maddie protested.

Jeanette merely lifted a brow.

"Well, there has to be a way," Maddie said. "Maybe the doctor can slip him antidepressants while he's in the hospital or at the rehab facility getting back on his feet."

"I don't think it's ethical for a doctor to give pills to patients against their will," Jeanette said. "But maybe the doctor will have better luck talking to my father than I would."

"An objective third party is sometimes all it takes," Maddie told her. "Especially if they're wearing a white coat."

Jeanette hoped it would be that easy, because she had a hunch Maddie was right in her diagnosis. She regarded Maddie with gratitude. "Thank you for being so supportive, but you really don't have to keep driving over here," she told her. "I'm only going to stay a couple more days—until my dad's settled at the rehab facility—then I'll be back at work. I really appreciate all the time off you've let me take. I know it's had an impact on spa business."

"Actually I need to talk to you about that," Maddie said. "I wasn't going to get into this until you came back, but since you've brought it up, Dana Sue, Helen and I think we need to hire another person to help with spa services."

Jeanette regarded her with alarm. "I can come back sooner if you need me."

"That's not the point," Maddie said. "It's not just because you've taken a few days off. The spa business is booming. We're turning people away. It's time to expand. And Helen is thinking maybe we ought to open a second spa. If we go forward with that, you'll be overseeing the expansion. Your plate will be pretty full."

"I had no idea you were even considering a new location. Do you know where?"

"No, neither of us has thought that through and we wanted your input, anyway. We all need to sit down and discuss this thoroughly. There are a lot of pros and cons to consider. We'll do that when you're back. In the meantime, I wonder if you know anyone you'd like to hire. Or do you want to advertise? You don't have to tell me now, but let's get on this soon, okay?"

"Yes, sure." Her head was reeling.

Maddie must have noticed her reaction. "Jeanette, are you okay? This is all good news, you know that, don't you?"

Yes, she supposed she did. But it seemed as if the ground was once again shifting beneath her feet. She'd found the stability she wanted in Serenity. She'd found a home and friends. Maddie hadn't said anything to her before about opening this new location and her being in charge.

She was confused. They'd been so pleased about her buying a house because it meant she planned to stay in Serenity. But now…

She looked at Maddie. "I don't want to move," she blurted.

Maddie seemed startled. "Sweetie, you're not moving anywhere. I didn't mean that. I just meant we'd be counting on you to help us plan this. You might have to do a little traveling, but we're not letting you get away, not from the spa and not from us. I thought we made that clear when we celebrated you buying your house in Serenity."

Relief flooded through Jeanette. "I'm sorry. I guess I jumped to conclusions. I'm not thinking too clearly these days. There's been so much happening and I'm having a little difficulty keeping up."

"Which is exactly why you can count on us for backup," Maddie said. "And Tom, too, I imagine. He seems pretty committed."

"He's been great," Jeanette said, thinking of all the hours he'd spent at the hospital, the kindness he'd shown toward her mother, the food he'd brought over from Sullivan's and from some of the finest Charleston restaurants. She suspected Howard was about to have a conniption over the amount of time Tom was away from the office, but if he was pressuring Tom, Tom had never shown it when he was with her.

"Not every man is good in a crisis," Maddie commented. "Something to think about, don't you agree?"

Jeanette grinned at her lack of subtlety. "Yes, Maddie, he gets points for this."

"A lot of points, I hope."

"I haven't kept a running tally," Jeanette said wryly.

Maddie leaned down and kissed her cheek. "Maybe you should," she said. "See you in a couple of days. Call if you need anything."

"Thanks."

"Don't forget that Thanksgiving is coming up soon and you're expected at my house," Maddie reminded her. "Tom, too, if he's not going to be with his family. I'll leave that invitation up to you."

Jeanette laughed. "Since you're so eager to see us together, I'm surprised you're leaving it up to me."

"I can't run your life for you. I can only nudge," Maddie replied.

"And it's killing you, isn't it?" Jeanette teased.

"You have no idea."

Jeanette was still chuckling as she watched her friend walk away. Then she sobered and went to spend a few minutes with her father, who'd finally been moved into a regular room. This sign that he was truly improving had been enough to persuade her mother to run back to the farm for the entire day, rather than the few hours she'd been spending there at night.

Jeanette found her dad staring blankly at the TV, which was tuned to an afternoon talk show she doubted he'd ever watched at home.

"Hi, Daddy," she said cheerfully, pulling a chair up beside the bed.

He barely spared her a glance before turning his gaze back to the TV.

She tried hard not to be daunted by his utter lack of welcome. She noted that his color was better and he'd made an effort to comb his hair. Someone had shaved him, too, so his sunken cheeks were no longer shadowed by stubble.

"The doctor says you're much better. You'll probably be going to rehab in a day or two, so they can help you get back on your feet."

That got his attention. He turned to her with a scowl. "I'm not going to any rehab place. Your mother can take care of me just fine at home."

"Not until you can get around on your own, she can't," Jeanette said firmly. She'd had to fight her mother on this, as well, but she was determined not to give in. The doctor agreed with her. "It'll be too much for her, Dad. She's not strong enough to lift you if you fall or to help you to the bathroom, much less run up and down the stairs all day long."

"Whatever," he muttered. Anger flitted across his face

and he pounded his fist against his cast. "This never should have happened."

"How did it?" she asked. "You're usually so careful."

"My mind wandered, that's all," he said defensively. "Probably not even a few seconds and the next thing I knew, I was down in that drainage ditch by the highway with the tractor on top of me." His eyes turned moist. "Probably how it happened with Ben, too. Now I see that. It only takes an instant to change your life forever. Or end your life."

Jeanette reached for his hand, but he jerked away. "I don't need your pity."

"Dad, I don't pity you," she said indignantly. "I love you. I'm sorry you're hurting so much."

"I'm not in pain," he snapped.

Though she didn't believe that, she hadn't been referring to physical pain. "I meant that your heart is still aching for Ben."

"Well, of course it is," he said with annoyance. "He was my son."

"And you blame yourself for letting him drive that night when the roads had ice on them," she said with sudden insight. Why had she never realized that before? "Dad, what happened was not your fault. The roads were just fine when we left the house for church. We were already at midnight mass when they iced over."

"But the steps were slippery when we came out of the service. I knew the roads would be bad and that your brother wasn't experienced enough to handle it. I should have insisted he leave his car at the church and ride home with us."

"Dad, stop it!" she said, then reminded him, "Ben had already left by the time we got outside. There was nothing you could have done. Nothing!"

"I was his father," he argued, growing more agitated. "It was my job to protect him."

This time when she reached for his hand, she clung to it tightly so he couldn't jerk away. "Dad, you were the best father anyone could ever have. It was an accident, the same way what happened to you was an accident. You have to let it go."

He lifted his stricken gaze to hers. "Your mother still blames me."

"No, she doesn't," Jeanette said, then wondered if that was true. Was it possible that her mother had silently blamed her father all these years and that he'd known that? Was that yet another reason the atmosphere at home had been so tense?

Her father turned away. "You don't know anything about it."

"I know *this*," she said quietly. "Even if you were the tiniest bit responsible for what happened to Ben—which I don't believe you were—you have long since paid the price for it. You need to forgive yourself. And if Mom does blame you, then she needs to move on, too."

Her words were greeted with silence, but then he asked in a voice barely above a whisper, "What about you?"

She stared at him in shock. "Dad, I never blamed you. Not once."

He regarded her with skepticism. "But you've been so angry. You've stayed away for years now, except for those visits when you flit in and out like a hummingbird, moving so fast it's hard to get a glimpse of you."

Jeanette hadn't expected to get into any of this, especially not now, but her father had opened a door that had been shut and locked for years. "I stayed away because you and mom acted as if I didn't matter anymore. It wasn't enough for you that you still had me. It was all about the son you lost." She leveled a look into his eyes. "And don't you dare think for one second that I didn't love Ben. It broke my heart when he died. I needed comfort as much as you and Mom did, but neither of you was there for me. I understood that, at least at first. But it never got better."

She couldn't seem to keep the bitterness out of her voice. "Do you remember when Ben was alive how we celebrated every birthday, how we always went a little overboard at Christmas?"

Her father nodded, really listening for once.

"After Ben died, I never even had a birthday cake again," she said, tears tracking down her cheeks. She swiped at them angrily. "You wouldn't allow me to put up the Christmas tree, much less play any holiday music in the house. The first year, I got that. I really did, but it went on, year after year, right up until I graduated from high school. We didn't even celebrate that. I felt as if I was invisible, as if I'd died right along with Ben."

Her tears flowed unchecked and she buried her face in her hands. "I'm sorry. I shouldn't have gotten into all this now. You're supposed to be recovering."

She felt her father's hand stroke her hair. At first the touch was so light, she thought she must have imagined it.

"I had no idea," he whispered in a choked voice. "None. I was so lost in my own pain, I never gave a thought to what I was doing to you or your mother."

Sensing that there was an opening that might not happen again, she lifted her gaze to his. "Dad, will you do something for me, just one thing?"

"Anything."

"Tell the doctor how you've been feeling since Ben died, let him help you."

His gaze narrowed suspiciously. "Help me how?"

"I'm not sure what he'll recommend," she admitted. "But whatever it is, I want you to promise me you'll do it. Not just for my sake, but for yours. Promise me, okay?"

Stubbornness and pride settled on his face and for what seemed like an eternity, she thought he was going to balk, but then he stroked her hair again and his expression turned sad. "I'll talk to him," he told her.

It was a concession, but she needed more. This was too important for half measures. "And listen to what he says?" she prodded.

He turned away from her, reaching for the pitcher of water on the stand beside his bed. He poured it with a hand that shook.

"Dad," she said. "Please."

He took a sip of water, then frowned at her. "You going to pester me till I say yes?"

"I am," she said.

"Okay, then, I'll listen," he said.

This time she was the one filled with suspicion. She sensed she'd inadvertently left a loophole in there. "Let me rephrase," she said, her heart suddenly lighter. "You'll do what he says."

"I'll listen," he repeated.

"Daddy!"

"Okay," he said at last. "For you I'll follow his advice."

She leaned down and rested her head on his chest. "Thank you, Daddy."

His arms came around her in an awkward embrace. "I love you, sweetheart. I really do. And I am so sorry for not having said that nearly enough."

"You said it now," she whispered, her heart full.

CHAPTER EIGHTEEN

Tom was worried sick about Jeanette. She'd sounded more and more exhausted each time he spoke to her, but to his relief she was finally coming home today, this time for good. She'd made it home for a few hours on Thanksgiving, but had returned almost at once to Charleston to oversee her father's rehab until he was recovering to her satisfaction both physically and emotionally.

Maddie had gone to pick her up this morning because he couldn't get away. Howard wanted the whole committee on the town square while the Christmas decorations were being put into place, even though the work was being done by town employees under Ronnie's supervision.

"I've never decorated a tree in my life," Tom had protested in a vain attempt to get out of standing around observing. "Much less installed snowflakes on light poles."

His words fell on deaf ears.

"You lived in a house that was on the holiday tour every year in Charleston," Howard had reminded him. "I saw pictures of it in the paper. Some of that expertise must have rubbed off."

"It didn't," Tom had said.

"What if there's some sort of crisis or a problem crops up? As town manager, it's your duty to be there tomorrow to deal with it, and that's that," Howard had said. "The tree's being delivered first thing in the morning. I want you on the square when it's unloaded."

Which was why Tom was standing outside at 7:00 a.m. on an unseasonably cold morning that felt more like New York than South Carolina. He could see his breath in the air and not even his thickest sweater and heavy coat could keep the chill out of his bones. Ronnie, thank heaven, had brought a huge Thermos of coffee from Sullivan's, which was helping somewhat. Erik had gone in early to brew it for them.

"Do you look so miserable because you don't want to be here, because you're cold or because you're missing Jeanette?" Ronnie asked as the tree was hoisted off the truck and into place in the center of the square. As its webbing was cut away, the branches spread out in all their fullness. It was impressive, no question about it. It wasn't the tree at Rockefeller Center or the White House, but it wouldn't fit inside any building in town, that's for sure.

"All of the above," Tom said. "I'm the one who should be picking Jeanette up this morning."

"Maddie's capable of bringing her home safely."

"Not the point," Tom muttered.

Ronnie grinned. "You hoping to score more points? I have it on good authority that your balance is already pretty high."

Tom frowned. "Also, not the point."

"Exactly how long has it been since you laid eyes on her?"

"Four days," Tom admitted. "I ran over to the rehab center a couple of days after Thanksgiving, but since then Howard's had me jumping through hoops. You'd think Christmas in Serenity depended on me single-handedly overseeing every detail. You'd think he'd care more about whether the potholes are filled or the bridge is going to fall down."

"You're the town manager," Ronnie reminded him with an amused expression. "He has you to worry about all of those things…and this."

Tom ignored the comment and focused on the huge tree, which was wobbling precariously. "How the devil are they planning to anchor that thing securely? I can see our liability rates soaring if it falls over and crushes a bunch of kids."

"Now, there's a cheery thought," Ronnie said. "You're just what every holiday celebration needs—a genuine Ebenezer Scrooge."

"Believe me, you, Howard and Mary Vaughn more than make up for it. Someone needs to be practical."

Ronnie didn't even try to hide his amusement. "This from the man who dug into his own pocket just to get a Christmas tree that Jeanette had her heart set on."

Tom frowned. "How did you find out about that?"

"Teresa told me you wrote a personal check to the tree farmer when the bill came in."

"That woman has a big mouth. I should fire her."

"But you won't," Ronnie predicted. "She's too good at her job."

"True," Tom conceded just as his cell phone rang. He glanced at caller ID and saw Jeanette's number. He felt his shoulders relax for the first time all morning. "Hey," he said softly. "You on your way home?"

"Maddie's picking me up in a few minutes. I should be there in an hour or so."

"Want to have lunch?"

"I should probably go straight to work."

"Not before you eat," he said. "I know you haven't been

eating properly since you've been hanging around the hospital and I doubt that improved after you got your dad settled in rehab."

"I ate every bit of food you brought me," she said.

"One meal every few days, that's hardly saying much. We'll go to Sullivan's and let Dana Sue fuss over you."

"Aren't you supposed to be supervising the installation of the Christmas decorations?"

"Even a prisoner gets a lunch break," he said. "But come to the square when you get to town. You can chime in with your two cents on everything that's happening. I might as well hear one more opinion."

"Is the tree there?"

"Wobbling around as we speak," he confirmed.

"Is it beautiful?" she asked, her voice suddenly soft and wistful.

"It's the perfect tree," Tom said. "You need to see it for yourself."

"I'll be there soon."

Tom flipped his phone closed, then caught the smug expression on Ronnie's face. "What?" he demanded.

"You are such a goner," Ronnie said. "You've been grumbling from the minute you got here, but less than two minutes on the phone with Jeanette and you go all mushy."

"I did not go mushy," Tom protested.

"Mushy," Ronnie repeated, then grinned. "It's a wonderful thing to see. You've officially joined the club."

"The club?"

"Men Who Love the Sweet Magnolias," Ronnie said. "It's an exclusive group. Damn lucky, too."

Tom thought about the way Jeanette made him feel. Maybe he had gone a little mushy, after all. To be perfectly honest and much to his amazement, it wasn't all bad.

* * *

Dana Sue was hovering over Jeanette as if she'd been gone for a year, rather than the better part of three weeks. Even though Jeanette had ordered only a salad, Dana Sue had brought out meat loaf and mashed potatoes, as well, and insisted that she eat every bite.

"You've lost weight you couldn't afford to lose," Dana Sue said. "I know since dealing with Annie's anorexia I'm a little compulsive about people's eating habits, but you'll float away on a stiff breeze without a little more meat on your bones."

Jeanette squeezed her hand sympathetically. They all knew what she'd gone through with her daughter, but happily Annie was now away at college and had her eating disorder under control. They were certain of it, because her dorm counselors had been alerted to keep an eagle eye out for her and Dana Sue checked in with them regularly. Annie knew she was being watched and, though she'd grumbled about the invasion of privacy, she also understood why it was necessary—for her health and for her mom and dad's peace of mind.

"Dana Sue, stop worrying. I just missed a few meals," Jeanette reassured her. "I'll put the weight back on in no time, now that I'm getting back into my routine."

"I intend to see to that," Tom said.

Dana Sue beamed at him. "Good. Now, I'm going to see if Erik has that apple pie out of the oven. If it's ready, I'm bringing you a slice with ice cream on top."

"Dana Sue, I can't eat another bite," Jeanette protested.

"Tom will help, won't you?" Dana Sue said to him.

"Absolutely."

Dana Sue headed for the kitchen and Jeanette turned to

Tom. "Why did you agree to that? I don't think I can swallow anything else."

"Do you want her worrying about you?"

"No."

"Or me, for that matter. I have a town to decorate. I can't be worrying that you're about to be lifted up by a breeze and blown to the next county."

"I've hardly lost that much weight," she said in exasperation.

He touched a finger to her cheek. "Not quite, but close," he insisted, his expression solemn. "I've missed you. I'm glad you're back."

She swallowed hard under his intense gaze. "I'm glad to be back."

"Things going okay with your father at rehab?"

"He hadn't bolted as of this morning, but that's about all I can say. He's still not happy about being there."

"How are things between the two of you and between you and your mother?"

"Better," she said. "The doctor actually convinced my dad to try an antidepressant. You would have thought he was being forced to swallow poison, but he did it. It's too soon to tell if it will make a real difference, but I have my fingers crossed. The doctor said they might have to try more than one medication to find the best one for my dad." She shook her head. "To think that we wasted all this time when he could have gotten help. I guess neither my mother nor I realized that his grief had crossed the line into depression."

"You were just a kid when this started," Tom reminded her. "And recently you haven't been around. As for your mother, I suspect she's not the first person who didn't know how to handle depression in a loved one, especially when it was much easier to blame it all on grief. That was something she could relate to because she was going through it herself."

Jeanette smiled at his defense of her mother. "She liked you, you know. I could tell. She admired the way you showed up with food and stayed with me." She wasn't putting her own spin on her mother's reaction, either. They'd talked about Tom after most of his visits. She gave him a sideways glance. "She says you're a keeper."

He grinned. "Really? How about you? What do you think?"

"I think I've missed you a lot more than I expected to," she said, her gaze locked with his. "A *lot* more."

He regarded her hesitantly. "Okay," he said slowly. "Just how much are we talking about?"

She kept her gaze steady, then said boldly, "You haven't kissed me yet."

"Easily corrected," he assured her, clasping her head and covering her mouth with his.

What began as a soft, tender kiss quickly escalated into a duel of tongues and gasping breath.

"Holy…" he murmured, breaking away, his expression dazed. "What's gotten into you?"

Her lips curved. "You, I think."

His cell phone rang, but he ignored it.

"Don't you think you ought to get that?" she said, amused by his unfocused gaze.

"You're propositioning me," he began, then looked at her hopefully. "At least I think you are."

"I am."

"And you want me to answer my phone?"

"It's the responsible thing to do," she reminded him. "You are the town manager and today you're in charge of Christmas. That's very important stuff."

"Not compared to you," he insisted as the phone continued to ring.

Jeanette reached into his pocket and pulled the phone out. "Answer it."

He took it from her and shut if off. "Now, what were we discussing?"

"Christmas," she suggested.

"Seduction," he corrected.

"Ah, yes," she said, then sighed. "But I have to go to work."

Tom looked stunned. "Work? You want to go to work *now*?"

"I don't want to, but I really can't put it off any longer."

"You could," Dana Sue said, regarding them with amusement as she stood at the end of the table with a serving of pie in her hand.

Jeanette frowned at her. "How long have you been there?"

Dana Sue grinned and held out the plate of apple pie. "Long enough for the pie to get cold and the ice cream to melt," she said. "To tell you the truth, I got a little warm myself." She met Jeanette's gaze. "I can call Maddie. Tell her you had to go to your apartment to rest. That I *ordered* you to go home to rest."

"Do that," Tom said, his gaze still on Jeanette.

"But—" Jeanette began.

"Do it," he repeated.

Dana Sue looked at her expectantly. "Up to you."

Jeanette felt Tom's hand creep slowly up her thigh under the table. She swallowed hard as heat shot through her. "Do it," she murmured, sliding out of the booth, dragging her coat behind her. Right now she was so warm, she hardly needed it.

Dana Sue fanned herself with a cloth napkin. "Well, damn," she said as they walked away.

Jeanette glanced over her shoulder and grinned. "Be sure you make that call before you go looking for Ronnie."

Dana Sue blushed. "How'd you know?"

"I think it's something in the air," Jeanette responded. Whatever it was, it had her feeling downright giddy with anticipation. One of these days she'd have to think about why she was so ready to sleep with a man she'd been refusing for weeks to date. All she knew at the moment was that it felt right, as if it had been inevitable. She'd work out all the rest of her conflicted emotions later.

Tom kept glancing sideways toward Jeanette as he sped through the streets of Serenity toward her apartment. "You're not going to change your mind, are you?"

She returned his gaze with a solemn expression. "I don't think so."

"Be sure," he suggested. "Otherwise I need to jump in a cold shower, or maybe the lake."

"You'd catch pneumonia in the lake," she said. "We can't have that."

When he cruised to a stop in the parking lot outside her place, he cut the engine, then faced her. "Jeanette, what's changed? Every time I've asked you to go out with me you've had an excuse. Now you're suddenly ready to skip that step completely."

She chuckled. "Do you really want to question this?"

"I don't want to, but I think I have to. Is this because you're grateful that I stood by you while your dad was in the hospital?"

"I appreciated that," she agreed. "But not enough to sleep with you."

He was still bewildered. "Then why? A couple of weeks ago you were still claiming you were not going to get involved with me."

"I think we both know that plan was doomed," she said wryly.

"Really? I thought you were pretty determined to keep me at arm's length."

"I was," she conceded. "That never slowed you down, though." She met his gaze. "You are one fine kisser. Has anyone ever told you that?"

"It's been mentioned," he said. He had no idea why he felt this need to discuss this to death, but something told him they were here for all the wrong reasons, that if he took advantage of this mood she was in, it would backfire in the end. "So, that's what this is about? You like the way I kiss?"

She smiled slowly. "Oh, yeah."

For some idiotic reason, he found that annoying. "I think I need to drop you off at the spa and get back to the town square."

She stared at him in confusion. "Why? What did I say? I just paid you a compliment."

"No, you told me that the prospect of sex with me appeals to you."

"That's a compliment," she insisted.

He frowned at her as he turned the key to start the car. "How would you take it if I told you I was only after you for your body?"

She stared at him, openmouthed with dismay. "That's not what I said," she protested.

"Isn't it?"

She hesitated so long, he could practically see the wheels turning in her mind. "I thought you'd be happy," she murmured. "You'd be getting what you want."

His gaze narrowed. "What is it you think I want?"

"Sex, something casual to fill in the time while you're living in Serenity."

Her words chilled him. "Dammit, Jeanette, do you really believe I think so little of you? God knows I want to sleep with you. I've been wanting that from the first time I set eyes on you, but even then I knew it was going to be about more than that between us."

She regarded him with bewilderment. "You said... I thought... Tom, you're not going to stay here. You've said so. It took me a while to accept that, but now I have. I can deal with it."

Her willingness to settle for so little made him even angrier—at her, at himself, he couldn't be sure which. "You can live with a casual fling?"

She nodded, though she looked miserable.

"Not only do you not know me, you don't even know yourself, if you honestly believe that," he said, throwing the car into Reverse. He had to get away from her before his desire started to outweigh his sense of decency.

He didn't say another word until he pulled up in front of The Corner Spa. Then he turned to her. "This isn't just about sex for me, Jeanette. God help me, but I'm falling in love with you. Let me know when you get on the same page."

She stared at him, her expression stricken, then bolted from the car. He watched her go, then sighed. Well, that had gone well, he thought sourly. And now he had to go deal with a bunch of cheery holiday fanatics. Ho-damn-ho-ho.

Jeanette was still reeling from Tom's words when she blindly made her way into the spa. She stuck her head into Maddie's office.

"Margaritas at my place tonight, okay?" she said, a desperate note in her voice.

"Why are you here?" Maddie asked, then regarded her worriedly. "Never mind. Should I call the others?"

Jeanette nodded. "Please." She didn't think she could deal with all their likely questions right now—especially Dana Sue's—not if she was going to get through the afternoon without falling apart.

"Do you want to talk now?" Maddie asked.

Jeanette shook her head. "Tonight, okay?"

"We'll be there at seven," Maddie promised.

It was what they did. When one of them had a crisis, the others rallied. They listened and offered advice and support, whether it was requested or not. Jeanette looked forward to their unsolicited opinions, because right now she had absolutely none of her own. She was still in shock. Tom thought he loved her? He'd actually said the words. Thrown them in her face, in fact.

She went through the motions with her first client, nodding appropriately, asking an occasional question, but her head wasn't in it. That appointment went reasonably well since the client was new and had no expectations beyond a good facial. She left happy, her skin glowing, her shopping bag filled with expensive products.

Unfortunately Mary Vaughn was next. She took one look at Jeanette and frowned.

"You look awful," she said tactlessly.

Despite her mood, Jeanette smiled. "Gee, thanks."

"Sorry," Mary Vaughn said. "I guess it's understandable with all you've been going through with your dad. I heard he's better, though."

"He is, thanks."

Jeanette concentrated on applying cleanser to Mary Vaughn's face to remove every trace of makeup.

"Did you get a chance to see the decorations going up?" Mary Vaughn asked.

"I caught a glimpse of them before I went to lunch."

"With Tom," Mary Vaughn said, her gaze meeting Jeanette's in the mirror. "I saw the two of you leaving together. I must say, you looked a lot happier then than you do now. Did something happen? You two didn't have a fight, did you?"

"Tom and I are fine," Jeanette said, hoping it wasn't a total lie. They might be on pages so far apart they were in different books, but otherwise they were fine. Really. "Tell me how everything's coming for the festival. Are we ready?"

Mary Vaughn seemed reluctant to drop the subject of Jeanette's relationship with Tom, but she finally relented. "The choirs were battling it out for a while. All of them wanted to sing 'Silent Night,' but I think I finally managed to get through to the directors that there are plenty of familiar choices to go around. I swear it was like dealing with a bunch of superstar divas. I wanted to tell them to get out their stupid hymnals and choose something before I did it for them."

"That would have pretty much ruined the whole holiday spirit of goodwill and cooperation," Jeanette said, amused.

"You're telling me."

"How's it going with Sonny? Are the two of you cooperating for Rory Sue's sake?"

Mary Vaughn's eyes started to shimmer and Jeanette realized she was about to cry. "What is it? Did I say the wrong thing?" she asked.

Mary Vaughn waved off the question. "No, you didn't say anything wrong. It's just that we've been getting along really well."

"And that's a bad thing?"

"It is if you're divorced and your ex-husband has moved on."

"Moved on? You mean he's seeing someone else?"

Mary Vaughn nodded, her expression miserable. "I had no idea, either, until I saw the two of them together at Sullivan's last night," she confided. "She works for him. She used to be a bookkeeper or secretary or something, but she's recently been promoted to sales associate. Judging from the way Sonny was looking at her, I think I know how she got that promotion."

"Mary Vaughn!"

"Well, that's exactly how some women operate," Mary Vaughn said.

Jeanette studied her closely. "Why do you care? The two of you have been divorced for a long time."

"I know," Mary Vaughn said with a sigh. "But lately, since we've been talking again and spending some time together, I've started wondering if maybe it wasn't a mistake. The divorce, I mean."

"You have feelings for Sonny?" Jeanette asked incredulously.

"I do," Mary Vaughn admitted. "How's that for a shocker? And, please, you can't tell another soul. It would be too humiliating. Years of dating and marriage and now, all of a sudden, after we've been divorced forever, I'm realizing what a great guy he is. I mean, I always knew he was great. I'm just realizing how we mesh. We have all this history, which means we don't have to explain every little thing. He gets me. He really gets everything about me. Do you realize how rare that is?"

Jeanette gave her a penetrating look. "Do you?"

"I do now. I have no idea why it took me so long to figure this out. Maybe I had to lose him—not the divorce, but to another woman—before I could see it."

"Do you want him back?"

Mary Vaughn nodded. "I think I do."

Jeanette heard the note of uncertainty and seized on it. "Look, I'm the last person to give anyone advice on relationships, especially today, but you don't sound one hundred percent sure that you want Sonny back. Until you are sure, don't try to break up this relationship you think he's in. Don't try to start something with him yourself."

"I know you're right. I've hurt him more times than you can possibly imagine. I can't do it again." She turned to meet Jeanette's gaze. "But how am I supposed to know for sure if we don't give it another try?"

"Maybe spending all this time with him during the holidays will give you the answers you need," Jeanette suggested.

"Sitting back and waiting isn't my style," Mary Vaughn said. "I favor the direct approach."

"Your decision, of course," Jeanette said. She thought about how well the direct approach had worked for her earlier. It had been a disaster. "But don't risk it unless you're prepared for rejection."

"Sweetie, I've been rejected more times than you can imagine. It's practically a lifestyle."

"Then maybe it's time to go a different way," Jeanette said. "Try the wait-and-see approach."

"I'll think about it," Mary Vaughn promised, then got a worrisome glint in her eyes. "But I will not let that little twit steal my man in the meantime."

Jeanette had to hide a smile at her friend's fierce declaration. Sonny's current relationship, whatever it might be, with this other woman, was doomed.

CHAPTER NINETEEN

—◆—

Jeanette was in her kitchen pouring frozen margaritas into glasses when Dana Sue came into her apartment without knocking.

"What the heck happened?" she demanded as she set a big bowl of guacamole and a bag of chips on the table. "When you left the restaurant this afternoon, you and Tom were practically steaming up the place."

"I know," Jeanette said just as Maddie came in with a plate of thick, decadent brownies.

"Don't say anything until Helen gets here," Maddie said, grabbing her own drink. "You'll just have to start over."

"I'm here," Helen announced. She was taking out assorted cheeses and crackers and putting them on the plates Jeanette had removed from the box in which she'd packed them for her upcoming move. "Now, will somebody tell me why?"

Overwhelmed with gratitude that they'd all come, actually believing for the first time that she really was a Sweet Magnolia, Jeanette looked at each of her three friends, then burst into tears.

"Well, hell," Helen said, reaching for her. The least demonstrative of the group, she patted her awkwardly on the back, then handed her off to Maddie.

Dana Sue stuffed a handful of tissues into her hand. "Let's go in the other room and sit down. Then take a sip of your drink and start at the beginning."

Everyone picked up some of the snacks and Jeanette trailed behind with the pitcher of margaritas, which was probably a mistake. She seemed to be a little unsteady on her feet, to say nothing of having her vision blurred by tears.

"Okay, then," Dana Sue said when they were seated. "You and Tom were headed straight to bed last time I saw you."

"You and Tom were planning to have sex?" Maddie said, sounding shocked. "Today? How did I miss that? I thought you were just having lunch. Then Dana Sue called and told me you were going home to rest… Oh, I get it."

Dana Sue grinned and, since Jeanette seemed incapable of speech, added, "Exactly. One thing led to another."

"So I gather," Maddie said. "It must have been some lunch."

"Then what happened?" Helen prodded. "Wasn't he any good at it?"

Jeanette choked back a laugh, or maybe it was a sob. "I don't know," she admitted. "He… This is so humiliating."

"He what?" Helen demanded impatiently, falling into her courtroom style of interrogation, which was effective on witnesses but hell on friends.

"Let her talk," Maddie commanded, nudging Helen in the ribs.

"He turned me down," Jeanette admitted sheepishly. "And then he said he loved me. Or thought he did. Or something like that. I was too embarrassed by then to pay much attention to what he was saying."

"The man said he loved you and you didn't hear the details?" Dana Sue asked incredulously.

"*After* he refused to sleep with me," Jeanette reminded her.

"Okay," Maddie soothed. "Did he say why he didn't want to sleep with you? He must have had a reason. Everyone in town knows he's been lusting after you since he got here."

Helen nodded. "They were taking bets in Wharton's on how soon you'd cave in."

Jeanette regarded her with dismay, though she wasn't sure why. They took bets on everything at Wharton's. They'd had a pool on whether she'd go out with him, so why not one on whether she'd have sex with the man?

Maddie frowned at Helen. "Did you have to bring that up now? It's hardly the time."

"I was just reporting the facts," Helen grumbled.

Maddie held Jeanette's hand tightly. "Pay no attention to her. If she's listening to gossip, then she's clearly had too much time on her hands lately. What did Tom *say* to you?"

Jeanette gulped down the rest of her margarita, then blurted, "He…he said I only wanted him for his body."

The other three women stared at her, then turned to each other. Maddie was the first to try futilely to suppress a laugh. Then all three of them were laughing at her…or maybe with her. It was kind of hard to tell, since she finally saw the humor in it and began laughing, too. She laughed until her stomach ached.

"I think I'm a little tipsy," she finally murmured.

"Not on one margarita!" Helen declared. "Even if these are strong enough to rouse the dead."

"I think you've missed the most important part of what

happened this afternoon," Maddie said when the laughter finally died. "Tom said he's in love with you. Isn't that what counts?"

Jeanette poured herself another margarita, then sighed. "I really, really wanted to sleep with him, even if he does have the mother from hell." She gave them a wobbly smile. "Did I tell you that my mother likes him and he likes her? That is so much better than me hating his mother."

"Maybe she *is* drunk," Helen murmured. "Is this your second margarita, Jeanette?"

"No, I believe I had one or two before you got here."

Helen rolled her eyes. "Then this conversation is probably pointless. You should go to bed and we can try it again tomorrow."

"But I need advice now," Jeanette argued.

"Why? Is Tom on his way over tonight?" Helen asked.

"No, but..."

They watched her expectantly.

"I don't know why," she finally admitted.

"That's it," Helen said, standing up. "Take a shower and go to bed."

"I'll stay," Dana Sue volunteered. "To make sure she doesn't drown. After all, this is partly my fault. I practically gave them my stamp of approval and sent them on their way this afternoon."

Jeanette rested her spinning head against the back of the sofa as Maddie and Helen cleaned up the snacks, then kissed her good-night.

"Okay, let's go," Dana Sue said, tugging on her arm.

"Go where?"

"Shower, then bed."

Jeanette balked. "Don't want to sleep with you," she murmured.

"Heaven forbid," Dana Sue responded.

Jeanette sighed. "Just Tom," she said as she stepped beneath the icy water that Dana Sue had turned on. She jumped right back out. "That's cold," she protested, shivering.

Dana Sue pushed her back in. "You'll thank me in the morning."

A few minutes later, wearing an oversize T-shirt, she crawled into bed and accepted the aspirin Dana Sue held out.

Dana Sue touched her cheek. "You and Tom will work this out," she promised.

"Don't know how."

"You'll talk. You'll get your signals straight."

"Same page," Jeanette murmured sleepily, then closed her eyes. They just needed to get on the same page. If her head didn't hurt so much, maybe she could figure out which one that was.

Tom was sitting behind his desk, staring morosely at a report on the town's failing infrastructure, when Cal, Ronnie and Erik walked in, their expressions grim.

"What happened to the three of you? Bad news?" he asked.

"You hurt Jeanette," Cal declared.

Tom blinked at his somber tone. "And now what? You have to hurt me?"

Ronnie grinned. "Something like that. We're supposed to have a come-to-Jesus talk with you."

"Though for the life of me, I'm not entirely sure why any of this is your fault," Erik said. "You told her you love her, didn't you?"

"I did," Tom agreed, not the least bit surprised that they

knew that. He was beginning to understand the Serenity grapevine. Even the Internet operated at a slower pace.

He regarded them with a challenging expression. "Why is any of this your business?" He waved off the question as soon as he'd uttered it. "Never mind. Stupid question. It's all about Sweet Magnolia unity or something like that."

"Exactly," Cal said. "There was apparently quite a party at Jeanette's last night. It involved margaritas and whatever else these occasions require. Jeanette cried. That was enough to get you in trouble, my friend."

"Jeanette cried?" Tom echoed.

"That's the way I heard it, too," Erik confirmed.

"So what happens now?" Tom asked. "Tar and feathers?" He wasn't entirely joking. These men might strike him as reasonable human beings, but their wives, collectively, scared the daylights out of him.

"Beats me," Ronnie said. "I think we're supposed to make sure you don't do it again."

"Will my promise suffice?" Tom asked.

Erik shrugged. "Works for me."

"Me, too," Cal said.

"Okay, then," Ronnie said, apparently satisfied, as well. "I need to get to work."

"Me, too," Cal said.

Erik sighed heavily. "Which leaves me to report in that the deed is done, right? You guys do know that Helen is the queen of skepticism, don't you?"

"You could just tell Dana Sue when you see her at work," Ronnie suggested. "Let her spread the word."

"And hear about that for a month from my wife?" Erik demanded. "I don't think so. I'll tell Helen." He gave Tom a warning look. "If she's not satisfied, she might be on your doorstep before the day is out. Prepare yourself. That woman has interrogation skills that make the Inquisition look tame."

"Duly noted," Tom said. "How about shooting a few hoops tonight? You guys game?"

"Shouldn't you be making amends tonight?" Cal asked.

Tom thought about that. "I think maybe I need to see how the rest of the day goes before trying that. I can still fit in a game of hoops."

"Count me in," Ronnie said.

"I'll be there," Cal said. He glanced at Erik. "You off tonight?"

Erik nodded. "I'll be there as long as Helen doesn't decide to shoot the messenger." He grinned at Tom. "You mind if I work a little spin on this, tell her you're ready to grovel, that you looked downright miserable?"

"Spin away," Tom said. Whatever Erik said, it probably wouldn't be far from the truth. Once his anger had vanished, he'd been left feeling foolish and miserable. He'd had an opportunity to sleep with the woman he was falling in love with and he'd blown it. Okay, maybe an innate sense of decency and a desire for her to actually reciprocate his feelings had called for that, but his body was still ticked off as hell about it.

"And we can still count you in to help Jeanette move on Saturday, right?" Cal asked. "Now that she's back, the closing's been rescheduled for Friday, so Saturday is the big day."

"Of course," Tom assured him.

Erik nodded. "I'll tell Helen that, too. You need all the points you can get."

"I thought I'd accumulated a lot of points already."

Cal regarded him with pity. "You made her cry, man.

There aren't enough points in the world to make up for that."

Tom shook his head. For a man who'd always had a way with women, it appeared he had a lot to learn when that woman was a Sweet Magnolia.

Jeanette had heard about the chat her friends' husbands had had with Tom. She had no idea what they'd been told to get them all riled up or what they'd said to Tom, but it was just one more humiliating moment in a string of them she seemed to be having lately. Fortunately, though, she didn't have a lot of time to think about it. When she wasn't at work, she was packing for the move to her new house.

The closing had gone smoothly yesterday afternoon and the move was slated for first thing this morning. All the guys were pitching in. Though Maddie had assured her that Tom still intended to help, Jeanette wasn't convinced he'd show up. Nor was she sure she wanted him to. In fact, right now, she wasn't sure she ever wanted to set eyes on him again, excellent kisser or not. This whole thing about him thinking he was falling in love with her had confused her.

She heard the rumble of the rental truck and looked outside to see Cal and Erik piling out of the cab. Ronnie and Tom were nowhere to be seen.

"I knew it," she muttered, unable to contain a sigh of disappointment.

Since she didn't want either of the men to see her dismay, she smiled brightly as they came inside.

"I have coffee and pastries in the kitchen," she told them. "I'm so grateful you're helping. I think everything's pretty well packed up, so hopefully it won't take long. I didn't make the boxes too heavy, so I can carry those down, if you'll deal with the furniture."

Cal gave her a chiding look. "You're not carrying anything. That's why we're here. In fact, you should probably head on over to the house and figure out exactly where you're going to want all this stuff when we get there."

"I marked the boxes," she told him.

Erik shook his head. "But you don't want piles of boxes in every room. It's overwhelming. Pick one room and let us put all the boxes in there. We can stack 'em according to where they're to go eventually. Then you take one box at a time wherever it belongs and unpack it. That way ninety-nine percent of the house will feel as if it's livable."

She beamed at him. "That's an excellent idea. I wish I'd done it that way on other moves."

"Okay, then, you head on over and decide about that room. You probably need to supervise the others, too."

She regarded him blankly. "The others?"

"Helen, Maddie and Dana Sue are scrubbing the place, and Ronnie and Tom are painting. They'll help us unload when we get there."

"But…" She'd had no idea they were planning to do any of that. All she'd counted on was a little muscle to help with the actual move. "They're cleaning and painting?"

"As we speak," Cal said. "And Tom was making noises about painting one of the bedrooms navy blue. I'm not sure that's what you had in mind, but he said it suited him."

"What on earth…?" Then she remembered his determination to share the house with her. She'd been certain she'd squelched that idea weeks ago. And, if not then, her attempt to seduce him and his reaction to it should have killed his scheme completely. Apparently she'd been wrong.

She grabbed her purse off the dining-room table. "You're sure you don't need me here?"

Erik grinned. "Not as badly as you're needed over there," he said.

"We have this under control," Cal assured her.

She was almost out the door when Cal called after her. "Hey, Jeanette, if you decide to strangle him, don't do it before we get there, okay?"

"So you can protect him?"

Cal shook his head. "No, so we can watch."

"Yeah, it's kinda enjoyable not being on the receiving end of anger for a change," Erik added. "The rest of us paid our dues, so why not him?"

Jeanette shook her head. "Who are you two trying to kid? Your wives adore you."

"Doesn't mean we don't tick 'em off from time to time," Cal said. "You might want to remember that."

"Meaning?"

"An occasional tiff goes with the territory," Erik explained. "Love's complicated."

"And rocky," Cal added.

"Nobody said anything about love," Jeanette retorted.

Cal grinned. "Yeah, they did. At least that's the way I heard it."

"Me, too," Erik confirmed.

"Your wives have big mouths," she said.

Erik laughed. "Tell us something we don't know. You gotta love 'em, though."

Jeanette sighed. "Yes, I do."

Apparently they were going to protect her interests in whatever way they thought the situation required, even if it meant spilling all her humiliating secrets.

Tom had already put one coat of navy blue paint on the walls of the downstairs guest room when Jeanette came flying in and screeched to a halt, her eyes wide, her expression indignant.

"What do you think you're doing?" she demanded.

"Isn't it obvious?"

"Navy blue? Who wants to sleep in a room that dark?"

"I do," he said.

"You are not sleeping in this room, or in this house, for that matter."

"Not what you were suggesting the other day," he reminded her.

"A gentleman would not bring that up."

"Then I guess we know what that makes me," he replied as he kept right on rolling the paint.

"An obnoxious pig," she suggested sweetly.

Tom hid a smile. At least she was speaking to him. He hadn't been sure she would.

She marched up and stared at him. "Are you smiling? Please tell me you are not smiling."

"I'm not smiling," he said, though his lips kept twitching.

"Tom McDonald, this is not even one tiny bit amusing. I don't want you getting ideas about me or about this room."

"Too late," he said. "I have plenty of ideas. You gave me most of them."

"Well, get rid of them."

"Sorry, darlin', I can't do that, especially not with you standing right up in my face breathing fire. That kind of makes me want to kiss you."

She backed up a step, looking alarmed. "No kissing."

He regarded her solemnly. "You seem to be having trouble making up your mind lately."

"Oh, go to hell," she said, and flounced out.

This time he couldn't stop the grin that spread across his

face. He didn't even try. That had gone well. Better than he'd expected, in fact.

He'd been thinking a lot about his own stupidity the other day. Next time she made him an offer, he had no intention of refusing it. Of course, given the outcome last time, coaxing her into making another offer might take a while. Since he wasn't an especially patient man, he was just going to have to do everything in his power to speed up the process. Riling her from time to time to get her juices stirring looked as if it might work out nicely. Just now she'd appeared to be about one taunt away from another very memorable lip-lock.

Though Jeanette didn't have nearly enough furniture to fill the house, what she did have was in place and gleaming with furniture polish. The hardwood floors shone and the downstairs rooms had all been freshly painted, including that ridiculous navy blue guest room. It actually looked nice with the shiny white woodwork, but she was not about to admit that to another living soul. In fact, she'd deliberately chosen that room to store all the boxes, to make sure Tom knew he wasn't welcome to move into it. It was almost impossible to squeeze past the door.

The empty pizza boxes and beer bottles had been taken away with a full load of trash and the first batch of empty packing boxes. Now she was all alone in her new house. She gazed around and her eyes filled with tears. It was a little overwhelming to realize this belonged to her, that she actually had a cozy home in which she could build whatever kind of life she wanted.

The last of the CDs finished playing and silence fell. After so many years in cramped apartments, with neighbors only a couple of layers of wallboard away, it felt a little eerie to be so totally alone. When someone knocked lightly on the front door, she jumped nervously.

She pulled aside the lacy curtain on the door to peek through the glass panel. Tom stood on the front porch, a bottle of champagne and a bouquet of flowers in hand. Her heart lurched at the sight of him. He wasn't supposed to be back here, not when she was feeling a little too alone and vulnerable.

She opened the door a crack. "What are you doing here?"

"I wanted to help you celebrate your new home."

"You were here when we toasted earlier. That'll do."

"I thought a more private celebration was in order."

She couldn't seem to tear her gaze away from the hopeful gleam in his eyes. "You confuse me," she murmured.

His mouth curved. "Ditto."

She considered her options and finally stepped aside to let him pass. "You can stay for a few minutes. Long enough for one glass of champagne."

"Okay," he said solemnly.

"What's in the bag?"

"Champagne glasses. I wasn't sure if you had any or if they were unpacked." He withdrew two elegant crystal flutes. Something told her they were old and valuable.

"You been raiding your mother's china cabinet?"

He laughed. "Something like that."

She spotted the Waterford mark on the bottom. "Nice taste."

"Glad you approve," he said as he popped the cork on the champagne and filled the glasses to the brim. He grinned at her reaction. "Since you're limiting me to one, I want to make it last."

He handed a glass to her, then lifted his own. "To you finding all the happiness you deserve in your new home."

"Thank you," she said and touched her flute to his, then sipped the champagne.

Finally she risked looking into his eyes and asking the question that had been on her mind all day. "What are you really doing here? I mean the whole day, not just right this second."

"Isn't that obvious?"

"Not to me."

"I'm trying to apologize."

"For?"

"Turning you down. Embarrassing you. Making you think for one single second that I didn't want you." He met her gaze. "How am I doing?"

"It's a nice start. Keep going."

He leaned forward, his expression solemn. "You took me by surprise. I'd wanted you for so long and there you were, all eager and willing, and then I had to go and question your motives. It was stupid."

She sighed. "No, actually, it wasn't. You were right to question me. And you were right that I was going to wind up regretting what we did if it didn't mean anything."

"It would have meant something," he told her emphatically. "There's no way it couldn't, not between us."

"But it wouldn't have meant what it should," she argued. "It wouldn't have been a commitment. It wouldn't have been the first step toward forever."

"You sound so sure of that."

"I am sure. You're an ambitious man. You have your entire future mapped out. And I admire that, I really do. It just seems there's no place in that future for me."

She half expected him to argue, but he didn't. He nodded, which confirmed everything she feared.

"A few weeks ago I didn't understand how you could reach that conclusion," he said. "I think I do now."

"Oh?"

"You told me what happened after your brother died," he said simply. "I know how your folks pushed you aside in their grief, how they made you believe you didn't matter. That must have hurt terribly."

"You have no idea how much," she said.

"That kind of hurt leaves scars," he said. "It makes you tough. You're not about to let anyone do that to you again, make you feel less important than you deserve to be."

"You're wrong," she said. "For a long time, I thought that's what I deserved. I walked straight into relationships I knew from the first were doomed. And, of course, I got exactly what I'd expected. I was second-best to a career, to some other woman, to all sorts of things. When I moved here after one more disastrous relationship, I made a vow to myself that I was done with that."

"So to protect yourself, you decided not to let anyone get close," he said. "Especially a bad risk like me."

"Exactly."

"What if I could prove to you that I'm not as bad a risk as you think?"

"I don't think you can. You've already spelled out your future plans. You can't take it back now."

"Will you let me try?"

"I don't think there's any way to unring that particular bell. Your plans are your plans," she said miserably.

"Plans change," he said simply.

"Not overnight, they don't."

"True," he said. "It's going to take time for me to convince you that we can work this out."

"But don't you see? That's the one thing we don't have.

You're moving on, maybe not tomorrow or next month or even next year, but you will go. I've found the place where I want to stay forever."

He seemed momentarily daunted by her words, but then he reached for her hands and clasped them in his. "What if I could prove to you that the place you want to be forever is in my heart? If I can prove that, then where we wind up living won't matter."

Jeanette was tempted by the sweetness of his words, the earnestness in his expression, but the risk was flashing neon red right in front of her eyes, too. She'd taken that leap of faith before, too many times. She'd trusted her heart and ignored the facts. She couldn't do that this time.

"It's not just about a house, or even a town," she told him.

"I know that. It's about you mattering more than anything else," he said. "And what I'm telling you is that I think you do. There's only one way we can find out for sure, and that's time."

"There are so many obstacles," she said.

"Name one."

"Your mother."

"An annoyance, not an obstacle." He made a gimme movement with his hand. "What else?"

"You're a Christmas grouch."

He laughed at that. "So are you."

She shook her head. "Not so much. For the first time in years, I'm finally remembering how much I loved Christmas when I was little. I think the tree was the turning point for me. One whiff of that scent, one look at that magnificent tree, and it all came flooding back."

"Okay, then, if Christmas is that important to you, it's a couple of weeks of the year. I can fake it."

"Remind me to use that line on you if we're ever in bed together," she said dryly.

Her words seemed to give him pause. But after a moment he went on, "How about this, then? From now through New Year's we act like a couple. We do the whole holiday thing however you want. We spend time together and with our respective families. We hang out with our friends. I'll even suck it up and go Christmas caroling if that's what you want."

"Now, there's a noble sacrifice," she said. "I have to be nice to your mother and you have to sing in public. Where's the fairness in that?"

"I'll throw in a lot of ho-ho-ho's when we kick off the Christmas festival," he added. "I will be the epitome of good cheer."

The thought of seeing him trying to stuff his bah-humbug attitude was too tempting to resist. At least that was her excuse for relenting.

"Okay," she said at last.

His expression brightened. "Can I move in?"

"I don't remember sex or my guest room being included in the negotiations," she told him.

"Are you sure? I thought they were implied."

She gave him a wry look. "You're a seasoned negotiator. I doubt you leave anything open to interpretation. No sex, no room."

"You sure you don't want to amend our verbal contract?"

"One hundred percent sure," she assured him. "But check back with me from time to time."

As she took in that appealing grin on his face and the heat in his eyes, something told her it was going to be way too easy for him to change her mind.

CHAPTER TWENTY

The Christmas festival committee gathered in the town hall conference room for its last meeting on the Monday before the event was to kick off on the second Saturday in December. Howard was in his element, as anxious as a child for the time when the tree lights would be turned on, the town square filled with vendors and all of downtown Serenity would be subjected to nonstop holiday music. He was clearly driving Tom nuts with his nitpicking attention to detail.

Listening to him go on and on, Mary Vaughn wondered why she'd ever found her father-in-law so intimidating. He was just an overgrown kid.

"Has anybody checked to see exactly what time it gets dark now?" Howard asked, directing yet another question toward Tom. "This thing needs to be scheduled right down to the second. We want to be sure to throw the switch on the tree and all the other lights right then and not a minute too soon. Maximum effect, that's the ticket. We want to wow the crowd."

Before Tom could reply, Howard turned to Mary

Vaughn. "Is Rory Sue coming home this weekend? She used to love the lighting of the tree."

"She says she has to study for her last two finals," Mary Vaughn told him. "They're next week. She'll be home right after that."

Howard didn't even try to hide his disappointment. "I suppose there's no way around that," he grumbled. "It's a shame, though. Having her here would have gotten the season off to a good start."

Mary Vaughn was beginning to have her doubts about whether that was possible. Rory Sue had refused to give up on the ski trip. Every conversation had turned into a battle. None of the plans Mary Vaughn and Sonny had been making seemed to please her. Mary Vaughn was beginning to fear her daughter would stubbornly refuse to have a good time just out of spite.

"That is so lame" was her most frequent comment. Mary Vaughn had heard it so often, she'd had to bite her tongue to keep from ordering Rory Sue to adjust her attitude or else. Or else what? That was what had kept her silent. She could hardly ground her. And if she told her not to bother coming home if she couldn't be pleasant, Rory Sue would probably whoop with joy and head straight to Colorado with her friend.

As the meeting dragged on, Mary Vaughn sank even deeper into her funk. She'd really wanted this holiday season to be special for her daughter, for her whole family, for that matter. As the weeks had passed and she and Sonny had made their plans for an old-fashioned Christmas filled with nostalgia and tradition, she'd found herself looking forward to recapturing what had once been such a special time for all of them. For the first time in years, they would have a real family celebration. She hadn't realized until recently how much she'd missed that. Nor had she realized how much she'd missed making plans with Sonny, having someone who actually listened to her ideas and wanted to please her.

She had taken so much for granted during her marriage. After it had ended, she'd told herself that none of it mattered, that she was capable of doing just fine for herself and Rory Sue on her own. And she was. Financially she'd done better than fine. But it had been so damn lonely.

When at last the meeting ended, Jeanette turned to face her. "What's going on?" she asked. "You look miserable."

Mary Vaughn was so used to covering up her feelings, she almost denied it, then sighed instead. "I am."

"Come on," Jeanette said. "Let's go to the spa and get some tea and you can tell me what's going on."

"Why?" she asked, bemused by the offer.

"Because you look as if you could use a friend," Jeanette said simply.

Totally unexpected tears welled up in Mary Vaughn's eyes. A friend? That was exactly what she needed. After too many years of pouring her energy into finding a man, she realized once again how desperate she was for a friend. She longed for someone who could give her honest advice, share confidences with her and make her laugh the way the Sweet Magnolias all did for each other.

"You don't need to pretend to be my friend," she told Jeanette out of habit. She'd spent a lifetime trying not to let anyone see her neediness.

"I'm not pretending," Jeanette said impatiently. "I thought we'd settled that ages ago. Just because we haven't managed to schedule time for the movies or lunch doesn't mean we're not friends. Now let's get out of here before someone else, namely your ex-father-in-law, sees you crying and starts asking questions you don't want to answer."

"I'm not crying," Mary Vaughn said with a sniff, then disproved the claim by wiping tears from her cheeks.

Jeanette set a brisk pace for the walk from Town Hall to the spa, then slipped around the side of the building and pointed to a table. "Sit. It's a little chilly to be sitting outside, but we won't be interrupted out here. I'll get our drinks and be right back."

Mary Vaughn sat down at the wrought-iron table and waited. Jeanette returned with two glasses of sweet tea and two muffins filled with plump blueberries.

"I can't eat that," Mary Vaughn protested automatically.

Jeanette set the muffin in front of her anyway. "Comfort food," she said succinctly. "Now tell me what's going on. Does this have something to do with Rory Sue?"

It did…and it didn't. Mary Vaughn tried to figure out exactly how to explain it. She broke off a piece of muffin and thought as she chewed it, practically sighing at the moistness and the burst of blueberry flavor.

"It started with Rory Sue," she said eventually. "She wanted to go away for the holidays."

"Skiing," Jeanette recalled.

"Exactly," she said, then distractedly put more of the muffin into her mouth. "And since I didn't want her to go, I got together with Sonny and we started making all these plans, you know, to make this the best Christmas ever."

Jeanette nodded. "Okay. I'm with you so far. Hasn't that turned out the way you wanted it to? Isn't Sonny cooperating? You told me he had been."

"Sonny's been great," she said, then added with emphasis, "Really, really great."

Jeanette's eyes widened. "You're sleeping with him?"

"No," she admitted, though she could feel heat climbing into her cheeks. She lowered her voice, even though there was no one else on the patio. "But I want to. All of a sudden I want my ex-husband. How bizarre is that?"

"Come on, Mary Vaughn, there's nothing bizarre about it. Did you see me act shocked when you told me the other day that you wanted him back? He's attractive, successful, funny," Jeanette said, not sounding nearly as horrified as Mary Vaughn had expected her to be. "Finding yourself attracted to him shouldn't be a huge shock."

"But I wasn't this attracted to him when we were married," Mary Vaughn confessed before swallowing another bite of the blueberry muffin. "I didn't appreciate him. He was just Sonny, the guy who'd loved me forever, my safe haven."

"And now?"

"He's sexy. He makes me laugh. And he gets me, you know? He knows my whole history. I used to think that was a drawback, but now I really value not having to explain myself or hide what I'm feeling. I can be completely open with him because I know he'll never judge me." She buried her face in her hands. "I told you all this before, didn't I? You must be sick of listening to me. It's just that there's no one else I can talk to about it, try to work it out, you know? Sometimes you have to say things aloud, test them out. Walking around the house talking to myself isn't getting the job done. It's just not the same."

"I know," Jeanette said soothingly. "Sounds to me as if you've grown up and fallen in love."

Mary Vaughn sighed heavily. "Yeah, that's what I'm afraid of."

"Afraid? Why?"

"Because Sonny's moved on. I told you I saw him with

a woman, didn't I? I still don't know exactly what's going on with the two of them. I've tried to find out, but no one I've asked seems to know anything about it. All I know for sure is that he doesn't want me anymore. I killed whatever it was he once felt for me."

"How can you be sure of that if you haven't told him how you feel?" Jeanette asked reasonably.

"I just know, okay?" Mary Vaughn said. "He's not picking up on any of my signals."

"What are they? Smoke signals?" Jeanette joked. "Come on. He's a guy. You have to be direct."

Mary Vaughn shook her head. "Look, I floated the idea past him, asked him if he'd ever thought the divorce was a mistake and he said no. I can't push this. I won't let him laugh in my face."

"Maybe he won't laugh now that you've spent all this time together," Jeanette countered. "Relationships evolve. People change. They start looking at things differently over time. Whatever was true once might not be any longer. You won't know unless you have a serious conversation with him about this."

Mary Vaughn wished she could believe that. She reached for more of the muffin, then realized that only crumbs were left on the plate. "I'm telling you he's moved on," she said despondently. "He's the one who wanted the divorce. I know everyone in town thought I dumped him, but it wasn't that way. He left me."

"Has he remarried?"

"Of course not," she said indignantly. "I would never go after a married man." She frowned at Jeanette's doubtful expression. "Ronnie Sullivan was *not* married to Dana Sue when I went after him. Why does everyone keep forgetting that? They were divorced."

"Okay, but that's beside the point, anyway," Jeanette said. "Let's stick to you and Sonny. So, you think he's seeing someone seriously…"

"I'm not a hundred percent sure about the woman from work. Maybe."

"Yet he's going to spend all this time with you during the holidays," Jeanette said. "So what if they've been on a few dates? I thought you were determined to fight for him. He can't be that serious about her if he's spending the holidays with you. She wouldn't stand for it. That tells me he hasn't moved on, at least not beyond the point of no return. If you really want him back, if you really think the divorce was a mistake, then you're going to have to take a risk and put your feelings on the line. Not long ago, you were ready to do that."

For a woman who could be totally direct in business, Mary Vaughn had little experience with taking that kind of risk in her personal life. Well, except for Ronnie, and look how that had turned out. The whole town had laughed at her behind her back.

"Have you ever done that?" she asked Jeanette.

Jeanette grinned, her expression sheepish. "Fairly recently, as a matter of fact."

"How did it go?"

"Not so well, to be perfectly honest."

Mary Vaughn regarded her with dismay. "Not exactly the encouragement I was hoping for."

"Yeah, well, it wasn't a big thrill for me, either, but it *did* open the lines of communication. And it reminded me of something my mother used to tell me all the time—that anything worth having is worth fighting for."

The familiar words struck a chord with Mary Vaughn. How many times had she said those exact words to herself years ago when she was struggling to make a life for herself after the hell of her childhood? She'd continued to scramble and fight for the things she wanted over the years, but somehow, when the goal mattered the most, she'd lost sight of that message. She'd talked herself out of fighting for what she wanted because she was afraid of losing.

She finished the last of her tea, then stood up and gave Jeanette a fierce hug. "Thank you so much."

"All I did was listen."

"No, you were a friend when I really needed one," Mary Vaughn said. "I can't begin to tell you what that means to me. Look, we're having an open house at my place after the tree-lighting ceremony. I hope you'll come. Bring Tom."

"I'd like that," Jeanette told her. "I'll discuss it with him and get back to you."

"No need. Just show up if you can."

"Will Sonny be there?"

"That's the plan," Mary Vaughn said. And she knew she could count on it, because he was the most reliable man she'd ever known.

Of course, if she told him all the things she'd been feeling lately, it was entirely possible he'd take off and spend the holidays as far away from Serenity—and her—as he could get.

The thick invitation arrived with the afternoon mail. Tom stared at the formal calligraphy and knew without even glancing at the return address that it was from his parents. They always launched the holiday season on the second Saturday in December with a lavish party that he was expected to attend. Since that was the opening night of the Christmas festival, he was going to have to decline this year and the resulting scene was likely to be unpleasant. He might as well get it over with now.

He picked up the phone and dialed his mother's private line. During this busy social season, she had a secretary answering their home phone and keeping track of her schedule.

"Hello, Mother," he said when she picked up at once.

"Darling, how are you?" she said, sounding pleased. "I was expecting to hear from you today. Did you get your invitation?"

"It just came."

"And you'll be here, of course. Will you be bringing someone?" she asked. "Or shall I arrange for a dinner partner for you?" There was an unmistakably hopeful note in her voice with that last query.

"I'm really sorry, Mother, but I can't make it this year."

Stunned silence met his announcement. Then she said, "What on earth do you mean you can't make it? We hold this party on the same Saturday every year. It's not as if I pulled the date out of a hat. Of course you'll be here. Whatever it is you're planning on doing instead can't possibly be as important as this. Just cancel it."

"I can't cancel, Mother. This is a business obligation. The town's Christmas festival begins that night. I have to be here."

"To do what? Make sure the tree lights come on?" she scoffed.

"Actually, yes, and to see that the vendors are happy and that everything runs smoothly."

"That's absurd. They don't need someone like you to deal with that. Delegate it. Let that little friend of yours handle it."

"If you're referring to Jeanette, she has her own responsibilities for that night. She can't take on mine."

"Thomas McDonald, I can't believe you would place more importance on some ridiculous ceremony in that nothing little town than you do on your own mother."

He'd been expecting the guilt card, but he still had to take a deep breath before responding. He might not care about these kind of social obligations, but his mother did. "It's not a competition. This is my job," he stressed. "If I could be there, you know I would be, because I know it matters to you."

"Just wait until I tell your father," she complained. "He's going to have a thing or two to say about this."

"I don't doubt it," Tom murmured. His father had acted as her unofficial enforcer as far back as Tom could remember. He'd never quite figured out the dynamics of their marriage or why his otherwise strong father so readily did his mother's bidding.

"What did you say?" his mother demanded irritably.

"Nothing, Mother. Look, I'm sorry about the conflict, but there's nothing I can do about it. We'll get together another time."

"The following weekend," she said at once, seizing on the opening. "I'm having another dinner party that Friday. Something smaller and more intimate for a few of your father's business associates. I intended to discuss that with you when I saw you, but since you're obviously so busy these days, I'd better get it onto your calendar now."

Tom was no more inclined to accept that invitation than he was this one, but he knew better than to offer another excuse. If he expected his mother to respect the things— and people—that mattered to him, then he had to show her the same courtesy, at least often enough to keep peace.

"We'll be there," he told her.

"We?" she asked suspiciously.

"Jeanette and I."

"Tom, that's entirely inappropriate."

"Inappropriate?" he repeated, his tone icy. The last of his good humor vanished. "If Jeanette's not welcome in your home, then perhaps I should rethink whether I belong there, either."

"Oh, for heaven's sake, bring her," she said impatiently. "But don't blame me if she doesn't fit in."

"I will blame you if you don't do everything you possibly can to make her feel welcome," he warned. "Please, Mother, do this for me."

"I can only do so much," she claimed, though with far less antagonism.

"Mother, we both know that your guests will take their cues from you. See that you send the right signals, or you can count me out for the rest of the holiday festivities."

"You are an incredibly stubborn and willful young man," she accused, but there wasn't much heat behind the words.

"I learned from two masters," he replied. "Tell Dad hello for me, okay?"

"Of course, though I don't think I'll mention how obstinate you've been."

Tom laughed. "Of course you will. You won't be able to resist. I love you, Mother."

She sighed dramatically. "And I you," she said.

Despite her words, it was obvious that he'd put that love to the test. Something told him that as long as Jeanette was in his life, there were going to be a lot more tests. What he didn't understand was why his mother had taken such a dislike to her. He knew in his gut that it went beyond that ridiculous incident at Chez Bella's. And he also had this odd feeling that it wasn't even about Jeanette personally, but about what she represented.

That's where he got hung up. What could his relationship with Jeanette possibly have to do with his parents? Did they see her as some kind of threat to his relationship with them? That would only happen if they persisted in being antagonistic toward her.

Obviously if things with Jeanette progressed the way he hoped they would, then he was going to have to sit his mother and father down and work this out. He wanted them to appreciate her as he did. If they couldn't, well, he didn't want to think about what that might mean. He would wait and cross that road when he got to it.

Jeanette was finishing up a huge stack of paperwork in her office when she looked up to see a vaguely familiar man standing in the doorway. That he looked like an older version of Tom was even more of a shock. Even if she hadn't seen him at a distance weeks ago, she would have recognized Tom's father, though what he was doing here was beyond her.

"Mr. McDonald, what can I do for you?"

He seemed surprised that she'd guessed his identity. "You know who I am?"

"You and your son look a lot alike. And we almost met on your first visit to Serenity. Would you like to come in and sit down? Or we could go out on the patio if you prefer."

"Here will do," he said, striding into the small office and making it feel even more cramped.

He perched on the edge of a chair across from her and regarded her with blatant curiosity. "I can see what my son sees in you," he said eventually. "You have a certain elfin appeal."

Jeanette had no idea how to take the comment, so she said nothing.

"You're all wrong for him, you know."

"A few weeks ago I would have said the same thing," she responded.

"Really?" He sounded startled by her candor.

"Our worlds are pretty far apart," she continued. "But Tom's almost convinced me that we can bridge the divide."

He seized on her phrasing. "Almost?"

"He's a pretty persuasive man."

Her comment clearly distressed him. His gaze narrowed. "What would it take for you to have a change of heart?" he asked.

"Excuse me?" Surely she hadn't heard him correctly, or at least he hadn't meant what the question implied.

"My wife tells me you've lived in Paris, so you're not just some little country girl who naively believes that love conquers all, am I right? You know how the world works."

"I'd like to think so," she said cautiously.

"Okay, then, what will it take for you to break things off with my son?"

"What will it take?" she echoed. "Are you actually offering me money to stop seeing Tom?"

"Money, a job in some other city, whatever it takes," he confirmed. "My son has a brilliant future ahead of him, once he gets this crazy idea about working for local government out of his head. To achieve his full potential, though, he needs the right woman by his side, someone with social stature."

Jeanette had been so taken aback by the entire visit up until now that she hadn't had time to get seriously offended, but Thomas McDonald was rapidly crossing a line. She stood up.

"I think you should go," she told him.

"Not until we have a deal."

"Then you're going to be sitting here by yourself for a very long time," she said. "I have no intention to listening to any more of this. It's insulting not only to me, but to your son. It's obvious to me that you don't respect the kind, decent, hardworking man he is. He loves the work he's doing and it's important work."

"He's planning Christmas festivities," he scoffed. "A man like Tom should be passing laws, making the world a better place, not worrying about the decorations on some ridiculous tree."

"Because that's the kind of thing you and your wife pay some lowly person to do for you, is that it?" Jeanette retorted. "I've heard all about the holiday spectacle that goes on at your home, so that must matter to someone. Your wife, maybe? Not that she would hang a single ornament herself, of course. That's what the peons are for."

"The point is—"

"The point is that you're a snob, Mr. McDonald. And I won't listen to another word you have to say about me or about your son. What goes on between Tom and me is none of your business."

"You're wrong," he said heatedly. "I will not allow him to throw his life away on the likes of you."

"You don't even know me," she said. "Now, get out."

"I will tell my son how rude and disrespectful you've been," he announced haughtily.

She smiled at that. "And I'll tell him how insulting and offensive you've been. Which do you think will make him angrier?"

He looked surprised. "You've got spunk, I'll give you that," he said grudgingly.

"Something you should probably keep in mind," she said.

"I told Clarisse this was a bad idea," he muttered, looking defeated.

Discovering that his wife had been behind the visit was less of a shock than it should have been. Jeanette knew there was no love lost there. She just didn't know what had triggered the woman to send her husband over here to try to buy her off.

"We're agreed on that much," Jeanette told him. "It was a lousy idea."

His eyes sparked with a hint of respect. "Under other circumstances..." he began, but his voice trailed off.

"What?" she prodded.

"This bad blood between you and my wife, it runs deep," he said.

"Tell me something I don't know. What I don't entirely understand is why. Or what would make you come over here to try to pay me off to get out of Tom's life. It's not about what happened at Chez Bella, is it?"

Mr. McDonald shook his head. He seemed to be weighing the benefit of giving her a more complete answer, so Jeanette simply waited.

"You know that my son and I have been at odds over his future for a long time now," he said eventually.

"He's mentioned that," she said.

"It's not about me wanting to control him or even about me giving two hoots about social standing or anything like that."

"But your wife obviously does," Jeanette said.

He gave her a rueful look. "You say that as dismissively as my son does. What neither of you understand is how important status is in certain circles. Clarisse came from money. Her family's reputation was sterling, something

I couldn't say for my own. Oh, we'd had money, social stature and respectability at one time, but my father had pretty much squandered the money and our reputation by the time I was an adult. He made bad business decisions. He gambled. And he had affairs. A lot of men may do that, but they're far more discreet about it than my father was. Everyone in Charleston knew. He humiliated my mother and left me and my brother to scramble to keep the family from losing everything."

"That must have been hard," Jeanette said quietly. She thought she was beginning to understand.

"You have no idea unless you've been there. Here I was a young man with good connections, but barely two cents to my name, when I met this amazing woman who could have married anyone. Clarisse's parents knew the state of my family's finances, to say nothing of all the stories about my father. They were adamant that there would be no wedding."

His expression turned nostalgic. "Clarisse was formidable even back then. She wouldn't take no for an answer. She loved me and believed in me. She saw the future we could have even when I was far from certain about it. When her parents wouldn't bend, we eloped. That's how much faith she had in me." He met Jeanette's gaze. "So you can understand why I would do anything for her."

"I think I can," she said. "And I can also see why she would view someone like me as a threat to everything she's wanted for your family. She wants Tom to marry someone who can make his life easier, not someone he might need to defend at every turn, someone who doesn't fit into his world."

He seemed surprised. "It's generous of you to try to see

her point of view, especially after how badly I've behaved today," he said. "I'm truly sorry for that."

Jeanette believed him. "Have you ever told Tom any of this?"

"No. When he and his sisters were young, we didn't want to worry them unnecessarily. We wanted them to have the happy, normal childhood to which they were entitled as McDonalds."

"It might help if he understood what happened back then."

"You're probably right. Clarisse and I like to think we've put that time behind us, but obviously it's not as deeply buried as we'd hoped. It still has the capacity to influence the way we react to certain things today."

"Tell him," Jeanette urged.

"I'll do that if you'll do one thing for me," he bargained.

"I won't break things off with your son," she warned.

He smiled. "Of course not. Just please give my wife some time to get used to the idea. I think once she gets to know you, she'll appreciate that you're exactly the right woman for our son. You have real integrity and that's something she treasures."

"Thank you for saying that."

He regarded her hopefully. "Can we forget all about this visit?"

"I don't think I want to forget all of it," she said. "You've given me a perspective I really needed to have."

"Then some good came out of it?"

She smiled. "Some."

"Fair enough. Will you come with him to the dinner party? It's important that he be there, and my wife is under the impression that he won't come without you."

She didn't want to admit that Tom hadn't mentioned

anything about a dinner party, so she merely nodded. "If he wants me to."

He shook his head at her response, a faint smile on his lips. "You remind me of someone."

"Oh?"

"It's ironic, really, but you're a lot like my wife."

She frowned. "And here we were getting along so well," she said.

He laughed. "No, it's true. You're both stubborn and willful. And when you love, you're going to do it with everything in you and damn the consequences. No wonder my son's infatuated with you. I almost feel sorry for him."

"I beg your pardon?"

"Take it from a man who's been married to a woman like that for forty years. It keeps life interesting. Challenging, but interesting."

He walked past her then and left her with her mouth open. The encounter had been eye-opening. If someone had predicted an hour ago that she could actually like a man who'd just tried to buy her off, she would have laughed. Somehow, though, with his candor, Mr. McDonald had won her over. And she thought maybe she'd earned his respect as well. All that remained was to see if that made any difference whatsoever in how things went from here on out.

CHAPTER TWENTY-ONE

⟡

Tom had been calling Jeanette on her cell phone for hours, but she hadn't been picking up. Frustrated, he walked over to the spa and saw a light still shining in her office. He knocked on the front door. When no one responded, he walked around and tapped on her office window. She had a ten-pound weight in her hand and was holding it up threateningly when she lifted the shade to peer out.

"You!" she exclaimed, lowering the weight and setting it on a chair. "Are you trying to scare me to death?"

He gestured toward the front of the building. "Let me in."

She frowned at the request. "I'm busy."

"Five minutes," he argued. "We need to talk."

"I need to work," she countered. "Maddie needs these reports on her desk in the morning and I have supplies to order. Everything piled up while I was spending time with my dad."

"None of that is as important as us needing to talk."

"Okay," she finally said. "I can spare five minutes. I'll meet you on the porch."

Since the last time he'd seen her she'd been in a far more

receptive mood, he had to wonder what had happened in the interim. Whatever it was couldn't have been good.

She unlocked the front door and stood just inside, blocking his way. "What's on your mind?"

"That seems to be evolving," he replied. "I came over here to discuss one thing, but now it appears we should be talking about whatever put you into this snit you're in."

She regarded him indignantly. "I am not in a snit."

"Really?"

She scraped her hand through her hair, leaving it in spikes that only made her look younger and more alluring. He really, really wanted to end this ridiculous argument they seemed to be having and kiss her, but in her current mood that might get him slugged. Since she was no longer holding that weight, it might be worth the risk.

"Look, I really am busy," she said. "Let's do this another time."

He ignored the request and tried to get a fix on the situation. "Have you had dinner?" he asked. Maybe low blood sugar had sent her into this dark mood.

"No. I'll grab something when I get home."

Just as he'd thought. That might not be the total explanation, but it was something he could grab on to. He shook his head. "Nope, dinner can't wait. You need food now. Let's go."

"Speaking of moods," she grumbled, "when did you turn all dictatorial?"

"About two minutes after I got here," he replied. "If you'll just close up, we can go to Sullivan's for dinner and then maybe we can have a rational conversation. After that, if you need to work, I'll bring you back here."

She scowled at him. "Rational? What are you implying?"

"Jeanette, would you just let me in on why you're so

annoyed? You're obviously determined to pick a fight with me."

"So what if I am? I certainly do not want to do it at Sullivan's where Dana Sue will be poking into our business."

"Okay, then," he said with exaggerated patience. "We'll stop by there and pick up something to go. We can eat at your place. If that still doesn't suit you, we can order a pizza."

"Why are you so intent on feeding me?"

Tom was rapidly losing his fragile hold on his own temper, but he did it because he didn't want this silly argument to escalate. Even so, he didn't choose his next words as carefully as he should have. "I'm hoping it will improve your mood before I ask you what I originally came over here to ask you."

Her gaze narrowed. "My mood is just fine or it would be, if you'd stop nagging me about it. Is this about the dinner party at your parents' house?"

Tom regarded her with dismay. Pieces suddenly slid into place, giving him a clearer picture of what was going on. He could think of only one way she could have known about that dinner party. And that would have put her into this mood in a heartbeat.

"Has my mother been in touch with you? What did she say? Did she upset you? Tell you to turn me down? Is that why you're acting like this?"

She flushed guiltily. "I haven't spoken to your mother."

"Then how the hell do you know about the dinner party?" he asked, then was struck by the obvious. He knew exactly how his mother operated. When she couldn't interfere without stirring Tom's ire, she would delegate the task to his father. Of course.

He turned away and started to pace. Now his temper

was about to skyrocket out of control. When he thought he had a grip on it, he paused in front of her, determined to get to the bottom of what had happened. "She sent my father over here, didn't she? Please tell me that my father did not come barging in here and give you a rough time."

"Tom, it's okay. Leave it alone," she said, a pleading note in her voice.

Tom took that for a confirmation. "How can I leave it alone? I won't have them interfering in my life or trying to intimidate you. It's past time for us to have this out."

"I handled your father," she said with a touch of pride. "In fact, I think he and I totally understand each other now."

He shuddered just imagining how that had played out. "Was it anything like the way you *handled* my mother?"

For the first time since his arrival, she grinned. "I was a tiny bit more diplomatic. So was he—in the end, anyway."

"What did he say to you?"

"It doesn't matter. And your reaction just now is exactly why I promised him I wouldn't say anything to you about the visit." She looked flustered. "I thought I'd have more time to figure out how to avoid slipping up. Now I've gone and broken my word to him."

"You should never have given him your word in the first place," Tom said, yanking his cell phone out of his pocket and punching in a number.

"What are you doing?"

"Calling him, of course."

She snatched the phone out of his hand. "No, you can't do that. He and I made peace, more or less. If you call, it will blow the truce to smithereens. He'll never trust me again."

He could see her rationale, but he didn't like it. He didn't like it one damn bit.

"Okay, fine," he conceded reluctantly. "But obviously we can't go to that dinner party now."

"Yes, we can," she said quietly. "I gave him my word about that, too. I want to make peace with your parents, Tom. I really do. Today was a big step toward doing that."

He regarded her in confusion. Where had this conciliatory attitude come from? "My mother, too?"

She nodded. "I understand her a lot better now."

"You do? How?"

"Your father and I really talked. There's a lot you don't know."

"About my own family?" he said incredulously.

"Yes. You need to sit down with them, have a real heart-to-heart. It's long overdue. I think it would make a huge difference in how you get along."

"Why don't you just fill me in?"

"It's not up to me. The three of you need to deal with this."

"This is quite a change of heart," he commented, not sure how he felt about it. Could achieving peace be as simple as she was suggesting? He doubted it, but he was willing to give it a shot. "You're sure about this?"

"I am." She regarded him solemnly. "I won't get between you and your parents, Tom. I know what it's like to have your family split apart by hard feelings and I won't be the cause of it in yours. If anything's going to happen with you and me, we have to try to get along with your parents." She reached up and rested a hand against his cheek. "Besides, you promised."

With that simple touch he pretty much forgot what they were discussing, much less something he'd apparently promised some time ago. "What did I promise?"

"That the holidays would be different this year, that

you'd really try with the whole 'peace and good will toward all men' philosophy."

"I didn't anticipate anything quite like this," he grumbled.

"Sure you did. After all, these are your parents we're talking about. You had to know it wouldn't be easy. If I can give them a chance, surely you can."

He shook his head. "I don't know if you're insane or a saint."

"Neither one." She smiled. "But I am starved, so let's go to Rosalina's and have that pizza there."

Her willingness to put the whole incident with his father behind her was baffling. Too baffling to deal with on an empty stomach. "And all that paperwork you were so worried about when I got here?"

She shrugged. "It can wait."

He looked into her eyes. "Can I make a suggestion then?"

"Sure."

"If we have the pizza delivered to your place, I could light a fire and open a bottle of wine," he suggested hopefully. "How does that sound?"

She hesitated, though she looked tempted. "Romantic," she admitted finally, a hitch in her voice.

"And?"

"You're still not moving in."

"Of course not." He lowered his head and covered her mouth with his, lingering until she uttered a sigh. "But maybe we could discuss a sleepover, just for tonight."

Her lips curved slightly under his. "We're not twelve."

He laughed. "Believe me, I know."

"Oh, you want to have *that* kind of sleepover," she teased.

He brushed his thumb along her lower lip. "What do you think?"

"I think we're wasting time talking about it when we could be on our way to my place."

Tom grinned. "As your town manager, I must tell you how much I appreciate your desire for efficiency."

"I knew that trait would serve me well one of these days," she said, making a quick dash to her office for her purse and keys. When she'd locked the door behind them, she held his gaze and asked, "Are we walking? It's a nice night."

Lost in the depths of her dark brown eyes, he murmured, "My car's faster."

"Then by all means, let's take that," she said, sounding vaguely breathless. She studied him warily. "You're not going to change your mind on me, are you?"

"No. I try never to repeat my mistakes."

She looked relieved. "Good to know."

Jeanette ordered the pizza as they drove the few blocks to her house. She must have sounded vaguely desperate, because it arrived within minutes after they did. Usually Rosalina's operated at a slower pace.

At any rate, by the time it arrived, Tom had already lit a fire and all the candles in her living room and popped the cork on a bottle of red zinfandel she'd been saving for a special occasion. This definitely qualified, she thought with anticipation. He'd also piled all the cushions from the sofa on the floor in front of the fireplace. Clearly he'd had some experience at this whole romantic seduction thing. Another time she might question that, but not now. Now she would go with the flow.

"It looks cozy," she said as she brought the food, plates and napkins over to join him.

"I was going for romantic," he said as he drew her down beside him.

She trembled under the intensity of his gaze. "That, too."

"Jeanette…" His voice trailed off as if he'd lost his train of thought.

"What?" she murmured as he cupped one hand behind her neck and leaned in to kiss her. The slow, simmering kiss drove all thoughts of food and everything else right out of her head.

When he pulled back, he looked as dazed as she felt. Still, he reached for the wine and poured two glasses, though she noticed that his hand was shaking. He held out one. She accepted it, took a sip, then set it aside.

"Tom…" she began, her gaze locked on his lips.

He studied her intently as if not entirely certain of the signal she was sending. "I thought you were starving."

"My priorities have changed."

He looked more hopeful. "Really?"

"Oh, yeah."

"Then dinner can wait?"

She nodded. She could eat anytime, but she'd waited way too long for this moment. "I think it should. I mean, the pizza smells great, but I'm pretty sure you could distract me if you put your mind to it."

His lips curved into a slow smile that was all male. "I'll certainly give it my best shot." he said, sealing his mouth over hers again.

Jeanette let herself drift into the kiss. For the first time, she let go of all her doubts about the future and her memories of the past and allowed herself to live entirely in the moment. It was quite a moment, too. Heat swept through her, followed by a yearning so intense it nearly overwhelmed her. She'd known he was an excellent kisser, but she'd had no idea how inventive he could be when he threw himself into the task, no idea how many nuances there could be to that one simple act between a man and a woman.

One minute his lips were soft and gently persuasive, the next he seemed to be devouring her, his tongue plundering in a way that turned her insides to molten lava. Even when he scattered tender little kisses across her brow, along the curve of her neck, it made her knees go weak.

Why in heaven's name had she been denying herself this? she wondered as his fingers got into the act, reaching for the buttons of her blouse, skimming along bare flesh. As he touched and explored—a gentle caress here, a more intimate stroke there, he kept his gaze on her as if assessing what she wanted, what she needed, then accommodating her.

Sometimes he made her wait, made her long for something more—a deeper kiss, a more intimate touch, something. Eventually, when she was about to push his hands aside and undo the last of the buttons herself, he flicked open the final one, then pressed a soft kiss to the skin he'd revealed. He did the same to every inch of flesh exposed as her blouse drifted down her shoulders. Completely bare except for the lace of her bra, she trembled under his dark gaze.

He leaned forward then and took the tip of her breast in his mouth, teasing the nipple through the lace until she could feel moisture gathering and her hips rose off the floor, seeking him. This moment, so long coming, now couldn't happen fast enough. She wanted it all, wanted him buried inside her, wanted to experience that astounding instant when they became one.

Tom, unfortunately, was in no rush. He seemed determined to savor every second, to draw it out until she was quivering beneath his touch.

"You are so beautiful with the firelight dancing across your skin," he murmured, his fingers following the light, dipping into the shadows until she thought she would come apart just from the reverence of his gaze and the exquisiteness of his touch. He seemed just as eager to give her that satisfaction, but now she was the one who wanted to savor.

"Wait," she whispered, stilling his hand in place on her thigh. "Let me."

She made quick work of unbuttoning his shirt and tossing it aside, then lifting his T-shirt over his head to reveal a muscular chest and solid abs that felt warm and unyielding under her eager fingers. He moaned softly as she explored, then gasped when she unbuckled his belt and reached lower, her hand encasing his impressive arousal. He moved restlessly, his impatience now a match for hers. That was what she'd wanted, what he'd claimed to want not that long ago— to be on the same page.

His pants came off, then her slacks and then they were back together, skin on skin, heat seeking heat, their hands and mouths everywhere, teasing and taunting until both of them were breathless and hungry with need.

"Now," she pleaded. "I've waited so long for this." What an idiot she'd been to wait so long! And yet she knew that weeks ago it wouldn't have been like this at all, wouldn't have been two people in tune with each other on so many levels. Then, it would have been just sex. Now, maybe, just maybe, it was love.

She shivered as Tom removed the scrap of lace that passed for panties, then tossed aside his own boxers. He lifted himself over her, gazing deep into her eyes as he plunged into her, filling her, then withdrawing slowly before plunging again. The rhythm took on a life of its own, building a sweet, delicious urgency that carried Jeanette higher and then higher still before erupting into spasms that spread through her, leaving behind heat and pleasure.

Just as she was recovering from the wonder of that, Tom began to move again, taking her to a whole new place before his own release ripped through him and then her again in a way she'd never experienced before. Two people as one, just as she'd always imagined it could be. The wonder of that made her want to weep.

She didn't realize a tear had fallen until she saw him regarding her with concern.

"Are you crying?"

"No," she insisted, despite the tears that kept falling on his chest.

"What's wrong?"

"Nothing. Everything's perfect."

"Are you sure? You haven't said much."

"I don't think I can," she said. "My mind's gone."

He grinned at that, his expression smug. "Is that a compliment?"

She nudged him in the ribs with her elbow. "Do you need to have everything spelled out for you? Isn't it enough that I can barely move or catch my breath?"

"Just checking. And, in case you were wondering, you were pretty amazing yourself."

"I wasn't wondering," she assured him pertly. "I know I'm good."

He laughed. "Confidence is one of the first things I noticed about you."

"And here I thought it was my body."

"That was the second thing," he said. "Right after you banished me from the spa."

Without covering herself, she propped herself up and looked at him. "What else?"

"What else?" he echoed blankly.

"Why are you attracted to me? Please tell me it's not just because your parents don't approve."

"That's irrelevant," he insisted. His heated gaze lingered on her. "Believe me, you have plenty to recommend you. I like the way your mind works. I like your sense of humor. You're not impressed with me, which is annoying but challenging. And you're not half-bad at this sleepover stuff, either."

She winked at him. "Play your cards right and there will be very little sleeping happening here tonight."

He feigned dismay. "In that case, I need that pizza."

Jeanette sat up and reached for the box. "Stamina is definitely called for," she said, taking a slice of the pizza before handing the rest over to him.

The pizza was stone-cold now, but it had definitely been worth the wait.

Mary Vaughn was having yet another dinner with Sonny tonight, but this time it had been his idea. She had no idea what had sparked the invitation, but she was looking forward to it. Maybe she'd actually get up the nerve to put her feelings on the line just as Jeanette had suggested. She'd have to play that by ear after she found out what was on Sonny's mind. It surely couldn't be Christmas, because they'd gone over their plans for the holidays so thoroughly that not one single detail was left that hadn't been nailed down.

Of course, maybe he was planning to tell her that he'd

gotten seriously involved with that other woman, the one from the dealership. Maybe he'd even insist on including her in all of their holiday plans. The thought made her jittery.

She studied him across the table. He was still a good-looking man, no doubt about it. And she'd finally realized that men like Sonny Lewis only came along once in a blue moon. If only she'd realized that before the divorce.

Well, maybe it wasn't too late. The only way to find out was to lay her cards on the table. The wicked twinkle in his eyes when he looked at her gave her courage.

"Sonny, I've been wondering about something," she began slowly, searching for exactly the right approach.

"You have?"

Her words, usually so glib, had to be carefully thought out if this was going to turn out the way she wanted it to. "Have you ever regretted…" Her voice faltered. "I mean, do you think we were too hasty when we got divorced?"

He stared at her, his mouth agape, his fork poised with a piece of steak on the tip. "Say that again."

"You heard me," she said with a touch of impatience. "Was our divorce a mistake?"

"No," he said with such absolute finality that she blanched.

"Oh, okay." She could feel a humiliating blush creep up her neck. "I was just wondering." She took a bite of her now-tasteless meal and murmured, "The steak is good, isn't it?"

He regarded her with exasperation. "I don't want to talk about the damn steak. Why would you ask such a thing now?" he inquired.

"I shouldn't have," she said quickly. "Forget I mentioned it."

He acted as if she hadn't spoken. "You never bothered to

question me years ago when I told you I wanted a divorce," he reminded her. "You acted as if you'd been expecting it."

Mary Vaughn bit back a sigh. She'd opened this can of worms. Now she had to deal with it. "I suppose I had been," she admitted. "I was never good enough for you. I always thought you'd figure that out sooner or later."

"Hogwash!" he said. "Mary Vaughn, you were never lacking in self-esteem, though God knows you had reason enough to, given your background. Growing up the way you did would have shattered someone without your strength."

"If you admired me so much, why did you leave?"

"You know the answer to that, but I'll explain it again if you want me to. Before I do, though, I want you to tell me why you're bringing this up now. Did you just wake up this morning and decide to go digging around in the past to stir things up?"

She didn't want to answer, didn't want to risk further embarrassment, but he was studying her with genuine curiosity, so she replied, "It wasn't like that. We've been getting along really well lately, you know, enjoying each other's company. We have all this history in common, and a daughter. It made me think. It seemed maybe we let it all slip away too easily."

He nodded. "Yep, *you* did exactly that."

She regarded him with astonishment. "*Me?* I'm not the one who asked for a divorce."

"No, but you didn't say no. You barely even blinked, then offered to help me pack my things."

She was confused by his reaction. "Did you want me to try to stop you?"

"I was hoping for exactly that, as a matter of fact. I was hoping you'd wake up and take a good long look at me and really see me for the first time, maybe appreciate the life we had. I always knew you loved Ronnie, but I loved you enough to overlook that. I thought I loved you enough to give us a real chance at happiness, but the truth was, after a few years when nothing changed, I got tired of being second best. I knew as long as I stayed I was going to have to swallow my pride and pretend it didn't matter. I couldn't do that any longer."

"I'm sorry," she whispered, seeing their life from his perspective for the first time. It wasn't as if she'd ever cheated on him, but she hadn't given him her heart. She'd been content, if not happy, with the way things were and thought he had been, too. How had she lied to herself for so long? "I am so very sorry."

"Me, too."

"I'd like to try to change that, if you'll let me," she said, taking on the risk of another humiliating rejection. "I'm not saying we should jump into anything, just keep seeing each other, see if we can have a fresh start. If it'll help, I know I was a fool back then."

Sonny's expression wasn't encouraging. "I don't know, Mary Vaughn. It's taken me a long time to get over you. I don't know that I want to get back on that emotional roller coaster."

"Not back to anything," she insisted. "Forward, to something new. Build on what was good about the two of us and not repeat the rest."

He looked skeptical. "It's not that easy to forget about the past."

"No, of course not. In fact, it's important to remember, so we won't repeat it." She met his gaze and did something she'd vowed never to do. She begged for this chance she didn't deserve, but wanted desperately. "Please, Sonny. All I'm asking for is another chance. Let me prove I've changed, that I can love you the way you ought to be loved. I think I'm finally mature enough to appreciate the man you are, the man you've always been."

"I don't know," he said, regarding her with wariness.

"Are you hesitating because you're seeing someone else?"

"Dammit, it's not about anyone else, Mary Vaughn. You've always been the only woman for me, more's the pity."

She covered his hand with hers. "Then take this chance," she said, then added simply, "Please."

He turned her hand over, twined his fingers through hers, staring at their interlocked fingers, then at her with a troubled expression. "It would have to be different this time," he said quietly.

She seized on the tiny opening. "It will be. I promise."

"Let me finish," he said. "I won't settle again, Mary Vaughn. I just won't do it."

With that simple declaration, that refusal to settle for anything less than what he deserved, he won not only her respect, but the heart she'd once withheld from him.

Unfortunately, with so many mistakes behind them—most of them hers—proving that she loved him with all her heart wasn't going to be easy. Fortunately, years of clawing and scratching to get what she wanted had made her tough. She *would* win him back. She was as sure of that as she was that the battle would be worth it.

CHAPTER TWENTY-TWO

$\cdot$─────◆◆◆─────$\cdot$

If Howard barged into his office one more time to ask if everything was ready for the festival kickoff tonight, Tom was going to shove his head in a vat of eggnog. He wouldn't even have to go far to find it, since a supply had arrived in front of Town Hall a few hours ago courtesy of the mayor, who seemed oblivious to how inappropriate it was for the town to be serving an alcoholic beverage even if extra care was being taken not to serve it to minors. His attempt to explain that had fallen on deaf ears.

"It's tradition," Howard had told him. "Get with it. Besides, there's not enough alcohol in that stuff to hardly count. Ask the sheriff. Nobody in this town has ever driven drunk after one toast with a little eggnog. Look at the size of those cups. They don't hold but a thimbleful."

Jeanette walked in just as Howard walked out, took one look at Tom's expression and asked, "What's our illustrious mayor done now?"

"Eggnog," Tom told her succinctly.

She grinned. "Yeah, it's a tradition."

"So he said. It's a bad one. There's no telling what kind

of lawsuit we could be setting ourselves up for if someone got into an accident on the way home."

"That's been discussed. The supplier barely waves the bottle of liquor over the eggnog. Nobody's gotten drunk on it yet. They'd have to drink gallons of it, and personally I think it's way too disgusting for anyone to even consider doing that. Nobody serves it to the kids. You're getting worked up over nothing."

"It's my job to protect the town," he reminded her.

She wrapped her arms around his waist. "And we appreciate your efforts." She stood on tiptoe and pressed her lips to his.

His bad mood was rapidly disintegrating. When she traced his lips with her tongue, he forgot what they'd been talking about.

"You taste good," he said.

"I ate a candy cane before I came inside," she said.

He winced. "Someone's giving away candy canes? Are they individually wrapped? Did I know about that?"

"Molly Flint has been giving away candy canes during the festival for seventy years. Nobody's gotten sick yet. And yes, worrywart, they are individually wrapped and meet all health department requirements. I'm sure of it. She buys them at the Piggly Wiggly." She shook him gently. "Now, relax."

"I can't. There are too many loose ends to worry about. The vendors—"

"Are registering as we speak," Jeanette assured him. "Dana Sue is showing them to their assigned spaces. They'll be all set up by four o'clock this afternoon, well ahead of the five-o'clock starting time for the festival. Anything else?"

"The choirs—"

"Mary Vaughn has the schedule. She's double-checked

with all the choir directors. No one's mentioned any glitches. Tully McBride will play the piano like always. The piano's been tuned and is already right in front of the stage. Tully's banging away on it right this second to make sure. The programs have been printed and Sonny will be here at four-thirty to hand them out."

He swiped his hand through his hair. "I hate this," he muttered. "Have I mentioned how much I hate this kind of thing?"

"More than once," she told him. "It's getting tiresome. Everything is going to go beautifully. The decorations are the best ever. Ronnie's checked every electrical connection and switch. The tree will light up right on schedule. You know all this. Why are you in such a panic?"

"It's not panic. It's annoyance that I have to deal with any of this. I was not hired to run Christmas. I was hired to run a town."

She frowned at him. "Well, in Serenity, Christmas is part of the job."

"It doesn't mean I have to like it. I'm obsessing over the kind of stuff my mother obsesses over, inconsequential junk that doesn't matter."

"It matters to the kids. It matters to the town," she reminded him. "Therefore it needs to matter to you. As for your mother, maybe you should ask her why all these things matter so much to her. I think you'd be surprised."

"Well, none of it matters to me." He frowned. "And when did you turn into such a cheerleader for the holidays? To say nothing of defending my mother?"

"I think I understand her a little bit better since that talk I had with your father," she said.

The response only served to remind him of yet another

thing that was still sticking in his craw. Before he could say anything, though, her expression turned nostalgic.

"You know, I really do have a whole new outlook on the holidays," she said. "I think it started when I finally made peace with my parents. I let all the rest go, too. I realized I didn't have to be miserable during the holidays as some sort of penance for being alive when my brother wasn't. The day we bought the tree helped, too. That tree farm smelled so good. And then you agreed to buy the perfect one for the festival." She sighed happily. "That was a wonderful day."

Tom stared at her, thinking what an idiot he'd been today. "I'm sorry. Here I am going on and on about a bunch of nonsense and spoiling your enjoyment."

"You haven't, trust me. A few weeks ago I would have been as grumpy as you," she admitted. "The prospect of being involved with the festival literally made me feel sick, but now, I don't know, it makes me feel hopeful. Like I'm reclaiming something special that was lost to me for a long time."

She looked at him worriedly. "I just wish you could relax and get into the spirit of this, too. You promised me you'd try."

"Yes, I did. Let me get through the next couple of hours and I swear to you I will be the cheeriest man you've ever met."

"Because it's the holiday season or because your part in the festival is over?"

He grinned. "Do I have to answer that?"

Her sigh now was one of frustration. "That's what I thought. I'll see you outside."

"Save me some eggnog," he said as she left.

He'd meant to make her smile, but instead she walked

away looking sad, as if he'd just popped her holiday balloon. He'd have to find some way to make it up to her....

The giant snowflakes on the light poles in downtown Serenity were sparkling. Vendors lined the streets, selling arts and crafts, quilts, jewelry and homemade jams and jellies. Kids, excited in anticipation of Santa's arrival, were inhaling cotton candy and hot dogs. Any minute now, Santa would arrive atop the town's fire truck as a local choir sang "Here Comes Santa Claus", the lights on the tree in the square would be turned on and the Christmas festival would be officially under way.

Next to Jeanette, Maddie grinned and squeezed her hand. "You did good! It's absolutely beautiful and there are more vendors than we've ever had before. I can't wait for the choirs to start singing. That's my favorite part. And the kids can't wait to see Santa. At least Jessica Lynn can't and Katie's pretending she still believes for her sister's sake. Kyle's too old and Cole's too young, but it's nice to have at least one kid who still believes in Santa."

"Where's Helen?" Jeanette asked. "I thought she'd be here by now with Sarah Beth."

"Last time I saw her she was in the kitchen at Sullivan's telling Erik how to decorate the Christmas cookies he's bringing over here for Santa to give away."

Jeanette chuckled. "How was that going?"

"Erik just tunes her out and does his thing."

"Really?"

"Oh, did I forget to mention that he gave her some icing and told her to do whatever she wanted with it? Last time I saw him, he was trying to get red icing out of his hair." Maddie turned to her, her expression sobering. "You and I haven't had much time to ourselves to talk lately. Right after the first of the year, we have to get serious about expanding the spa. Meantime, what's going on with you and Tom? We're taking bets he'll be giving you a ring for Christmas, or Valentine's Day at the latest. I know it may seem fast, but he doesn't strike any of us as the kind of man who likes to wait around. And he has said he loves you."

Jeanette wasn't quite as certain as Maddie that she and Tom were anywhere near ready for that big a commitment. They'd taken a huge step when they'd slept together and she'd taken an even bigger leap of faith after talking with his father, but marriage or even an engagement? It was too soon for that kind of talk.

"I think you're all jumping the gun," she told Maddie.

"Come on. I've seen you two together. Everything clicks."

Jeanette barely resisted the urge to sigh again. "It does, doesn't it?"

"So what's the problem?"

"If you can believe it, Christmas. The worst memories of my life are all tied up with the holidays and I've managed to overcome that and really find my way back to loving the season the way I did as a child. He's still so cynical and jaded, it's driving me nuts. You should have heard him going on and on a couple of hours ago. You would have thought the entire season was invented just to annoy him."

"Maybe he's just the kind of guy who obsesses over details, and right now there are a hundred of them related to getting this event off the ground."

Jeanette shook her head. "It runs deeper than that. It's all tied up with the phony excess his mother insists on, but please, that doesn't begin to compare with what I went through."

"You've never explained about that," Maddie reminded

her. "I've hoped you would, but I swore to myself I wouldn't pressure you to tell me."

Jeanette couldn't help grinning at the pious note in her voice. "That must have just about killed you."

"You have no idea," Maddie replied just as Cole began to wail. "Hold on. Don't you dare leave," she ordered Jeanette as she reached for her son. "Give me a minute to find Cal in this mob scene and turn our baby boy over to him. Then you and I can talk."

"Maddie, this isn't the best time," Jeanette protested. "It will only bring you down. Heck, talking about it will bring *me* down and I'm in a halfway decent place right now."

"You're not if you're thinking that you and Tom don't have a future because you disagree about the holidays," Maddie said, then turned to Kyle. "Take your brother." She handed the baby over to the horrified teenager.

"Mom!" Kyle protested, even as he snuggled the baby against his chest with the ease of someone who'd grown used to caring for his new siblings.

"Find Cal," Maddie ordered, giving him no sympathy. "He can take over for you."

"This sucks," Kyle grumbled, but he went off in search of his stepfather.

"You are putting a serious dent in your son's social life," Jeanette told Maddie, who merely grinned.

"Don't let him fool you. The girls are drawn to him like a magnet when he's babysitting. He just hates admitting how much he likes having them fawn all over him and Cole."

"So the baby is a babe magnet?"

"Absolutely," Maddie said. "Last time Ty was home, he kept pleading to take the baby for a walk in the park. At first I thought it was all about bonding with his new brother, but then Kyle filled me in."

"Wait a minute," Jeanette said. "Isn't Ty dating Annie? I thought they were a couple."

"Something's going on there, but I'm trying to stay out of it. So is Dana Sue. Those two kids have been thick as thieves for a while now, but over Thanksgiving they weren't even speaking. I have no idea if they fought, broke up or what."

"It must be hard not going to the same college and trying to maintain a relationship," Jeanette mused.

"We all warned them about that, but Ty said they'd do okay. Annie'd adored him practically forever and he was great with her when she was dealing with her eating disorder, so we backed off. Whatever's going on, they have to work it out for themselves. It won't help for Dana Sue or me to get involved."

"Yet another of your frustrations, I'm sure," Jeanette said.

"Yes, and since I can't fix their issues, let's deal with yours," Maddie said. "Why did you react so badly when I asked you to work on the festival? And what does that have to do with what's going on now between you and Tom?"

Since Maddie was as tenacious as a pitbull, Jeanette gave her the condensed version of the Christmas Eve accident and its aftermath.

Maddie's eyes welled with tears. "Oh, sweetie, I had no idea. I would never have forced you into doing all this if I'd understood why you were so against it. You should have told me right then."

"It's worked out better this way," Jeanette admitted. "I needed to face what happened and let go of all the pain. I actually think I can go to church on Christmas Eve this year with an open heart. I wish Tom were in the same place."

"Come on, sweetie. This is not that big a deal. You'll

figure this out. You two have too much going for you not to overcome your differences over the holidays," Maddie said adamantly.

Jeanette tried to come up with an explanation for her gut feeling that would make sense to Maddie. "It's not the holidays, per se," she said eventually. "It's that I don't think I can be with someone who's so negative."

Maddie clearly didn't buy it. She regarded her knowingly. "You're making excuses, Jeanette. This isn't about Christmas or negativity. What's *really* stopping you from grabbing on to what the two of you have found with each other?"

Jeanette wasn't really surprised that Maddie had called her on it. Maddie was an intuitive woman. The problem was, she didn't have a straightforward answer. "It's not just one thing," she said eventually. "I could give you a whole list of reasons we don't belong together."

"Starting with?"

"His mother and I don't get along." She decided not to mention Mrs. McDonald's attempt to get her out of Tom's life permanently by sending her husband over here on a mission to buy her off. It hadn't worked and now that she understood why it had happened in the first place, she could forgive the whole misguided incident. Maddie might not.

"You planning to live with the woman?" Maddie asked wryly.

"No, but come on, even if she and I find a way to make peace, she is not the kind of person to stay out of our lives. Do I really want a lifetime of dealing with her?"

"If it comes with a man as great as Tom, don't you think it would be worth it?"

Jeanette thought of how Tom made her feel when they were alone and grinned. "Now that you mention it, maybe it does. Meantime, though, in the spirit of holiday goodwill I agreed to show up at some fancy dinner party at their house next weekend."

"Is that your punishment for existing?" Maddie inquired tartly.

"It's my pitiful attempt to extend an olive branch yet again," Jeanette said.

"Give it time. They'll come to appreciate you for the wonderful woman you are," Maddie assured her.

"You are such an optimist."

"Well, of course I am. A few years ago, when Richard walked out on me, I thought I'd never be happy again. Then Cal came along and just look at my life. It's better than ever. I have two little ones I'd never dreamed in a million years that I'd have at this stage of my life. I have a husband who adores me. I have a son who's excelling in college and is destined to play pro baseball. I have two other kids who are getting smarter and more mature every day. And I have a business I enjoy and friends who support me and make me laugh. All that can be yours, too. You just have to reach out and grab what you want."

"I'd be hard pressed to come up with five kids overnight, but I see your point," Jeanette said. "I need to count my blessings."

"And Tom could be one of those if you'll open your heart to him," Maddie reminded her. "Work this out, sweetie. I know you want to."

"Yeah, I do," Jeanette admitted, her gaze searching the crowded square before finally finding Tom near the stage. He and Santa—Howard—were arguing, yet again. Then Howard plunked an extra Santa hat on Tom's head and Jeanette found herself chuckling at his obvious discomfort.

Maddie nudged her with an elbow. "You've gotta love a man in a Santa hat."

Jeanette sighed. "Yeah, I suppose I do."

But that didn't seem to stop her from wondering if she was going to live to regret it.

Tom looked around the town square at the awed expressions on the kids' faces and shook his head. Maybe only someone under twelve could truly enjoy Christmas, he mused.

He turned to share his thoughts with Jeanette and realized that she was gazing around at all the lights with that same look of awe on her face. He frowned.

"You really have gotten into this, haven't you?"

"Don't make it sound like an accusation," she responded. "I have gotten into it. Just look at all these people, Tom. Look at how happy the kids are. Even Howard's in his element up there handing out candy canes and Érik's cookies and letting the kids whisper their Christmas wishes in his ear."

"How are they going to feel on Christmas morning when they don't get what they asked for?"

She whirled on him. "Would you just give it a rest? Look how the town has come together for this event. That's a good thing. Lighten up, okay?"

"You know, I really don't understand you anymore," he said, genuinely bewildered by her change in attitude.

"Ditto," she said, walking away.

Years ago, faced with his parents' total lack of interest in ensuring their children enjoyed the holiday season, using it mainly as a time to enhance social connections, Tom had learned to be independent, not to rely on anyone for his happiness. Tonight, though, for the very first time he felt well and truly alone. It scared him to think that Jeanette might use this as yet another reason to keep their relationship from moving forward. Things had been going well recently, and now, it seemed he was about to ruin it. He had to get a grip, remember what really mattered.

"You look as if someone just stole your Christmas presents," Ronnie noted, joining him. "Where's Jeanette?"

"I have no idea."

Ronnie gave him a knowing look. "Did you two have a fight?"

"Apparently," he said.

Ronnie nodded sagely. "Ah, one of those. They're the toughest kind to handle. Did she give you any clues?"

"It had something to do with my bah-humbug attitude."

Ronnie grinned. "Yeah, you really do need to work on that. The whole town's talking about what a grump you are. It probably doesn't bode well for your future as town manager."

Tom stared at him incredulously. "You think I could be fired because I'm not filled with the Christmas spirit?"

"Serenity does have certain expectations for its town officials," Ronnie said solemnly.

"You can't be serious!"

Ronnie chuckled. "Okay, I'm kidding. Your job is probably safe, but you really do need to loosen up about the holidays."

Tom sighed. "I know."

"Then maybe you should get a clue," Ronnie suggested. "Go find some mistletoe, drag Jeanette under it and kiss her like there's no tomorrow."

"And you think that will fix things?"

"Probably not, but it might be a good start."

"Given her current mood, she'll probably slug me."

"That's why we have paramedics on standby," Ronnie said.

"I thought that was in case somebody choked on a hot dog," Tom muttered.

"They multitask," Ronnie assured him. "Find the woman and kiss her before all of this gets blown out of proportion."

"Kissing can't solve this problem," Tom said.

"Maybe not, but it can remind you both that what you have is worth fighting for."

Tom regarded him with envy. "How'd you get to be so smart?"

"By blowing my marriage to smithereens and having to fight like hell to get it back," Ronnie said. "Take it from me, it's smarter to appreciate what you have before it gets away from you."

Appreciating Jeanette wasn't the problem. *Understanding* her was the hard part, but Ronnie was right about one thing. He didn't want to lose her and take a chance on spending the rest of his life without her.

Jeanette was standing alone under a tree watching Mary Vaughn and Sonny. They'd set up chairs side by side in front of the stage and were seemingly listening to the concert by the town's choirs, though from what she could tell, neither one of them had glanced at the stage in the past half hour. They were totally, one hundred percent absorbed in each other. She envied them.

"What are the odds at Wharton's on those two getting back together?" Tom asked, coming up beside her.

"Probably higher than the bets they're placing on the two of us," she reported glumly.

He turned her to face him. "I'm sorry about earlier. For too many years just the sound of Christmas music was enough to put me in a foul mood. You have no idea how much hypocrisy there was in my house. Our celebration didn't have anything to do with love or goodwill. It was materialistic in the extreme. There were mountains of presents on Christmas morning, though they had little to do with anything my sisters or I wanted. Instead my parents bought what they thought we should have so they could gloat to their friends that they'd found the impossible-to-find latest toy or technology gizmo. You would have thought the holidays were invented to advance my mother's personal social agenda."

"Didn't you ever wonder why that mattered so much to her?" Jeannette asked.

He regarded her with puzzlement. "There you go again, hinting that there's some deep dark secret I'm missing. If you know something, tell me."

"It's not my place."

"Then excuse me if I go on hating the holidays."

"Okay, you were a classic poor little rich boy," she said. "Am I supposed to feel sorry for you?"

Tom winced. "No. I'm just trying to make you understand."

"I *do* understand. We all have things in our pasts we'd like to forget, things that didn't go the way we thought we deserved or the way we hoped they would. Grow up. Get over it."

"The righteousness of the recently converted," Tom commented.

Jeanette stared at him in shock. "What does *that* mean?"

"Not all that long ago, you were letting the past rule your life, too," he reminded her. "Now you've found a way to reconcile with your parents and to look at the holiday season from a new perspective. And that's wonderful. It really is. I wouldn't want anything less for you. Just give the rest of us time to catch up."

"I never meant to..." Her voice trailed off.

What *had* she meant? Maybe she *had* been judging him too harshly for not adapting and rejoicing at the same pace she had—especially when she knew about his mother and why she placed so much emphasis on status when he didn't. What was wrong with her? She of all people knew that pain and heartache were individual. What her father and mother had felt wasn't the same thing she'd experienced. Their grief had taken them in one direction, leaving her out and causing her to suffer in a different way entirely.

Perhaps Tom hadn't suffered the major loss she and her family had, but she knew all too well how being disconnected from those you loved could hurt. Chances were, his relationship with his family had been awkward and difficult all year long, but it had probably felt a thousand times worse during the holidays when other families were celebrating together. She had no right to minimize any of that.

"I'm sorry," she whispered. "I just wanted us to be able to share this, to enjoy the magic of the holidays together."

"And we will," he promised. "I will get there, maybe not before we run out of eggnog tonight, but I will get there."

She pulled his head down and kissed him slowly, feeling the tension in his shoulders ease, breathing in the scent of him, which mingled with the scent of pine in the air.

"You know," he said softly, his lips against hers, "I think some of the magic of the season is rubbing off on me, after all."

Mary Vaughn felt as if she'd never thrown a party before in her life. She'd been dashing around the house for the past hour double-checking every detail, making sure that the caterer had the food displayed just right for the buffet, that there wasn't a speck of dust on the chandelier in the dining room, that not one single bulb had blown out on the dozens of strands on the massive tree in the living room.

"Will you settle down?" Sonny pleaded, trailing behind her in a way that seemed wonderfully familiar. "Everything's perfect."

"What if no one comes?"

"Don't be ridiculous. Your parties are always the highlight of the season. And every single person we spoke to at the festival tonight said they planned to drop by."

"I know, but people get tired. They think it will be packed and no one will miss them."

He stopped her as she was about to count the cloth napkins for the second time. With his hands on her shoulders holding her in place, he looked into her eyes. "Why are you so nervous?"

"Because..." she began, then couldn't bring herself to finish.

"Because people are going to know we're back together?" he asked. "Is that it?"

She nodded. "I want to make you proud."

"You've always made me proud."

"But I want people to see that I finally really get what an amazing man you are."

He tilted her chin up. "The only one who needs to believe that is me."

"And quite likely your father," she said ruefully. "He may not be thrilled that we're getting back together."

"You're wrong about that. He's wanted this for a long time."

"But he never liked me," Mary Vaughn protested.

"No, he never liked that you didn't love me the way he

thought you ought to. He wasn't blind, Mary Vaughn, and it's a small town. He knew you never got over Ronnie."

"I have now, you know," she said, meeting his gaze directly. "You're the only man I want."

"I'm actually starting to believe that," he told her. "In fact, I have an early Christmas present for you."

He reached into his pocket and withdrew a box. "It's not a ring," he warned when he handed it to her. "I'm telling you that so you won't be disappointed. It's too soon for that kind of commitment, but I wanted you to know how I feel about you just the same. I have faith in what's happening between us."

She opened the box to find a piece of estate jewelry inside, a locket. Her fingers trembling, she opened it to find a snapshot of Sonny and Rory Sue on one side. The other side had been engraved with a single word: *Forever.*

"That's what I want for us, Mary Vaughn. This time I want it to be forever."

"Oh, Sonny, so do I," she whispered against his cheek. "So do I."

"Shall I put it on for you?" he asked.

She nodded and lifted her hair out of the way as he dealt with the delicate clasp. The brush of his fingers across the nape of her neck made her shiver with anticipation.

For the first time, she was glad Rory Sue wasn't home from college, that she wouldn't be here for a few more days. It meant she and Sonny would have the house to themselves once the party was over. And if she had her way, they'd make good use of as many bedrooms as they possibly could. She smiled at the thought.

CHAPTER TWENTY-THREE

———————•◦•———————

Even though she'd committed to going with Tom, Jeanette wasn't entirely sure how smart it was to attend the dinner party at his parents' home the week after the kickoff of the Christmas festival. Tom was on edge, too, which made her even more nervous. There were easily half a dozen ways this night could be a disaster.

Even as Tom was parking the car in the brick-paved, circular driveway, she was scrambling for an excuse to cut and run. She didn't trust the truce she'd made with his father, and his mother was too darn unpredictable.

"This is a bad idea," she said.

"You're just coming to that conclusion now?" Tom said, his own tone dire.

"You could go alone," she suggested.

"While you do what? Hide in the bushes?"

"You could drop me off at a restaurant and pick me up later."

"Not a chance. They're expecting you. Besides, need I remind you that this was part of our deal? I drop the bah-humbug attitude and you try to get along with my folks."

"Whatever," she said, not nearly as entranced with the idea now that she was on their doorstep.

"Look, my parents need to get used to the idea that we're seriously involved. Let's just go inside and do this," he said.

"Whoa!" she protested. "We are not seriously involved. We're sleeping together, but that's not the same thing."

Tom scowled. "We most certainly are seriously involved. And do you really want to sit out here and debate this when we both know I could prove you wrong if I really wanted to?"

His confident words made her feel a little reckless…or maybe it was knowing they were practically sitting under his parents' watchful eyes. She met his gaze. "Oh, yeah?" she challenged.

He blinked, but then his eyes turned dark and dangerous. "Are you sure you want to challenge me about this right now?"

"I believe I do," she said as a little shiver of anticipation scooted up her spine.

He was out of the car and around to her side in a split second. He yanked open the door and seized her hand. "Let's go."

She saw now that she might have pushed him a tiny bit too far. "Go where?"

"There's a guesthouse out back. Nobody's staying in it." He was walking so fast, she had to run to keep up with him.

"Tom, wait," she protested.

"I've been waiting for this ever since I saw that dress you're wearing tonight."

"We can't sneak off and get all hot and sweaty in your parents' guesthouse when they're expecting us for dinner. It would be rude." To say nothing of courting disaster. She was skating on very thin ice with his parents as it was.

He laughed. "Do you really want to discuss etiquette now?"

"Your mother already has an exceptionally low opinion of me. I don't want to make it worse."

"My opinion's the one that counts," he reminded her, though he did slow down and back her into a wrought-iron fence. Then he grabbed the railings on either side of her and leaned in to cover her mouth with his.

Jeanette gasped, as his tongue plunged inside. With all his hot, very male hardness pressed against her, she forgot why this was such a bad idea. Her hands cupped his face, ensuring that the kiss didn't end. His hips ground into hers. He reached down, lifted the hem of her dress and slid his hand along her bare thigh until it found the moist core of her. She jerked at the intimate touch and almost flew apart right then and there.

"Stop," she murmured, then, "No, don't stop. Don't… Tom?" His clever fingers dived inside her and then she did come undone. Her eyes wide, her breath coming in quick pants, she met his gaze. "That wasn't supposed to happen. It…we shouldn't be doing this." She buried her head in his shoulder. "Tom, how can I possibly go inside now? Everyone will know what we've been doing."

He touched a finger to her cheek, brushed back a wayward curl. "There's a bathroom in the guesthouse. You can check yourself out in the mirror in there, though I happen to think you look amazing, all tousled and glowing."

Her hand immediately went to her hair, which was curling wildly after all her earlier attempts to tame it. "Oh, no."

"Stop," he commanded. "The look suits you. Please don't fix it."

"We'll see," she said. "Where's this guesthouse?"

He led the way to what had once been a gatekeeper's cottage, guarding the main entrance to the large property. It was only slightly smaller than her new house and had been decorated with a masculine touch in burgundy and navy blues, accented with beige. She studied it, then turned to him. "Your mother did this for you, didn't she?"

He nodded. "They had some crazy idea I'd move back home if I had my own place on the property, at least until I married and settled down to the life they envisioned for me."

"Did you ever live here?"

He shook his head. "But they haven't given up hope. I keep telling them to rent it out, but they refuse to do it. My father says I'm bound to come to my senses one of these days and move back to Charleston, where a good address really matters."

Just then she glanced at the clock sitting over the fireplace mantel and realized they were late. "Look at the time. Your mother is going to kill us...or me, anyway. She'll blame this on me."

"I'll tell her it was my fault," Tom promised.

"Two minutes," Jeanette said and ran for the bathroom.

Tom had been right, her cheeks were glowing and her hair was mussed, but in a way that some women paid a lot of money to achieve. She straightened her clothes, washed up and replaced the lipstick that had been lost to his kisses. In exactly two minutes, she returned to the living room.

"Will I do?"

"You're gorgeous," he assured her.

She rolled her eyes at the biased comment. "Thanks, but you'd better find an explanation for our tardiness that has absolutely nothing to do with what actually happened."

"Not a problem. I'll tell her that we left a bit late, got

stuck in traffic." He led the way along a path to the brightly lit house.

It was a rare warm evening for this time of year, and music and laughter poured from the open windows and the French doors that led to the terrace. They slipped inside through the open doors.

"Well, there you are!" his mother said, zeroing in on them at once. "I thought perhaps you'd forgotten the way home." She frowned as she surveyed Jeanette, but her greeting was polite enough.

"Thank you for including me," Jeanette said, even though Mrs. McDonald looked as if she'd just tasted a slice of lemon. That sour expression was getting to be way too familiar.

"Tom, you need to find your father and let him know you're here. There's someone he wants you to meet."

"Okay," Tom said. He started to reach for Jeanette's hand, but his mother stepped between them.

"Jeanette will be just fine with me. I'll see that she meets everyone, though I imagine she's met quite a few of them since they were regulars at Chez Bella."

Tom froze. "Mother, if you've done anything to deliberately make Jeanette feel uncomfortable…"

"She's a guest in my home," his mother said stiffly. "McDonalds do not embarrass their guests."

He gave her a hard look, then nodded. "I'll take your word on that."

Jeanette watched him walk away with dismay, but since there was no other choice, she drew herself up, plastered a smile on her face and said, "Your decorations are beautiful, Mrs. McDonald. I love the nutcracker theme. I'm sure you've been working on it for weeks."

It was true. This room absolutely sparkled with twinkling, multicolored lights. It was filled with the fragrance of evergreens, even though Tom had told her the boughs on display were artificial, and the nutcracker theme had been carried out with enthusiasm. There were hundreds of them on the tree, larger ones on the mantel and life-size nutcrackers at the entrance to the room.

Across the hall the decor—from what she could glimpse of it—was the Sugarplum Fairy with pale pink, purple and silver ribbons woven through the boughs and accompanied by thousands of tiny white lights.

Jeanette had been in department stores with less attention to holiday detail.

"This house has always been a showcase during the holidays," Mrs. McDonald said proudly. "It's a tradition I've been happy to continue."

"Are your daughters here? I'd love to meet them," Jeanette said.

"Not tonight. This is a business dinner, not a family celebration," she said pointedly.

Jeanette winced at the distinction and the less-than-subtle implication that she wouldn't have been included had it been for family.

For the next half hour she endured curious glances and cool greetings from women who'd once told her some of their most intimate secrets. They weren't used to meeting her on an equal footing and it was plainly awkward for all of them. Not that any of them were outright rude. They simply didn't know what to make of her presence, especially without Tom by her side and past gossip about the lawsuit threat from Mrs. McDonald still ringing in their ears.

Jeanette held her head up, chatted briefly and then found her way to the bar, where she asked for a glass of wine. She took it onto the terrace, intending to stay only long enough to regroup, when she heard raised voices coming from another room. Since Tom's was one of them, she drifted in that direction.

"Dad, how many times do I have to tell you that I am not joining a law practice in Charleston?" Tom demanded heatedly. "Do you have any idea how embarrassing that conversation was for Dwight Mitchell and for me?"

"And do you know what a fool you'd be to turn him down? Mitchell and McLaughlin is one of the oldest, most prestigious firms in Charleston. In the state, for that matter. If you join that practice, you'll be set for life, not just financially, but for whatever political career you want to pursue."

"I'm not going to practice law and I'm not going to run for office," Tom said emphatically. "I don't know how to make that any clearer."

"When are you going to stop making decisions just to spite me?" his father retorted.

"Dad, my decisions have nothing to do with you. I'm doing work that I love. Please accept that so we don't have to keep having this conversation."

"And the same thing is true of Jeanette? You really care for her?"

"You know I do. I want you and Mother to get to know her. She's very important to me. So are you, whether you believe that or not. I'd like us all to get along."

His father sighed heavily. "I want that, too. I just had such high hopes for your future, as did your mother."

"Dad, I'm working toward the future I want. It's a perfectly honorable one, even if it's not the one you would have chosen for me. That's what matters. And I'm with a woman I love, a woman who makes me happy."

"Even though she's not one of us?"

Tom laughed. "Because she can't trace her ancestors back to English royalty or whatever the hell matters so much to Mother? Come on, Dad. Mother's always been a bit of a snob, but not you."

Silence fell for a moment, then Mr. McDonald spoke, his tone weary. "You're right. I have no room to talk. My ancestors worked hard for what they achieved and then my father nearly squandered everything with his drinking, his gambling and his affairs. I've spent my life trying to restore what he almost lost. It wasn't about the money. It was about our reputation. That's all I care about, Tom. I want our good name to continue, to matter in Charleston the way it once did. Your mother took a huge risk when she married me after all my father's scandalous behavior. I promised her she'd never have cause to regret it. Lately, she's been embarrassed to show her face."

"Given the amount of entertaining the two of you seem to be doing during the holidays, she can't be too embarrassed," Tom replied. He hesitated. "Dad, Jeanette's been hinting that there were things you and Mother had been keeping from me, things that would explain why all of this matters so much to you. Is this it? Is it because of Grandfather?"

"He nearly ruined us, not just our finances, but our reputation," his father said. "I know you think all the things your mother cares so much about are frivolous, but they matter because we've had to fight so hard to get them back."

"I see."

"Do you really, son?"

"I think I'm starting to."

"Cut your mother some slack, okay?"

"If the two of you will cut *us* some," Tom agreed. "I love Jeanette. I intend to marry her, if she'll have me."

"Please, don't do this, Tom. It will kill your mother."

"Only if she refuses to take the time to get to know Jeanette. In the end, that will drive us away," Tom said. "I guarantee you that. Dad, I'm sorry about what Grandfather did, but it has nothing to do with me. It was in the past. I'm sure people have forgotten all about it. I've certainly never heard a word said against him."

"Because your mother and I didn't want you or your sisters to know. We did everything we needed to do to live down the mess my father had created, and eventually people forgot or at least allowed us to put it behind us. You have a legacy you can be proud of. A lot of the credit for that goes to your mother for taking a chance on me."

"Dad, I've always been proud of you. I don't always agree with you and I can't live my life to please you, but that doesn't negate the way I feel about you."

His father's expression was weary as he gestured around the room. "All of this was supposed to be yours."

"I don't need it," Tom said gently. "I've found what I need. I have work I enjoy, a woman I love."

"And you won't reconsider?"

Tom shook his head. "No. This is the life I want. Can you please try to accept that?"

"I'll try," his father replied, sounding defeated. "Go on back to the party. It's almost time for dinner. Tell your mother I'll be out in a minute."

"Dad, I'm sorry if I've hurt you. I really am."

"Don't be. I know better than most that a man has to choose the path that suits him. My whole life has been spent trying *not* to take the one my father took."

Tom stood beside him, hesitant. "You're sure you're okay?"

His father smiled ruefully. "I've weathered worse set-backs than this one. Go on now. I'll be right along."

As Tom reached the door, he called out to him. "Son?"

"Yes?"

"Just so you know, I like your young woman. I'd hoped that you'd find someone right here in Charleston and I felt I had to try to make that happen, but in the end this is your decision. Jeanette has backbone. If you do decide to marry, I hope you'll be as happy together as your mother and I have been."

As Tom stepped outside, he saw Jeanette just going back inside the other room. He followed, and when Jeanette tried to slip inside, Tom caught up with her.

"You heard, didn't you?" he demanded.

She nodded. "I didn't mean to eavesdrop. I went outside to get some air and I heard raised voices."

"I'm sorry about some of the things my father said." He smiled. "You did hear him say, though, that he likes you."

"I heard. It actually means a lot, because I know how hard it was for him to say it." She smiled brightly. "Now all I have to do is win over your mother."

"We could do that another night," he suggested. His gaze held hers. "Want to get out of here? This house suddenly seems unbearably stuffy and overcrowded."

Jeanette was tempted, but good manners dictated they stay. "I'd love to, but I don't think we should. Your mother will be offended. That's no way for me to win points."

"Actually she'd probably be relieved. There'd be a lot less tension over dinner."

She shook her head. "Nice try, but we're staying."

He leaned down and stole a kiss. "The things I'm willing to do for you," he murmured. "First the Christmas festival, now this."

"If that's all you ever have to do for me, you'll be getting off lightly."

A maid announced just then that dinner was being served. In the dining room, with its glittering chandelier, polished silver and sparkling crystal, white tapers shimmered amid clusters of bright green holly. The meal went surprisingly well. Not only was Mrs. McDonald civil, but Mr. McDonald actually made a real attempt to include Jeanette in the conversation.

Perhaps it was the wine, combined with the excellent rack of lamb and decadent chocolate dessert, but there was plenty of laughter. Everyone seemed perfectly mellow by the time coffee was served.

On the way into the living room, Tom leaned down to Jeanette. "Can we make our excuses now? It's getting late and we do have to be at the festival first thing in the morning."

"You sound surprisingly happy about that," she noted.

"Amazingly enough, I'm feeling happy about it."

She beamed at him. "That's what I like to hear. Let's say goodbye to your mother."

They wove through the crowd until they found her, her cheeks glowing with the success of the party.

"Mother, I have to apologize," Tom said. "We need to duck out early."

"It's been a lovely evening," Jeanette said with sincerity. "Thank you again for including me. I'm sorry we have to go, but our Christmas event starts again early tomorrow morning and we both need to be there."

"I thought that was last weekend," his mother said, turning to Tom as if she'd caught him in a lie.

"It kicked off last weekend," Tom explained.

"It lasts for two weeks and it's one of the town's biggest

events of the year," Jeanette told her, ignoring Tom's less than subtle poke in her ribs. "You should drive over. There will be vendors there all day. Church choirs will perform. The tree's already lit in the town square, the stores are decorated, and it's really beautiful at night."

"It sounds charming."

Jeanette listened closely for a derisive note in her voice, but she sounded as if she meant it. "You really should come," Jeanette persisted. "Tom's worked really hard on it and the tree is amazing."

"Perhaps we will," she said at last. She turned to Tom, her expression oddly hesitant. "Would that be okay with you?"

Tom summoned a smile. "Of course. Jeanette and I will be around somewhere. Be sure to look for us."

"And thanks again for tonight," Jeanette said.

His mother hesitated, as if searching for the right words. "I'm happy you could come," she said, the words awkward but seemingly sincere. Then she stood on tiptoe to kiss Tom's cheek. "I'll tell your father about the festival. Hopefully we'll see you tomorrow."

"Good night, Mother."

Outside, Jeanette heaved a sigh of relief. "I can breathe again."

"Me, too," Tom said, loosening his tie.

"It wasn't as awful as I was afraid it would be," she admitted.

"I think my parents were really trying."

She reached for his hand. "So do I." She studied his face, then asked, "Did you mean what you said to your father about marrying me?"

He grinned. "Ah, you heard that, too."

"It's not as if you whispered it in his ear. So?"

"It's definitely on my agenda," he said. "But when I get around to proposing, it will not be in my parents' driveway. It will be in a romantic setting."

A smile tugged at her lips. "Good to know."

When Dana Sue needed help decorating Sullivan's for the holidays, Jeanette was the first to offer to pitch in. When Maddie mentioned that they ought to have a Christmas event at the spa for their clients, Jeanette volunteered to plan it. Then she decided to throw her own holiday party, her first in her new home. She bought fancy invitations, spread out every one of her cookbooks looking for the most festive recipes and bought a tree that barely fit into her living room. Tom actually lugged it in for her without complaint, though he begged off before it was time to hang the first decoration.

On the Monday after the invitations went out, Maddie pulled her aside. "Let's have a cup of tea," she said, guiding her onto the patio where the sun had created a pool of warmth and allowed them the privacy Maddie obviously wanted.

"Okay, what's going on with you?" Maddie asked. "I got the invitation to your party."

"You'll come, won't you? Cal and the kids, too?"

"Of course, we'll be there, but sweetie, do you think maybe you're going a little overboard with the whole Christmas thing? You spent all your spare time for two days helping Dana Sue decorate Sullivan's. You planned our party, which was a huge success. And now you want to do your own party. Is this about making up for lost time, or are you doing some kind of in-your-face thing as a test for Tom?"

Jeanette blinked at the question. "That's crazy. Why would I test Tom?"

"You tell me."

Jeanette sipped her tea and thought about what Maddie was asking. Had she gone overboard? Was she testing Tom? She didn't think so. "Tom and I have been doing okay ever since we went to see his parents. I finally feel as if we have a real chance."

"Okay, then you know what I think?" Maddie said. "I think you're trying to fill a void. What you really want is what you used to have with your parents. Is that possible?"

Jeanette hadn't considered it, but now that Maddie had voiced the idea, she realized it was exactly what she was doing. After so many years, she'd finally recaptured her own love for the holiday season, but she wanted more. She wanted things to be the way they'd once been. Of course, that wasn't possible, so she was substituting all these other activities for what was going to be missing from the holidays—her family.

"Things are so much better with my parents," she said slowly. "We've been talking at least once a week, but they haven't said a word about Christmas. I don't think they're ready to deal with that yet."

"Have you asked them? Maybe invited them here?" Maddie suggested. "It might be easier for them to get back into the holidays in a new place where they can create brand-new memories. You know they'd be welcome at Sullivan's on Christmas Day with all the rest of us."

"I could at least ask, I suppose," Jeanette said.

"And if they turn you down, just remember it has nothing to do with you. It's all about what they can handle."

"You're right." Jeanette nodded. "I can do this. If

I've reached out to Tom's parents, I ought to be able to strengthen my bonds with my own."

Maddie grinned. "Not the same. You had very low expectations where they were concerned. The way I heard it from Tom, that they even showed up last Saturday for festival was nothing short of a miracle. Miracles don't ever seem to be that easy with your own folks, not with all that emotional baggage."

"True, but I owe it to them and to myself to try," she said decisively. "I think I'll go inside right now and call them."

"Good luck," Maddie called after her. "And no matter what happens, remember that you have people all around you here who love you and consider you family."

"Thanks," she said, her eyes misty. Knowing that Maddie had been one hundred percent sincere was enough to give her the courage to reach out. If it were any other occasion, the risk would be minimal, but Christmas had a lot of pitfalls. Maybe, finally, they'd be ready to let go of the heartache that had been associated with the holiday for too long now.

CHAPTER TWENTY-FOUR

❖

With Maddie's support still echoing in her head, Jeanette picked up the phone in her office and called her parents. As always, her mother sounded surprised to hear her voice.

"Jeanette," her mother said. "Is that you?"

"It's me, Mom."

"Is anything wrong?"

"No, everything's fine. How's Dad?"

"He's getting better every day. That medicine has made all the difference in the world. He's like a new man." She paused. "No, I take that back. He's like the man I married."

"I'm really glad, Mom. What about you? Are you getting back into your routine?" The last time they'd spoken, her mother had mentioned that she intended to become more active in the women's group at her church, something she'd given up when Jeanette's dad was injured. Jeanette had thought that her desire to reach out to the friends who'd once been so important to her was proof that things were finally improving at home.

"I went to the Wednesday meeting at church last week," she told Jeanette.

"And how was it to be back?"

"It was wonderful to catch up with everyone. We never had time when I saw them at services. I swear, even though I've only missed the meetings for a couple of months, half of them have grandbabies I didn't know about. We talked so much, we didn't get a bit of business accomplished. I'm baking a chocolate cake with caramel frosting for the coffee hour after services on Sunday. Everyone kept telling me how much they'd missed it."

"That's wonderful, Mom. You sound good."

"I am good, better than I've been in a very long while. Now tell me about you," her mother said. "How's that young man of yours?"

"Tom's good."

"And work's going well?"

"It is. We had a holiday party at the spa the other night. I planned the whole thing and it was packed. Now I'm planning my own open house for Christmas Eve. That's why I called you, actually. I'd like you and Dad to come to Serenity for Christmas. Now that I have the house, I have a guest room. You could stay for a couple of days and meet all my friends."

The silence that greeted the invitation wasn't a surprise, but it hurt just the same.

"You know we don't celebrate the holidays," her mother finally said. "Not since your brother died."

Determined not to be deterred by the old argument, Jeanette pressed her. "That was years ago, Mom. I miss him, too, but he wouldn't want us to be like this. Ben loved the holidays. We should celebrate as a family. You won't have to lift a finger to help with the open house here. It's all under control. And friends have invited us for Christmas dinner, so there's no worry about cooking, either. I'd just like you and Dad to meet the people who are important to me. Please. And Tom will be here. You already know him. I'd really like us to have a family Christmas again."

Her mother's hesitation seemed endless. "Well, I suppose I could ask your father. Don't count on it, though."

"Tell him it would mean the world to me," Jeanette said, praying that enough time had passed that hearing that would be enough for him. Perhaps, with a little holiday spirit on her side, she could reclaim her rightful place in her family and together they could finally move on.

"I'll call you tomorrow, okay?" she told her mother. "Talk to Dad tonight and we can discuss it again tomorrow."

"It's really that important to you?" her mother asked.

"It really is. I'm happy here, Mom. I have great friends. Serenity is a wonderful town. And it's all decorated for Christmas right now, so it's looking its very best. The spa is amazing and we've even made it look festive, too. And my house is cozy and warm. I learned how to make it that way from you. I want to share all this with both of you. I want you to be a part of my life again."

"Then I'll do my best to persuade your father," her mother promised.

Jeanette breathed a sigh of relief. "Thanks, Mom. Love you."

"We love you, too," her mother responded. "I know it hasn't always seemed that way, but we do."

Having her mother say the words aloud was a better present than Jeanette had ever expected. Even if her parents turned down the invitation for this year, those words were enough to make her keep reaching out. Maybe, at long last, she'd reclaim the family she'd thought for so long was lost to her.

* * *

Tom was actually starting to warm up to the whole concept of the holidays. He was pretty sure it was Jeanette's enthusiasm rubbing off on him. Or maybe it was because everyone in town seemed to have the holiday spirit. He'd even caught himself pausing in the town square before walking home to admire the tree and enjoy the sound of carols, which were now blasting from loudspeakers set up at Ronnie's store.

He was about to leave his office when Teresa stuck her head in, her expression disapproving, and announced that he had a visitor. "He doesn't have an appointment, but he says it's important. Shall I tell him to call first and schedule a better time?" She sounded as if she really wanted to do exactly that. She did not like disruptions to her routine any more than Tom usually did. Today, however, he was in such a good mood, he saw little reason to be difficult just for the sake of his schedule. He could spare a few minutes.

"No, it's okay. Send him in. Did he give you a name?"

"Dwight Mitchell."

Tom wished he hadn't acted so hastily. Dwight Mitchell was the last person he wanted to see. Still, he plastered a formal smile on his face and held out his hand when the high-powered attorney from Charleston walked into his office.

"What brings you all the way to Serenity?" Tom asked, gesturing toward a chair.

"You, of course. I thought we should talk again after that abbreviated conversation we had with your father."

Tom frowned. "I certainly appreciate you taking the time to come here, but I think I made my position clear. I have no interest in practicing law."

Dwight grinned. "You made that clear. Have to say it

was good to see your father flustered for once. I didn't think that was possible."

"If you understand I'm not interested in practicing law in Charleston or anywhere else, then why are you here?"

"Actually I'm head of the search team for a new financial person in Charleston. I know you held that position in another town not long ago. Now, as town manager here, you have even more experience in all aspects of government. After listening to how committed you are to this kind of work, I think you're exactly the kind of man we've been looking for. I thought I should check with you, though, see how you'd feel about me tossing your hat in the ring for the job. Are you interested?"

For once Tom didn't have to feign his enthusiasm. To have an opportunity like this drop into his lap was amazing. An image of Jeanette's likely reaction gave him pause, but he couldn't deny that he was interested. Surely it made sense to at least explore the opportunity. That was reasonable, wasn't it? He fought off the sensation that Jeanette wouldn't see it the same way and met Dwight's gaze. "I'm interested," he said.

"Glad to hear it."

"It's exactly the kind of move I'd been hoping to make eventually."

"Well, sooner's better than later, don't you think? This strikes me as a nice little town, but all the real action is in a city."

That was precisely what Tom had always thought. Of course, just because Dwight Mitchell was here to test the waters didn't mean he'd get the job. Still, he owed it to himself—and to Jeanette and their future—to explore the possibility of moving into a position that could really take him one more rung up the ladder to the kind of job he eventually wanted as manager of a major city. He winced as he realized he was trying to mentally justify moving forward on something that was bound to upset her.

"Tell me something, though," he said, suddenly struck by a thought. "Does my father have anything to do with this?"

"Not a thing," Dwight assured him. "I doubt he even knows I'm on the search committee. We've been pretty low-key up till now. John Davis isn't leaving the job until February, so we have a little time to get all the right candidates lined up. You'd be at the top of my list."

"I appreciate that," Tom said. "And, yes, I'd definitely like to be considered."

"Then we'll schedule an interview. What about day after tomorrow? Can you get over to Charleston? I realize that this time of year schedules are crazy, but I don't want to wait until after the holidays."

Tom glanced at his calendar and saw that was the day that Jeanette's parents would be arriving, and only two days before Christmas. She'd asked him to join them for dinner, but he could probably make it back in time for that.

"What time?" he asked.

"Let's say two o'clock," Dwight said. "You'll be the first person we've talked with, so if you make the kind of impression I'm expecting you to, we can wrap this up right then and there. That would give you time to give people here plenty of notice that you're leaving."

Two o'clock would be cutting it close, but Tom figured the interview wouldn't last more than an hour, two at the outside. That would still give him enough time to make it back for dinner. If things went well, he could sit down with Jeanette afterward and fill her in. They could make the final decision together. No need to worry her before that.

"I'll be there," he told Dwight. "And thanks again for thinking of me."

As soon as he'd walked Dwight to his car, he considered calling Jeanette and discussing the potential job right then, but something held him back. Perhaps it was the hundred percent certainty that she wasn't going to be nearly as happy about this as he was. She was all caught up in her plans for her open house. Why bring her down when there was a chance this would come to nothing?

Poor excuse, and he knew it. But the truth was he needed time, time to come up with an overwhelmingly sound argument to convince her that his getting this job was all good for both of them.

He sighed. He was lying to himself. She was going to be mad as hell, and also hurt that he hadn't discussed it with her immediately.

Oh, come on, the cowardly side of him countered. He wasn't talking about postponing the conversation indefinitely. It was a couple of days. He'd have all the facts then. And maybe by then his powers of persuasion would kick into high gear and he'd find all the words he needed to win her over.

Jeanette was a nervous wreck as she watched out the window for the arrival of her parents. That they'd agreed to come was as much of a Christmas miracle as she'd dared to hope for. That she couldn't share this moment with Tom was a disappointment, but it only cast a slight pall over her anticipation. He would be here later for dinner, for the open house tomorrow night and for Christmas dinner at Sullivan's.

She glanced around her house one more time to reassure herself that there wasn't a speck of dust on anything, that every light on the tree was sparkling brightly, that the stray cat she'd taken in a few days ago hadn't knocked any more ornaments to the floor. The orange tabby—she'd named him Marmalade—glanced up at her as if to reproach her for even thinking he'd do something so uncivilized. In fact, his meow radiated indignation.

"Okay, okay, you're on your best behavior," Jeanette said. "I'm just nervous."

This time the meow was more sympathetic. Limping on his injured paw, the cat rubbed up against Jeanette, then gave her hand a scratchy lick. After that, Marmalade settled down on the bright green Christmas pillow on the sofa as if it had been meant for him. His contented purr made Jeanette smile. For years she'd wanted a pet, but her lifestyle hadn't permitted it. Marmalade's arrival a few days before Christmas seemed like yet another sign that her life was coming together exactly as she'd always wanted it to.

Still anxious, she went into the kitchen to check on the coffee she was brewing for her dad and the kettle she'd filled with water to make tea for herself and her mom. She filled a plate with Christmas cookies she'd baked using her mother's favorite recipe. Though she'd done most of her baking a few days ago, she'd made one last batch this morning just to fill the house with the scent of warm cookies.

Back in the living room, she peered out the window just in time to see her parents turn into the driveway. Opening the door, she ran out to greet them.

"Mom, Dad, I'm so glad you came," she said, hugging them both. "Let's get your things inside so you can rest a bit."

Her father shook his head. "We haven't been traveling for days, you know. It's only a two-hour drive, at least the way your mother insisted we go. Could have made it in ninety minutes if we'd taken the interstate." Even as he spoke, though, he gave her mom's hand an affectionate squeeze.

"I'm surprised you let Mom get behind the wheel," Jeanette said.

"My leg's still bothering me some," he admitted. "I'm starting to like being chauffeured around."

"Well, don't get too used to it, old man," her mother teased. "The service ends as soon as you get back on your feet a hundred percent."

"Seems like a good incentive to take my time," he said, chuckling.

Jeanette listened to the exchange with amazement. It sounded exactly like the kind of cheerful banter that had gone on in their house years ago. It was wonderful to see.

Inside, they made a fuss over the house, even the navy blue guest room.

"Now, this is the kind of room a man can feel comfortable in," her father said. "Doesn't have all that frilly stuff your mama likes."

"Tom picked the color," Jeanette admitted. "I had my doubts, but it does look good."

Her father eyed her curiously. "Just how serious is this thing between you two? If you're letting him decide on paint colors in your house, it sounds as if he's fairly important. Do I need to ask his intentions?"

"Heavens, no!" Jeanette said. "But things are good between us right now. He'll be here later for dinner. I'm glad you're going to get to spend some time with him."

She showed them where they could find extra towels, then left them to unpack. "Come on into the kitchen whenever you're ready. I have tea, coffee and cookies."

"Your mama's sugar cookies, smells like," her dad said.

"That's right."

Her mother gave him a resigned look. "I imagine that means I'll be unpacking on my own. Your daddy never could resist my sugar cookies, especially when they're fresh out of the oven."

He chuckled again. "I'll be with Jeanette in the kitchen if you need me."

As soon as they were alone and Jeanette had poured his coffee, she met his gaze. "Dad, I can't tell you how glad I am that you came."

"We should have done this a long time ago," he said, regarding her with real regret. "We've let too much time pass without taking an interest in your life."

She pressed a kiss to his cheek. "You're here now. That's all that matters."

He took a bite of a cookie, then smiled. "You might have gotten your brains from me, but you got your mama's knack for baking."

Jeanette laughed. "Don't let her hear you say that. She's every bit as smart as you."

"So she is," he agreed, sobering. "And I thank my lucky stars every day that she's stuck by me all these years. It can't have been easy for her, or for you."

"We both love you," Jeanette told him simply.

And in the end, that was all that mattered.

At six o'clock, when Jeanette took the roast out of the oven, there was still no sign of Tom. Nor had he called. She was torn between worry and exasperation. Trying not to let on just how upset she was, she put the rest of the meal on the table and plastered a bright smile on her face.

"I think we should go ahead and eat," she told her parents. "Tom's obviously been held up."

"We can wait a while longer if you want to," her mother said, studying her worriedly.

"No," Jeanette said more sharply than she'd intended. "The food will be ruined if we wait."

Her mother gave her a sympathetic look. "Sweetie, nothing's going to be ruined. The roast will be okay for a little while in the oven, if you set it on warm. Everything else can be heated up in the microwave."

"No," Jeanette said stubbornly. "He knew what time we were eating. He should be here."

"You could call him," her mother suggested. "He has a cell phone, doesn't he?"

Jeanette debated with herself about calling, then decided it was ridiculous not to. She started with his office, even though it was past closing time. Even so, Teresa answered.

"Teresa, it's Jeanette. I'm looking for Tom. Is he still there?"

"He hasn't been here all afternoon," Teresa told her. "He had some kind of meeting over in Charleston."

"Charleston?" Jeanette echoed, letting her shock show.

"He didn't tell you?"

"No, he didn't mention a thing," she said, a sinking sensation in the pit of her stomach. "Thanks, though. I'll try him on his cell phone."

"I'll leave a message on his desk that you called in case he stops in here," Teresa promised.

"Thanks."

She hung up, then dialed Tom's cell number. When he picked up, there was so much noise on the other end she could hardly hear him.

"Tom, it's me. Where *are* you?"

He muttered an expletive, then asked, "What time is it?"

"After six," she said tightly. "Where are you?"

"I had a meeting in Charleston. It ran longer than I expected and then we went out for a quick drink. Time got away from me."

"So I gather," she said. "And if you've been drinking, then you shouldn't be driving, so perhaps you ought to consider staying at your folks' place tonight."

"But your parents—"

"Forget it," she said. "You'll see them tomorrow, that is if you can tear yourself away from whatever's going on in Charleston."

"But I want to tell you about all this," he said. "Just wait until you hear what's happened."

She fell silent and did exactly that—waited.

"Jeanette, you still there?"

"Yes."

"I've been offered a job. It's exactly what I was hoping for. I just wasn't expecting it to happen this fast. I can't wait to tell you all about it."

"You've been offered a job," she echoed dully. "In Charleston?"

"Yes."

"And you've accepted? Without even discussing it with me?"

"Not formally. I was going to talk to you about it tonight, then give them my answer. It's the opportunity I've always wanted."

Jeanette could read between the lines. He was going to say yes.

"Congratulations," she said, barely managing to choke out the word. Everything she'd feared was coming true. He'd chosen something else over her. "By the way, don't bother rushing back tomorrow. There's no need for you to waste your time being here for my open house."

"Hey, hold on a minute. Are you uninviting me?" he asked incredulously.

"That's exactly what I'm doing. I don't want you here."

"It's because of the job, isn't it? Dammit, I knew I shouldn't have blurted the news out like this."

"How intuitive," she said sarcastically. "I can see why they're desperate to hire you."

The background noise faded as he apparently moved to someplace quieter. "Come on, Jeanette. At least listen to what I have to say. This is going to be a great thing for both of us."

"No, thanks," she said. "If you'd mentioned any of this before you went to Charleston, we might have had something to discuss. Since you didn't, I can only assume that my opinion doesn't count. You've known all along how I felt about taking a backseat in anyone's life. I thought you got it."

"I did. I do. Come on, you know I value your opinion. I wanted all the details before we talked about this."

"It will hardly be much of a discussion if you've already made your decision, will it? Trust me, Tom, I do wish you well, but I'm done."

She hung up before he could reply. Then, despite the ringing of the phone, she put dinner back on the table and managed to choke it down without once bursting into tears in front of her parents. To their credit, neither of them mentioned Tom's absence, and when the meal ended, her mother shooed her away.

"Let me clean up in here for you," she told Jeanette. "Maybe then you'll finally answer that phone that's been ringing off and on all evening."

"Not a chance," Jeanette said, then gave her a hug. "Thanks for not asking a lot of questions, though."

"It's not me you need to worry about. If your daddy crosses paths with Tom anytime soon, you can bet there will be questions."

Jeanette's lips twitched slightly. "Tell Daddy he can slug him if he wants to."

Her mother feigned dismay. "Please, I am not going to give him any ideas. He'd like nothing better than to slug a man who's hurt you."

"I'm not hurt," Jeanette said. "I'm furious."

Her mother patted her hand. "Sometimes it's real hard to tell the difference."

Tom walked into Sullivan's on Christmas Day, not sure what to expect. Dana Sue had called to repeat the invitation, she'd even included his parents, but there was no question that Jeanette would be here. There was also no question that she still wasn't speaking to him. The one time she'd actually picked up the phone in the past two days, she'd hung up as soon as she heard his voice.

He knew he'd made a mess of things by not telling her in advance about the job interview. Warning bells had gone off in his head, but he'd ignored them. He wondered if they'd be able to make peace or if she really was through with him. He had a ring in his pocket that he hoped would persuade her to give him another chance. If that didn't work, he was counting on the arrival of the big guns—his parents—to do the trick. He'd finally gotten through to them that Jeanette meant everything to him. He hoped their promise to come and share in today's celebration would be enough to convince Jeanette that he was serious about their future and that his parents wouldn't be a roadblock to their happiness.

Of course, the real issue was the job in Charleston, and he had a feeling there was nothing he could say about that

that would appease her. Turning it down might do the trick, but he hadn't been able to bring himself to do that. He was holding off on that to use it as a last resort, a way to prove that she mattered more to him than any job, even an ideal one.

"What are you doing here?"

The icy question was spoken behind him. Apparently she hadn't mellowed.

"Dana Sue insisted I come," he said, drinking in the sight of her. Though she still looked angry, the dark circles under her eyes suggested she'd been sleeping no better than he had.

"Yet another person making decisions that affect me without discussing them," she said bitterly. "I would have told her I didn't want you here."

"Apparently Dana Sue has a more generous spirit."

"Look, you can stay or go, that's up to you, but don't stay on my account and don't stay if you're going to ruin it for everyone."

"That's definitely not my intention," he said. "In fact, I was hoping to grab a minute alone with you."

"Why?" she asked, her tone still unyielding.

"I have a gift for you," he said.

For just an instant, she looked nonplussed. "I didn't get you anything. Well, I did, but I returned it yesterday."

"Actually you've already given me a gift," he told her. "You brought something into my life I never expected. Look, I know I've really botched this up, but I swear to you that I had every intention of discussing the whole job thing with you as soon as I got home that night. I thought I could make you see that it was a great offer."

"Yeah, I got that part. You might not have accepted, but it was plain you intended to."

"I wanted to," he corrected. "There's a difference. Please tell me you know I think that you're more important to me than any job," he said.

She shook her head. "Sorry, I'm not getting that. Words are easy. Your actions speak volumes."

"What about this action?" he asked, reaching in his pocket for a foil-wrapped package with bright red ribbon. "Will this convince you?"

She backed up a step, even as her eyes stayed glued to the package. "Tom?"

"Yes, Jeanette," he said solemnly.

"What does that mean?"

He chuckled. "I think if you open it, the meaning will be clear."

Her gaze narrowed. "Do you still want the job in Charleston?"

"I do, but it's negotiable."

She blinked at that. "Really?"

"You're more important to me than any job. Look, I know I screwed up. I should have told you before I went to the interview, discussed what it might mean with you, but it all happened so fast. I'm sorry."

"So, instead I got blindsided," she said.

"Again, sorry."

"If we're going to be together, we have to talk things through, make big decisions together."

"I know that. And if you will hear me out about the job and you still disapprove and think we can't make it work, I'll tell them I'm not taking it."

"But you want it," she said, sounding resigned. "That's the truth, isn't it?"

"Yes."

"Then how can I be the one to ruin it for you?"

"Because you matter more." He tucked his finger under her chin and forced her to look at him. "I mean that, Jeanette. You matter more!"

She seemed startled by his vehemence. "Okay, so say we can work through that, what about your parents? We've made some progress..."

"They'll be here shortly to make a little more progress."

Her eyes widened. "Your parents are coming here?"

He glanced at his watch. "In about fifteen minutes."

"Does Dana Sue know you invited them?"

"Her idea," he admitted. "I wasn't clever enough or brave enough to think of it."

"I see."

"Do you really? We can make this work, Jeanette. I believe that with everything in me."

She still looked doubtful. "I won't leave Serenity," she said.

"Did I ask you to?"

"This job you want is in Charleston. A move is implied."

"But not absolutely necessary. I can commute. Or we can arrange our hours so we can split our time between both places. We already have the guesthouse at my parents' place in Charleston and we can keep your house here."

"You really have given this a lot of thought, haven't you?"

He nodded. "Looking at things from every angle is one of my skills as a manager."

"It may turn out to be a bit annoying in a prospective husband," she noted.

"I'll change," he offered. "I'll be obnoxiously single-minded, if that's what you want."

"Hardly."

"Then tell me what you *do* want."

"I want it all," she admitted. "You, Serenity, my house and you doing what makes you happy."

"You make me happy."

"But you need to do work that's satisfying, too," she conceded, then sighed. "I suppose we can talk about commuting."

"Thank you. Anything else we need to negotiate before you accept my proposal?"

She considered the question, her expression thoughtful. "You won't grumble about Christmas ever again?"

"Never," he said, then amended, "Well, other than having to deal with Howard if you volunteer me to help with the festival."

"Acceptable," she said.

"Ready to open your present yet?" he inquired hopefully.

She gave him an impish look. "Not just yet. My dad's around here somewhere. I think you two should have a talk."

"You want me to ask for your father's blessing?"

"No, I want you to talk to a man who's just rediscovered the meaning of Christmas. He's the one in the Santa suit."

"But I thought—"

She grinned. "I know. He wasn't too wild about the idea, either, but then Howard decided to take Mary Vaughn, Rory Sue and Sonny to Aspen to celebrate the fact that Sonny and Mary Vaughn are on their way to a reconciliation. Somebody had to fill in."

"And you convinced your dad to do it?"

She shook her head. "I called in some help."

"Oh?"

"Maddie, Dana Sue and Helen. They ganged up on him the second he came in the door. They told him how disappointed the kids would be if there was no Santa to hand out presents."

She shrugged as her gaze went to her dad, who was surrounded by a couple dozen kids, many of them belonging to her best friends. Two college-age youngsters—most likely Maddie's son Ty and Dana Sue's daughter Annie, whom Tom had heard so much about—were trying to organize the little ones into a line, while not even glancing at each other.

Tom pointed out the pair. "Ty and Annie, right?"

Jeanette followed the direction of his gaze. "Yes."

"Looks as if they have some issues to work out, too," he said.

"I know," Jeanette said. "Neither Maddie nor Dana Sue knows what's going on between them these days, just that they're not speaking."

"Maybe the holidays will work their magic on them, too," Tom said.

Jeanette regarded him with surprise. "You actually mean that?"

He nodded. "By the way, your dad really seems to be in his element."

"He always had a soft spot for kids and for Christmas. He just lost sight of that for a while." She grinned. "You should be very grateful to him, by the way. You were their next choice to fill in as Santa."

"I'll be sure and thank him for saving me from that," Tom said, though somehow the prospect wasn't nearly as disturbing as it once would have been.

He brushed a stray wisp of hair back from Jeanette's cheek. "Sounds to me as if we have a lot to celebrate," he said.

She stood on tiptoe and kissed him. "Are you feeling that holiday spirit yet?"

Tom laughed. "Well, I'm feeling something, all right."

"Hey, watch it. It's Christmas and this is a PG-rated, family celebration. To say nothing of the fact that I will not have your parents walking in here and finding us in a lip-lock."

"Later, then," he said dutifully.

"Definitely later. Merry Christmas, Tom."

"The very merriest, darlin'."

* * * * *

*The Sweet Magnolias legacy continues for
a new generation of women!*

Keep reading for a sneak peak of Home in Carolina
by #1 New York Times *bestselling author
Sherryl Woods.*

CHAPTER ONE

Settled at her usual table near the kitchen of her mom's restaurant, Annie Sullivan ate the last of her omelet and opened the local paper to the sports section. Even though she and major league pitcher Tyler Townsend, a hometown boy, had been apart for a long time now, it was a habit she hadn't been able to break. She kept hoping that one day she'd see his name in print and it wouldn't hurt. So far, though, that hadn't happened.

Today, with the baseball season barely started in mid-April, she was expecting nothing more than a small jolt to her system from the local weekly. Instead, her jaw dropped at the headline at the top of the page: Star Braves Pitcher Ty Townsend on Injured Reserve. The article went on to report that after pitching just three games, the baseball sensation from Serenity would be out indefinitely following surgery two weeks ago for a potentially career-ending injury to his shoulder. He'd be doing rehab, possibly for months, and he'd be doing it right here in town. He was, in fact, already here.

Clutching the paper in a white-knuckled grip, Annie had to draw in several deep breaths before she could stand.

Shouting for her mother, she headed straight for the restaurant kitchen, only to be intercepted by sous-chef Erik Whitney.

Regarding her with concern, Erik steadied her when she would have dashed right past him. "Hey, sweetheart, where's the fire?" he asked.

"I need to see my mother," she said, trying to wrench free of his grasp.

"She's in her office. What's wrong, Annie? You look as if you've seen a ghost."

Though she'd poured out her heart to Erik as a teenager, right this second she was incapable of speech. Instead, Annie simply handed him the paper.

Erik took one look at the headline and muttered a curse. "I knew this was going to happen," he said.

Annie stared at him, her sense of betrayal deepening. "You knew about this? You knew Ty was back in town?"

Erik nodded. "Since the day before yesterday."

"Mom, too?"

He nodded again.

Now it was Annie who uttered a curse, made a U-turn and headed back to the table to grab her purse. What had everyone been thinking, conspiring to keep something this huge from her? Especially her mom, who knew better than anyone the damage secrets, lies and betrayal could do.

Erik stuck with her. "Come on, Annie, don't blame your mother for this. Go to her office. Talk to her," he urged as she stormed past him through the kitchen. "She was just trying to protect you."

At the door, she turned and asked angrily, "So I could be blindsided, instead? Ty had surgery two weeks ago, Erik! He's been in town how long—a couple of days? A week? It's not as if this happened yesterday."

"I'm sure Dana Sue thought it wouldn't make the paper here before she had a chance to tell you."

"Forget the stupid newspaper. We're talking about Serenity in an age of cell phones and the Internet," Annie said incredulously. "Gossip spreads in minutes, and around here Ty's big news. Heck, even *you* knew, and you're not tapped into the grapevine. You all knew before one word of this hit the paper."

"Helen's tapped in and I'm married to her, to say nothing of working for your mom. Not much gets past the Sweet Magnolias. And in this case, they all knew what was going on the instant Maddie found out Ty had to have surgery."

"Which begs the question," Annie said bitterly. "Why didn't anyone think I had a right to know?" A thought suddenly struck her. "That's where Maddie went a couple of weeks ago, isn't it? She went to be with Ty when he had his surgery."

Erik nodded. "Look, it's not about you deserving to know," he said reasonably. "You've been pretty touchy about anything to do with Ty for quite a while now. Nobody's known quite how to handle it."

Okay, that was fair. In fact, Annie totally understood the dilemma. She and Ty had been together on a casual basis during her senior year in high school and for a couple of years after that. Since their mothers, Dana Sue and Maddie, were best friends, she and Ty had been friends forever, as well. The ties binding them had been tight on many levels.

And then it had all unraveled. Annie supposed the breakup had been as inevitable as the fact that they'd fallen in love in the first place. After all, a superstar professional athlete had beautiful women falling at his feet in every city. How was Annie, the quiet hometown girl struggling every day to beat an eating disorder, supposed to compete with that, especially when she was still in college?

The official disintegration of their relationship had dragged out over an entire year, partly because neither of them had known how to dash all those parental expectations that they'd marry and live happily ever after.

For months they'd seen the handwriting on the wall, but they'd both been in denial. When tensions had been running especially high, they'd tried to avoid coming back to Serenity at the same time. On the rare occasions when family get-togethers couldn't be avoided, they'd tried to deal with the awkwardness with carefully orchestrated polite indifference. They'd both understood how a bitter split could potentially damage the lifelong friendship between their mothers, and they'd wanted to avoid inflicting that kind of collateral damage. At least they'd agreed on that much.

Of course, all of that was before the real damage had been done, before Ty's infidelity had become public knowledge in the worst possible way. After that, all bets had been off. There'd been no more pretense that things had ended amicably.

Fortunately, neither her mom nor Ty's had asked too many questions once the facts were out there. It went beyond sensitivity. Annie suspected Dana Sue and Maddie had made a pact years earlier to leave the two of them alone. Goodness knew, the Sweet Magnolias, as Dana Sue and Maddie and Helen had been known since high school, meddled in everyone else's lives, but over the years they'd barely mentioned Ty in Annie's presence or her to him. More recently, the silence had been deafening.

Annie supposed their current avoidance of the subject was part of the same old pattern, though she was in no mood to cut them any slack this time. Didn't they think she'd care that Ty had sustained a serious injury? Didn't they know what it would do to her for him to be right back here, in her face every single day? Couldn't they at least have warned her?

As she started out the door, Erik tried once more to stop her.

"Wait!" he commanded. "Come on, Annie. If you won't talk to your mother, talk to me. I swear I'll just listen. You can rant and rave all you want."

She regarded him with a bleak expression. "There's nothing to say." Ty had as much right to come home to Serenity as she did, even if it would turn her life upside down.

"Where are you going?"

She shook her head. She honestly didn't know. Not to work, that was for sure. She worked at The Corner Spa, owned by her mom, Helen and Ty's mom. Maddie, in fact, ran it. Annie didn't want to face her right now, either. Though they both tried, it had been awkward between them ever since the breakup. Now it would be a thousand times worse. She wasn't sure she could bear another of Maddie's pitying looks.

Ironically, Annie worked at the spa as a sports injury therapist and personal trainer. Armed with her degree as a physical therapist and two years of experience at a sports injury facility in Charleston, she'd had the idea to add a physical therapy component to the spa's services.

And while the spa was open only to women, there wasn't a doubt in her mind that Ty intended to do his rehab there in the off-hours when no one else was around. He could be counting on his stepfather and former coach, Cal Maddox, to oversee his rehab, or even the spa's other personal fitness instructor, Elliott Cruz, but Annie suspected that sooner or later someone was going to suggest she get involved. She was the one with the expertise in sports injuries, after all.

Just the thought of seeing Ty again was enough to make her want to throw up. It had been years since she'd won her battle with anorexia, and though she'd never been bulimic, right this second any thought of food made her nauseous. The little bit she'd already eaten churned in her stomach.

Even as the dark thoughts registered, Annie gasped. No way! she thought fiercely. She was not going to let Ty's return send her back into the kind of self-destructive eating pattern that had nearly killed her. She was stronger than that. And he was a pig. In fact, that might have to become her mantra, one she repeated at least a dozen times a day.

"I am strong, and Tyler Townsend is a pig!" she said aloud, testing it.

Yes, indeed, that ought to keep her from backsliding. And if she felt herself slipping on either front, well, she could always take an extended vacation somewhere far away from Serenity until Ty's shoulder had healed and he was back to his glamorous, self-indulgent lifestyle, the lifestyle he'd chosen over her.

Satisfied with her plan, she considered going to work, after all, but concluded it might be a bit too soon to test herself. Instead, she called the spa and asked Elliott to take any of her appointments he had time for and to cancel the rest.

"I'm taking a mental health day," she informed him, falling back on an excuse she hadn't used since high school.

"Ah, you heard about Ty," he said, sounding sympathetic. "Anything I can do?"

"Has he been sneaking in there after hours?" she asked, hating the fact that there were virtually no secrets in this town except those kept from her.

"Just a couple of times," he admitted. He hesitated, then

added, "I've started working with him, but he'd do better with you."

"Hell will freeze over before that happens," she said heatedly.

"Think about it, Annie," Elliott urged. "His career's on the line, and he was once your friend."

"He was more than a friend and he blew it," she retorted, unyielding. "Will you deal with my appointments today or not?"

"Of course I will," he said. "I'm sorry you're hurting."

Annie sighed. "I just wish I knew if I'm more hurt because Ty's back or because everyone apparently conspired to keep it from me."

"A little of both, I suspect," Elliott said. "Do something totally spontaneous today, something a little crazy. Blow off some steam. You'll feel better."

Annie considered the suggestion, then dismissed it. The only thing that might make her feel marginally better would be having Elliott—or anyone else—agree to punch Ty's face in. She smiled at the thought and suddenly knew exactly where she needed to go—to the one person who might actually do that for her.

Ten minutes later, she was sitting on a stool behind the counter at her dad's hardware store on Main Street, while he waited on a customer. Ronnie Sullivan had a history of being quick-tempered and protective. This might work to her advantage today.

As soon as they were alone, her father surveyed her intently. "You don't look so good, kid."

"You could make me feel better," she suggested.

"By punching Ty's lights out?" he guessed, proving he, too, had been in on the town's worst-kept secret. "I don't think so."

She sighed. "Why not? He deserves it."

Ronnie laughed. "No question about it, but can you imagine the ruckus that would stir up between your mom and Maddie? They'd be forced to take sides, and so would Cal and I. Then Helen and Erik would be drawn into it, and eventually the entire town would likely follow suit. Pretty soon, everybody would have to wear buttons or ribbons to declare which side they're on. Sorry, sweetie, it just wouldn't be good for business, and in the end, you'd be consumed by guilt for stirring it all up."

Despite herself, Annie chuckled at her dad's logic. It was true: Serenity did have a tendency to take sides, and there was no way this feud between her and Ty would stay quiet for long, even without her dad beating Ty up for her. And, damn her soft heart, she *would* feel guilty about it.

"I guess I'll just have to deal with this," she said morosely.

Her dad pulled a stool up next to hers and studied her with a frown. "Is there anything else I can do to help?"

"You can tell me why men are such idiots," she said. The question wasn't rhetorical. She really wanted to know.

"Hormones and a lack of common sense," Ronnie said at once. "Just look how I messed things up with your mom for no good reason. Weigh that against how long it took me to make things right. Idiocy definitely played a role in that." He slanted a look at her. "You want to talk about what happened? I know it's a touchy subject, but you've never said a word about how you felt when things blew up and all Ty's dirty laundry was spread all over the tabloids."

"I think my feelings are pretty obvious without dissecting them," she told him.

"Sometimes talking does help."

She shook her head. "Not likely."

"Sweetie, I know how badly he hurt you, and if I really thought it would help, I would punch him." He hesitated, then added, "I also know how important his friendship was to you for a long time before that. Do you really want to lose that, too?"

"I lost our friendship a long time ago," she said mournfully. That, as much as anything else, was what had broken her heart. "I just have to face it, Dad. It's over. Not just the relationship, but also the friendship. I'll never be able to trust Ty again."

"Your mom learned to trust me again," he reminded her gently.

"Not the same," she said.

Her dad was right about one thing, though. Cheating was something he and Ty had in common. The big difference was that Ronnie had recognized his mistake after one careless, irresponsible slip. Ty not only hadn't acknowledged it, he'd compounded it by cheating over and over until he'd finally gotten caught. He had a three-year-old son as proof of his infidelity.

Annie might have been able to get past the cheating with enough time, but that precious little boy? No way. Any babies Ty had were supposed to be with her, not some gold digger who'd slept with Ty a couple of times, then dumped her kid with him in exchange for a big payoff when he wouldn't marry her.

Oh, Annie knew all the gory details. Not because Ty had told her, but because they'd been tabloid fodder for weeks. Obviously if Ty was home, so was his little boy. Now everyone in Serenity who'd been living on Mars when the story first broke would know just how big a fool she'd been to give her heart to some hotshot sports superstar.

Worst of all, despite everything—the betrayal, the hurt,

the humiliation—she still loved him. And that made her an
even bigger idiot than he was.

"You need to call Annie," Maddie told Ty after seeing
the headline about his return in the Serenity newspaper.
"It was crazy to think we could keep your being back here
quiet for long."

"Don't you think Dana Sue probably filled her in?" he
said, torn between dread and anticipation at the thought
of speaking to Annie. Their relationship had ended really
badly, and it had been all his fault. "Besides, Annie doesn't
want to talk to me. She made that plain three years ago."

"When Trevor was born," his mother guessed.

Ty nodded. He loved his son to pieces, but he knew that
Annie would never in a million years get past the fact that
he'd not only cheated, but fathered a child with someone
else. There wasn't an explanation in the world good enough
to make her see past that one huge mistake.

Claiming that they hadn't been exclusive certainly hadn't
worked. Reminding her of the countless times they'd talked
about how reasonable it was to date others while she was
still in college and he was on the road with the team had
only backfired.

"That didn't include getting another woman pregnant,"
she'd retorted, her eyes filled with the kind of hurt he hadn't
seen since her mom had kicked her dad out for cheating
when Annie was fourteen. "How am I supposed to forgive that?"

"I don't know," he'd told her, defeated. "I honestly don't
know."

Truthfully, he still didn't. But when he'd been injured,
the one bright spot had been the chance to come back to
Serenity and maybe take a stab at making things right

with Annie. He could have done the rehab anywhere, had the best trainers in the world working with him, but he'd refused every option the team had proposed, packed up Trevor and come home. He wasn't entirely sure why making amends to Annie was so important right now, but it was. One of the lessons he'd learned the hard way was that friendships were more valuable and lasting than casual sex. Too bad he'd had to lose his best friend before he'd figured it out.

Now that he was here, though, he had no idea what the next step should be. Maybe his mom was right. Maybe it just needed to start with a phone call.

"Does she ever mention me?" he asked, looking for some sign that Annie's attitude had mellowed.

Maddie shook her head. "Certainly not to me. Can you blame her?"

"I suppose not."

"I so wish things had turned out differently, Ty. You two—"

"Are over," he said flatly. "Her decision."

"If you honestly believe that, then why did you come back here?"

"I thought it would be good for Trevor to spend some time with his family." That, at least, was true. His son needed more stability than he could get even from the most doting nanny and a dad who was on the road for days—sometimes weeks—at a time.

His mother studied him skeptically. "Really? And that thought only occurred to you after I mentioned that Annie had moved back home?" Before he could respond, she continued, "Because it certainly didn't cross your mind during the off-season last year, or the year before that."

"Coincidence," he claimed.

"Oh, Ty," she chided. "At least be honest with yourself. You're here because of Annie. Why bother denying it, at least with me? Now, what are you going to do to make things right?"

He glanced across the table and saw the lingering disappointment in his mother's expression. That was as hard to take as losing Annie. After the way his dad had cheated on his mom and the way Ty had hated him for it, surely he should have behaved more responsibly. Instead, he was apparently a chip off the old block, after all.

"I have no idea what I can do," he admitted.

"Well, you need to come up with a plan. The two of you are bound to cross paths. Not only is this a very small town, but our families are connected. Dana Sue and I are friends. We're in business together. Annie works for me, for heaven's sake."

Ty winced at the complicated mess he'd managed to create. "I'm sorry, Mom. If this is going to become some big thing between you and Dana Sue, I can go somewhere else for rehab. There are plenty of facilities in Atlanta."

"No," she said, backing down at once. "Having you back home is such an unexpected joy for me and for your brothers and sisters. It's giving us a chance to spend time with Trevor, too."

She drew herself up. "Dana Sue and I will figure out a way to deal with this," she said confidently. "We've been friends a long time, and we've always known that something might come between you and Annie. That's why we tried so hard to stay out of it."

"How about you and Annie, though?" he asked worriedly, wishing he'd thought his decision through before disrupting everyone's lives. Coming back had been selfish, he could see that now. "She's been like another daughter to you, and you work together. It's going to freak her out knowing I'm around. What if she quits just to avoid me?"

"Annie's more mature than that," Maddie said with certainty. "She's a strong young woman. She'll cope."

"What if it, you know…?" He hesitated, then voiced his greatest fear, the one that had nagged at him since the day they'd parted. "What if she goes back to being anorexic?"

Maddie regarded him with dismay. "No, Ty! She won't do that."

"She could, Mom." He shook his head. "What the hell was I thinking? The stress of Ronnie taking off is part of what triggered her eating disorder in the first place. She felt like her life was a mess, and food was the only thing she could control. Now, having me in her face could do the same thing. I'd never forgive myself if that happened."

"It's not going to happen," Maddie said emphatically. "She was just a teenager when she got so sick. She's twenty-three now. It's been years. Believe me, Dana Sue and Ronnie know all the signs. Annie still sees Dr. McDaniels from time to time. They'll be all over her if there's even a hint that her anorexia is back. Besides, she didn't fall apart when you two split up, so there's no reason to think she will now just because you're here in Serenity."

"I suppose." Still, he couldn't help worrying about Annie. She'd never been half as tough as she'd wanted everyone to believe she was. He was one of the few who'd seen her vulnerability way before she'd been diagnosed with anorexia. She'd looked up to him, trusted him, talked to him…fallen in love with him.

Then he'd betrayed her. And for what? A string of casual flings that had meant nothing. He'd wanted to prove he was hot stuff. Hanging out with groupies had been a rite of passage into the big leagues. All the guys liked to unwind after the games. There were always eager women around.

Unfortunately, it had taken too long for him to realize just how empty and meaningless all that was. Compared to what he had with Annie—the real deal, he knew now—it was just sex and a few laughs with women who liked to brag they'd hooked up with a baseball player.

To his very deep regret, Trevor's mom had barely stood out from the crowd. When they'd met after a road game in Cincinnati, she'd struck him as shy, with her big brown eyes and corn silk hair. She was quieter than most of the others, less aggressive. She'd actually been able to hold up her end of a conversation. Ironically, he'd seen a vulnerability in her that had reminded him of Annie.

The next time he'd been in Cincinnati, Ty had seen Dee-Dee again, spent three nights with her. On his third trip to town, she'd told him she was pregnant.

The news had hit him like one of his own fastballs in the gut, left him slack-jawed and sputtering. He realized he didn't even know her last name.

Nor could he be sure the baby was his. He wanted proof, insisted on it, which set off their first huge fight. Dee-Dee, whose last name turned out to be Mitchell, was insulted he would even ask. He was appalled that she thought he was so stupid he wouldn't.

Struggling with years of conditioning to take responsibility for his own actions, Ty had turned to a buddy on the team for advice.

"You in love with her?" Jimmy Falco had asked.

"No," Ty admitted. "I barely know her."

"Then you wait. You get a paternity test. If the kid turns out to be yours, you go from there."

Dee-Dee had been furious when he'd told her the plan.

She'd threatened to go to the tabloids if he didn't marry her immediately. Despite all the potential for very public ugliness, Ty held firm. That was when he should have gone to Annie and confessed everything, but he'd waited. And, of course, the news had leaked out.

By the time Trevor was born, any faint feelings he might have had for Dee-Dee were dead and buried. The positive paternity test didn't change that. In court, he acknowledged being the boy's father, relinquished custody to Dee-Dee with visitation rights for himself, arranged to pay child support, and even agreed to a generous lump-sum payment to get Dee-Dee her own place, a two-bedroom condo in a very nice building.

Two months later, he'd opened the door to his hotel room on a road trip to Denver to find Trevor in a basket on the doorstep, and Dee-Dee nowhere in sight. In an instant, he took on the role of single dad.

Because of the prior arrangement and Dee-Dee's disappearance, it had taken a year of wrangling in court to change their custody agreement so that he had sole custody. He'd struggled to balance parenthood with a physically demanding career that took him away from home too often. Finding a nanny he'd trusted had been a nightmare, but eventually he'd found Cassandra, an older woman who'd raised four children of her own and doted on Trevor as if he were one of her own grandchildren. To Ty's amusement, she treated him as a son who'd gone astray and needed firm moral guidance. Cassandra had been a godsend for both of them.

In the meantime, the whole thing had played out in the tabloids. He imagined that Dee-Dee had gotten a pretty penny for the inside scoop, to say nothing of what she must have gotten for tipping off a photographer before she left the baby outside his hotel room.

And it had all hit the fan before he'd been able to work up the nerve to tell Annie about any of it. He'd been the worst kind of coward.

What Annie thought of him—what he thought of himself—didn't matter, though, not as long as she didn't fall back into her old anorexic eating pattern. He didn't think he could handle that. Hurting her was bad enough. He'd never be able to live with destroying all the progress she'd made, the normal, healthy life she was leading.

Then, again, maybe he was exaggerating the pain he'd caused her. Maybe she'd made peace with what had happened, considered herself lucky to be rid of him. She could have moved on by now. It was certainly what he deserved, but the thought depressed him just the same.

Because Annie Sullivan had slipped into his heart about a million years ago, and she was still there...despite everything he'd done to show her otherwise.

Don't miss Home in Carolina
A Sweet Magnolias novel
Available wherever MIRA books are sold!

Catch up with all things Sweet Magnolias from
#1 *New York Times* bestselling author

SHERRYL WOODS

Read the books that inspired the hit Netflix series!

Raise a glass and treat yourself to the official cookbook of the Sweet Magnolias, with original recipes celebrating the flavor and fragrance of the South.

Get 4 FREE REWARDS!

We'll send you 2 FREE Books plus 2 FREE Mystery Gifts.

FREE Value Over **$20**

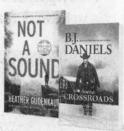

Both the **Romance** and **Suspense** collections feature compelling novels written by many of today's bestselling authors.

YES! Please send me 2 FREE novels from the Essential Romance or Essential Suspense Collection and my 2 FREE gifts (gifts are worth about $10 retail). After receiving them, if I don't wish to receive any more books, I can return the shipping statement marked "cancel." If I don't cancel, I will receive 4 brand-new novels every month and be billed just $7.24 each in the U.S. or $7.49 each in Canada. That's a savings of up to 28% off the cover price. It's quite a bargain! Shipping and handling is just 50¢ per book in the U.S. and $1.25 per book in Canada.* I understand that accepting the 2 free books and gifts places me under no obligation to buy anything. I can always return a shipment and cancel at any time. The free books and gifts are mine to keep no matter what I decide.

Choose one: ☐ **Essential Romance**
(194/394 MDN GQ6M)

☐ **Essential Suspense**
(191/391 MDN GQ6M)

Name (please print)

Address _____ Apt. #

City _____ State/Province _____ Zip/Postal Code

Email: Please check this box ☐ if you would like to receive newsletters and promotional emails from Harlequin Enterprises ULC and its affiliates. You can unsubscribe anytime.

> Mail to the **Harlequin Reader Service:**
> **IN U.S.A.:** P.O. Box 1341, Buffalo, NY 14240-8531
> **IN CANADA:** P.O. Box 603, Fort Erie, Ontario L2A 5X3

Want to try 2 free books from another series! Call 1-800-873-8635 or visit www.ReaderService.com.

---

*Terms and prices subject to change without notice. Prices do not include sales taxes, which will be charged (if applicable) based on your state or country of residence. Canadian residents will be charged applicable taxes. Offer not valid in Quebec. This offer is limited to one order per household. Books received may not be as shown. Not valid for current subscribers to the Essential Romance or Essential Suspense Collection. All orders subject to approval. Credit or debit balances in a customer's account(s) may be offset by any other outstanding balance owed by or to the customer. Please allow 4 to 6 weeks for delivery. Offer available while quantities last.

Your Privacy—Your information is being collected by Harlequin Enterprises ULC, operating as Harlequin Reader Service. For a complete summary of the information we collect, how we use this information and to whom it is disclosed, please visit our privacy notice located at corporate.harlequin.com/privacy-notice. From time to time we may also exchange your personal information with reputable third parties. If you wish to opt out of this sharing of your personal information, please visit readerservice.com/consumerschoice or call 1-800-873-8635. **Notice to California Residents**—Under California law, you have specific rights to control and access your data. For more information on these rights and how to exercise them, visit corporate.harlequin.com/california-privacy.

STRSMAX22